Danger lives at the top of the Earth,
where nothing can survive . . .
except fear.

ICE HUNT

JAMES ROLLINS

ICE HUNT

HARPER

An Imprint of HarperCollinsPublishers

"A History of Secret Human Experiment" copyright by Healthnewsnet. All rights reserved. Used by permission.

Station schematics by Steve Prey. All rights reserved. Used by permission of Steve Prey.

HARPER

An Imprint of HarperCollins*Publishers*
10 East 53rd Street
New York, New York 10022-5299

Copyright © 2003 by Jim Czajkowski
Excerpt from *The Judas Strain* copyright © 2007 by Jim Czajkowski
ISBN: 978-0-06-052160-8
ISBN-10: 0-06-052160-0

First Harper paperback printing: March 2007
First Avon Books paperback printing: July 2004
First William Morrow hardcover printing: July 2003

HarperCollins® and Harper® are trademarks of HarperCollins Publishers.

Printed in the United States of America

Visit Harper paperbacks on the World Wide Web at
www.harpercollins.com

30 29 28 27 26 25 24 23 22 21

To Dave Meek,

the next star on the horizon

ACKNOWLEDGMENTS

A book is seldom the work of the author alone, but usually the collaborative effort of many folks. This novel is no exception. First, Steve Prey must be mentioned as the chief engineer and draftsman for this novel, whose painstaking work on constructing the station schematics both inspired and changed the story. Then I had a posse of language experts who helped with countless details. Carolyn Williams, Vasily Dcrcbcnskiy, and William Czajkowski helped with the Russian translations, while Kim Crockatt and Nunavut.com were integral to finding my Inuit translator: Emily Angulalik. I also must thank John Overton of the Health News Network for his assistance in collating historical information used in this novel.

Additionally, I must heartily acknowledge my friends and family who helped shape the manuscript into its present form: Carolyn McCray, Chris Crowe, Michael Gallowglas, Lee Garrett, David Murray, Dennis Grayson, Penny Hill, Lynne Williams, Laurel Piper, Lane Therrell, Mary Hanley, Dave Meek, Royale Adams, Jane O'Riva, Chris "the little" Smith, Judy and Steve Prey, and Caroline Williams. For the map used here, I must acknowledge its source: *The CIA World Factbook 2000*. Finally, the four folks who continue to remain my most loyal supporters: my editor, Lyssa

Keusch; my agents, Russ Galen and Danny Baror; and my publicist, Jim Davis. Lastly and most importantly, I must stress that any and all errors of fact or detail fall squarely on my own shoulders.

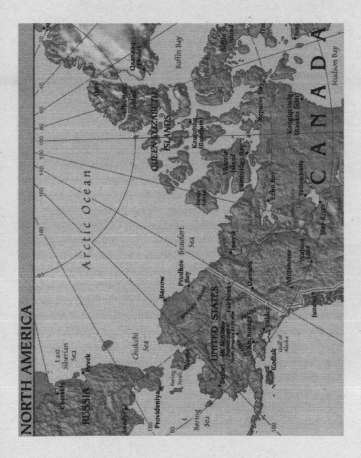

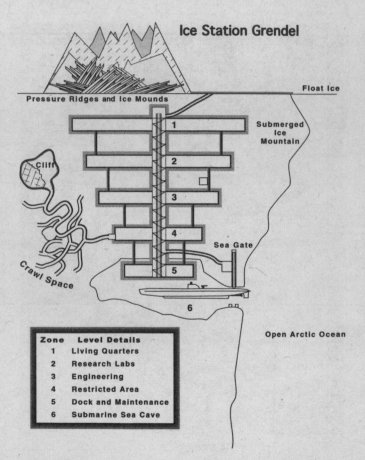

Ice Station Grendel

Float Ice

Pressure Ridges and Ice Mounds

Submerged Ice Mountain

Cliff

Crawl Space

Sea Gate

Open Arctic Ocean

Zone	Level Details
1	Living Quarters
2	Research Labs
3	Engineering
4	Restricted Area
5	Dock and Maintenance
6	Submarine Sea Cave

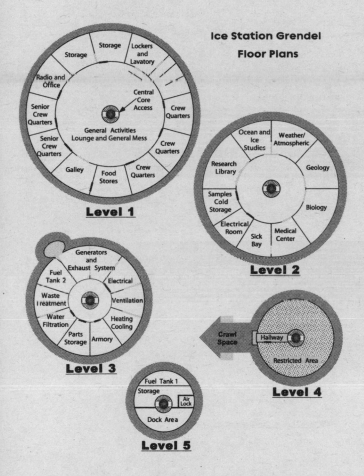

Ice Station Grendel
Floor Plans

Level 1

Storage
Storage
Lockers and Lavatory
Radio and Office
Central Core Access
Senior Crew Quarters
Crew Quarters
Senior Crew Quarters
Crew Quarters
General Activities Lounge and General Mess
Galley
Food Stores
Crew Quarters

Level 2

Ocean and Ice Studies
Weather/Atmospheric
Research Library
Geology
Samples Cold Storage
Biology
Electrical Room
Sick Bay
Medical Center

Level 3

Generators and Exhaust System
Fuel Tank 2
Electrical
Waste Treatment
Ventilation
Water Filtration
Heating Cooling
Parts Storage
Armory

Level 4

Crawl Space
Hallway
Restricted Area

Level 5

Fuel Tank 1
Storage
Air Lock
Dock Area

PERSONNEL

CIVILIAN

(1) Matthew Pike, an Alaska Fish and Game warden
(2) Jennifer Aratuk, sheriff for the Nunamiut and Inupiat tribes
(3) Junaquaat (John) Aratuk, retired
(4) Craig Teague, reporter for the *Seattle Times*
(5) Bennie and Belinda Haydon, owners of an ultralight sightseeing company
(6) Bane, retired search-and-rescue dog, wolf/malamute cross

OMEGA RESEARCHERS

(1) Dr. Amanda Reynolds, an American engineer
(2) Dr. Oskar Willig, a Swedish oceanographer
(3) Dr. Henry Ogden, an American biologist
(4) Dr. Lee Bentley, a NASA researcher in material sciences
(5) Dr. Connor MacFerran, a Scottish geologist
(6) Dr. Erik Gustof, a Canadian meteorologist
(7) Lacy Devlin, a geology postgrad
(8) Magdalene, Antony, and Zane, biology postgrads

UNITED STATES MILITARY

(1) Gregory Perry, captain of the *Polar Sentinel*
(2) Roberto Bratt, lieutenant commander and XO of the *Polar Sentinel*
(3) Kent Reynolds, admiral and commander of the Pacific Fleet
(4) Paul Sewell, lieutenant commander and head of base security for Omega
(5) Serina Washburn, lieutenant
(6) Mitchell Greer, lieutenant
(7) Frank O'Donnell, petty officer
(8) Tom Pomautuk, ensign
(9) Joe Kowalski, seaman
(10) Doug Pearlson, seaman
(11) Ted Kanter, master sergeant, Delta Forces
(12) Edwin Wilson, command sergeant major, Delta Forces

RUSSIAN MILITARY

(1) Viktor Petkov, admiral and commander of the Russian Northern Fleet
(2) Anton Mikovsky, captain first rank of the *Drakon*
(3) Gregor Yanovich, diving officer and XO of the *Drakon*
(4) Stefan Yurgen, member of Leopard ops

ARCHIVED RECORD:
THE TORONTO DAILY STAR,
NOVEMBER 23, 1937

ESKIMO VILLAGE VANISHES!
RCMP Confirms Trapper's Story

Special to the Star,

Lake Territory, November 23. The inspector for the Royal Canadian Mounted Police returned today to confirm the disappearance of an Eskimo village in the Northern Lakes region. Ten days ago, fur trapper Joe LaBelle contacted the RCMP to report a chilling discovery. While running a trapline, LaBelle snowshoed out to an isolated Eskimo village on the shores of Lake Anjikuni only to discover every inhabitant—man, woman, and child—had vanished from their huts and storehouses. "It was as if every one of them poor folk up and took off with no more than the shirts on their backs."

Inspector Pierre Menard of the RCMP returned with his team's findings today and confirmed the trapper's story. The village had indeed been found abandoned under most strange circumstances. "In our search, we discovered undisturbed foodstuff, gear, and provisions but no sign of the villagers. Not a single footprint or track." Even the Eskimos' sled dogs were found buried under the snow, starved to death. But the most disturbing discovery of all was reported at the end: the Eskimos' ancestral graves were found excavated and emptied.

The RCMP promises to continue the search, but for now the fate of the villagers remains a mystery.

ICE HUNT

PROLOGUE

FEBRUARY 6, 11:58 A.M.
538 KILOMETERS NORTH OF ARCTIC CIRCLE
FORTY FATHOMS UNDER THE POLAR ICE CAP

The USS *Polar Sentinel* was gliding through the dark ocean. The sub's twin bronze screws churned silently, propelling the Navy's newest research submarine under the roof of ice. The warning bells of the proximity alarms echoed down the length of the vessel.

"Sweet mother, what a monster," the diving officer mumbled from his post, bent over a small video monitor.

Captain Gregory Perry didn't argue with Commander Bratt's assessment. He stood atop the control room's periscope stand. His eyes were fixed to the scope's optical piece as he studied the ocean beyond the sub's double hull of titanium and plate-carbon steel. Though it was midday, it was still winter in the Arctic. It had been months since anyone had seen the sun. Around them the waters remained dark. The plane of ice overhead stretched black as far as he could see, interrupted only by occasional blue-green patches of thinner ice, filtering the scant moonlight of the surface world. The average thickness of the polar ice cap was a mere ten feet, but that did not mean the roof of their world was uniform or smooth. All around, jagged pressure ridges jutted like stalactites, some delving down eighty feet.

But none of this compared to the inverted mountain of ice that dropped into the depths of the Arctic Ocean ahead of them, a veritable Everest of ice. The sub slowly circled the peak.

"This baby must extend down a mile," Commander Bratt continued.

"Actually one-point-four miles," the chief of the watch reported from his wraparound station of instruments. A finger traced the video monitor of the top-sounding sonar. The high-frequency instrument was used to contour the ice.

Perry continued to observe through the periscope, trusting his own eyes versus the video monitors. He thumbed on the sub's xenon spotlights, igniting the cliff face. Black walls glowed with hues of cobalt blue and aquamarine. The sub slowly circled its perimeter, close enough for the ice-mapping sonar to protest their proximity.

"Can someone cut those damn bells?" Perry muttered.

"Aye, sir."

Silence settled throughout the vessel. No one spoke. The only sound was the muffled hum of the engines and the soft hiss of the oxygen generator. Like all subs, the small nuclear-powered *Polar Sentinel* had been designed to run silent. The research vessel was half the size of its bigger brothers. Jokingly referred to as Tadpole-class, the submarine had been miniaturized through some key advances in engineering, allowing for a smaller crew, which in turn allowed for less space needed for living quarters. Additionally, built as a pure research vessel, the submarine was emptied of all armaments to allow more room for scientific equipment and personnel. Still, despite the stripping of the sub, no one was really fooled. The *Polar Sentinel* was also the test platform for an upcoming generation of attack submarine: smaller, faster, deadlier.

Technically still on its shakedown cruise, the sub had been assigned to the Omega Drift Station, a semipermanent U.S. research facility built atop the polar ice cap, a joint project between various government science agencies, including the National Science Foundation and the National Oceanographic and Atmospheric Administration.

The crew had spent the last week surfacing the sub through open leads between ice floes or up through thinly iced-over lakes, called polynyas. Their task was to implant meteorological equipment atop the ice for the scientific base to monitor. But an hour ago, they had come upon this inverted Everest of ice.

"That's one hell of an iceberg," Bratt whistled.

A new voice intruded. "The correct term is an ice *island*." Perry glanced from the periscope.

A gray-haired man with a neatly trimmed beard stooped through the hatch to enter the control room from the forward research decks. It was Dr. Oskar Willig, the Swedish oceanographer. He was accompanied by an ensign. The aging but wiry and hard-eyed Swede waved a dismissive hand toward the video monitor and nodded to Captain Perry. "It's a much more spectacular view from Cyclops. In fact, Dr. Reynolds asked to see if you'd join us there. We've discovered something intriguing."

After a long moment, Perry nodded and folded up the periscope grips. He twisted the hydraulic control ring, and the stainless-steel pole with its optic module descended into the housing below. "Commander Bratt, you have the conn." He stepped down from the periscope stand to join Dr. Willig.

Commander Bratt raised one bushy eyebrow as he passed by. "You're going to Cyclops? With all this ice around? You're a braver man than I am, Captain. True balls of brass."

"Not brass." Perry tapped a knuckle on a wall plate. "Titanium."

This earned a chuckle from his second-in-command.

The Swedish oceanographer's eyes were bright with excitement as Perry joined him. "In all my years, I've never seen such a spectacular example of an ice island."

Perry ran a hand over the stubble of his red hair, then motioned the older doctor ahead of him.

The doctor nodded, turning, but he continued to speak rapidly, lecturing as if still in his classroom at the University of Stockholm. "These islands are rare. They originate when giant icebergs calve off the mainland glaciers. Then ocean currents drive these floating mountains into the polar ice cap, where they're frozen in place. Eventually, during the years of thawing and refreezing, they become incorporated into the cap itself." Dr. Willig glanced back at the captain as he climbed through the forward hatch. "Somewhat like almonds in a chocolate bar, you might say."

Perry followed, bending his own six-foot frame through the opening. "But what's so exciting about such a discovery? Why did Dr. Reynolds insist upon us mapping around this embedded almond?"

Dr. Willig bobbed his head, leading the way down the main passage and through the research section of the sub. "Besides the rarity of these ice islands, because they have been calved from glaciers, they contain very old ice and many even hold boulders and sections of terra firma. They're frozen glimpses of the distant past. Can you just imagine?"

Perry followed, urging the doctor onward.

"We dare not lose this chance. We may never find such an example again. The polar ice cap covers an area twice the size of your United States. And with the cap's surface worn featureless by winter winds and summer melts, such islands are impossible to discern. Not even NASA satellites could pinpoint such discoveries. Stumbling upon this mountain is a scientific gift from God."

"I don't know about God, but it is intriguing," Perry conceded. He had been granted command of the *Sentinel* because of his background and interest in the Arctic region. His own father had served aboard the USS *Nautilus,* the first submarine to cross the Arctic Ocean and pass under the North Pole back in 1958. It was an honor to be adding to his father's legacy up here, to captain the Navy's newest research vessel.

Dr. Willig pointed to a sealed hatch at the end of the corridor. "Come. You need to see this with your own eyes."

Perry waved him on, glancing over his shoulder. The *Polar Sentinel* was divided into two sections. Aft of the control station were the crew's living quarters and the engineering levels. Forward of the bridge lay the research labs. But ahead, in the nose of the boat, where normally the torpedo room and sonar boom would be on a Virginia-class submarine, was the strangest modification of a naval sub.

"After you," Dr. Willig offered as they reached the sealed door.

Perry opened the hatch and pushed his way into the room. The muted lighting of the *Sentinel* ill prepared him for the blinding brilliance of the next chamber. He shielded his eyes as he entered.

The upper shell of the former torpedo room had been replaced with a canopy of foot-thick Lexan polycarbonate. The clear plastic shell arched overhead and in front, allowing an uninterrupted view of the seas around the *Sentinel,* a window upon the watery world. Viewed from outside, the Lexan canopy looked like a single glass eye, hence its nickname: *Cyclops*.

Perry ignored the handful of scientists off to the sides, bent over equipment and monitors. The Navy men stood straighter and nodded to their captain. He returned their acknowledgment, but it was impossible to truly break his gaze from the view out Cyclops.

Ahead, a voice spoke from the heart of the glare: "Impressive, isn't it?"

Perry blinked away his blindness and spotted a slender figure in the room's center, limned in aquamarine light. "Dr. Reynolds?"

"I couldn't resist watching from here." He heard the warm

smile in the woman's voice. Dr. Amanda Reynolds was the nominal head of Omega Drift Station. Her father was Admiral Kent Reynolds, commander of the Pacific submarine fleet. Raised a Navy brat, the doctor was as comfortable aboard a submarine as any sailor wearing the double dolphins of the fleet.

Perry crossed to her. He had first met Amanda two years ago when he was granted his captain's bars. It had been at a social function given by her father. In that one evening, he had inadvertently insulted her potato salad, almost broken her toe during a short dance, and made the mistake of insisting that the Cubs would beat the San Francisco Giants in an upcoming game, losing ten dollars in the bargain. Overall it had been a great evening.

Perry cleared his throat and made sure Amanda was looking at him. "So what do you think of Cyclops?" he asked, speaking crisply so she could read his lips. She had lost her hearing at the age of thirteen as a result of a car accident.

Amanda Reynolds glanced overhead, turning slightly forward. "It's everything my father dreamed it would be."

She stood under the arch, surrounded on all sides by the Arctic Ocean. She appeared to be floating in the sea itself. Presently she leaned on one hip, half turned. Her sweep of ebony hair was snugged into an efficient ponytail. She wore one of the Navy's blue underway uniforms, crisply pressed.

Perry joined her, stepping out under the open ocean. Being a career submariner, he understood his crew's discomfort with this room. Although fire was the main fear on any submarine, no one completely trusted the foot-thick plastic shell as an alternative for a double hull of titanium and carbon plate—especially with so much ice around.

He had to resist the urge to hunch away from the plastic canopy. The weight of the entire Arctic Ocean seemed to hang overhead.

"Why did you call me up here?" he asked, touching her arm to draw her eyes.

"For this . . . something amazing." Amanda's voice tremored with excitement. She waved an arm forward. Beyond Cyclops, the sub's lamps illuminated the wall of ice slowly passing by the front of the vessel. Standing here, it felt as if they were motionless, and it was the ice island instead that was turning, revolving like a giant's toy top in front of them. This close, the entire cliff face glowed under the illumination of the sub's xenon spotlights. The ice seemed to stretch infinitely up and down.

Without a doubt, it was both a humbling and starkly chilling sight, but Perry still did not understand why his presence had been requested.

"We've been testing the new DeepEye sonar system," Amanda began to explain.

Perry nodded. He was familiar with her research project. The *Polar Sentinel* was the first submarine to be equipped with her experimental ice-surveying system, a penetrating sonar, a type of X ray for ice. The device had been based on Dr. Reynolds's own design. Her background was in geosciences engineering, specializing in the polar regions.

She continued, "We were hoping to test it on the island here and see if we could discern any boulders or terrestrial matter inside."

"And did you find something?" He still could not take his eyes off the slowly turning cliff of ice.

Amanda stepped to the side, toward a pair of men hunched over equipment. "Our first couple passes failed to reveal anything, but it's like peeling an onion. We had to be careful. The sonar waves of the DeepEye cause minute vibrations in the ice. They actually heat it up slightly. So we had to proceed one layer at a time as we scanned the island. Slow, meticulous work. Then we discovered—"

Perry still stood under the eye of Cyclops. He was the first to see the danger as the sub edged around a thick ridge of ice. Ahead, boulder-sized chunks of ice floated and bounced up the cliff face, an avalanche in reverse. But ahead, a large dark crack skittered across the face of the ice. A monstrous section of cliff face suddenly leaned toward the slow-moving ship, toppling out toward them. They were going to collide with it.

With a gasp, he dove for the intercom. "Captain to the bridge!" he yelled.

"On it, Captain," Commander Bratt answered, tense. "Flooding negative."

Instantly Perry felt the familiar tug on the sub as thousands of pounds of water drowned the emergency tanks.

The sub dropped, diving at a steep angle.

Perry stared out of Cyclops, unblinking, unsure if they would avoid a collision as the wall of ice dropped from the cliff like a blue ax. It was now a race between the buoyancy of the falling ice and the weight of their own emergency ballast. The submarine canted nose first. Handholds were grabbed. A notebook slid down the slanted floor.

Small cries echoed, but Perry ignored them. He watched, powerless. A collision here would be disastrous. There was nowhere to surface for miles around. Though the *Polar Sentinel* had been built to handle the rigors of the Arctic, there were limits.

The toppling wall of ice filled the world ahead of them. The sub continued to dive. Seams popped and groaned from the sudden increase in pressure as the sub plunged into the frigid depths.

Then open water appeared ahead, just under the slowly falling slab of ice. The submarine dove toward it.

The section of cliff face slid past overhead—no more than inches. Perry craned his neck, following it past the arch of Lexan above his head. He could read the pictographic lines of algae across the ice's surface. He held his breath, ready for the screech of metal, ready to hear the emergency klaxons blare. But the continual low hiss of the oxygen generators persisted.

After a long half minute, Perry let out a deep breath and

turned to the intercom. "Captain to the bridge," he said. "Good job up there, men."

Commander Bratt answered, relief and pride in his voice, "Shutting the flood. Venting negative." The sub began to level. After a moment, Bratt added, "Let's not do that again."

"Aye to that," Perry agreed. "But let's do a slow circle back around and inspect the area—from a safe distance. I wager that breakaway may have been triggered by the DeepEye sonar." He glanced to Amanda, remembering her concern about the new sonar's vibration signature and heating effect. "We should get some pictures since we're testing the darned thing."

Commander Bratt acknowledged and ordered his bridge crew, "Helmsman, left full rudder. Ahead slow. Take us around."

The submarine eased away from the ice mountain in a slow circle. Perry crossed to the bank of video monitors. "Can we get a close-up of the fracture zone?"

One of the technicians nodded. "Yes, sir."

Amanda spoke, her words slightly slurred, her enunciation slipping with her anxiety. "We should've anticipated such a fracturing."

He patted her hand. "That's why we call this a shakedown cruise. If you're not shook up a time or two, then you're not doing your job."

Despite his poor attempt at humor, her face remained tight.

Then again, his own heart still pounded from the close call. He bent closer to the screen as the technician manipulated a toggle to bring the exterior cameras into focus on the fractured area. The shattered chunk of cliff shimmered into clarity.

"What's that?" Amanda asked. She pointed to a dark blemish on the screen. It was in the center of the fracture zone. "Can you zoom in?"

The technician nodded and twisted a dial. The section of

cliff swelled. The blemish grew in detail and depth. It was not ice or rock, but something unusual. As the sub turned, the *Polar Sentinel*'s spotlights illuminated it. It was black, angular. *Man-made*.

As they swung closer, Perry knew what he was seeing: the stern end of another sub, frozen like a stick in a Popsicle. He crossed over to the canopy of Lexan glass and stared out. He could just make out the sub poking from the ice. It was old, ancient.

The *Polar Sentinel* glided past at a safe distance.

"Is that what I think it is?" Dr. Willig asked, his voice weak.

"A sub," Perry answered with a nod. He could recognize any submarine from just a casual glance. "I'd say a World War Two–era sub. Russian I series."

Amanda, her face less pale now, spoke from where she now stood with two researchers. "This supports our earlier discovery. The reason I called you down here."

Perry turned to her. "What are you talking about?"

She pointed to a different monitor. "We mapped and taped this earlier from the DeepEye." The screen displayed a three-dimensional image of the ice island. The resolution was amazing, but Perry didn't see anything significant.

"Show him," Amanda continued, placing a hand on one of the technician's shoulders.

He tapped a few keys, and the image of the ice island dissolved from solid to ghostly. Within the interior of the island, passages and distinct tiers sectioned the iceberg, rising up layer by layer toward the top.

"What is it?" Perry asked.

The technician answered, "We think it's an abandoned ice base built inside the berg." He tapped a few keys and the image swelled to concentrate on one tier. There appeared to be rooms and corridors. It was definitely not a natural formation.

"A *Russian* ice base if you're right about that sub,"

Amanda added, lifting an eyebrow toward Perry. "The vessel is docked at the lowest level."

He pointed to several darker objects scattered here and there on the display. "Are those what I think they are?"

The technician overlaid a cursor atop one of them and tapped a key, zooming in on it. The shape of the form was unquestionable.

"Bodies, Captain," he answered. "Dead bodies."

A flicker of movement drew Perry's attention to the edge of the screen—then it vanished. He frowned and glanced to the others. "Did anyone else see that?"

Amanda's eyes widened. "Rewind the tape."

The technician shuttled the recording backward and zoomed slightly outward. He forwarded to the blurred movement on the screen. He slowed it down. On the lowest tier of the station something stirred, then disappeared into the deeper depths of the ice mountain, retreating beyond the reach of the sonar. Though visible only for a moment, there was no doubt.

Amanda whispered, "Something's alive in there . . ."

Act One

SNOW FLIGHT

ᐊᐳᖅᒥ ᓈᖅᕓᖅ

Blood Lure

ᐊᐅᖅᑰᒃ ᒥᒃᑭᐱᓇ

APRIL 6, 2:56 P.M.
BROOKS RANGE, ALASKA

Always respect Mother Nature . . . especially when she weighs four hundred pounds and is guarding her baby.

Matthew Pike faced the grizzly from fifty yards away. The massive she-bear eyed him back, chuffing into the breeze. Her yearling cub nosed a blackberry briar, but it was too early in the season for berries. The cub was just playing in the brambles, oblivious to the six-foot-two Fish and Game officer standing, sweating, in the afternoon sun. But the youngster had little to fear when watched over by his mother. Her muscled bulk, yellowed teeth, and four-inch claws were protection enough.

Matt's moist palm rested on his holstered canister of pepper spray. His other hand slowly shifted to the rifle slung on his shoulder. *Don't charge, sweetheart . . . don't make this day any worse than it already is.* He'd had enough trouble with his own dogs earlier and had left them tethered back at his campsite.

As he watched, her ears slowly flattened to her skull. Her

back legs bunched as she bounced a bit on her front legs. It was clear posturing, a stance meant to chase off any threat.

Matt held back a groan. How he wanted to run, but he knew to do so would only provoke the she-bear to chase him down. He risked taking a single slow step backward, careful to avoid the snap of a twig. He wore an old pair of moose-hide boots, hand-sewn by his ex-wife, a skill learned from her Inuit father. Though they were three years divorced, Matt appreciated her skill now. The soft soles allowed him to tread quietly.

He continued his slow retreat.

Normally, when one encountered a bear in the wild, the best defense was loud noises: shouts, catcalls, whistles, anything to warn the normally reclusive predators away. But to stumble upon this sow and cub when topping a rise, running face-to-face into *Ursus arctos horribilis,* any sudden movement or noise could trigger the maternal beast to charge. Bear attacks numbered in the thousands each year in Alaska, including hundreds of fatalities. Just two months ago, he and a fellow warden had run a tributary of the Yukon River in kayaks, searching for two rafters reported late in returning home, only to discover their half-eaten remains.

So Matt knew bears. He knew to watch for fresh bear signs whenever hiking: unsettled dung, torn-up sod, clawed trunks of trees. He carried a bear whistle around his neck and pepper spray at his belt. And no one with any wits entered the Alaskan backcountry without a rifle. But as Matt had learned during his ten-year stint among the parks and lands of Alaska, out here the unexpected was commonplace. In a state bigger than Texas, with most of its lands accessible only by floatplane, the wildernesses of Alaska made the wild places of the lower states seem like nothing more than Disney theme parks: domesticated, crowded, commercialized. But here nature ruled in all its stark and brutal majesty.

Of course, right now, Matt was hoping for a break on the *brutal* part. He continued his cautious retreat. The she-bear kept her post. Then the small male cub—if you could call a a hundred-and-fifty-pound ball of fur and muscle *small*—finally noticed the stranger nearby. It rose on its hind legs, looking at him. It shimmied and tossed its head about, male aggression made almost comical. Then it did the one thing Matt prayed it wouldn't do. It dropped on all fours and loped toward him, more in play and curiosity than with any aggressive intent. But it was a deadly move nonetheless.

While Matt did not fear the yearling cub—a blast of pepper spray would surely stop it in its tracks—its mother's response was a different matter. The pepper spray would be no more than a tenderizing seasoning when her pile-driver strength pounded down on him. And forget about a head shot, even with his Marlin sport rifle. The bear's thick skull would only deflect the bullet. Not even a shot square through the heart was a safe bet. It would take ten minutes for such a shot to kill a bear, and the shooter would be bear scat by then. The only real way to kill a grizzly was to aim for the legs, bring her bulk down, then keep on shooting.

And despite the personal danger, Matt was loath to do this. The grizzlies were his personal totem. They were the symbol of this country. With their numbers dwindling to less than twenty-five thousand, he could not bring himself to kill even one of them. In fact, he had come to Brooks Range on his own personal time to help in the cataloging and DNA mapping of the parkland's population of awakening grizzlies, fresh out of winter's blanket. He had been up here collecting samples from hair traps stationed throughout the remote areas of the park and freshening their foul-smelling scent lures when he found himself in this predicament.

But now Matt was faced with the choice of kill or be killed. The cub bounded merrily in his direction. His mother growled in warning—but Matt was not sure if she was talking to him or her cub. Either way, his retreat sped up, one foot fumbling behind the other. He shrugged his rifle into one hand and unholstered his pepper spray.

As he struggled with the spray's flip top, a fierce growl rose behind him. Matt glanced over his shoulder. On the trail behind him, a dark shape raced at him, tail flagging in the air.

Matt's eyes grew wide with recognition. "Bane! No!" The black dog pounded up the slope, hackles raised, a continual growl flowing from his throat. The dog's keen nose must have scented the bears . . . and maybe his own master's fear. "Heel!" Matt yelled in a barked command.

Ever obedient, the dog halted the charge and stopped at his side, front legs braking, hind legs bunched. With one resounding bark, he crouched, teeth bared. A wolf cross, Bane was broad of chest and bulked out just shy of a hundred pounds. A short length of chewed leather tether hung from his collar. Matt had left Bane, along with his three other dogs, back at his temporary campsite while he went to freshen the scent lure of a nearby hair trap. The lure—a mixture of cow's blood, rotted fish guts, and skunk oil—drove the dogs crazy. He had learned his lesson this morning when Gregor had rolled in a freshly laid lure. It had taken repeated baths to get the scent off the dog. He had not wanted a repeat of the event this afternoon and had left the dogs behind. But always his companion, Bane had clearly chewed through his lead and tracked after him.

Bane barked again.

Matt turned to see both bears—mother and cub—frozen in place at the sudden appearance of the large dog. The she-bear snuffled the air. Up here in the Brooks Range, she was surely familiar with wolves. Would the threat be enough to chase the bears off?

Closer, only fifteen yards away, the cub danced a bit on its feet. Then with a toss of its head, it bounced toward them, heedless of any threat. The mother now had no choice. She opened her mouth and bellowed, dropping down to begin her charge.

Matt thought quickly. He jammed the can of pepper spray

into its holster and snatched a jelly jar full of blood lure from the side of his backpack. He leaned back and tossed it with all the strength in his arm and upper back. The fist-sized bottle flew with the accuracy of a Yankee pitcher's fastball and shattered against the bole of a cottonwood thirty yards up the trail. Blood and guts splattered out. Usually two thimbles of the contents were enough to freshen a lure, capable of attracting bears from miles around. With the entire bottle emptied, the concentrated scent immediately swelled out, ripening the air.

The cub stopped its ambling approach, dead in its tracks. It lifted its nose high, sniffing and snuffling. Its head swung like a radar dish toward the source of the delicious smell. Even the she-bear interrupted her charge to glance toward the smeared cottonwood. The cub turned and bounded up the slope. For a hungry cub, fresh from hibernating in its winter den, the reek was a thousand times more interesting than blackberry briars or a pair of woodland strangers. The cub loped happily away. His mother eyed them warily still, but she sidled back on her haunches, guarding her cub as it trundled past her toward the fouled tree.

Matt sensed now would be a good time to make a hasty retreat. "Heel, Bane," he whispered. The dog's nose was in the air, sniffing at the lure. Matt reached down and grabbed the chewed end of the lead. "Don't even think about it."

He backed over the ridge and down the far side, leaving the bears to their prize. He kept walking backward, one eye on the trail behind him, one eye on the ridge above, just in case mama decided to follow. But the bears stayed put, and after a quarter mile, Matt turned and hiked the two miles back to camp.

Camp had been set by a wide stream, still iced over in patches as full spring was late to come. But there were signs of the warmer weather to follow in the blooming wildflowers all around: blue Jacob's ladder, yellow fireweed, blood-red wild roses, and purple violets. Even the frozen stream, framed in willows and lined by alders, was edged in blooming water hemlock.

It was one of Matt's favorite times of the year, when the Gates of the Arctic National Park climbed out of winter's hibernation, but too early for the tourists and rafters to begin their annual pilgrimage here. Not that there were that many folks even then within the confines of the eight million acres, a reserve the size of Vermont and Connecticut combined. Over the entire year, fewer than three thousand visitors braved the rugged park.

But for the moment, Matt had the region all to himself.

At the camp, the usual cacophony of yips and barks greeted his safe return. His roan mare—half Arabian, half quarter horse—nickered at him, tossing her nose and stamping a single hoof in clear feminine irritation. Bane trotted ahead and bumped and nosed his own mates in canine camaraderie. Matt loosed the three other dogs—Gregor, Simon, and Butthead—from their tethers. They ran in circles, sniffing, lifting legs, tongues lolling, the usual mischief of the canine species.

Bane simply returned to his side, sitting, eyeing the younger dogs. His coat was almost solid black, with just a hint of a silver undercoat and a white blaze under his chin.

Matt frowned at the pack leader, ready to scold, but he shook his head instead. What was the damn use? Bane was the lead of his sled team, quick to respond to commands and agile of limb, but the mutt always had a stubborn will of his own.

"You know that cost us an entire bottle of lure," Matt griped. "Carol is going to drain our blood to make the next one." Carol Jeffries was the head researcher running the DNA bear program out of Bettles. She would have his hide for losing the jelly jar. With just one bottle left, he could bait only half the sampling traps. He would have to return early, setting her research behind by a full month. He could imagine her ire. Sighing, he wondered if it wouldn't have been better simply to wrestle the four-hundred-pound grizzly.

He patted Bane's side and ruffled the dog's thick mane, earning a thump of a tail. "Let's see about getting dinner." If the day was wasted, he might as well have a hot meal tonight as consolation. Though it was early, the sky was beginning to cloud up, and this far north, the Arctic sun would soon set. They might even get a bit of rain or snow before nightfall. So if he wanted a fire tonight, he'd best get to work now.

He shrugged out of his coat, an old Army parka, patched at the elbows, its green color worn to a dull gray with a soft alpaca liner buttoned inside. Dressed in a thick wool shirt and heavy trousers, he was warm enough, especially after the long hike and the earlier adrenaline surge. He crossed to the river with a bucket and cracked ice from the stream edge. Though it would be easier simply to scoop water from the stream itself, the ice was distinctly purer. Since he was going to make a fire, it would melt quickly enough anyway.

With practiced ease, he set about the usual routine of preparing his camp, glad to have the woods to himself. He whistled under his breath as he gathered dry wood. Then, after a moment, a strange silence settled around him. It took him half a breath to realize it. The dogs had gone quiet. Even the twittering of golden plovers from the willows had ceased. His own lonely whistle cut out.

Then he heard it, too.

The rumble of an airplane.

It was a soft sound until the single-engine Cessna crossed the ridgeline and swooped over the valley. Matt strained up. Even before he saw the plane, he knew something was wrong. The sound of the engine was not a continual whine, but an asthmatic sputter.

The plane tilted on one wing, then the other. Its height bobbled, engine coughing. Matt could imagine the pilot struggling to look for a place to land. It was outfitted with floats, as were most bush pilot planes. It only needed a river wide enough upon which to set down. But Matt knew none would be found up here. The tiny stream beside his camp would eventually drain into the wider Alatna River that ran through the center of the park, but that was a good hundred miles away.

He watched the Cessna scribe a drunken path over the valley. Then with a grind of the engine, it climbed enough to limp over the next ridgeline. Matt winced as he watched. He would've sworn the floats brushed the top of a spruce tree. Then the plane was gone.

Matt continued to stare, ears straining to listen for the fate of the plane. It was not long in coming. Like the sound of distant thunder, a splintering crash echoed from the neighboring valley.

"Goddamn it," he mumbled under his breath.

He watched the skyline, and after a long moment, he saw the telltale streak of oily smoke snake into the dirty-white sky.

"And I thought I had a bad day." He turned to his camp. "Saddle up, boys. Dinner will to have to wait."

He grabbed up his Army jacket and crossed to his mare, shaking his head. In any other place in the world, this might be a rare event, but up here in Alaska, the bush pilot myth was alive and well. There was a certain macho bravado in seeing how far one could push oneself or one's aircraft, leading to unnecessary chances. Over the course of a year, two hundred small planes crashed into the Alaskan wilderness. Salvage operators hired to recover the planes were backlogged for almost a full year. And it was a growth industry. Every year, more planes fell. "Who needs to dig for gold," a salvage operator once told him, "when money falls out of the damn sky?"

Matt saddled his mare. Planes were one thing, people were another. If there were any survivors, the sooner they were rescued, the better their chances. Alaska was not kind to the weak or injured. Matt had been reminded of this fact all too well himself today when he went eyeball to eyeball with a four-hundred-pound grizzly. It was an eat-or-be-eaten world out here.

He secured his tack with a final tug and tossed on his saddlebag with the first-aid kit. He didn't bother with his one handheld radio. He had traveled beyond range three days ago.

Slipping his moosehide boot into a stirrup, Matt pulled himself into the saddle. His dogs danced around at the edges of the camp. They knew they were heading out. "C'mon, boys, time to play heroes."

SEVEROMORSK NAVAL COMPLEX
MURMANSK, RUSSIA

Viktor Petkov stood at Pier Four, bundled in a long brown greatcoat and fur cap. The only markings of his rank were on the red epaulets and the front of his cap: four gold stars.

He smoked a cigar, Cuban, though it was all but forgotten. At his back rose the Severomorsk Naval Complex, his home and domain. Bounded in razor wire and concrete blast barriers, the small city housed the massive shipyards, dry docks, repair facilities, weapons depots, and operations buildings of the Russian Northern Fleet. Positioned on the northern coast, the city-complex faced the Arctic Ocean and braved the harsh winters of this hostile land. Here were forged not only mighty seagoing vessels but even harder men.

Viktor's storm-gray eyes ignored the ocean and focused on the rush of activity down the length of the pier. The submarine *Drakon* was almost ready to be tugged away from her berth. The shore-power cables were already being hauled and secured.

"Admiral Petkov," the young captain said, standing at attention. "On your orders, the *Drakon* is ready to be under way."

He nodded, checking his watch. "Once aboard, I'll need a secure landline before we leave."

"Yes, sir. If you'll follow me."

Viktor studied Captain Mikovsky as he was led down the pier to the gangway. The *Drakon* was the man's first command assignment. He recognized the pride in the other's gait. Captain Mikovsky had just returned from a successful shakedown cruise of the new Akula class II vessel and was now taking the admiral of the Northern Fleet on a mission whose specifics were still sealed from all eyes. The thirty-year-old captain—half Viktor's own age—strode down the pier like the cock of the walk.

Was I ever this foolish? Viktor wondered as they reached the gangway. Only a year from retirement, he could hardly remember being so young, so sure of himself. The world had become a less certain place over the past decades.

The captain preceded him, announcing the admiral's arrival shipboard, then turned back to him. "Request permission to be under way, sir."

He nodded and flicked the stub of his cigar into the waters below.

The captain began issuing orders, relayed through a bullhorn by the officer of the deck positioned atop the sail's bridge to the crew on the pier. "Lose the gangway. Take in line one. Take in line two."

A crane hauled the gangway up and away. Line handlers scurried among the bollards and ropes.

Mikovsky led the way up the steel rungs of the conning tower. Once there, he gave final orders to his officer of the deck and junior officer of the deck, then led Viktor down into the submarine itself.

It had been almost two years since the admiral had been aboard a submarine, but he knew the layout of this boat down to every screw and plate. Since he was an old submariner himself, the designs had passed through his office for inspection and comment. Despite this knowledge, he allowed Mikovsky to walk him through the busy control station and down to the captain's stateroom that he was commandeering for this voyage.

Eyes followed him, respectfully glancing away when caught. He knew the image he presented. Tall for a sub-mariner, lean and lanky. His hair had aged to a shock of white, worn uncharacteristically long to his collar. This, along with his stolid demeanor and ice-gray eyes, had earned him his nickname. He heard it whispered down the boat.

Belyi Prizrak

The White Ghost.

At last, they reached his cabin.

"The communication line is still active as you requested," Mikovsky said, standing at the door.

"And the crates from the research facility?"

"Stored in the stateroom, as you ordered." The captain waved to the open door.

The admiral glanced inside. "Very good." He slipped off his fur cap. "You're dismissed, Captain. See to your boat."

"Yes, Admiral." The man turned on a heel and departed.

Viktor closed the stateroom door and locked it behind him. His personal gear was piled neatly by the bed, but at the back of the small room was a stack of six titanium boxes. He crossed to the sealed red binder resting atop the stack. One finger checked the seal against tampering. It was secure. Across the face of the binder was stenciled one word:

ГРЕНДЕЛ

It was a name out of legend.

Grendel.

His fingers formed a fist over the folder. The name for this mission had been derived from the Nordic tale *Beowulf.* Grendel was the legendary monster that terrorized the north-ern coasts until defeated by the Norse hero Beowulf. But for Petkov, the name carried a deeper meaning. It was his own personal demon, a source of pain, shame, humiliation, and grief. It had forged the man he was today. His fist clenched harder.

After so long . . . almost sixty years . . . He remembered his father being led away at the point of a gun in the middle of the night. He had been only six years old.

He stared at the stack of boxes. It took him a long moment to breathe again. He turned away. The stateroom, painted green, contained a single bunk, a bookshelf, a desk, a wash-basin, and a communication station that consisted of the bridge speaker box, a video monitor, and a single telephone.

He reached and picked up the phone's receiver, spoke rapidly, then listened as his call was routed, coded, and rerouted again. He waited. Then a familiar voice came on the line, frosted with static. "Leopard, here."

"Status?"

"The target is down."

"Confirmation?"

"Under way."

"You know your orders."

A pause. "No survivors."

This last needed no validation. Admiral Petkov ended the call, settling the receiver down into its cradle. Now it started.

5:16 P.M.
BROOKS RANGE, ALASKA

Matt urged his horse up the ridgeline. It had been a hard climb. The neighboring valley was a thousand feet higher in elevation. Up here, snow still lay on the ground, thicker in the shadow of the trees. His four dogs were already loping ahead, sniffing, nosing, ears perked. He whistled to keep them from getting too far ahead.

From the ridgeline, Matt surveyed the next valley. A spiral of smoke, thinning now, marked the crash site, but the forest of spruce and alder blocked the view of the crumpled plane. He listened. No voices were heard. A bad sign. Frowning, he tapped his heels on his mare's flanks. "Off we go, Mariah."

He walked his horse down, mindful of the ice and snow. He followed a seep creek trickling through the forest. A mist hung over the thread of water. The quiet grew unnerving. Mosquitoes buzzed him, setting his teeth on edge. The only other noise was his horse's steps: a crunching sound as each hoof broke through the crust of ice over the snow.

Even his dogs had grown less ebullient, drawing closer, stopping frequently to lift noses to the air.

Bane kept a guard on point, sticking fifty paces ahead of him. The dark-furred wolf mix kept to the shadows, almost lost in the dappling. As the companion of a Fish and Game warden, Bane had gone through a canine search-and-rescue program. The dog had a keen nose and seemed to sense where Matt was headed.

Once they reached the valley floor, their pace increased. Matt could now smell burning oil. They headed toward it as directly as the terrain would allow, but it still took them another twenty minutes to reach the crash site.

The forest opened into a meadow. The pilot must have been aiming for it, hoping to land his craft in the break in the forest. He had almost made it, too. A long gouge crossed the meadow of yellow milk vetch, directly across the center of the clearing. But the landing field had been too short.

Off to the left, a Cessna 185 Skywagon lay smashed into the forest of green spruce. It had jammed nose first into the trees, wings crumpled and torn away, tilted tail end up. Smoke billowed from the crushed engine compartment, and the stench of fuel filled the valley. The risk of fire was great.

Walking his way across the meadow, Matt noted the clouds, heavy and low, that hung overhead. For once, rain would be welcome up here. Even more encouraging would have been any sign of movement.

Once within a few yards, Matt yanked the reins and climbed off his horse. He stood another long moment staring at the wreckage. He had seen dead bodies before, plenty of them. He had served six years in the Green Berets, spending time in Somalia and the Middle East before opting out to complete college through the GI Bill. So it was not squeamishness that kept him back. Still, death had touched him too deeply, too personally, to make it an easy task of stepping amid the wreckage.

But if there were any survivors . . .

Matt proceeded toward the ruined Cessna. "Hello!" he yelled, feeling foolish.

No answer. No surprise there.

He crept under a bent wing and crunched through broken safety glass. The windows had shattered out as the fuselage crumpled. From the engine compartment ahead, smoke continued to billow, choking him, stinging his eyes. A stream of gasoline flowed underfoot.

Matt held his arm over his mouth and nose. He tried the door. It was jammed and twisted tight. He stretched up and poked his head in the side window. The plane was not empty.

The pilot was strapped into his seat, but from the angle of his neck and the spar piercing his chest, he was clearly dead. The seat next to the pilot was empty. Matt began to crane around to check the backseats—then a shock passed through him as he recognized the pilot. The mop of black hair, the scraggly beard, the blue eyes . . . now glazed and lifeless.

"Brent . . ." he mumbled. Brent Cumming. They had played poker regularly back when Matt and Jenny were still together. Jenny was a sheriff for the Nunamiut and Inupiat native tribes, and because of the vast distances under her jurisdiction, she was of necessity a skilled pilot. As such, she knew the other pilots who serviced the region, including Brent Cumming. Their two families had spent a summer camping, their kids romping and playing together. How was he going to tell Cheryl, Brent's wife?

He shook himself out of his shock and poked his head into the back window, numbly checking the rear seats. He found a man sprawled on his back, faceup. He wasn't moving either. Matt started to sigh when suddenly the man's arms shot up, a gun clutched between his hands.

"Don't move!"

Matt startled, more at the sudden shout than the threat of the gun.

"I mean it! Don't move!" The man sat up. He was pale, his green eyes wide, his blond hair caked with blood on his left side. His head must have struck the window frame. Still his aim did not waver. "I'll shoot!"

"Then shoot," Matt said calmly, leaning a bit against the plane's fuselage.

This response clearly baffled the stranger. His brow pinched together. From the man's brand-new Eddie Bauer Arctic parka, he was clearly a stranger to these parts. Nonetheless, there was a hard edge to him. Though having just crashed, he clearly had kept his wits about him. Matt had to give him credit there.

"If you'll put that *flare* gun down," Matt said, "maybe I'll even think about finishing this rescue mission."

The man waited a full breath, then lowered his arms, sagging backward. "I . . . I'm sorry."

"Nothing to be sorry about. You just fell out of the sky. In such rare cases, I have the tendency to forgive a lack of gracious hospitality."

This earned a tired grin from the man.

"Are you hurt?" he asked.

"Head took a good crack. And my leg's caught."

Matt leaned through the window, having to stretch up on his toes. The front section of the plane had crimped back, trapping the man's right leg between the copilot's seat and his own. So much for just having the man crawl through the window.

"The pilot . . ." the man began. "Is he . . ."

"Dead," Matt finished. "Nothing we can do for him at the moment." He tugged again at the door. He wouldn't be able to free it with brute strength alone. He tapped one knuckle on the fuselage, thinking. "Hang on a sec."

He crossed back to Mariah, grabbed the horse's reins, and walked her closer to the wreckage. She protested with a toss of her head. It was bad enough being pulled away from the pasture of milk vetch, but the burning engine smell spooked her, too. "Easy there, gal," Matt soothed.

His dogs simply remained where they lay sprawled. Bane sat up, ears perked, but Matt waved the wolf down.

Once close enough, Matt ran a rope from the saddle to the frame of the plane's door. He didn't trust the handle to be secure enough. He then crossed back to the mare and urged her to follow. She did so willingly, glad to leave the vicinity of the foul-smelling wreckage, but once she reached the length of her tether, she stopped.

Matt coaxed her with tugs on her reins, but she still refused. He slid behind her, biting back a curse, then grabbed her tail and pulled it up over her hind end. He hated tailing her like this, but he had to get her to pull. She whinnied at the pain and kicked a hoof at him. He tumbled away, letting go of the tail and landing on his backside. He shook his head. He and the female species never did know how to communicate.

Then Bane was there, barking, snapping at the horse's heels. Mariah might not respect Matt, but a half wolf was another thing. Old instincts ran deep. The mare leaped ahead, yanking on the tether.

A groan of metal erupted behind him. Matt rolled around. The entire tilted fuselage of the Cessna canted to the side. A shout of alarm arose from inside. Then, with the popping sound of an opening soda can, the crumpled door broke away.

Mariah reared up, but Matt returned to calm her. He undid the saddle hitch and walked her away, waving Bane off. He settled her at the edge of the clearing, then patted her flank. "Good girl. You've earned yourself an extra handful of grain tonight."

He strode back to the wreckage. The stranger was almost out of the plane. He was able to slide his trapped leg along the edge of the two crammed seats until he reached the open door. Then he was free.

Matt helped him down. "How's the leg?"

The man tested it gingerly. "Bruised, and the worst damned charley horse, but nothing feels broken." Now that the man was free, Matt realized he was younger than he first appeared. Probably no more than his late twenties.

As they hobbled away from the wreckage, Matt held out a hand. "Name's Matthew Pike."

"Craig . . . Craig Teague."

After they were well away from the plane, Matt settled the man to a log, then shoved away his dogs when they came up to nose the stranger. Matt straightened a kink from his back and glanced back to the plane and his dead friend. "So what happened?"

The man remained silent for a long moment. When he spoke, it was in a whisper. "I don't know. We were heading to Deadhorse—"

"Over in Prudhoe?"

"Prudhoe Bay, yes." The man nodded, gingerly fingering his lacerated scalp. Deadhorse was the name of the airport that serviced the oilfields and township of Prudhoe Bay. It was located at the northernmost edge of Alaska, where the North Slope's oil fields met the Arctic Ocean. "We were about two hours out of Fairbanks when the pilot reported something wrong with the engine. It seemed he was losing fuel or something. Which seemed impossible since we had just tanked up in Fairbanks."

Matt could smell the fuel still in the air. They had not run out of juice, that's for sure. And Brent Cumming always kept his plane's engine in tip-top shape. A mechanic before becoming a bush pilot, Brent knew his way around the Cessna's three-hundred-horsepower engine. With two kids and a wife, he depended on that craft for both his livelihood and his lifeline, so Brent maintained his machinery like a finely tuned Rolex.

"When the engine began to sputter, we tried to find a place to land, but by that time we were among these damn mountains. The pilot . . . he . . . he tried to radio for help, but even the radio seemed to be malfunctioning."

Matt understood. There had been storms of solar flares this past week. They messed with all sorts of communication in the northern regions. He glanced back to the wreckage. He could only imagine the terror of those last moments: the panic, the desperation, the disbelief.

The man's voice cracked slightly. He had to swallow to continue speaking. "We had no choice but to try to land here. And then . . . and then . . ."

Matt reached over and patted the man's shoulder. The rest of the story was plainly evident. "It's okay. We'll get you out of here. But I should see about that head wound of yours first."

He crossed over to Mariah and retrieved the first-aid kit. It was really a full med kit. Matt had assembled it himself, utilizing his experience in the Green Berets. Besides the usual gauze rolls, Band-Aids, and aspirin, he had a small pharmacy of antibiotics, antihistamines, antiprotozoals, and antidiarrhetics. The kit also contained suture material, local anesthetic, syringes, splinting material, even a stethoscope. He pulled out a bottle of peroxide and cleaned the man's wound.

Matt talked as he worked. "So, Craig, what was your business up in Prudhoe?" he asked, studying the other. The fellow certainly didn't have the look of an oil rigger. Among such hard men, black oil and grease were indelibly tattooed into the creases and folds of their hands. Contrarily, this man's palms were free of calluses, his nails unbroken and neatly trimmed. Matt supposed he was an engineer or geologist. In fact, the man had a studious look to his countenance, keenly assessing his surroundings, glancing to Matt's horse, his dogs, the meadow, and the surrounding mountains. The only place he avoided looking was back to the wreckage.

"Prudhoe Bay wasn't my destination. We were to refuel there, then hop out to a research base on the ice cap. Omega Drift Station, a part of the SCICEX research group."

"SCICEX?" Matt smeared antibiotic cream on the wound, then covered it with a Teflon-coated gauze sponge, wrapping it in place.

" 'Scientific Ice Expeditions,' " Craig explained, wincing as Matt secured the wrap. "It's a five-year collaborative effort between the U.S. Navy and civilian scientists."

Matt nodded. "I think I remember hearing about that." The group was using Navy subs to collect data from over a hundred thousand miles of ship track in the Arctic, delving into regions never before visited. Matt's brow crinkled. "But I thought that ended back in 1999."

His words drew the man's full attention, his eyes widening slightly in surprise as he turned to Matt.

"Despite appearances," Matt explained, "I'm Fish and Game. So I'm generally familiar with many of the larger Arctic research projects."

Craig studied him with cautious, calculating eyes, then bobbed his head. "Well, you're right. Officially SCICEX ended, but one station—Omega—had drifted into the ice cap's Zone of Comparative Inaccessibility."

No-man's-land, Matt thought. The ZCI was the most remote part of the polar ice cap, hardest to reach and most isolated.

"For a chance to study such an inaccessible region, funding was extended to this one SCICEX station."

"So you're a scientist?" Matt said, fastening up his med kit.

The man laughed, but there was no real humor behind it. "No, not a scientist. I was on assignment from my newspaper. The *Seattle Times.* I'm a political reporter."

"A political reporter?"

The man shrugged.

"Why would—" Matt was cut off by the buzzing sound of

a plane's engine. He craned his neck. The lowering sky was thick with heavy clouds. Off to the side, Bane growled deep in his throat as the noise grew in volume.

Craig climbed to his feet. "Another plane. Maybe someone heard the pilot's distress call."

From the clouds, a small plane appeared, dropping over the valley but still keeping high. Matt watched it pass. It was another Cessna, only a larger version than Brent's. It appeared to be a 206 or 207 Skywagon, an eight-seater.

Matt whistled Mariah closer to him, then plucked his binoculars from the saddlebag. Lifting the scopes, he searched a moment for the plane, then focused on it. It appeared brand-new . . . or freshly painted. Rare for these parts. The terrain was hard on aircraft.

"Have they spotted us?" Craig asked.

The plane tilted on a wing and began a slow circle over the valley. "With the trail of engine smoke, it'd be hard to miss us."

Still, Matt felt a tingle of unease. He had not spotted a single plane in the past week, and now two in one day. And this plane was too clean, too white. As he watched, the rear cargo door craned open. That was the nice thing about that size of Skywagon. Such planes were used around these parts to shuttle the injured to various outlying hospitals. The rear cargo hatch was perfect for loading and unloading stretchers, or, in worst cases, coffins. But there was another useful and common application for the Skywagon's large rear hatch.

From the cargo bay, a shape flew free, and a second quickly followed. Sky divers. Matt had a hard time following them with his binoculars. They were plummeting fast. Then chutes ballooned out, slowing them, making them easier to focus upon. Parawing airfoils, Matt recognized, used in precision parachuting for landing in tight places. The pair swung around in tandem, aiming for the meadow.

Matt focused on the divers themselves. Like the plane and

chutes, they were outfitted in white, no insignia. Rifles were strapped to their backs, but he was unable to discern make and type.

As he spied on them, cold dread settled in the pit of his stomach. It was not the presence of the guns that trickled ice into Matt's blood. Instead, it was what was *under* each sky diver. Each man was strapped into the seat of a motorcycle. The tires were studded with metal spikes. Snow choppers. They were muscular vehicles, capable of tearing up terrain, chasing anything down in these mountains.

Matt lowered the binoculars. He stared over at the reporter, then cleared his throat. "I hope you're good at riding a horse."

2

Cat and Mouse

ᐹᓯᓗ ᐊᑳᓐᖓᒐᕐᖓ

APRIL 6, 5:36 P.M.
ZCI REGION OF THE POLAR ICE CAP
OMEGA DRIFT STATION

Will I ever be warm again . . . ?

Captain Perry crunched across the ice and snow toward Omega Drift Station. The wind whistled around him, a haunted sound that spoke to the hollowness in his heart. Here, at the end of the world, the wind was a living creature, always blowing, scouring the surface like a starving beast. It was the ultimate predator: merciless, constant, inescapable. As an old Inuit proverb says, "It's not the cold that kills, it's the wind."

Perry marched steadily forward into the teeth of the blustery gale. Behind him, the *Polar Sentinel* floated inside a polynya, a large open lake within the ice. The Omega Drift Station was constructed on its shoreline, the site having been chosen for the stability of the nearby polynya, allowing easy ingress and egress of a Navy sub. The polynya owed its permanence to the ring of thick pressure ridges that surrounded the lake, climbing two stories high and delving four times as deep below the surface. These battlements of packed ice held the lake open against the constant crush of the surrounding floes. The research station was built on a relatively level ice plain a quarter mile away, a long hike in the subzero cold.

He marched with a small party of his men, the first of four rotations to be allowed shore leave. The sailors chattered among themselves, but Perry remained hunched in his Navy parka, the edge of his fur-lined hood pulled tightly over his face. He stared off to the northeast, to where the Russian ice base had been discovered two months ago, only thirty miles from here. A shiver trembled through him, but it had nothing to do with the cold.

So many dead . . . He pictured the Russian bodies, the old inhabitants of the ice base, stacked like cordwood after being chopped or thawed out of their icy tomb. Thirty-two men, twelve women. It had taken them two weeks to clear all the bodies. Some had looked starved to death, while others looked as if they had met more violent ends. They found one body hung in a room, the rope so frozen it shattered with their touch. *But that wasn't the worst . . .*

Perry pushed this thought away.

As he climbed a ridge of ice, made easier by the steps chopped into it, the drift station came into view. It was a small hamlet of red Jamesway huts. The assembly of fifteen red buildings appeared like a bloody rash on the ice. Steam smoked from each hut, misting over the base, giving it a deceptively sultry appearance. The rumble of twenty-four generators seemed to vibrate the mists. The smell of diesel fuel and kerosene hung over the site. A single lone American flag hung from a pole, snapping in the occasional fiercer gusts.

Scattered around the semipermanent settlement, a handful of Ski-Doos and two sealed Sno-Cats stood ready to service the scientists and personnel of the base. There was even an iceboat, a catamaran resting on stainless-steel runners.

From the top of the ridge, Perry stared out toward the horizon. He saw the worn trail snaking across the ice, heading from Omega out to the old Russian base. Ever since the discovery, the personnel here had been shuttling back and forth across the ice cap, using whatever vehicles were on hand. Currently a quarter of the drift station's manpower had shifted over to the buried Russian base and was encamped inside the inverted mountain of ice.

Perry stared another long moment. The path to the Russian base was easy to see. This area of the ice cap was covered with a layer of scalloped snow, what was called *sastrugi,* little curled waves of frozen snow formed by winds and erosion. "Like the top of a lemon meringue," his XO had commented. But the path made by the Sno-Cats and Ski-Doos had ground the lemon meringue *sastrugi* flat, leaving a worn track through the crisp waves.

Perry understood the interest of the men and women here. They were scientists with an avid curiosity. But none of them had been the first to enter the base as he had been, crossing the thirty miles overland from Omega to the defunct station. None knew what he and a small group of his men had found in the heart of the station. He had immediately ordered his men silent and stationed a complement of armed guards to keep that one section of the base off-limits to the Omega personnel. Only one member of the drift station knew of Perry's find: Dr. Amanda Reynolds. She had been with Perry when he had entered the base. For the first time, the strong and independent woman had been shaken to her core.

Whatever had shown up on the DeepEye sonar—the flicker of movement seen on the recording—was never discovered. Maybe it had been just a sonar ghost, a mirage created by the sub's own motion, or maybe it was some scavenger that had vacated the station, like a polar bear. Though this last was unlikely, not unless the beast had found an entrance that they had yet to discover. Two months ago, they had been forced to use thermite charges to melt a way down into the buried station. Since then, extra heat charges and C4 explosives had been used to open an artificial polynya nearby for the *Polar Sentinel* to service the newly reoccupied base.

As Perry climbed down the ice ridge, he wished they had simply sunk the entire Russian station. No good would come of it. He was certain of that. But he had orders to follow. He shivered as the winds kicked up.

A shout drew his attention back to the assembly of Jamesway huts. A figure dressed in a blue parka waved an arm in their direction, encouraging them forward. Perry crossed down the ridge toward the figure. The man hurried forward to meet him, hunched against the cold.

"Captain." The figure was Erik Gustof, the Canadian meteorologist. He was a strapping fellow of Norwegian descent, characterized by whitish-blond hair and tall build, though at the moment, all that could be discerned were the man's two eyes, goggled against the snow's glare, and a frosted white mustache. "There's a satellite call holding for you."

"Who—?"

"Admiral Reynolds." The man glanced to the skies. "You'd best be quick. There's a big storm headed our way, and that last bevy of solar flares is still wreaking havoc with the systems."

Perry nodded and turned to his junior officer. "Dismiss the men. They're on their own until twenty hundred. Then the next team gets their turn ashore."

This was met with general whoops from the men. They scattered in various directions, some to the station's mess hall, others to the recreation hut, and others still to the living quarters for more personal dalliances. Captain Perry followed Erik to an assembly of three joined huts, the main base of operations.

"Dr. Reynolds sent me out to hurry you along," Erik explained. "She's speaking with her father right now. We don't know how long communication will hold."

They reached the door to the operations hut, kicked off snow and ice from their boots, then ducked through the doorway. The heat of the interior was painful after the frigid cold. Perry shook off his gloves, then unzipped his parka and threw back his hood. He rubbed the tip of his nose to make sure it was still there.

"Nippy out, eh?" Erik said, remaining in his parka.

"It's not the cold, it's the humidity," he grumbled sarcastically. Perry hung up his parka among the many others already there. He still wore his blue jumpsuit with his name stenciled on a pocket. He folded his cap and tucked it into his belt.

Erik stepped back to the door. "You know the way to the NAVSAT station. I'm going to check on some instruments outside before the storm hits tonight."

"Thanks."

Erik grinned and yanked the door open. Even in such a short time, the wind had kicked up outside. A gust whipped inside and struck Perry like a slap to the face. Erik hurried out, shoving the door shut.

Perry shivered a moment, rubbing his hands. *Who the hell would volunteer to stay in this godforsaken land for two years?*

He crossed the anteroom and went through another set of doors into the main operations room. It held all the various offices of the administration, along with several labs. The main purpose of the research in this building was to measure the seasonal rate of growth and erosion of the ice pack, measuring the heat budget of the Arctic. But other labs in other huts varied greatly, from a full mining operation that sampled cores of the ocean floor to a hydrolab that studied the health of the phyto- and zooplankton under the ice. The research was continuous, running around the clock as the station drifted along, floating with the polar current and traveling almost two miles every day.

He nodded to various familiar faces behind desks or bent over computer screens. He crossed through a set of airlock-type doors that led into one of the adjoining huts.

This hut was extra insulated and had two backup generators. It was Omega's lifeline to the outside world. It contained all their radio and communication equipment: shortwave for maintaining contact with teams on the ice, VLF and ULF for communication with the subs assigned here, and NAVSAT, the military satellite communication system. The hut was empty, except for the lone figure of Amanda Reynolds.

Perry crossed to her. She glanced up from where she leaned over a TTY, a text telephone unit. The portable keyboard device allowed her to communicate over the satellite. She could speak into the microphone and answers would come out on the LCD screen.

Amanda nodded to him, but spoke to her father, Admiral Reynolds. "I know, Dad. I know you didn't want me out here in the first place. But—"

She was cut off and leaned closer to read the TTY. Her face reddened; obviously an argument had been under way. And it was an old argument from the looks of it. Her father hadn't wanted Amanda to take this assignment in the first place, worried about her, about her disability. Amanda had defied him, coming anyway, asserting her independence.

But Perry wondered how much of her fight was not so much to convince her father as herself. He had never met a woman so fiercely determined to prove herself in all things, in all ways.

And it was taking its toll.

Perry studied the worn look in her eyes, the bruised shadows beneath them. She appeared to have aged a decade over the past two months. Secrets did that to you.

She continued, speaking into the phone, heat entering her voice. "We'll discuss this later. Captain Perry is here."

As she read her father's response, she held her breath, biting her lower lip. "Fine!" she finally snapped, and ripped off the headset. She shoved it at him. "Here."

He took the headset, noting the tremble in her fingers. Fury, frustration, or both? He palmed the microphone to keep his next words private with her. "Is he still keeping the information under lock and key?"

Amanda snorted and stood. "And electronic padlock and voiceprint recognition and retinal scan identification. Fort Knox couldn't be more secure."

Perry smiled at her. "He's doing his best. The bureaucratic machinery under him grinds slowly. With such sensitive matters, diplomatic channels have to be handled with delicacy."

"But I don't know why. This goes back to World War Two. After so long, the world has a right to know."

"It's waited for fifty years. It can wait another month or so. With the already strained relations between the U.S. and Russia, the way has to be greased before letting the information out."

Amanda sighed, stared into his eyes, then shook her head. "You sound just like my father."

Perry leaned in. "In that case, this would be very Freudian." He kissed her.

She smiled under his lips and mumbled, "You kiss like him, too."

He choked a laugh, pulling back.

She pointed to the headset. "You'd best not keep the admiral waiting."

He slipped the headset in place and pulled up the microphone. "Captain Perry here."

"Captain, I trust you're taking good care of my daughter." His voice cut in and out a bit.

"Yes, sir . . . very good care." One hand reached over and squeezed Amanda's hand. Their affection for each other was no secret, but it had grown deeper over the past two months, slipping past fondness to something more meaningful. For propriety's sake, they restricted any outward displays to private moments. Not even the admiral, Amanda's father, knew of the escalation of their affections.

"Captain, I'll keep this brief," the admiral continued. "The Russian ambassador was contacted yesterday and given a copy of your report."

"But I thought we weren't going to contact them until—"

Now it was Perry's turn to be cut off. "We had no choice," the admiral interrupted. "Word had somehow reached Moscow about the rediscovery of the old ice station."

"Yes, sir. But what does this mean for those of us out here?"

There was a long pause. Perry was momentarily unsure if the solar storm had cut off communication—then the admiral spoke again, "Greg . . ."

The informal use of his first name instantly drew him to full alert.

"Greg, I need you to be aware of something else. While I may be out here on the West Coast, I've been in this business long enough to know when the hive back in D.C. is buzzing. Something is going on over there. Midnight meetings between the NSA and the CIA over the matter. The secretary of the Navy has been recalled from a junket in the Middle East. The entire cabinet was recalled early from their Easter break."

"What's it all about?"

"That's just it. I don't know. Something broke high in command, higher than my station. Word has yet to reach me . . . if it ever will. Some political shit storm is brewing over this. D.C. is locking up hatches and battening down. I've never seen its like before."

A cold finger of dread ran up Perry's spine. "I don't understand. Why?"

Again his words stuttered in the electronic chop. "I'm not sure. But I wanted to give you heads-up about the escalation down here."

Perry frowned. It all sounded like the usual politics to him. He would note the admiral's concern, but what else could he do?

"Captain, there's one other thing. A strange tidbit that has trickled down to me; actually it was passed by an aide to the undersecretary. It's a single word that seems to be the center of the shit storm."

"What's the word?"

"Grendel."

Perry's breath went out of him.

"Perhaps a code name, a name of a ship, I don't know," the admiral continued. "Does it mean anything to you?"

Perry closed his eyes. *Grendel* . . . The discovery had only been made today. The steel plaque had been covered in ice and hoarfrost and was easy to miss. It was near the main surface entrance into the buried ice station.

ЛЕДОВАЯ СТАНЦИЯ ГРЕНДЕЛ

"Greg?"

His mind continued to spin. *How did Washington know . . . ?* Omega's translator and the *Sentinel*'s own linguistic expert had argued over the plaque's translation, especially the last word, until finally coming to the same conclusion.

It was the name of the buried base: *Ice Station Grendel*.

"Captain Perry, are you still there?"

"Yes, sir."

"Does the word mean something?"

"Yes, sir, I believe it does." His voice remained tight. Besides the word being etched on the plaque, Perry had seen the same Cyrillic lettering in one other place, on one of the station's doors . . . a door before which he himself had posted armed guards.

ГРЕНДЕЛ

Until today, he had not known the meaning of the Cyrillic letters stenciled upon that monstrous door.

Now he did.

But he hadn't been the first.

6:26 P.M.
BROOKS RANGE, ALASKA

Matt led the way up the steep slope, guiding Mariah by the reins. Craig rode on top, hunched down, clinging to the saddle horn. Matt dared not ride double, at least not yet, not until they were headed downhill or at least on flat land. He feared taxing the horse too soon.

Ahead, his four dogs ranged toward the top of the valley. They all had to get out of these steep peaks. Only Bane seemed to sense his master's fear, sticking close, ears perked.

Matt glanced behind. The sky divers had surely landed by now, but there was no growl of motorcycle engines. No sign of a chase, but the dense forest of spruce and aspen obscured his view.

Already a twilight gloom had settled over the valley, the sun disappearing both into the surrounding peaks and the stacks of dark clouds overhead. Being April, the days had begun to lengthen from the continual dark of winter toward the midnight sun of summer.

Squinting, Matt watched over his shoulder. But there was no telling what was going on. He frowned. Maybe he had been wrong . . . maybe he had grown too paranoid out here in these empty woods.

Craig must have noticed his concerned expression. "Could it have been a rescue party? Are we running for no good reason?"

Matt opened his mouth to speak—then an explosion took his words away. Both men stared downhill. From the gloom below, a fiery ball rolled skyward. The blast echoed away.

"The plane . . ." Craig mumbled.

"They destroyed it." Matt's eyes grew wide. He pictured Brent Cumming's body razed.

"Why?"

Matt squinted, thinking. He could come up with only one reason. "They're covering their tracks. If the plane had been sabotaged, they'd need to destroy the evidence—and that includes any witnesses." Matt pictured the clear trail of hoof, boot, and paw prints heading away from the crash site. He'd had no time to mask their path.

From below a new noise cut through the forest like a band saw. A motorcycle engine roared to life, growling fiercely, then settling to a low rumble. A second soon joined the chorus.

Bane echoed the motors, rumbling deep in his chest.

Matt stared at the weak glow of the fading sun. The clouds were lowering still. They'd get more than a sifting of snow overnight. A fact he was sure their pursuers knew, too, which meant the saboteurs would attempt to run them down before the sun set.

"What can we do?" Craig asked.

As answer, Matt tugged Mariah's lead and headed for the top of the rise. He had to find a way to delay them . . . at least long enough until the skies opened.

"Is there somewhere we can hide?" Craig's voice trembled. He hunched farther over the saddle as Mariah clambered up a tumble of talus rock.

Matt dismissed Craig's question for now. Foremost in his mind was simply to survive until nightfall. They were at a distinct disadvantage. One horse, two men. Their pursuers each had a snow chopper. Not good odds. Already the rumble of the cycles throttled up as the chase began.

Matt tugged Mariah up to the ridgeline. At the top, a sudden wind gusted from the southwest, frigid with the promise of ice and sleet. Without hesitating, he headed down the slope, toward where he had set up his camp. There was no refuge to be found there, so he weighed other options. He knew of some caves, but they were too far, and there was no certain safety to be found in them. Another plan was needed.

"Can you ride on your own?" Matt asked Craig.

A weak nod answered him, but fear shone in the man's eyes.

Matt reached and slid his rifle from behind the saddle, then shoved a box of rifle cartridges into a pocket.

"What are you planning?" Craig asked.

"There's nothing to worry about. I'm just going to use you as bait." He then bent down to his dog. "Bane."

The dog's ears perked up, his eyes on Matt.

Matt pointed his arm down the ridge. "Bane . . . to camp!" he ordered sharply.

The dog spun back around and started down. The other dogs followed. Matt slapped Mariah's rump, starting her down after them. Matt trotted beside them for a few paces. "Keep after the dogs. They'll get you to my camp. Take cover as well as you can. There's also an ax by the woodpile. Just in case."

Craig's face blanched, but he nodded, earning Matt's respect.

Matt slid to a stop, watching a moment as horse, rider, and dogs trotted down the wooded and bouldered slope. They were soon gone, vanished into the thick woods.

Turning, he climbed back up the trail until he was twenty yards from the ridgeline. He then leaped from the muddied trail of hoofprints to a granite outcropping, then leapfrogged to another stone. He wanted no evidence of his side trail. Once well off the churned track, Matt settled under the limbs of a spruce, tucking into the shadows, shielding himself behind the trunk. He had a clear view to the ridgeline. If the pursuers followed their same path, they would be momentarily silhouetted against the sky as they crossed the ridge and began their descent into the next valley.

Crouching to one knee, Matt wrapped his rifle's sling

around his wrist, positioned the walnut stock against his shoulder, and took aim down the barrel. He was confident he could take out one of the riders at such close range, but could he take out both of them?

From over the ridgeline, the grumbling of the two engines grew closer and closer, a pair of maddened animals on the trail of prey.

Kneeling now, blood pounding in his ears, Matt recalled another time, a decade ago, another life, being holed up in a mortar-blasted building in Somalia. Gunfire all around. The world reduced to green shadows and lines by his nightvision goggles. It hadn't been the firefights that unnerved most men. It was the waiting.

Drawing a slow breath through his lips, Matt forced himself to relax, to stay loose and ready. Tension could throw off one's aim better than poor marksmanship. He let his breath out, centering himself. This was not Somalia. These were his woods. The crisp scent of the crushed spruce needles under his knee helped sharpen him, reminding him where he was. He knew these mountains better than anyone.

Across the ridge, the noise of the motorcycles ratcheted up, filling the world with their growls and sputters. Matt made out the sound of branches breaking under the studded tires. *Close* . . . He moved his finger from the trigger guard to the trigger and leaned closer to the rifle, his cheek against the wooden stock.

The wait grew to a timeless moment. Despite the cold, a bead of sweat rolled down his right temple. He had to force himself not to squint one eye. Always shoot with both eyes open. His father had drilled that into him when deer hunting back in Alabama, reinforced later by his boot camp sergeant. Matt breathed shallowly through his nose, concentrating.

Come on . . .

As if hearing him, a cycle shot over the ridgeline at full throttle, catching Matt by surprise. Rather than riding cautiously to the top of the rise, the rider had gunned his cycle and flew high across the ridge, his tires lifting free of the ground.

Matt shifted his hip, following its course. He squeezed the trigger, the rifle blasted, answered immediately by the ping of a slug on metal.

The airborne cycle fishtailed. He had struck the rear tire guard. Rider and cycle struck the ground askew, bounced once, then cartwheeled into a tumble. The rider leaped free, rolling down the slope and into dense bushes.

"Damn it," Matt mumbled. He kept his gaze fixed on the ridgeline. He had no idea if the first rider was unharmed, injured, or dead, but he dared not take his attention from the ridgeline. There was still the second cycle. Matt levered the spent cartridge out the side of the rifle and snapped the next one home, wishing for his old M-16 automatic from his Green Beret days.

He covered the top of the rise.

His hearing, after the rifle blast and tumbling crash of the first cycle, was confused. The grumble of the second cycle echoed all around. Movement to the left caught his eye. He swung his rifle in time to see the second cycle shoot over the ridge a short distance down from the other.

He aimed, more desperately than with any true marksmanship, and fired. This time there was not even the ping of slug on metal. The cycle landed smoothly, the rider tucked hard between the handles of his bike, then both disappeared behind an outcropping.

Matt fell back behind the spruce's trunk. He popped the spent cartridge and cranked another in place. These were no amateurs. They had anticipated an ambush, sending the first cycle at breakneck speed over the ridge to draw his attention while the second wheeled around from the other side.

Crack.

A limb of the spruce shattered a foot above Matt's head, pelting him with splinters. Matt slammed lower, sliding to his back, rifle cradled over his chest. A rifle shot . . . it had come from the direction of the first rider. So the bastard wasn't dead.

Biting back panic, Matt kept his position. The sniper must not have had a clean shot at him; otherwise he'd be dead. The splintering blast had been an attempt to flush him out. The sniper must have gained his approximate position when Matt had fired at the second cycle.

"Damn it . . ." Matt was now pinned between them: one rider down to the left in the bushes and the other still on his cycle among the stones.

Matt listened, gasping between clenched teeth. The growl of the other cycle had died to a steady rumble. What was going on? Was the man waiting? Had he abandoned the cycle, leaving it idling, while he snuck into better position?

He couldn't take the chance. He had to move.

Swearing under his breath, Matt slid on his back down the slope, his flight made easier by the thick layer of fallen spruce needles. Without lifting his head, he surfed the slick needles and reached a nearby snowmelt channel, no more than a shallow gully. He slipped into the relative shelter of the trickling waterway. The water soaked through his wool pants, but his patched Army jacket kept his torso dry.

He lay for a moment, listening. The single remaining cycle still idled ominously. But no other sound could be heard. His pursuers were not giving themselves away. Military or mercenary, Matt had no way of knowing, only that they were professional and worked as a team. That meant that the reporter was out of immediate danger. The pair would not leave an armed assailant at their back. They would have to dispatch Matt before continuing on.

Matt considered his own options. They were few. He could escape on his own and leave Craig to the gunmen. He wagered they were more interested in silencing the reporter than him, and he had no doubt that he could disappear into these woods on his own. But this was not a real option.

He had his dogs to think about.

Matt continued crabbing his way down the worn channel. The cold helped dull the panic. Nothing like dumping your ass in ice water to clear the mind.

He moved as silently as he could.

Thirty yards down, the snowmelt channel tipped over a ledge. It was a short drop, seven feet. He rolled onto his belly in the channel and dropped feetfirst over the edge, careful to protect his rifle from the water and the mud.

That was his mistake.

As he fell over the lip, a shot struck the rifle, tearing it from his stinging fingers. In his foolish attempt to protect it, he had held the rifle too high, too exposed, giving himself away. Matt landed hard in a shallow pool of ice melt and cradled his jarred hand.

He quickly searched and found the rifle lying on the bank. The black walnut stock was a splintered ruin, cracked away. He hurried and collected the trashed weapon. The gun itself was still intact, just the stock ruined. Palming the weapon, he ran along the short cliff face. He didn't bother masking his flight. He shoved through bushes, snapping branches underfoot. The cliff he followed ended at a broken area of rock and tumbled talus, the path of an ancient glacier. The scarp was a tangle of gullies, boulders, and ravines.

Behind him, there were no sounds of pursuit, but he knew the men were closing in on him, racing down the slope to the cliff's edge, weapons on shoulders, ready to dispatch their quarry.

Spurred, Matt flew faster, sticking close to the cliff face. Ahead, the shadows thickened as the sun crept away and the clouds descended upon the peaks. Night could not come soon enough. He reached the scrabbled terrain and ducked behind a boulder.

He risked a glance behind him. The deep shadows now aided his pursuers. An inky gloom masked the terrain. He studied the edge of the cliff. Nothing. He turned away and almost missed it. A shift of shadows. Matt dropped lower.

Someone was climbing down the cliff, half shielded by a fall of rock. Before Matt could raise his ruined rifle, the figure vanished into the darkness at the base of the cliff.

Matt continued to point his rifle, positioning it as well he could without the steadying support of the stock. He held it at arm's length. The barrel wavered. He could not trust his accuracy.

Up the slope, the single motorcycle engine suddenly roared back to life, growling, throttling, then it was off.

Matt cocked an ear. The other pursuer was heading off to the left, intending to circle around the scarp and get behind Matt again. Closer, the other hunter had vanished away. He could be anywhere. Matt could not trust his position.

Twisting back behind the boulder, he searched the terrain. Few trees grew here, mostly just low bushes, weedy grasses, and scrabbles of reindeer lichen. A swift rocky stream tumbled down through the center in a series of waterfalls. A mist hovered and traced the waterway as the day cooled toward twilight.

He ran down the scarp's slope, keeping low, aiming for the stream. He had to shake the immediate tail behind him. He hopped and climbed to the stream. With his boots wet and muddy from his previous slide, he left a clear trail across the bare rock.

Once at the stream, he waded into the water, stifling a gasp at the chill. The depth was only up to his knees, but the current tugged at his legs. The rocks were slippery. He fought for balance and climbed upstream, back up the slope he had just fled down. Crouching, he hurried, dragging his legs through the water as silently as possible.

He listened for any sign of the nearby hunter, but the world was filled with the roar of the other motorcycle and the burbling crash of water over rock.

Ten yards up the stream, he reached one of the cataracts, a waterfall over a five-foot drop of rock face. He prayed for one small bit of luck on this long, chilling day. On legs numbed by the icy waters, he stepped up to the cascade of water and jammed his arm through the fall. Many of these cataracts had small spaces behind them as the granite rock face was worn away by the churn of the waterfall that ebbed and flowed with the seasons.

Matt wiggled his fingers.

This one was no exception.

He pivoted around and shoved his back through the waterfall. The bracing flow covered him for a painful breath, then he was leaning against the rock wall, legs splayed to either side, half crouched. The flow of the cataract was a curtain before his face. The cascade was sheer enough to peer through, but it turned the world beyond into a watery blur.

Hugging his rifle to his chest, Matt waited. Now that he had stopped fighting the current and crouched still, the cold bit into him. His teeth chattered uncontrollably, and an ache reached all the way to his bones. Hypothermia would set in quickly. He hoped his trackers were skilled and wouldn't leave him waiting too long.

As Matt shivered, a memory of another day, another icy waterway, intruded. He had been even colder and wetter then. Three years ago, late winter, an unusually warm spell had everyone in Alaska out, enjoying the unseasonably temperate weather. He and his family had been no exception. A winter camping trip to ice-fish and hike the snowy mountains. Then a moment's inattention . . .

Despite the danger now, Matt squeezed his eyes closed against the sudden stab of pain.

He had used a wood ax to break through the ice. He had searched and searched the cold river, almost dying himself from hypothermia, but his eight-year-old son's body wasn't found until two days later, far down the waterway.

Tyler . . . I'm sorry . . .

He forced his eyes open. Now was not the time to mourn the boy. Still, the water's icy embrace had awakened the memory. He could not escape it. His body remembered the cold, the icy water. Memories frozen in every fiber of his being were loosened. Unless someone had lost a son or daughter, none could imagine how a mere memory could stab like a dagger: agonizing, blinding, down to the bone.

Tyler . . .

Movement drew him back to the present. Off to the right, a figure shifted between boulders along the bank. As he watched, old anger trembled his legs, along with a numbing despair that made one fearless.

The hunter had followed Matt's muddy trail, but he was taking no chances, sticking to shadows. His rifle was slung over his shoulder, but he bore a pistol in one fist. The man had also shed his snowy outerwear and wore only a camouflaged uniform and black cap, easier to hide.

Matt lifted his rifle, parting the fall of water with his barrel. He didn't point it toward the slinking figure. With his gun compromised, he couldn't trust a keen shot between the sheltering rocks. Instead, he aimed for the wet bank of the stream, where he had waded into the channel a few minutes ago. Only ten yards away, bare of boulders.

The camouflaged hunter reached the spot, easing out of the rocks. He crouched low. Matt watched him eye the far bank. No wet trail led away. The fellow stared downstream. Matt could guess what he was thinking. Had his quarry fled down the channel like he had earlier down the smaller snowmelt gully? The hunter raised higher, searching down the course. He was a tall man, linebacker build.

Matt moved his finger to the trigger, using all the muscles in his forearm and shoulder to hold the rifle steady. Some innate sense drew the man's attention. He swung around, his face a pale look of surprise. He spotted the rifle at the same time Matt pulled the trigger.

The blast was loud in the tiny space. The recoil almost tore the weapon from his grip. Something tiny pinged past his ear. Matt ignored it all. He concentrated on his target.

The hunter pitched backward as if shoved in the chest. His

pistol spun from his hand, arms outflung. He struck a granite extrusion and sat down hard.

Even before the man hit the ground, Matt was out of his hiding place. He yanked on the rifle to eject the spent cartridge, but he found it jammed. He tugged harder, but no success. The damage to the weapon must have been worse than he had thought. He was lucky the rifle hadn't exploded in his face when he had fired.

He raced down the stream toward the fallen hunter. The man, though down, struggled to free his rifle behind him. It was a race, but the channel's current now worked in Matt's favor. He flew the ten yards, leaping from the current.

He was too late.

The rifle came around and pointed at his chest.

In midair, Matt jerked his body aside and swung his damaged weapon like a club. He felt metal strike metal as the gunman's rifle exploded. Flaming pain seared Matt's shoulder.

He cried out . . . then his weight hit the other. It was like striking a brick wall. The man outweighed Matt by a good thirty pounds. But the impact knocked the assailant's rifle away. It skittered across the rocks and into the stream.

Matt rolled off the guy and kicked his foot around to smash into the man's face. But the attacker was already dodging aside. He seemed unfazed by the chest wound. In fact, there was no blood.

Kevlar vest, Matt thought.

The other crouched an arm's length away, his face a mask of fury. One hand fingered the hole in his camouflage.

Still hurts like a son of a bitch, though, doesn't it, asshole?

A flash of silver and a dagger appeared in the man's other hand. The bastard was a friggin' Swiss Army knife of weapons.

Matt lifted his rifle, holding it like a fencing sword. His shoulder burned, but he ignored the pain. He turned one side to the man, keeping his silhouette small against the dagger.

Eyes bright with bloodlust, the assassin smiled, feral. Perfect white teeth. Whoever the man worked for, they had a good dental plan.

With no warning, the man lunged at him, dagger held low, professional, skilled. His other arm was raised to parry Matt's rifle.

Matt danced back two steps. His free hand rested on his hip, on his belt. He yanked free the holstered can of pepper spray and thumbed the safety cap off. He swung it around and sprayed. Meant to ward off bears, the spray had a shooting distance of twenty feet.

It struck his steel-eyed attacker full in the face.

The effect was the same as if he had shot a cannonball at point-blank range.

The assailant fell to his knees, head thrown back, dagger forgotten. A stunned moment, then an inhuman howl flowed from the man's throat. It was a garbled sound. The man must have inhaled just as the spray hit, burning larynx and throat. He clawed at his eyes and face, ripping tracks across his cheeks.

Matt stood back. The bear spray was ten times more potent than that used in law enforcement, a combination of pepper and tear gas. It was meant to drop grizzlies, not just common thugs. Already the man's eyelids blistered. Blinded by the pain, he flipped around, wild, like a marlin landed on a fishing boat deck. But there was purpose to his thrashing. He fought toward the icy stream. His body racked and vomit spilled over the rocks, choking. He collapsed yards from the stream, moaning, curled in on himself.

Matt simply walked over and collected the man's dagger. He considered slicing the man's throat, but he was not feeling generous today. The fellow was no further threat. There was a fair chance he would even die from the spray. And if not, he'd be disfigured and disabled for life. Matt felt no remorse. He remembered Brent Cumming, his friend's neck broken as his Cessna crashed.

Matt turned away while checking his own wound. The rifle shot had grazed his shoulder, more a burn than a wound.

Distantly, the grumble of the motorcycle had throttled down. Had the rider heard his partner's wail? Did he know it was his friend? Or was he wondering if it was their quarry?

Matt checked the stream for the other rifle, but the current had swept it away. He dared not tarry. He trusted the other pursuer would eventually come to search for his partner. Matt did not plan on being here. He'd trek back to camp, collect his dogs, horse, and the reporter—then he was heading to the only place he knew in the area. Invited or not, welcome or not, they would have to take him in.

He listened as the cycle growled more fiercely again. Of course, out there was one last snag to this plan. Matt crossed the scarp, away from the other pursuer. His camp was two miles away, but at least it was on this side of the rockfall. It would take a bit of time for the rider to find his partner, circle around, and chase them. By then, Matt planned on being well away.

With this goal in mind, Matt crossed back into the thicker woods and jogged down toward his camp. His wet clothes hung like sacks of cement on him, but after a few minutes, the exertion helped warm his limbs and staved off the threat of hypothermia. Once he reached camp, he could change into dry things.

As he continued down, a light snowfall drifted from the clouds overhead. The flakes were thick, heavy, heralding a more abundant fall to come. After ten minutes, this promise began to be fulfilled. The snow obscured the spruce forest, making it hard to see much past a few yards. But Matt knew these woods. He reached the ice-rimmed river on the valley floor and followed it downstream to his campsite. He found the horse trail.

The first to greet him was Bane. The dog all but tackled him as he slogged down the last of the trail.

"Yeah, I'm glad to see you, too." He thumped the dog's side and followed the way back to camp.

He found Mariah munching on some green reeds. The other dogs ran up, but there was no sign of the reporter. "Craig?"

From behind a bush, the reporter stood up. He bore a small hand ax in both fists. The relief on his face was etched in every corner. "I . . . I didn't know what happened? I heard the gunfire . . . the scream . . ."

"It wasn't me." Matt crossed and collected the ax. "But we're not out of the proverbial woods yet."

Across the valley, the whining growl of the lone motorcycle persisted. Matt stared into the dark, snowy woods. *No, they certainly weren't out yet.*

"What are we going to do?" Craig also listened to the motorcycle. The sound had already grown louder. The reporter's eyes drifted to his shattered rifle.

Matt had forgotten he was even carrying it. "Broken," he muttered. He turned back to camp and began to rummage through his supplies, quickly picking out what they would need for this midnight run. They would have to travel light.

"Do you have another gun?" Craig asked. "Or can we outrun the motorcycle on the horse?"

Matt shook his head, answering both questions.

"Then what are we going to do?"

He found what he was looking for. He added it to his bag. *At least this wasn't broken.*

"What about the other motorcycle?" Craig's voice edged toward panic.

Matt straightened. "Don't worry. There's an old Alaskan saying."

"What's that?"

"Up here, only the strong survive . . . but sometimes even they're killed."

His words clearly offered no consolation to the Seattle reporter.

10:48 P.M.

Stefan Yurgen wore nightvision goggles, allowing him to see in the dark without the motorcycle's lights, but the snow-storm kept his vision to no more than ten meters. The snow fell thickly, a green fog through the scopes.

He kept his snow-and-ice bike steady, grinding and carv-ing up the switchback trail. The snow might block his view, but it allowed him to follow his prey easily. The fresh snow clearly marked their trail. He counted one horse, four dogs. Both men were riding. Occasionally, one man hopped off and led the horse afoot across some trickier terrain, then re-mounted.

He watched for any sign of the pair splitting, but no prints led away from the main trail.

Good. He wanted them together.

Under the frozen goggles, a permanent scowl etched his features. Mikal had been his younger brother. An hour ago, he had found his brother's tortured body beside a small stream, nearly comatose from pain, his face a bloody wreck. He'd had no choice. He had orders to follow. It had still torn him to pull the trigger, but at least the agony had ended for Mikal.

Afterward, he had marked his forehead with his brother's blood. This was no longer just a search-and-destroy mission. It was an oath vendetta. He would return with the Ameri-can's ears and nose. He would hand them to his father back in Vladistak. For Mikal . . . for what had been done to his younger brother. This he swore on Mikal's blood.

Stefan had caught a brief glimpse of his target earlier through his rifle's scope: tall, sandy-haired, windburned face. The man had proven resourceful, but Mikal had been the newest member to the Leopard ops team, ten years his junior. His younger brother did not have Stefan's years of battle-honed experience. He was a cub compared to a lion. Now forewarned of his target's skill, Stefan would not underestimate his quarry. Upon his brother's blood, he would capture the American alive, carve his carcass while he still breathed. His screams would reach all the way back to Mother Russia.

As Stefan climbed through the wooded ravine, the trail left by his quarry grew more distinct. His features hardened. The distance between them was closing. No more than a hundred meters, he estimated. A skilled tracker, trained in the winter mountains of Afghanistan, Stefan knew how to judge a trail.

He manhandled the bike up another switchback, then throttled down. He climbed off the cycle, shrugging his rifle snugly in place. He reached next to the weapon holstered on the side of the vehicle. It was now time to begin the true hunt. Raised along the Siberian coast, Stefan knew the cold, knew snow and ice, and he knew how to chase prey through a storm.

From here, he would proceed on foot . . . but first he needed to shake his targets, panic them into acting instinctively. And like any wild animal, once panicked, people made mistakes.

He slid up his nightvision goggles, raised the heavy weapon, then read the distance and elevation indicators through the scope.

Satisfied, he pulled the trigger.

11:02 P.M.

Craig shivered, clinging close to the man saddled ahead of him. He tried to glean whatever warmth he could from the shared contact. At least he was shielded from the worst of the wind by the Fish and Game warden's broad back.

Matt spoke as they climbed through the snowstorm. "I don't understand," he said, pressing the issue. "There has to be a reason for all this. Does it have to do with your story? Or is it something else?"

"I don't know," Craig repeated for the tenth time, speaking through a wool scarf wrapped over his lower face. He didn't want to talk about it. He only wanted to concentrate on staying warm. *Damn this assignment . . .*

"If it's you, why go to all this trouble to keep you away from your story?"

"I don't know. Back in Seattle, I covered alderman races and tracked AP stories out of Washington from a local angle. I was given this assignment because the editor has a grudge. So I dated his niece once. She *was* twenty years old, for God's sake. It wasn't like she was twelve."

Matt mumbled, "A political reporter. I mean why would a scientific research station call in a political reporter anyway?"

Craig sighed. The man would clearly not give up. In a desire to end this line of discussion, he finally loosened his tongue and spilled what he knew. "A marine biologist from the drift station has a cousin who works for the paper. He sent a telegram, indicating a discovery of significant interest. Something to do with an abandoned ice base discovered by their researchers. Whatever they found has stirred up a lot of excitement, but the station was placed under a gag order by the Navy personnel there."

"A gag order? And this biologist was able to ferret this news out anyway."

Craig nodded. "I was being sent to see if there really is a story of national interest."

Matt sighed. "Well, it certainly stirred up someone's interest."

Craig snorted, but he was relieved when the man fell into a ruminative silence. Behind them, the growl of the motorcycle seemed to have ebbed. Maybe they were outdistancing their pursuer. Maybe he had turned back, giving up the chase.

Matt glanced behind them, slowing his horse.

With the cycle quieted, the woods seemed to have grown more still and a little darker. The snowfall drifted with a hushed whisper through the trees. Matt reined the horse to a stop. He stood in the stirrups, staring back, his eyebrows tucked together.

A sharp whistling suddenly pierced the quiet.

"What—" Craig began, twisting around.

Matt reached behind, grabbed him by the shoulders, and dragged them both out of the saddle. They fell to the snowy ground, knocking the wind from his chest.

Craig coughed, gasping. *What the hell is—*

Matt shoved his face into the snow, half covering his body with his own. "Stay down!" he growled.

An explosion rocked the wintry quiet. A score of yards up the trail, snow, dirt, and bushes plumed upward. Leaves and needles were shredded from the surrounding trees.

The mare bucked, whinnying in terror, eyes rolling white. But Matt was already up, grabbing the reins. Dogs barked and yipped from all around.

Craig began to sit up. Matt reached down and yanked him to his feet. "Up, up," he urged, shoving him toward the horse.

"What was—"

"Grenade . . . the bastard has a goddamn grenade launcher."

As the ringing in his ears died away, Craig tried to wrap his mind around this concept. He scrambled back up into the saddle. The mountains had gone quiet. Even the motorcycle's engine had gone silent.

"He's coming after us on foot," Matt explained. "We don't have much time." He whistled for his dogs, scattered by the explosion. They all returned, but one was limping. Matt bent to check the injured dog.

Craig was not so patient. "C'mon . . . leave the dog."

Matt glanced sharply at him, then back to the malamute. He ran his hands down the lame limb. "Just sprained, Simon," he whispered to the dog, relieved, and patted its head.

Standing, Matt grabbed the horse's lead and headed away from the deer trail they had been following.

"Where are we going?" Craig continued to search both ahead and behind him. His ears strained for any telltale whistle of another grenade.

"The jackass is trying to spook us."

In Craig's case, the fellow had surely succeeded.

They tromped through some denser woods, through deeper snow. Craig was forced to duck low branches, getting snow dumped on his back with their passage. It was hard going, slow, too slow, but Matt seemed determined in his direction.

"Where are we headed?" Craig asked, dusting off his shoulders.

"To see if some old friends are still around."

11:28 P.M.

Stefan crouched by the trail. Gloved, hooded, and cloaked in white, he blended perfectly with the snow. But to him, the world was traced and silhouetted in hues of green. Through his nightvision goggles, he examined the trail. His targets had struck off to the left, clearly scared from the trail by the grenade explosion ahead, just as he had hoped.

He turned to follow, moving swiftly and silently. He had hunted wolves in the rural hills around his hometown. He knew how to travel a wood silently, to use the available cover. Coupled with the tools of his ops training, he was a most skilled assassin.

Still, his targets needn't have feared another grenade. He had left the launcher back at the bike. His rifle was enough . . . along with his hunting knife, with which he planned to skin the American who had killed his brother. He set off down their new trail, watching to make sure the pair did not split up. But the track of hoof, paw, and footprints remained a steady single course.

Before leaving the cycle, he had radioed his superiors and reported the events. The storm was too severe to send in reinforcements, but Stefan had assured his lieutenant that they were not needed. Before midnight struck, he would have his quarry contained. His evacuation the next morning had already been coordinated.

He continued down the side trail, watching for any treachery. But the grenade seemed to have done its job. It had sent them into flight.

A quarter mile down the side path, he found a spot where the snow was churned up. It looked like the horse might have taken a spill on the icy terrain. Stefan hoped a few bones had been broken during the fall.

He quickly searched the area, but only one trail led off from here. The track was much fresher. Slush had not yet frozen in the hoofprints. He was no more than five minutes behind. The American continued to walk his horse.

Stefan straightened, noting the ripe smell of offal. Some animal must have died nearby. But before this night was over, there would be more for the scavengers to feed upon.

Anticipating he was close enough to use the infrared feature in his goggles, he reached to his lens and toggled a tab on its edge, switching out of the current nightvision mode, which amplified ambient light, and over to infrared, which registered heat signatures. The green hues vanished, and the world went dark. He scanned ahead, seeking any heat sources. The range of the scope was a hundred yards in good weather. With the snowfall masking any warmth, he could expect half that distance. As such, he faintly made out a reddish blob, poorly defined just at the farthest range of his goggles.

He smiled and switched back to his nightvision spectrum so he could see again and continue his pursuit. With his target in sight, he hurried onto the fresh path. In his drive, he failed to see the thin white thread stretched across the path, but he felt the faint tug on his pant cuff and the snap of the thread.

He dove aside into a small snowbank, expecting an explosion or booby trap to spring. He glanced behind, only to see a faint flash of green through his goggles as something fell from an overhanging tree limb and shattered against a rock under it.

He covered his face, knocking loose his goggles, and ducked away.

Something damp splashed his legs.

He glanced down. *Blood* . . . the red stain was stark against his white snowsuit. His heart pounded in his throat, but he felt no secondary flare of pain. He calmed. It wasn't his own blood.

Then the smell struck him. Back in Afghanistan, he had crawled through the rebel tunnels and come upon a group of dead soldiers, slaughtered, it appeared, by a nail bomb. Blood, ripped intestine, flies, maggots, the heat of the summer . . . it had festered and fermented for a week. This stench was worse.

Gagging reflexively, he tried to crawl away from it, but the stench clung to him, followed him, rising and swelling around him. Bile rose in his throat. He choked and emptied his stomach.

Still, he was a hardened soldier. He scrubbed his pant legs in the snow and fought to his feet. His eyes teared as the world swirled in black and white, shadow and snow.

He stumbled up the trail. If they thought a stench bomb would incapacitate him, the fuckers would learn otherwise. He had been trained to withstand assaults with tear gas and worse. Spitting, he clambered up the trail and reseated his nightvision goggles.

Reaching to the toggle, he checked infrared again and searched for his target. At first he saw nothing but blackness. He cursed, choking up bile. They may have delayed him, but their trail into the empty peaks remained clear through the snow. He would catch up with them.

He reached to his goggles, but before he could switch back to night vision, a reddish glow materialized against the dark background. The sudden infrared signature was bright and clear. The wind must have parted the snow enough to extend his field of view. He grinned. So they weren't that far. He headed toward it.

As he moved, the heat signature grew quickly . . . *too quickly*. He stopped. The rosy glow swelled larger in the scopes, larger than a single man. Were they headed back here on the horse? Did they think to subdue him after their crude attempt at chemical warfare?

His eyes narrowed. If so, they were in for a rude surprise. It was wrong to underestimate one of Russia's elite commandos. He swung around—then noticed a second heat signature approaching from the left. He spun, frowning, as a third and fourth bloomed into existence.

What the hell?

He crouched amid the reeking stench. It seemed to hang in the air. The shapes grew huge in his sights. The red signatures were massive, larger than any horse. A fifth and sixth shape shimmered into existence. They converged from all sides.

He now knew what they were.

Bears . . . grizzlies from their size.

He switched off the infrared and went to night vision again. The snow was falling thicker. The woods were cloaked in green fog. There was no sign of the approaching monsters. He switched back to infrared. They were closer still, almost upon him.

Lured here . . . the stench . . . A groan escaped him.

He toggled back and forth between infrared and night vision. Finally, he lifted his rifle and targeted one of the red blobs as it pounded toward him. The snap of twigs and crunch of snow echoed all around. He fired at the shape.

The blast paused the others, but the one he had fired upon let loose a tremendous roar—a bloodcurdling, primeval sound—and thundered toward him, faster, unfazed. The bellow of rage was answered by others. The group hammered down upon him.

He fired and fired again. But nothing slowed the monsters. His lungs burned, his heart pounded in his throat. He ripped away the goggles, crouching, rifle up.

The roaring filled his head, chasing away any thought and sense. He swung around and around, surrounded by the dark and the snow.

Where . . . where . . . where . . .

Then from the snow, dark shapes flowed, massive, creatures of nightmare, moving with impossible grace and speed. They set upon him, not in fury, but with the unstoppable momentum of predator and prey.

11:54 P.M.

Matt stood beside Mariah, lead in hand, and listened as the hunter's screams echoed up to him. They did not last long, cutting off abruptly. He turned away, walked his horse over the last rise, and set off toward the lower valleys. By morning, he wanted to be as far gone from the area as possible, vanished deep into the thicker, taller woods of the lower slopes of the Brooks Range. They still had at least two days of hiking to reach the single homestead he knew in the area, the only place with a satellite radio for a hundred miles.

Craig sat atop the mare, pale, shaking slightly. He finally spoke after they had crossed the rise. "Grizzlies . . . how did you know they'd be around here?"

Matt spoke dully, watching the dogs nose ahead. "I trashed a bottle of blood lure down in that hollow earlier. By now a good number of bears should be attracted to the area."

"And . . . and you walked us right through there?"

He shrugged. "The snowfall, the dark . . . they'd most likely leave us alone as long as we didn't bother them."

"And that bottle you set up in the tree?"

With his military background, he knew how to quickly rig a simple trap. "More blood lure," he explained. "I figured the fresh explosion of scent would draw those nearby and keep our grenade-toting friend occupied." Matt shook his head in regret—not for the hunter, only for the wounded bears.

They continued on. Matt trudged along, wondering for the thousandth time who the men were that had hunted them and why. If given the time or the opportunity, he would have liked the chance to interrogate one or the other. They were clearly professionals with a military background. But were they active service or hired mercenaries?

Matt slipped out the dagger he had confiscated from the first hunter. He flipped it around, examining it with a penlight. No insignia, no manufacturer's mark, no unique design. Purposefully void of any indication of origin. He wagered if he had examined the men's rifles and pistols, the same would have been true. This alone suggested the pair were more than just mercenaries. Such men didn't concern themselves with wiping all traces from their weapons.

But Matt knew who did.

A black ops team.

Matt remembered Craig's story of the Navy's gag order on the drift station. Could it be their own government? After spending eight years in an elite Green Beret team, he knew that sometimes hard choices, sacrifices, had to be made in the name of national security.

Still, Matt refused to believe it. But if not us, then who?

"Where are we going now?" Craig asked, interrupting his ponderings.

Matt sighed, expelling these worrisome thoughts for now,

and stared out at the snowy woods. "We're heading to some-place even more dangerous."

"Where's that?"

His voice tightened with regret. "My ex-wife's cabin."

3

Trap Lines

ᓇᓂ ᐊᖅᑐᕐᐱᑦ

Jennifer Aratuk stood, club in hand, over the trap. The wolverine glared at her, hissing a warning. Its rear end bunched up as it guarded its own catch. The dead marten, a cat-sized weasel, lay snared in her father's trap, its black pelt stark against the snow. It had been dead and buried in the fresh fallen snow, its neck broken, but the wolverine had reached the trap first and dug it up. The wolverine, a male, was not about to relinquish its frozen prize.

"Get outta here!" she yelled, and waved her cudgel of alder.

The white-masked beast snarled and jarred toward her a foot, then back. A display that basically meant "fuck you" in wolverine. Fearless, wolverines were known to stand against wolves when food was involved. They were also equipped with talonlike claws and sharp teeth set in bone-crushing jaws.

Frowning but cautious, Jenny considered clubbing the creature. A stout knock on its skull would either drive it off or addle it long enough for her to collect the marten. Her father collected the pelts and traded them for seal oil and other native wares. She had spent the last two days running his trapline. This consisted of hunting down his snares, collecting any catches, and resetting and baiting the traps. She did not relish the chore, but her father's arthritis had gotten worse the past year, and she feared for him alone in the woods.

"All right, junior," Jenny said, conceding. "I guess you did get here first." She used her club to reach and unhook the snare line from the branch of the cottonwood. With the line free, the marten was released. She nudged its body.

The wolverine growled and snatched at the marten, sinking its teeth into a frozen thigh. It backpedaled with its prize, hissing all the way as it retreated through the snow to some hidden burrow.

Jenny watched it waddle with its catch, then shook her head. She wouldn't tell her father about this, passing on a chance to get a marten *and* a wolverine pelt. He wouldn't be pleased. Then again, she was a county sheriff, not a trapper. He should be happy enough that she spent a week of her two-week vacation each year helping him with his damn traps.

She headed back to her sled, tromping in her Sherpa snowshoes. The overnight trip to run the traps was not wholly a chore. During the last three days, a storm had covered the national parklands with two feet of thick snow, perfect for her to run her team one last time before the true spring melt. She enjoyed these outings, just her and her dogs. It was still too early in the year to expect any tourists, hikers, or campers to be about. She had this section of the national park all to herself. Her family cabin was just at the outskirts of the parklands, in the lowland valleys. Her father, as a pure-blooded Inuit native, was still allowed to subsistence-hunt and -trap within certain areas of the park as a result of the Alaska National Interest Lands Conservation Act of 1980. Hence her current overnight trip with her dogs.

The usual barks and yips from her crew greeted her as she returned. She unsnapped her snowshoes' bindings and kicked them off. Collecting them up, she secured them atop the sled. Underneath were her sleeping bag, a change of dry clothes, a hatchet, a lantern, mosquito repellent, a plastic container of dry dog food, a soggy carton of Power Bars, a twist-tied bag of ranch-flavored Doritos, and a small cooler of Tab soda. She undid her shoulder holster, swung the service revolver over one of the sled's handles, and cinched it in place next to a leather-sheathed ax.

Next she shook free of her thick woolen overmitts. She wore a thinner, more manageable pair of Gore-Tex gloves underneath. "Okay, boys and girls, off we go."

At her command, those dogs still lounging in the snow climbed to their feet, tails wagging. The team was still harnessed to the gang line. She only had to go down and tighten their traces. As she did, she patted each dog in turn: Mutley and Jeff, George and Gracie, Holmes and Watson, Cagney and Lacey. They were all strays or rescue animals, a motley bunch of Lab mixes, malamutes, and shepherd crosses. She had more back at home, composing a full team of sixteen, with which she had run the Iditarod from Anchorage to Nome last year. She had not even placed in the top half of the sled teams, but the challenge and the time with her crew was victory enough for her.

With everyone ready, she grabbed the snub line and gave it a jostle. "Mush!"

The dogs dug into the snow. With a furious row of barking, they set off at an easy pace. Jenny walked behind them, steering. The wolverine-burgled trap was the last of the line. She had run a complete circuit, out and back. From here, it was an easy three miles to the cabin. She hoped her father remembered to leave a pot of coffee simmering this morning.

She guided the dogs along a slow sweeping set of switchbacks over a sparsely wooded rise. She stopped them at the top. Ahead, the world opened up. Ridge after ridge climbed to the horizon. Spruces, flocked with snow, shone emerald in the sunlight, while stands of hardwoods—alder and cottonwood—painted the landscape in subtler shades of greens and yellows. In the distance, a silver river ran over cataracts, dancing brightly.

She drew a deep breath of the cedar-scented air. There was a cold, barren beauty to the lands here. It was too much for some, not enough for others. The sun, rare in the past few days, shone sharply but warmly on her face. Across the clouded skies, a single hawk circled. She followed its path a moment.

These were the lands of her people, but no matter how much time she spent out here, she could not touch that past . . . not any longer. It was like losing a sense you never knew you had. But it was the least of her losses.

Turning attention back to her team, she lowered her snow goggles against the fresh glare, then climbed onto the sled's runners and called to the dogs, "Eyah!" She snapped the line.

The dogs leaped in their harnesses, racing down the far slope. Jenny rode the runners, steering and braking as needed. They flew across the snow. A sharp gust of wind tossed back the hood of her fur parka. She reached to yank it up, but it felt good for the moment to feel the rush of cold wind against her cheeks and through her hair. She shook her head, loosening and flagging a long trail of ebony hair.

She lifted her foot off the brake and let her rig fly down a long straight run. The wind whistled and the passing trees became a blur. She guided the team around a gentle curve along a wide stream. For an endless moment, she felt in perfect harmony with her dogs, with the steel and ash of her sled, with the world around her.

The crack of rifle fire startled her back into her own body.

She jumped with both feet onto her brake, casting up a rooster tail of snow behind the sled. The rig and team slowed. She stood straighter atop the runners.

Again an echoing blast of a rifle split the quiet of the morning.

Her experienced ears told her the direction from which the gunfire had come—her cabin!

Fear for her father flamed through her. *"Eyah!"* she yelled, and snapped the line.

Horrible scenarios played out in her head. Bears were out and about already, though they rarely ventured so low. But moose were often just as dangerous, and the cabin was near the river, where the thick willow browses attracted the yearling bulls. And then there were the predators that walked on two legs: poachers and thieves that raided outlying cabins. As a sheriff, she had seen enough tragedy in the wilds of the Alaskan backcountry.

Panic made her desperate, reckless.

She dug around a sharp bend in the river. Ahead, a narrow pinch squeezed between a cliff of granite and the rocky stream. She realized she was speeding too fast. She tried the brake, but a patch of ice betrayed her. The sled fishtailed toward the cliff.

There was no avoiding it.

She hopped to the runner farthest from the cliff and used all her weight and the momentum of the too-sharp turn to tilt the sled up on one runner. The underside of her rig struck the icy cliff face. Steel screeched across rock.

Clutching and praying the sled didn't tumble on top of her, she clung tight to her handles, giving up the dogs' snub line. With the line loosened, the dogs took off at a full sprint. The sled dragged behind the furious team.

Jenny held in a scream—then it was over.

The cliff fell away and the sled landed hard on both runners, almost throwing her off. She scrambled to maintain her perch. The dogs continued their relentless charge for home. They knew the cabin was only a couple hundred yards off.

She made no attempt to slow them.

Gasping, Jenny listened for gunfire, but all she heard was the blood pounding in her ears. She feared what she would find at her cabin. One hand unsnapped her pistol holster. She left the gun in the holster, not trusting herself to run the rig and hold a weapon.

The sled raced alongside the river. She was now following the same track upon which she had left yesterday. A final wide bend and her cabin suddenly appeared ahead. It was built in a meadow where the stream swung around and emptied into a swollen river. Beyond the cabin, her sheriff's plane floated at the end of a stout dock.

She quickly spotted her father standing before the cabin's doorway. He was dressed in traditional Inuit clothes: fur parka, fur pants, and mukluk boots. He clutched an old Winchester hunting rifle across his chest. Even from here she could see the angry spark in his eyes.

"Dad!"

He turned toward her, startled. She urged her dogs on, now kicking with one leg to keep the sled careening toward the cabin.

Once clear of the forest and sailing into the open, sunlit meadow, she yanked out her pistol and hopped off the rig, running to keep her momentum and her legs under her. She raced toward her father. Behind her, the unguided sled glanced over a boulder and toppled. She ignored the splintering crash and searched for danger, her eyes darting all around.

Then it lunged at her. A large black shape leaped toward her from the shadows of the porch.

Wolf, her mind screamed. She swung her pistol.

"No!" The shout was a bark of command from behind her.

Her eyes adjusted, changing focus. The large dark shape dissolved into the familiar.

"Bane," she cried with relief.

She lowered her weapon and dropped to one knee, accepting the exuberant attention and hot tongue of the huge dog. After being thoroughly slicked with saliva, she twisted around. Two men stood ten yards away in the fringe of the forest. Nearby, a horse chewed leaves from a low-slung branch of an alder.

Her father spoke from the doorway, harsh and angry. "I warned the bastard to get away from here. He's not welcome around these parts." He lifted his rifle for emphasis.

Jenny stared over at her former husband. Matthew Pike smiled back at her, but a trace of nervousness shone behind his white teeth. She glanced over to her ruined rig, then back to her father.

She stood up. "Go ahead and shoot him."

11:54 A.M.

Matt knew his ex-wife was only venting, but he still kept his post at the forest's edge. The two stared at each other for a long breath. Then she shook her head in disgust and crossed to her father. She took the rifle from him and spoke softly but sternly in Inuktitut. "Papa, you know better than to shoot a gun into the air. Even out here."

Matt studied her, unable to look away. Because of her mother's French-Canadian blood, Jenny was tall for an Inuit, almost six feet. But like her father, she was as lean as a willow switch. Her skin was the color of creamed coffee, soft, inviting to the touch, and she had the most expressive eyes of any woman. They could dance, spark, or smolder. He had fallen in love with those eyes.

Now, three years after their divorce, those same eyes stared at him with bald anger . . . and something deeper, something more painful. "What are you doing here, Matt?"

He couldn't find his tongue fast enough, so Craig spoke.

"We're sorry to disturb you, ma'am. But there was a plane crash." He fingered the fresh wrap that Matt had applied to his scalp wound. "We've spent the past two days hiking out from it. Matt here rescued me."

Jenny glanced back to him.

"It was Brent Cumming's plane," Matt added, finally finding his tongue. He paused as understanding slowly hardened Jenny's face. Brent was not standing with them. He answered the question that now shone in her eyes. "He's dead."

"Oh my God . . ." She raised a hand to her forehead, sagging as she stood. "Cheryl . . . what am I going to tell her?"

Matt tentatively walked forward, leading Mariah. "You'll tell her it wasn't an accident."

The lost look in her eyes sharpened. "What do you mean?"

"It's a long story." Matt glanced to the smoke rising from the chimney of the cabin. He had helped build the homestead ten years ago. It was constructed of unpeeled, green-cut logs and a sod roof. He had followed a traditional design. There was even a small *lagyaq,* or meat storehouse, out back. But to aid in heating the main dwelling, he had modernized the cabin's design with a propane tank and triple-paned windows.

As he stood, old memories superimposed over the present. He had spent many a happy time here . . . and one awful winter.

"Maybe we could discuss this inside," he said. "There are two other bodies out in the woods."

Concern crinkled her forehead, but she nodded.

His words, though, did little to soften her father's expression. "I'll see to the horse and dogs," John Aratuk said, stalking forward and taking Mariah's lead. He had calmed enough to rub a palm down the mare's nose, but the old man refused to make eye contact with Matt. He did, however, nod perfunctorily to Craig as they passed each other. He plainly bore the stranger no ill will, only begrudged him the company he kept.

Jenny shoved the cabin door open and set the bolt-action Winchester rifle just inside the doorway. "Come in."

Matt waved Craig ahead of him. The reporter passed inside, but Matt paused on the threshold. *It's been three years since I last stepped inside here.* He girded himself, licked his dry lips, and ducked through. A part of him expected to see Tyler's tiny body still sprawled on the pine table, bony arms crossed over his chest. At that time, Matt had stumbled inside on limbs leaden with grief, half frozen, frost bitten, his heart an icy stone in his chest.

But the cabin was not cold now. It was warm, scented with old smoke and a deep woody musk. Across the room, Jenny bent over a small cast-iron stove. She opened the door and used a poker to stoke the firebox and stir up the coals. A pot of coffee rested atop a griddle, steaming gently.

"There are mugs in the cupboard," Jenny said. "You know where they are."

Matt crossed to the sideboard and removed three earthenware cups. He straightened and stared around the great room, raftered with logs overhead. Nothing much had changed. The main room of the cabin was lit with three traditional *qulliq* oil lamps, half-moons of hollow soapstone. The cabin had electricity, but that required running the generator. A river-stone fireplace stood in one corner. The chairs and sofa were made by a native craftsman from caribou hide and fire-aged spruce. Pictures hung on the wall, taken by Jenny herself. She was a superb photographer. Around the room, bits of native artwork and artifacts finished the decorations: small totems, a carved figure of the Inuit sea god, Sedna, and a painted shaman mask used in healing ceremonies.

Each item had history. It was hard standing here. Tragedy seemed to follow him. During his first year at the University of Tennessee, his parents had both been killed in a home-invasion robbery. Left without resources, he was forced to join the Army. There, he channeled his anger and pain into his career, eventually joining Special Forces and becoming a Green Beret. But after Somalia, he could no longer stomach bloodshed and death. So he quit the service and returned to school, earning his degree in environmental sciences. After graduation, he came to Alaska because of its wide-open spaces and vast tracts of parklands.

He came here to be alone.

But that changed when he met Jenny . . .

With mugs in hand, Matt stood transfixed between the past and the present. Off the main room were two bedchambers. He turned away, not ready to brush against those more intimate memories. Still, some reached out and touched him.

In one room . . . reading Winnie-the-Pooh *to Tyler by lamplight, the entire family nestled in thick woolen pajamas . . .*

In the other . . . curled under heavy goose-down quilts with Jenny, her naked body an ember against his own skin

"Coffee's ready," Jenny said, drawing him back. With a worn oven mitt, she lifted the hot pot and waved the two men to the sofa.

Matt set the mugs on the knotty-pine table.

She filled them. "Tell me what happened." Her voice was emotionless, professional, a sheriff's voice.

Craig began, telling his side of the story. He related all that had transpired since he left his Seattle newspaper office. He finished with the harrowing plunge in the plane.

"Sabotage?" Jenny asked. She knew Brent as well as Matt did. If there was a problem with the plane, there had to be another reason besides neglect or simple equipment failure . . . not in Brent Cumming's plane.

Matt nodded. "I suspected as much. Then this second plane appeared." He gave her the call signs painted on the plane, but he wagered either the aircraft would be discovered stolen or the call signs were bogus. He told her as much. "As it circled, two commandos dove from the plane with ice choppers and rifles. They clearly didn't want to leave anyone behind to tell tales."

Jenny's brows knit together. Her eyes flicked to Craig, but the reporter was carefully inspecting his coffee as he swirled in some sugar. "What happened then?"

Matt detailed the fate of the two assassins as plainly as possible. She unfolded a topographic map of the area, and he marked down the plane crash site and roughly where the bodies of the two men could be found.

"I'll need to call into Fairbanks for this," she said as he finished.

"And I need to contact my newspaper," Craig added, perking up with a jolt of Jenny's strong coffee. "They must be wondering what happened. I was supposed to update them when I reached Prudhoe Bay."

Jenny stood up, flipping closed her notepad. "The satellite phone is over there." She pointed her pad to a desk. "Make it quick, then I'll need to reach my office."

Craig took his mug of coffee with him. "How do I use it?"

"Just dial like you would any other phone. You might get a bit more static due to the recent solar storms. They've been fritzing everything lately."

Craig nodded and sat at the desk. He picked up the receiver.

Jenny stepped to the fireplace. "What do you make of all this?" she asked Matt.

He joined her, leaning a hand on the hearth's mantel. "Clearly someone wants to keep the newspapers away from the drift station."

"A cover-up?"

"I don't know."

In the background, Craig spoke into the phone. "Sandra, this is Teague. Connect me to the big guy." A pause. "I don't care if he's in a meeting. I've got news that can't wait."

Matt imagined the reporter already had more story than he'd expected when he left Seattle.

Jenny turned her back a bit on Craig and lowered her voice. "Does this guy know more than he's telling us?"

Matt eyed Craig. "I doubt it. I think he just ended up here because he pulled the short straw."

"And these commandos . . . you're sure they were military?"

"Military background, at least." Matt recognized the tension building in Jenny as she stood by the fireplace. She kept her eyes averted from him, her words terse. She had a job to do here, but his presence kept her on guard.

He couldn't blame her. He didn't deserve any better. Still, he wanted to find some way past this unnaturally forced discourse. He wanted to tell her that he hadn't touched a drink in over two years, but would she even care? Did it even matter any longer? The damage had been done.

He studied a single framed picture of Tyler on the mantel: smiling, towheaded, a pup in his arms, Bane, then eight weeks old. Matt's heart clenched with joy and grief. He allowed himself to feel the emotion. He had long given up trying to drown it away. It still hurt . . . and in many ways, that was a good thing.

Jenny spoke. "Any other impressions?"

He took a deep breath to keep the pain out of his voice and stepped away from the fireplace. "I don't know." He rubbed his brow with a knuckle. "They might have been foreign nationals."

"Why do you say that?"

"They never spoke a word within earshot. In retrospect, it was like they were purposefully keeping silent, hiding their origin. Like they had done with their weapons."

"Could they be hired mercenaries?"

He shrugged. He had no idea.

"So far we don't have much to go on." Her gaze grew long as she began to plan. "We'll get forensics up there and see what they can dig up. But something tells me the real answers are going to be found over at the polar base. And if so, the FBI will need to be called in . . . and military intelligence if the Navy is somehow tied in with all this. What a mess . . ."

He nodded. "A mess *someone* wanted to clear up at the end of a rifle barrel."

She glanced to him. It looked like she wanted to say something, but then thought better of it.

Matt took a deep breath. "Jenny . . . look . . ."

Craig had been conversing in low tones, but his voice grew suddenly louder. "Prudhoe Bay, *why?*"

Jenny and Matt both turned toward him.

"I don't see why I have to—" A long pause. "Fine, but I'm with a sheriff now. I can't promise I'll be able to get there." Craig rolled his eyes and shook his head. Finally, he sighed and spoke. "I expect a big-ass raise after this, goddamn it." He shoved the phone down.

"What's wrong?" Matt asked.

Craig blustered for a moment, then collected himself. "They want me to stay here. Can you believe that? I'm supposed to meet with the paper's contact at Prudhoe and follow up on events. See if they're somehow connected to the research station."

Jenny crossed to the desk as Craig vacated it in disgust. "Either way, you'll have to stay here for now until Fairbanks clears you. We're still in the middle of an investigation."

"That's fine by me," he groused.

Jenny picked up the phone.

Before she could dial, the door to the cabin swung open. Her father stomped in, knocking snow off his boots. "Seems like we're going to get more unexpected visitors." He glared over at Matt. "Looks like a plane might be trying to land here."

With the door open, the rumbling of an engine echoed into them. Dogs barked in the background.

Matt met Jenny's gaze, and both hurried to the door.

From the shelter of the doorjamb, they studied the skies. A white Cessna slowly circled into view, drawing parallel with the wide river.

"Matt?"

He stared up at the plane. Blood drained into his legs. "It's the same one."

"Are you sure?" She shielded a hand over her eyes, clearly attempting to spot the call sign on the underside of the wings.

"Yes." He didn't need to read the stenciled letters and numbers.

"Do they know you're here?"

Matt spotted motion by one of the plane's windows. Someone leaned out, waving an arm at them. Then his eyes widened. Not an arm . . . a grenade launcher, a *rocket-propelled* grenade launcher.

He shoved Jenny back inside as a spat of flame spouted from the weapon.

"What—" she cried out.

The explosion cut off her words. A window on the south side of the cabin shattered inward. Glass sprayed the room.

As the blast echoed away, Matt dove to the ruined window. Just outside, the remains of the tiny *lagyaq* storehouse smoldered around a cratered ruin. The roof still sailed high in the air.

In the sky, the Cessna sped past, low over the trees, tilting on a wing for another pass.

Matt swung around and met Jenny's gaze. "I'd say they know we're here."

Jenny's expression remained hard. She already had the Winchester rifle in hand again. She stalked toward the open door, followed by everyone else.

Matt hurried after her. "What do you think you're going to do?"

Outside, Jenny had to yell to be heard above the racket of

barking dogs and the whine of the Cessna. "We're getting out of here." She raised the rifle and tracked the plane as it arced around. "Everyone get to the Twin Otter."

"What about running back into the woods?" Craig asked, staring doubtfully at the small sheriff's plane resting on its floats in the river.

"We escaped once that way," Matt said, shoving the reporter toward the dock. "We can't count on that kind of luck again. Not on such a clear day. And there's no telling if they dropped other commandos out there somewhere."

Together, the group fled across the yard toward the dock. Jenny helped her father, one hand on his elbow. Dogs ran all around, leaping, barking.

Suddenly Bane appeared at Matt's side and raced with his master as they hit the docks. Matt had no time to warn the wolf away.

Instead Matt held out a hand for Jenny's rifle. "Get the engine started. I'll try to keep them busy."

Jenny nodded to him. Matt was surprised by the lack of fear in her eyes. She passed the rifle into his palms.

Matt backed down the dock. Bane followed him.

The Cessna banked into another glide toward the homestead. Matt raised the rifle and followed its course. He squeezed off a shot to no effect. He yanked on the rifle's bolt to crank another round in place.

At the end of the dock, the Twin Otter's engine coughed once, then died. *Come on, Jen . . .*

The Cessna dropped its flaps and dove along the river's length, aiming for the foundering floatplane.

Matt aimed for the cockpit window and fired again. He missed. Undeterred, the plane continued its dive. "Damn it!" He pulled the rifle's bolt and shouldered the weapon, widening his stance.

Nearby, the Otter's engine's finally choked and caught. The rumble drowned out the barking dogs.

"Matt!" Jenny called out the side window. "Get in!"

The Cessna now glided no more than thirty feet above the river. A figure dressed in a white parka leaned out an open side door. The length of a black grenade launcher was balanced on his shoulder. They were coming in fast, going for a point-blank shot. There was no way the Otter could accelerate out of the way in time.

Their only chance was for Matt to get them to blow this shot, make them come around again, buying them time to get airborne themselves.

Biting his lower lip, he eyed through the sights and focused on the man with the launcher. He would swear the guy stared right back at him. Matt squeezed the trigger.

The crack of the rifle made him blink. The man on the Cessna ducked under one of the plane's struts. Matt had missed, glancing only the wing, but the close call had rattled the man.

Unfortunately, that was not enough. The grenade launcher quickly swung back into position. The Cessna was now only seventy yards away and coming in savage and low.

He readied the Winchester.

"Matt!" Jenny yelled. "Now!"

He glanced over. Jenny's father held open the plane's door. The man beckoned to him. "We're still tethered to the dock!" he bellowed, pointing to the rope.

Matt swore under his breath and ran to the plane, clutching the rifle in one hand. With his free hand, he tugged off the plane's rope tether and hopped onto the nearest pontoon.

At his heels, Bane leaped into the cabin in one graceful bound. From their years together, the dog was familiar with this mode of travel.

"Go," Matt yelled through the open door.

The Otter's engine roared. The twin props, one on each wing, chewed up the air. The plane swiveled away from the docks.

Jenny's father reached to help Matt inside as he balanced on the float. "No, John," Matt said, and met the elder Inuit's eyes. He flipped the rope tether around his own waist, then tossed the end to Jenny's father. "Tie me in!"

John's brows crinkled.

"Belay me!" Matt explained, pointing to a steel stanchion by the door.

The elder's eyes widened with understanding. He wrapped the rope loosely around the support. In the past, the pair had done some glacier climbing together.

As the Otter began to accelerate along the river, Matt worked down the port-side pontoon, leaning against the rope like a rappeller, using the loop as a brace. Jenny's father fed the rope, keeping the line taut through the stanchion.

Matt clambered out from under the wing's shadow.

The Cessna chased thirty yards behind their plane's tail, almost directly overhead, closing swiftly down on them. The Otter would not escape in time.

Matt raised his rifle and leaned far out, held only by the rope's loop, legs braced wide on the pontoon. Ignoring the commando with the grenade launcher, he aimed for the cockpit window.

As he pulled the trigger, a matching flash of fire exploded from the launcher. Matt cried out. He was too late.

But then the Cessna bobbled in the air: dropping suddenly, tilting on one wing.

With a gut-punching *whoosh,* a geyser of water and rock jetted high over the far side of the Twin Otter.

Matt craned around, twisting in his rope, as they passed the spot. Debris rained down into the river and shoreline.

The grenade had missed. The launcher's aim must've been jolted just as he fired.

The Cessna, unable to stop its momentum, roared past overhead, now chased by the Otter on the river. The other plane managed to steady its flight, but Matt had spotted the spiderweb of cracks on the cockpit window.

His aim had been true.

He danced back up the pontoon, the river racing past his

heels. The winds buffeted against him as John reeled him
back to the door. Matt reached the opening just as the pon-
toons lifted free of the water. The rattle under his soles
ceased in one heartbeat.

As the plane tilted, Matt lost his balance, falling backward. His arms flailed. He dropped the rifle as he snatched
for a handhold. The Winchester tumbled into the river
below.

Then a hand grabbed his belt.

He stared into his former father-in-law's black eyes. The
Inuit, secure and snugged in his seat belt, held him tight.
They matched gazes as the winds howled past the plane.
Then something broke in the older man's face, and he
yanked Matt inside.

He fell into the cabin and twisted to close the door. Bane
nosed him from the third row of seats, tongue lolling as he
greeted him. Matt roughed him away and slammed the
door.

Jenny called from the front, "They're coming back
around!"

Matt hauled himself up and crawled toward the copilot's
seat. Ahead, the Cessna banked sharply on a wingtip.

As Matt settled to the seat, he noticed his empty hands.
He silently cursed himself for losing the rifle. "Do you have
another gun?"

Jenny spoke as she worked the throttle. The plane fought
for height. "I have my Browning, and there's my service
shotgun bolted to the rear cabin wall. But you'll never hit
anything in the air."

He sighed. She was right. Neither weapon was accurate at
long range, especially in these winds.

Jenny climbed the plane. "Our only chance is to make for
Prudhoe Bay."

Matt understood. It was the closest military base. Whatever was going on was beyond their ability to handle. But
Prudhoe was four hundred miles away.

Jenny stared at the Cessna diving toward them. "This is going to get ugly."

"Message for you, Admiral."

Viktor Petkov ignored the young lieutenant at the stateroom door and continued to read the passage from the book on his desk: *The Brothers Karamazov* by Fyodor Dostoyevsky. He had often found this book by the dead Russian writer a comfort. In moments when his own soul was tested, he could relate to Ivan Karamasov's struggle with himself and his spirituality.

But it had never been a struggle for Viktor's father. He had always been Russian Orthodox, most devoutly so. Even after the rise of Stalin, when it became untenable to practice one's faith, his father had not abandoned his beliefs. It may have been for this reason, more than any other, that one of the most decorated scientists of the time had been exiled— stolen away from his family at gunpoint—and sent to an isolated ice station out in the Arctic Ocean.

Viktor finished reading the section titled "The Legend of the Grand Inquisitor," where Ivan dramatically repudiates God. It stirred him. Ivan's anger spoke to his own heart, his own frustration. Like Ivan, Viktor's own father had been murdered—not by the hands of one of his sons, as in the novel, but by treachery nonetheless.

And the misery had not ended there. After the base's disappearance in 1948, his mother had slipped into a black depression that lasted a full decade and ended one morning within the noose of a knotted bedsheet. Viktor had been eighteen years old when he walked in and discovered his mother hanging from a rafter in their apartment.

Without any other relatives, he had been recruited into the Russian military. It became his new family. Seeking answers to or some type of resolution for the fate of his father, Viktor's interest in the Arctic grew. This obsession and a deep-seated fury guided his career, leading to his ruthless rise within the Russian submarine forces and eventually into the command staff of the Severomorsk Naval Complex.

Despite this success, he never forgot how his father was torn from his family. He could still picture his mother hanging from her handmade noose, her toes just brushing the bare plank floors.

"Sir?" The lieutenant's feet shifted on the deck plating, drawing him back to the present. His voice stuttered, clearly fearful of disturbing *Beliy Prizrak,* the White Ghost. "We . . . we've a coded message marked urgent and for your eyes only."

Viktor closed the book and ran a finger along the leather-bound cover. He then held out a hand to the lieutenant. He had been expecting the message. The *Drakon* had risen to periscope depth half an hour ago and raised its communication array through a crack in the ice, sending out reports and receiving incoming messages.

The man gratefully held out a metal binder. Viktor signed for it and accepted it.

"That'll be all, Lieutenant. If I need to send out a reply, I'll ring the bridge."

"Yes, sir." The man turned sharply on a heel and left.

Viktor opened the binder. Stamped across the top was PERSONAL FOR THE FLEET COMMANDER. The rest was encrypted. He sighed and began the decryption. It was from Colonel General Yergen Chenko, directorate of the FSB, the Federal'naya Sluzhba Bezopasnosti, what the Americans called the Federal Security Service, one of the successors of the old KGB. *New name, same game*, he thought sourly. The message came from their headquarters in Lubyanka.

URGENT   **URGENT**   **URGENT**   **URGENT**

FM   FEDERAL'NAYA SLUZHBA BEZOPASNOSTI (FSB)
TO   *DRAKON*
//BT//
REF   LUBYANKA 76-453A DATED 8 APR
SUBJ   DEPLOYMENT/RENDEZVOUS COORDINATES

TOP SECRET   **TOP SECRET**   **TOP SECRET**
PERSONAL FOR FLEET COMMANDER
RMKS/
(1) NEW INTELLIGENCE HAS CONFIRMED US COUNTERINTELLIGENCE
OPERATION IS UNDER WAY. US DELTA FORCE MOBILIZED. OPERA-
TION CONTROLLER IDENTIFIED AND CONFIRMED. COUNTERMEA-
SURES HAVE BEEN ACCELERATED AND COORDINATED WITH
LEOPARD OPS.
(2) OMEGA DRIFT STATION HAS BEEN APPROVED AS TARGET ONE. CO-
ORDINATE ALPHA FOUR TWO DECIMAL SIX TACK THREE ONE DECI-
MAL TWO, CHART Z-SUBONE.
(3) *DRAKON* ORDERED TO RUN SILENT FROM HERE UNTIL MOLNIYA GO-
CODE IS TRANSMITTED.
(4) DEPLOYMENT GO-CODE SET FOR 0800.
(5) INTELLIGENCE UPDATE WILL BE RELAYED ALONG WITH GO-CODE.
(6) COL. GEN. Y. CHENKO SENDS.
    BT
    NNNN

Viktor frowned as he finished decrypting the message.

What had been stated in the missive was plain enough and
no surprise. The target and time of attack were established
and confirmed: *Omega Drift station, tomorrow morning.*
And clearly Washington was now aware of the stakes surrounding the old ice base.

But as usual with Chenko, there were layers of information hidden between the lines of his encryption.

U.S. Delta Forces mobilized.

It was a simple statement that left as much unspoken as was written. The United States Delta Force was one of the most covert groups of the U.S. Special Forces and, when deployed, operated with immunity from the law. Once out in the field, a Delta Force team functioned with nearly complete autonomy, overseen only by an "operational controller," who could be either a high-ranking military official or someone in significant power in government.

By the deployment of U.S. Delta Forces, the rules of the coming engagement were clear to both sides. The war about to be waged would never be played out in the press. This was a covert war. No matter the outcome, the greater world would never know what happened out here. Both sides understood this and had silently agreed to it by their actions.

Out on the polar ice cap, there was a vital treasure to be won, but also a secret to be buried. Both governments intended to be the victor.

Pity those who came between them.

Such covert conflicts were not new. Despite the outward appearance of cooperation between the United States and Russia, the politics behind closed doors was as rabid and retaliatory as ever. In today's new world, one clasped hands in greeting while palming a dagger in the other.

Viktor knew this game only too well. He was an expert at its stratagems and deceptions. Otherwise he wouldn't be where he was today.

He closed the metal binder and stood up. He crossed to the six titanium cases resting on the floor. Each was half a meter square. Stamped on the top were a set of Cyrillic letters, the initials for the Arctic and Antarctic Research Institute, located in St. Petersburg, Russia. No one, not even Moscow, knew what was in these crates.

Vikor's gaze narrowed and settled on the symbol emblazoned below the institute's initials, a trifoil icon known throughout the world.

Nuclear danger . . .
Viktor touched the symbol.
Here was a game he intended to win.

4

Airborne

ᐳᐸᑕᔪᒃ ᕿᓚᖕᒥ

APRIL 8, 2:42 P.M.
EN ROUTE OVER BROOKS RANGE

Jennifer Aratuk checked her airspeed and heading. She tried her best to ignore the Cessna banking through the skies toward her. It was difficult with Matt leaning forward in his seat, his nose all but pressed against the cockpit glass.

"They're coming around!" he yelled.

No kidding. She put the plane over on a wingtip and spun the Twin Otter away. As they turned, she saw her home below. The blasted storehouse still smoked and her dogs ran in circles, soundlessly barking. Her heart went out to her friends. They would have to fend for themselves until she could return or send someone to take care of them.

First, though, she and the others had to survive.

As she skimmed the Otter over the snow-tipped tops of trees, it sounded for a moment like the plane had run through a spate of hail. A pinging rattle vibrated through the cabin.

Bane barked from the row of backseats.

"They're shooting at us!" Craig cried, buckled beside her father.

Jenny checked her right wing. Holes peppered its surface. *Damn them!* She pulled back hard on the throttle, driving the nose of the plane up. The agile plane shot skyward, gaining height rapidly.

Beside her, Matt grabbed his chair arms to hold himself in place.

"Buckle in," she griped at him.

He hurriedly snapped his seat belt in place while he craned his neck around to search the skies for the Cessna. The other plane was pulling out of its dive and chasing after them.

"Hang on!" she warned as they crossed the top of the valley rise. She couldn't let the other plane get above them again, but she also knew her craft was not as fast as the Cessna behind her. It would take some artful flying.

She dropped her flaps and pushed the wheel in, shoving the nose of the plane down into the neighboring valley. Its sides were steep, more a gorge than valley. The plane dropped sickeningly. She used gravity to increase her speed. The Twin Otter swooped down, slicing toward the wide river that carved through the center of the canyon. She followed it downstream.

The Cessna appeared behind her. It stayed high, arcing over the river valley. It again tried to get above her.

Jenny banked tightly and followed the river's course as it wound through the gorge. "Come on, baby," she whispered to her craft. She had flown the Otter since joining the sheriff's department. It had gotten her out of many a jam.

"They're diving on us again!" Matt said.

"I hear you."

"That's good," he said.

She glanced to him, but he was staring out the window.

The plane sped over the river, arcing around a sharp bend where the river chattered over the series of rapids. *Close . . .* She stared ahead. A thick mist wafted over the river ahead, obscuring the way.

•

"Jen . . . ?" Matt was now staring ahead.

"I know." She brought the plane lower. The floats now glided three feet above the churn of boulders and frothing water. A rumble echoed into the cabin.

Then a new noise intruded. It sounded like firecrackers going off. A spray of bullets chewed across the rocky bank of the river and splattered into the water, slicing toward them. The Cessna flew overhead, slightly behind them.

"Machine gun," Matt mumbled.

A slug ricocheted off a boulder in the river and struck the plane's side window. Cracks spiderwebbed over its surface.

Craig gasped, ducking away.

Jenny ground her teeth. She had no choice but to stay her course. She had committed to this. The walls of the gorge had grown into cliffs and drawn inward on either side like vise grips.

Bullets again struck the wing, tugging the plane down on that side. Jenny fought her controls. The float on the same side hit the water, but bounced back. A single slug pinged through the cabin.

Then they were into the thick mists.

A sigh burst from Jenny. The world vanished around them, and a roar filled the cabin, drowning out the engines. The windshield ran with droplets. She didn't bother with the wipers. She was momentarily blind. It didn't matter.

She shoved the wheel forward, nosing the plane in a stomach-dropping dive.

Craig cried out, thinking they were crashing.

He needn't have worried. Their airspeed rocketed up as they plunged almost straight down, following the waterfall as the river tumbled over a two-hundred-foot drop. The mists parted and the ground came hurtling up toward them.

Jenny again put the plane over on a wing and shot away to the right, following the cliff face on her left.

Matt stared at the monstrous wall. Craig gaped, white-knuckled in his seat. "The Continental Divide," Matt said, turning to Craig. "If you're visiting the Brooks Range, it's something you really don't want to miss."

Jenny eyed the cliff face. The Continental Divide split the country into its watersheds, driving up from the Rocky Mountains in the south, through Canada, and down along the Brooks Range, ending eventually at the Seward Peninsula. In the Brooks Range, it split the flows between those that traveled north and east into the Arctic Ocean and those that drained south and west into the Bering Sea.

Right now, she prayed it split the course of her plane from her pursuers. She spotted the Cessna as it shot high over the falls, aiming straight out. A grim smile tightened her lips. By the time they spotted her and circled, she would have a significant lead.

But was it enough?

The Cessna was now a speck behind them, but she noted it swinging around.

Jenny made a course correction, aiming away from the cliff face and toward a wide valley that sloped out of the mountain range toward the lower foothills. It was the Alatna Valley. They were soon over the river that drained south out of the mountains. She continued straight ahead, leaving the Alatna River behind.

"Where are we going?" Matt asked, craning back. "We're heading west. I thought you wanted to head to Prudhoe Bay."

"I do."

"Then why aren't we heading straight north up the Alatna and over the Antigun Pass?" He pointed back to the river. "It's the safest way through the mountains."

"We'd never make it that far. They'd catch up with us again. After we clear the Antigun Pass, there is nothing beyond that but the open tundra. We'd be picked off."

"But—?"

She glared over at him. "Do you want to fly this thing?"

He held up a hand. "No, babe. This is all your game."

Jenny gripped the plane's wheel tighter. *Babe?* She had to fight the urge to elbow him in his face. Matt knew how to fly. She had taught him herself, but he was no risk taker. In some ways, he was too cautious a flier to ever truly excel. One had sometimes to give oneself over to the wind, to simply trust one's craft and the power of the slipstream. Matt never could do that. Instead he always fought and tried to control every aspect of flight, like he was trying to break a horse.

"Why don't you make yourself useful," she said, "and try the radio. We need to let someone know what's going on up here."

Matt nodded and pulled on a set of earphones with a microphone attached. He switched on SATCOM to bounce their signal off a polar-orbiting communication satellite. It was the only way to communicate in the mountains around here. "I'm just getting static."

Her frown deepened. "Solar storms kicking in again. Switch to radio. Channel eleven. Try to reach Bettles. Someone may still receive us. Signals cut in and out all the time."

He did as instructed. His words were terse, giving their location and direction. Once done, he repeated it again. There didn't seem to be any response.

"Where are we headed?" Craig asked behind her, his voice shaky. He stared out the cracked side window at the passing meadows and forests far below. Jenny could only imagine his terror. He had already crashed once this week.

"Do you know the area?" she answered, drawing his attention to her.

He shook his head.

"If we mean to lose our tail, then we're going to need some cover. We're too open here. Too exposed."

Matt overheard her. He glanced to her, then at her heading. Understanding suddenly dawned in his face. "You can't be serious?"

Her father spoke one word, knowing her goal, too. "Arrigetch."

"Dear God," Matt exhaled, cinching his seat belt tighter. "You do have parachutes somewhere in here, right?"

3:17 P.M.
POLAR ICE CAP

Amanda Reynolds flew across the ice. There was no other term for this mode of transportation. Though it was properly called ice sailing, such a description was a far cry from the experience itself.

Winds filled the twelve-foot sail, spreading in a bright blue billow before her. With her body crouched, but comfortable, in the fiberglass molded seat, her feet worked the two floor pedals. She kept one hand on the jib line's crank. Under her, the boat raced across the ice at breathtaking speeds, slicing through the frozen waves of snow.

Despite her speed, she glanced around her. There was no place more starkly empty and barren. It was a frozen desert, one even more formidable and inhospitable than the Sahara. Yet at the same time, there was a distinct spiritual beauty to the place: the continual winds, the dance of blowing snow, the subtle shades of ice. Even the jagged peaks of pressure ridges were sculptures of force given form.

She worked the pedals to arc around one of these ridges with a skill honed from a decade of practice. From a long line of sailors and shipbuilders, she was in her element here. Far though she was from the family-owned shop in Port Richardson, south of San Francisco.

With her brother's help, she had built the iceboat she rode now. Its sixteen-foot hull had been constructed from hand-picked Sitka spruce. Its runners were a titanium alloy. She had clocked the boat at sixty miles per hour on Lake Ottachi in Canada, but she had been limited by a run of only a thousand feet.

She stared out at the endless expanse around her and smiled.

One of these days . . .

But for now, she settled into her seat and appreciated this time alone, away from the cramped and humid station. Overhead, the sun was sharp and the day still subzero. Though the flow of winds continually chafed against her, she was oblivious to the cold. She wore a form-hugging thermal dry suit and hood, used by divers in the Arctic waters. Her entire face was covered by a custom-molded polypropylene mask, the eyeholes fitted with polarized lenses. Only as she inhaled was she reminded of the Arctic freeze, but even that could be warmed by breathing through a battery-generated air heater that hung from the suit. But she preferred to taste the air.

And to savor the experience.

Out here, she had no disability. She did not need to hear the wind or the knife-sharp hiss of her runners over the ice. She sensed the vibrations through the wood, felt the wind's press, saw the dance of snow over the ice's surface. The world sang to her out here.

She could almost forget the car accident. *A drunk driver . . . a basal skull fracture . . . and the world went silent and more empty.* Since then, she had struggled against pity, both from others and her own heart. But it was hard. A full decade had passed since the accident, and she was beginning to lose her ability to speak clearly. She read the confusion in others' eyes that required her to repeat herself or to sign. Frustrated, she had channeled her energies into her studies and research. A part of her knew she was isolating herself. But where was the distinction between isolation and independence?

After the loss of her mother, her father had hovered over her, kept her close, seldom out of his sight. And she suspected it wasn't all because of her deafness. He feared simply losing her. Concern turned into smothering. Her struggle for freedom wasn't so much to prove that she could live as a deaf woman in the larger world, but that she could simply live independent. Period.

Then Greg . . . Captain Perry . . . came into her life. His smiles, the clear lack of pity, his bumbling attempts at flirtation, all had worn her down. Now they were at the threshold of a deeper relationship, and she was not sure how she felt about it. Her mother had been a captain's wife. It was not a world of isolation or independence. She knew this. It was parties, formal naval dinners, weekly social events with other wives. But did she want that life?

She shook her head, pushing such thoughts aside for now. There was no need to make any decisions right now. Who knew where any of this would lead?

Frowning, she manipulated her pedals to glide the boat in a gentle swing toward her destination two miles ahead: the buried Russian ice station. Earlier in the morning, the head of the biology team, Dr. Henry Ogden, had radioed her, claiming some discovery at the station that had led to a clash with the geology team. He insisted she come out and settle matters.

As head of Omega, Amanda was often called in to arbitrate interdisciplinary disputes. At times, it was like wrangling with a bunch of spoiled children. Though she could have easily sidestepped such a demand on her time, it was a perfect excuse for her to escape the drift station for a day.

So she had agreed, setting out just after lunch.

Ahead, red flags were staked atop the giant peaks of a huge pressure ridge system that extended for miles in all directions. The flags fluttered in the wind, marking the opening down into the ice base. Not that the signal flags were necessary any longer. Parked in the shelter of the ridgeline were four Ski-Doos and two larger Sno-Cats, all painted red. And beyond the vehicles, a scar split the smooth terrain where the Navy had blown a hole through the ice for the *Polar Sentinel* to surface.

As she stared at the opening that led down into the Russian base, a sense of foreboding grew in her. From the mouth of the excavated ice tunnel, billows of steam misted as if from the throat of a sleeping dragon. As of last week, the new occupants of the station had succeeded in overhauling the old generators. Fifty-two of them, all preserved. Surprisingly the lights were found to be working—as were the space heaters. The well-insulated station was said to be quite balmy.

But Amanda remembered her first steps into the icy tomb below. Using metal detectors and portable sonar devices, they were able to find the main entrance and use melt charges and explosives to tunnel down to the sealed doors of the base. The entrance was locked both by ice and a thick steel bar. They had been forced to use an acetylene torch to cut their way into the dead base.

Amanda now wondered if all their effort was worth it. She slipped her sail and gently began to brake as she neared the mountainous line of pressure ridges. In a sheltered valley between two of the ice peaks, a temporary morgue had been set up. The orange storm tents hid the frozen bodies. According to her father, a Russian delegation was already en route from Moscow to retrieve their lost comrades. They would be arriving next week.

Still no one was talking about what else was found down below.

She worked the foot pedals and expertly brought her iceboat around and braked the craft in the makeshift parking lot.

There was no one to greet her.

Glancing around, she searched the mountains. They were valleyed in shadows. Beyond them, the terrain was a maze of bridges, overhangs, crevices, and pinnacles. She again remembered the strange few seconds of movement that registered on the DeepEye sonar. Maybe it *was* just a sonar ghost, but the supposition that maybe it was some scavenger, like a polar bear, made her edgy. She stared at the impassable territory beyond the entrance and shivered.

Amanda quickly cranked down her sails, tied them off, and used a hammer to pound in a snow anchor. Once everything was secured, she grabbed her overnight bag from the boat and set off the short distance to the misty tunnel opening.

The entrance looked like any other ice cave that pocked the glaciers of the polar region. It had been widened since she had last been here and was now expansive enough to accommodate an SUV. She reached the threshold and climbed down the chopped steps to the steel door, which hung crooked on its hinges after being forced open. The mist grew thicker here, where the warm air from the base seeped out into the cold. Over the entrance was the sign Captain Perry had described. It must have been discovered when the ice tunnel had been widened.

She studied it. Bold Cyrillic lettering marched across the thick riveted plate, naming the facility:

ЛЕДОВАЯ СТАНЦИЯ ГРЕНДЕЛ

Ice Station Grendel.

Why had the Russians named it so oddly? Amanda was versed enough in literature to recognize the reference to the monster in the Beowulf legend, but the knowledge brought no further understanding.

With a shake of her head, she turned her attention back to the door and had to shoulder her way through. Ice constantly re-formed around the hinges and edges of the door. With a popping of steel and ice, she stumbled across the threshold.

A young researcher down the hall glanced over to her. He was kneeling beside an open electrical panel. It was Lee Bentley, a NASA researcher specializing in material sciences. He wore only a T-shirt and jeans.

Was it that warm in the base?

Spotting her, the scientist lifted his arms in mock terror. "Don't shoot!"

Amanda frowned, then realized how she must look with her polypropylene mask in place. She unsnapped and tugged it off, hooking it to her belt.

"Welcome to Ice *Sauna* Grendel." Lee chuckled, standing. He was short, only an inch over five feet. He had once explained how he always wanted to be an astronaut, but missed the height requirement by a mere two inches, hence his assignment to NASA's material sciences lab. He was up here to test new composites in the extremes of temperature and weather in the Arctic.

Amanda crossed to him, tugging her hood back. "I can't believe how hot it is in here."

Lee pointed to the spread of tools on the grated metal floor. "That's what I'm working on. Everyone's complaining about the heat. We brought over some air pumps to circulate better, but we figured we'd better get this thermostat problem fixed or the base will start to melt down into the ice mountain."

Amanda's eyes widened. "Is that a danger?"

He chuckled again and tapped one of the steel-plate walls. "No. There is three feet of insulation beyond the physical structure of the station. We could turn this entire station into an Easy Bake oven, and it still wouldn't significantly affect the ice beyond." He glanced appreciatively around him. "Whoever designed and engineered this place knew their material sciences. The insulation is a series of interlocked layers of asbestos-impregnated cement and sponge blocks. The structural skeleton of the place is combinations of steel, aluminum, and crude ceramic composites. Lightweight, durable, and decades ahead of its time. I would say—"

Amanda cut him off. That was one thing about her fellow scientists. Once they got talking about their field of expertise, they could ramble on and on. And it was a strain reading lips when they slurred into technobabble. "Lee, I have a meeting scheduled with Dr. Ogden. Do you happen to know where he might be?"

"Henry?" He scratched his head with a screwdriver. "Can't say for sure, but I'd try the Crawl Space. He and the geology team got into quite a row this morning. You could hear them yelling all the way up here."

Amanda nodded and continued past the NASA scientist. The base was constructed in five circular levels, connected by a narrow spiral staircase that ran down the center of the structure. Each level had roughly the same layout: a central communal space surrounded by a ring of rooms that opened into it. But each successive level was smaller than the one above it. As a whole, it appeared like a giant toy top drilled into the ice.

The uppermost tier was the widest, fifty yards across. It housed the old living quarters: barracks, kitchen, some offices. Amanda slipped down the hall and entered the central area of this tier. Tables and chairs were scattered about. It must have served as the base's mess hall and meeting room.

She waved to a pair of scientists seated at one of the tables, then crossed to the central spiral staircase. The steps coursed around a ten-foot-wide open shaft. Heavy oiled cables dropped down into the depths. It connected to a crude barred cage, actually more a dumbwaiter than an elevator, used to haul material from one level to the next.

As she started down the stairs, the steel steps vibrated under her feet, in tune with the chugging generators and humming machinery below. It was strange, like the place was alive again, coming out of a long hibernation.

Amanda climbed down the stairs, winding around and around. She skipped past Levels Two and Three. They contained small research labs and the base's engineering plant.

There were only two other levels. The bottommost was the smallest, sealed with a single watertight door. It contained the old docking station for the Russian sub, now half flooded and frozen. The conning tower of the sub could be seen through the ice, covered completely over.

But Amanda's destination was the fourth level. This tier was unlike any of the others. There was no central communal workspace. The stairs here opened into a closed hall that radiated straight out across the level. To one side, a single door opened off this hall, the only access to this sealed floor.

She stepped into the steel-walled hall and spotted the two uniformed Navy guards posted at the door a few steps down the hall. They carried rifles on their shoulders.

The petty officer in charge nodded to her. "Dr. Reynolds." The other, a seaman second grade, eyed her snug blue thermal suit, his gaze traveling up and down her form.

She acknowledged the petty officer. "Have you seen Dr. Ogden?"

"Yes, ma'am. He mentioned you'd be coming. He asked us to keep everyone out of the Crawl Space until you arrived." The guard pointed down to the other end of the hall.

A door lay at that end, too, but it didn't lead into the lab on this floor. It was an exit, a doorway into the heart of the ice island. Beyond lay a maze of natural caverns and manmade tunnels, cored from the ice itself, which the researchers of the station had nicknamed the Crawl Space.

This region had all the glaciologists and geologists walking around with drunken smiles. They had been boring out samples, taking temperatures, and performing other more arcane tests. She couldn't blame them for their excitement. How many times did one get to explore the interior of an iceberg? She had heard that they'd found a cache of inclusions, a geologist's term for boulders and other bits of terrestrial debris. As a result of the find, the entire geology team had relocated here from Omega.

Why the clash with the biologists, though? There was only one way to find out.

"Thank you," she said to the guard.

As she crossed down the hall, she was happy to leave the sealed floor behind her. She'd had a hard time making eye contact with the guards. The guilt of her knowledge weighed on her, dulled her appreciation of the other discoveries here.

Among the researchers, speculations and rumors as to what lay on Level Four were rampant: alien spaceships, nuclear technology, biological warfare experiments, even whispers closer to the truth.

Other bodies found.

The actual truth was far more horrific than any of the wildest speculations.

As she reached the end of the hall, the double set of doors swung open ahead of her. A figure in a heavy yellow parka shambled through. Amanda felt the cold exhalation flowing through the open door, a breath from the heart of the ice island.

The figure shook back his hood and revealed his frosted features. Dr. Henry Ogden, the fifty-year-old Harvard biologist, looked surprised to find her there. "Dr. Reynolds!"

"Henry." She nodded to him.

"Dear God." He pulled a glove off with his teeth and checked his watch. He then ran a hand over his bald pate. Besides his eyebrows, the only hair on the man's head was a thin brown mustache and a tiny soul patch under his lower lip. He absentmindedly tugged at this little tuft of hair. "I'm sorry. I hoped to meet you upstairs."

"What's this all about?"

He glanced back to the door. "I . . . I found something . . . something amazing. You should—" As he turned away, she could no longer read his lips.

"Dr. Ogden?"

He turned back, his eyebrows raised quizzically.

She touched her lips with her fingers.

"Oh, I'm sorry." He now spoke in an unnaturally slow manner, as if speaking to someone with a mental defect. Amanda bit back her anger.

"You need to see this for yourself," he continued. "That's why I had you come." He stared a moment at the Navy guards down the hall. "I couldn't count on them keeping the rock hounds away for very long. The specimens . . ." His voice trailed off, distracted. He shook his head. "Let's get you a parka, and I'll take you."

"I'll stay warm enough in this," she said impatiently, running a hand over her thermal suit. "Show me what you found."

The biologist's eyes were still on the guards, his brows crinkled. Amanda wagered he was speculating like all the others. His gaze eventually swung back to her. "What I found . . . I think it's the reason the station was built here."

It took a moment for his words to register. "What? What do you mean?"

"Come see." He turned and headed back through the double doors.

Amanda followed, but she peered back to the guarded doorway. *It's the reason the station was built here.*

She prayed the biologist was wrong.

3:40 P.M.
OVER BROOKS RANGE

Staring out the windshield of the Twin Otter, Matt tried to focus on the beauty of one of the great natural wonders of the world. This section of the Gates of the Arctic National Park was the goal of thousands of hikers, climbers, and adventurers each year.

Ahead rose the Arrigetch Peaks. The name—Arrigetch—came from the Nunamiut, meaning "upstretched fingers of the hand." An apt description. The entire region was jammed with pinnacles and sheer spires of granite. It was a land of thousand-foot vertical walls, precarious overhangs, and glacial amphitheaters. Such terrain was a natural playground for climbers, while hikers enjoyed its verdant alpine meadows and ice-blue tarns.

But flying through Arrigetch was plain madness. And it wasn't just the rocks. The winds were a hazard, too. The air currents flowed from the glacial heights like a swollen river through cataracts, carving the winds into a raging mix of sudden gusts, shears, and crosswinds.

"Get ready!" Jenny warned.

The plane climbed toward the jumbled landscape. To either side, mountains towered, their slopes bright with snow and ice floes. Between them rose Arrigetch. There appeared no way to pass through the area.

Matt craned around. Their pursuers had almost caught up with them again. The Cessna buzzed about a quarter mile back. Would they dare follow into this maze?

Below, a stream drained from the broken heights above. A sparse taiga-spruce forest finally succumbed to the altitude and faded away. They were now above the continent's tree line.

Matt turned to Jenny, ready to try one last time to dissuade her from what she was about to attempt. But he saw the determined glint in her eye, the way her brows pinched together. There would be no talking her out of it.

Her father spoke from behind them. John had finished cinching Bane's dog collar to one of the seat harnesses. "Ready back here."

Beside the elder Inuit, Craig sat straight-backed in his seat. The reporter's eyes were locked ahead. He had paled since coming in sight of Arrigetch. On the ground, the view was humbling, but from the air, it was sheer terror.

The Otter raced over the last of the rocky slopes, impossibly high and impassable.

"Here we go," Jenny said.

"And here they come," Matt echoed.

The chatter of gunfire cut through the whine of their motors. Loose shale on the slope danced with the impact of the slugs. But the line of fire was well to the side. The other plane was still too far off for an accurate shot. It was a desperate act before they lost their quarry to Arrigetch.

As Matt watched the Cessna, a puff of fire rolled from one of the side windows. Though he heard nothing, he imagined the whistle of the incoming grenade. A trail of smoke marked its rocketed path, arcing to within two yards of their wingtip, then vanishing ahead. The explosion erupted against one of the pinnacles, casting out a rain of stone. A section of cliff face broke free and slid earthward.

Jenny banked from the assaulted pillar and turned up on one wing. Matt had a momentary view of the ground below as the Otter shot between the two spires.

"Ohmygod, ohmygod," Craig intoned behind him.

Once past the spires, Jenny leveled out. Surrounded on all sides by columns and towers, peaks and pinnacles, cliffs and walls. The heights were such that the tops could not be seen out the windows.

Winds buffeted the small plane, jostling it.

Matt clenched his armrests.

Jenny banked hard, tilting up on the other wing. Matt's eyes stretched wide. He wanted to close them, but for some reason, he couldn't. Instead, he cursed this firsthand view of Jenny's flying. Economy seating suddenly did have its appeal.

The Otter shot between a cliff face and a tilted column. To his side, Jenny began to hum under her breath. Matt knew she did this whenever she was fully concentrating on something, but usually it was just the *New York Times* crossword puzzle.

The plane skirted the pinnacle and leveled again—but only for a breath.

"Hang on," Jenny muttered.

Matt simply glared. His forearms were already cramped from clutching his seat. What more did she want?

She rolled the Otter over on a wing and spun tight around a spire. For the next five minutes, she zigzagged and barnstormed through the rock maze. Back and forth, up on one wing, then the other.

His stomach lurching, Matt sought any sign of the Cessna in the skies, but it was like searching through a stone forest. He had lost sight of the plane as soon as they entered Arrigetch—which had been Jenny's plan all along. There were a thousand exits from this region: passes, chutes, moraines, valleys, glacial flows. And with the lowering cloud cover, if the Cessna wanted to know where they were headed, it would have to follow, if it dared.

The plane entered a wide glacial cirque, a natural amphitheater carved from the side of one of the mountains. Jenny swung the Otter in a gentle glide along the edge of the steep-sided bowl. The lip of a glacier hung over the mountain's edge in an icy cornice. Below, the floor was covered with boulders and glacial till, powdery rock and gravel that had been left behind as the ice retreated.

But in the center lay a perfectly still mountain lake. The blue surface of the tarn was a mirror, reflecting the Otter as it circled around the bowl. The walls of the cirque were too steep for a direct flight out. Jenny began a slow spiral, heading up, trying to clear the mountain cliffs.

Matt let out a slow sigh of relief. They had survived Arrigetch.

Then movement in the tarn's reflection caught his eye.

Another plane.

The Cessna shot into the cirque, entering from an entirely different direction. From the way the plane bobbled for a moment, Matt guessed their pursuers were just as surprised to see them here.

"Jen?" Matt said.

"I don't have enough altitude yet to clear the cliffs." Her words for the first time sounded scared.

The two planes now circled the stone amphitheater, climbing higher, the tense pageant mirrored in the blue lake below. The door to the other plane shoved open. From seventy yards away, Matt spotted the now familiar parka-clad figure brace himself in place, shouldering the grenade launcher.

He turned back to Jenny. He knew he'd eventually regret his next words, but he also knew they would never clear the top of the cliffs before they were fired upon. "Get us back into Arrigetch!"

"There's not enough time!"

"Just do it." Matt unbuckled and climbed from the copilot seat. He scrambled over to the side window that faced the other plane.

Jenny banked toward the maze of rock, circling back toward Arrigetch.

Matt unhitched the window and slid it back. Winds blasted into the cabin. Bane barked excitedly from the backseat, tail wagging furiously. The wolf loved flying.

"What are you doing?" Jenny called to him.

"You fly," he yelled, and cracked open the emergency box by the door. He needed a weapon, and he didn't have time to free and load the shotgun. He grabbed the flare gun inside the emergency kit and jammed it out the window. He pointed it at the other plane. With the winds, prop wash, and shifting positions of the planes, it was a Hail Mary shot.

He aimed as best he could and pulled the trigger.

The fizzling trail of the flare arced across the cirque, reflected in the tarn below. He had been aiming for the parka-clad figure, but the winds carried the flare to the side. It exploded into brilliance as it sailed past the nose of the plane.

The other pilot, clearly tense from his transit through the jagged clutches of Arrigetch, veered off, pitching the plane suddenly to the side. The parka-clad figure at the plane's door lost his footing and tumbled out, arms cartwheeling. But a couple yards down, he snagged, tethered in place to the frame of the door. He swung back and forth under the belly of the Cessna.

It had to be distraction enough.

"Go!" Matt yelled, and slammed the window shut. He crawled back to the front seat.

Jenny's father patted him on the shoulder as he passed. "Good shot."

Matt nodded to Craig. "It was his idea." He remembered the reporter pulling the flare gun on him when he came to his rescue a couple days ago. It had reminded him of a lesson taught to him by his old sergeant: *Use whatever you have on hand . . . never give up the fight.*

Feeling better, Matt buckled into place.

Jenny was already diving back into the maze. "They're coming after us," she said.

Matt jerked around, surprised. He turned in time to see the flailing man cut free. His form tumbled through the air and splashed into the blue tarn.

Stunned, Matt sat back around. They had sacrificed their own man to continue the pursuit.

Jenny swung the plane over on one wing and sped away among the cliffs. But this time, they couldn't shake the other plane.

And Jenny was tiring. Matt saw how her hands had begun to tremble. Her eyes had lost their steady determination and shone with desperation. A single mistake and they were dead.

As he thought it, it happened.

Jenny banked hard around a craggy column.

Ahead a solid wall of stone filled the world.

A dead end.

They could not turn away in time. Matt braced himself, expecting Jenny to try, but instead she throttled up.

Matt's throat closed tight. He suddenly realized where they were and what she was about to attempt. "No, no, no . . ."

"Oh yes," she answered him. The nose of the plane dropped sickeningly. She spiraled out a bit and back around.

At the base of the cliff, a river flowed out. Eons ago, an earthquake had rattled Arrigetch, toppling one peak against another. This created a Devil's Pass, a breach left under the two tumbled peaks.

It was one of the exits from Arrigetch.

Jenny dove toward the river, aiming for the opening in the rock. Her angle was too steep. But at the last moment, she pulled hard on the wheel and throttled down, almost stalling the props. The Otter leveled out a foot above the stream, then shot into the Devil's Pass.

Instantly the world went dark, and the dull roar of their engines trebled—but daylight lay directly ahead. It was a straight passage, no longer than forty yards. But it was also tight, leaving only a yard to either side.

Jenny was humming again.

"They're still behind us!" Craig called out.

Matt turned as the Cessna ducked into the tunnel. The other pilot was determined not to lose his target.

Matt clenched a fist. Their last desperate maneuver had been for nothing. The other pilot matched Jenny trick for trick. It was hopeless. Beyond the tunnel lay the open mountains. There would be nowhere to hide.

"Hold tight, folks," Jenny warned as they neared the far end of the tunnel.

"What are you—?"

Jenny shoved the wheel. The plane dipped. The floats struck the stream hard and skidded over its surface, casting a flume of water behind them. As the plane bounced back up, they were out of the tunnel and sailing high into the air.

Matt searched behind them as Jenny banked away.

From the tunnel mouth, the Cessna appeared, tumbling out, rolling end over end, wings broken. One of the propellers bounced free and spun up the snowy slope.

Matt turned back to his ex-wife with awe. The sudden backwash from her bounce against the stream had struck the other plane's props and wings, causing the Cessna to bobble and brush against one of the tunnel walls.

A fatal mistake.

Jenny's voice trembled. "I hate tailgaters."

It was like stepping into a different world. The Crawl Space outside the Russian ice station was a natural warren of ice caverns and chutes. As Amanda passed over the threshold, she left not only the warmth of the station behind, but also all man-made structures.

Just outside the double doors to the base lay rusty piles of plate steel, bags of old concrete, stacks of conduit, and spools of wire. When it was first discovered, it was assumed the natural space in the ice was used as a storage annex, hence its nickname.

A structural engineer with the NASA group hypothesized that the station may have been constructed within a natural cavern inside the ice island, requiring less excavation. He suggested the Crawl Space might be the tiny remnant of the larger cavern system.

But outside such idle speculation, the Crawl Space held little fascination for most of Omega's scientists. To them, it was just the janitor's closet of the base. Only the geologists and glaciologists seemed truly fascinated by these back rooms and ice chutes.

"This way," Dr. Ogden said, zipping his jacket up to his chin and pulling the fur-lined hood over his bald head. The biologist grabbed a flashlight from a stack near the door, flicked it on, and aimed past the cluttered entrance hall to the dark passages beyond. When he stood a moment longer, Amanda thought he might be speaking to her, but with his back turned, she couldn't tell for sure. Before she could ask, he set off down toward the warren of tunnels.

Amanda followed. At least the geologists had spread sand on the ice floor for better footing. As she continued, leaving the lighted entrance behind, the air grew much colder. For some reason the motionless air seemed icier than on the surface. She lifted her warming mask from the belt of her thermal suit and flicked on the switch.

Henry Ogden continued, winding his way, passing side caverns, some empty, some stacked with gear. One alcove even contained butcher-wrapped packages and crates marked in Russian. Perishables, Amanda imagined. No need for freezers here.

As they continued deeper, she noted evidence of the scientists' handiwork here: walls pocked with bore holes, some survey stakes with little flags, some pieces of modern equipment, even an empty Hostess Ding Dong box. She kicked this last aside as she passed. The new inhabitants of Ice Station Grendel were certainly leaving their unique footprints here.

Distracted by her surroundings, Amanda quickly became lost. Passages crisscrossed in all different directions. Dr. Ogden stopped at one of the intersections and searched the walls with his flashlight.

Amanda noted small spray-painted marks on the ice. They seemed freshly painted and varied in colors and shapes: red arrows, blue squiggles, and orange triangles. They were clearly signposts left behind by the scientists.

Henry touched a green dot, nodded to himself, and continued in that direction.

By now, the tunnels had narrowed and lowered overhead. Amanda had to hunch as she followed after the determined biologist. In the strangely still air, sparkles of ice crystals shone in the flashlight's glow. Here the walls were so glassy that she spotted air bubbles trapped in the ice, glinting like pearls.

She ran gloved fingers along the wall. Silky smooth. Such tunnels and caves were formed as the surface ice melted in the summer's heat, and the warm water leaked through cracks and fissures, flowing downward and melting out these shafts and pockets. Eventually the surface froze again, sealing and preserving the cavern system below.

Amanda gazed at the blue glass walls. There was a beauty here that warmed the cold. As she craned around, her heel slipped. Only a frantic grab for a spar halted her tumble.

Dr. Ogden glanced back to her. "Careful. It's pretty slippery from here on."

Now you tell me, she thought, and pulled herself back to her feet. She realized the spar she had grabbed was not ice. It was a chunk of rock protruding from the ice. She stared at it a moment as Dr. Ogden continued. It was one of the many inclusions, she realized, described by the geologists. She touched it with a bit of reverence. Here was a rock from whatever landmass this glacial chunk had broken away from eons ago.

Gloom settled around her as the biologist rounded a bend with his flashlight. Amanda hurried after him, regretting that she hadn't collected one of the flashlights herself. She watched her footing now. Here the passages were not sanded. The geologists must not have ventured into this section of the Crawl Space yet.

Henry glanced back to her. "It's just ahead."

Amanda stared around her as the tunnel began to widen again. Within the glassy walls, boulders hung, an avalanche frozen in place. Deeper in the ice, other shadows darkened the upper reaches. They must be entering a cluster of inclusions.

Rounding a bend, the tunnel emptied into a large cave. Amanda lost her footing again and skated out of the tunnel. With her arms out for balance, she managed to stop herself.

She stood for a moment, stunned. The floor of the cavern was as large as an Olympic ice rink. But she quickly forgot the floor as she gaped at the chamber's breadth and width. Arched over and around her was a huge natural cathedral: half ice and half *stone*.

She stood, surrounded by ice, but the back half of the chamber was solid rock. A bowl of stone encompassed the far wall and overhung the ceiling.

Something touched her elbow, startling her. It was only Dr. Ogden. He drew her eyes back to him, his lips moving.

"It's the remnant of an ancient cliff face. At least according to MacFerran," Henry said, naming the head of the geology team. "He says it must have broken from the landmass as the glacier calved and formed this ice island. It dates back to the last ice age. He immediately wanted to blast away sections and core out samples, but I had to stop him."

Amanda was still too stunned to speak.

"On just cursory examination, I found dead lichen and frozen mosses. Searching the cliff pockets more thoroughly, I discovered three bird's nests, one with eggs!" He began to speak more rapidly with his excitement. Amanda had to concentrate on his lips. "There were also a pack of rodents and a snake trapped in ice. It's a treasure trove of life from that age, a whole frozen biosphere." He led the way across the cavern toward the stone wall. "But that's not all! Come see!"

She followed, staring ahead. The wall was not as solid as it had first appeared. It was pocked with cubbies and alcoves. Some sections seemed broken and half tumbled out. Deep clefts also delved into the rock face, but they were too dark to discern how far they penetrated.

Amanda crossed under the arch of stone and eyed with trepidation the slabs precariously balanced overhead. None of it seemed as solid as it had been a moment ago.

Dr. Ogden grabbed her elbow, squeezing hard, stopping her. "Careful," he said, drawing her eye, then pointing to the floor.

A few steps ahead lay an open well in the ice-rink floor. It was too perfectly oval to be natural, and the edges were scored coarsely.

"They dug one of them out from here."

Amanda frowned. "One of what?" She spotted other pits in the ice now.

Henry tugged her to the side. "Over here." He slipped a canteen of water from his belt. He motioned her down on a knee on the ice. They were now only a few yards from the shattered stone cliff. Hunched down, it was almost like they were on a frozen lake with the shore only a few steps away.

The biologist whisked the ice with his gloved hand. Then placed his flashlight facedown onto the frozen lake. Lit from on top, the section of ice under them glowed. But details were murky because of the frost on the ice's surface. Still, Amanda could make out the dark shadow of something a few feet under the ice.

Henry sat back and opened his canteen. "Watch," he mouthed to her.

Leaning over, he poured a wash of water over the surface, melting the frost rime and turning the ice to glass under them. The light shone clearly, limning what lay below in perfect detail.

Amanda gasped, leaning away.

The creature looked as if it were lunging up through the ice at her, caught for a moment in a camera's flash. Its body was pale white and smooth-skinned, like the beluga whales that frequented the Arctic, and almost their same size, half a ton at least. But unlike the beluga, this creature bore short forelimbs that ended in raking claws and large webbed hind limbs, spread now, ready to sweep upward at her. Its body also seemed more supple than a whale's, with a longer torso, curving like an otter. It looked built for speed.

But it was the elongated maw, stretched wide to strike, lined by daggered teeth, that chilled her to the bone. It gaped wide enough to swallow a whole pig. Its black eyes were half rolled to white, like a great white lunging after prey.

Amanda sat back and took a few puffs from her air warmer as her limbs tremored from the cold and shock. "What the hell is it?"

The biologist ignored her question. "There are more specimens!" He slid on his knees across the ice and revealed another of the creatures lurking just at the cliff face. This beast was curled in the ice as if in slumber, its body wrapped in a tight spiral, jaws tucked in the center, tail around the whole, not unlike a dog in slumber.

Henry quickly gained his feet. "That's not all."

Before she could ask a question, he crossed and entered a wide cleft in the rock face. Amanda followed, chasing after the light, still picturing the jaws of the monster, wide and hungry.

The cleft cut a few yards into the rock face and ended at a cave the size of a two-car garage.

Amanda straightened. Positioned against the back wall were six giant ice blocks. Inside each were frozen examples of the creatures, all curled in the fetal-like position. But it was the sight in the chamber's center that had Amanda falling back toward the exit.

Like a frog in a biology lab, one of the creatures lay stretched across the ice floor, legs staked spread-eagle. Its torso was cut from throat to pelvis, skin splayed back and pinned to the ice. From the frozen state of the dissection, it was clearly an old project. But she caught only a glimpse of bone and organs and had to turn away.

She hurried back out onto the open frozen lake. Dr. Ogden followed. He seemed oblivious to her shock. He touched her arm to draw her eyes.

"A discovery of this magnitude will change the face of biology," Henry said, bending close to her in his insistence. "Now you can see why I had to stop the geologists from ruining this preserved ecosystem. A find like this . . . preserved like this—"

Amanda cut him off. Her voice brittle. "What the hell are those things?"

Henry blinked at her and waved a hand. "Oh, of course. You're an engineer."

Though she was deaf, she could almost hear his condescension. She rankled a bit, but held her tongue.

He motioned back to the cleft and spoke more slowly. "I studied the specimen back there all day. I have a background in paleobiology. Fossilized remains of such a species have been discovered in Pakistan and in China, but never such a preserved specimen."

"A specimen of what, Henry?" Her eyes were hard on the biologist.

"Of *Ambulocetus natans*. What is commonly called 'the walking whale.' It is the evolutionary link between land-dwelling mammals and the modern whale."

She simply gaped at him as he continued.

"It is estimated to have existed some forty-nine million years ago, then died out some thirty-six million years ago. But the splayed out legs, the pelvis fused into the backbone, the nasal drift . . . all clearly mark this as distinctly *Ambulocetus*."

Amanda shook her head. "You can't be claiming that these specimens are so old. Forty million years?"

"No." His eyes widened. "That's just it! MacFerran says the ice at this level is only fifty thousand years old, dating back to the last ice age. And these specimens bear some unique features. My initial supposition is that some pod of *Ambulocetus* whales must have migrated to the Arctic regions, like modern whales do today. Once here, they developed Arctic adaptations. The white skin, the gigantism, the thicker layer of fat. Similar to the polar bear or beluga whales."

Amanda remembered her own earlier comparison to the beluga. "And these creatures somehow survived up here until the last ice age? Without any evidence ever being discovered?"

"Is it really so surprising? Anything that lived and died on the polar ice cap would have simply sunk to the bottom of the Arctic Ocean, a region barely glimpsed at all. And on land, permafrost makes it nearly impossible to carry out digs above the Arctic Circle. So it is entirely possible for something to have existed for eons, then died out without leaving a trace. Even today we have barely any paleological record of this region."

Amanda shook her head, but she could not dismiss what she had seen. And she couldn't discount his argument. Only in the past decade, with the advent of modern technology and tools, was the Arctic region truly being explored. Her own team back at Omega was defining a new species every week. So far, the discoveries were just new, unclassified phytoplankton or algae, nothing on the level of these creatures.

Henry continued, "The Russians must have discovered these creatures when they dug out their base. Or maybe they built the base here because of them. Who knows?"

Amanda remembered Henry's early claim: *It's the reason the station was built here.* "What makes you think that?" She flashed back again to the discovery on Level Four. This new discovery, amazing as it was, seemed in no way connected to the other.

Henry eyed her. "Isn't it obvious?"

Amanda scrunched her brow.

"*Ambulocetus* fossils were only discovered in the past few years." He pointed back to the cleft. "Back in World War Two, they knew nothing about them. So, of course, the Russians would come up with their own name for such a monster."

Her eyes grew wide.

"They named their base after the creature," Dr. Ogden explained needlessly. "A mascot of sorts, I imagine."

Amanda stared down at the frozen lake, at the beast lunging up at her. She now knew what she was truly seeing. The monster of Nordic legend.

Grendel.

Act Two

FIRE AND ICE

ᐃᖕᓇᖅᓗ ᓯᑯᓗ

5

Slippery Slope

ᔅᑯᖕᖁᐁᓇ᠊ᑐᖅ ᐱᖅᐅᐊᑎᒍᑦ

Matt slumped in his seat. Snoring echoed throughout the cabin of the Twin Otter. It came not from the sleeping reporter nor from Jenny's dozing father, but from the wolf sprawled on his back across the third row of seats. A particularly loud snort raised a ghost of a smile on Matt's face.

Jenny spoke from beside him. "I thought you were going to get his deviated septum fixed."

The ghost became a true smile. Bane had snored since he was a pup curled on the foot of their bed. It had been a source of amusement to both of them. Matt sat straighter. "The plastic surgeon out of Nome said it would require too extensive a nasal job. Too much trimming. He would end up looking like a bulldog."

Jenny didn't respond, so Matt risked a glance her way. She stared straight out, but he noted the small crinkles at the corners of her eyes. Sad amusement.

Crossing his arms, Matt wondered if that was the best he could manage with her. For the moment, it was enough.

He gazed out the window. The moon was near to full, casting a silvery brilliance across the snowy plains. This far north, winter still gripped the land, but some signs of the spring thaw were visible: a trickle of misty stream, a sprinkling of meltwater lakes. A few caribou herds speckled the tundra, moving slowly through the night, following the snowmelt waterways, feeding on reindeer moss, sprigs of lingonberry, and munching through muskeg, the ubiquitous tussocks of balled-up grass, each the size of a ripe pumpkin, rooted in the thawing muck.

"We were lucky to have radioed Deadhorse when we did," Jenny mumbled beside him, drawing his eye.

"What do you mean?"

After clearing Arrigetch, they had managed to raise the airstrip at Prudhoe Bay on Alaska's North Slope. They had alerted civil and military authorities to their chase through the Brooks Range. Helicopters would be dispatched in the morning to search for the debris of the Cessna. They should have answers on their pursuers shortly after that. Matt had also been able to reach Carol Jeffries, the bear researcher over in Bettles. She knew Jenny's cabin and would send some folks to take care of the animals left behind. Craig had also relayed word to his own contact at Prudhoe. Once questioned and debriefed, the reporter would have one hell of a tale to tell. After making contact, and with the story of their ordeal now passed to the outside world, they had all relaxed.

But now what was wrong? Matt pulled himself up in his seat.

Jenny pointed out the Otter's windshield—not to the tundra below, but to the clear skies.

Matt leaned forward. At first, he saw nothing unusual. The constellation Orion hung brightly. Polaris, the North Star, lay directly ahead. Then he spotted the shimmering bands and streamers rising from the horizon, flickers of greens, reds, and blues. The borealis was rising.

"According to the forecast," Jenny said, "we're due for a brilliant display."

Matt leaned back, watching the spectacle spread in colored fans and dancing flames across the night sky. Such a natural show went by many names: the aurora borealis, the northern lights. Among the native Athapascan Indians, it was called *koyukon* or *yoyakkyh,* while the Inuit simply named them spirit lights.

As he watched, the wave of colors flowed over the arch of the sky, shimmering in a luminous corona and rolling in clouds of azures and deep crimsons.

"We won't be able to reach anyone for a while," Jenny said.

Matt nodded. Such a dazzling display, created as solar winds struck the upper atmosphere of the earth, would frazzle most communications. But they didn't have very far to go. Another half hour at most. Already the northern horizon had begun to brighten with the lights of the oil fields and distant Prudhoe Bay.

They flew in silence for several minutes more, simply enjoying the light show in the sky, accompanied by Bane's snoring in the back. For these few moments, it felt like home. Maybe it was simply the aftereffects of their harrowing day, an endorphin-induced sense of ease and comfort. But Matt feared wounding it with speech.

It was Jenny who finally broke the silence. "Matt . . ." The timbre of her voice was soft.

"Don't," he said. It had taken them three years and today's life-and-death struggle to bring them into one space together. He did not want to threaten this small start.

Jenny sighed. He did not fail to note her tone of exasperation.

Her fingers tightened on the wheel, moving with a squeak of leather on vinyl. "Never mind," she whispered.

The moment's peace was gone—and it had not even taken words. Tension filled the cabin, raising a wall between them.

The remainder of the journey was made in total silence, strained now, bitter.

The first few oil derricks came into view, decorated in lights like a Christmas tree. Off to the left, a jagged silver line marred the perfect tundra, rising and falling over the landscape like a giant metal snake. The Trans-Alaska Pipeline. It ran from Prudhoe Bay on Alaska's north coast to Valdez on Prince William Sound, a river of black gold.

They were closing in on their destination. The pipeline led the way. Jenny followed it now, paralleling its run. She tried the radio, attempting to reach the airport tower at Deadhorse. Her frown was answer enough. The skies still danced and flashed.

She banked in a slow arc. Ahead, the township of Prudhoe Bay—if you could call it a town—glowed in the night like some oilman's Oz. It was mostly a company town, built for the sole purpose of oil production, transportation, and supporting services. Its average population was under a hundred, but the number of transient oil workers caused this number to vary, depending on the workload. There was also a small military presence here, protecting the heart of the entire North Slope oil production.

Beyond the town's border stretched the Beaufort Sea and the Arctic Ocean, but it was hard to tell where land ended and ocean began. Spreading from the shore were vast rafts of fast ice extending for miles into the ocean, fusing eventually with the pack ice of the polar cap. As summer warmed the region, the cap would shrink by half, retreating from shorelines, but for now, the world was solid ice.

Jenny headed out toward the sea, circling Prudhoe Bay and positioning herself for landing at the single airstrip. "Something's going on down there," she said, tipping up on one wing.

Matt spotted it, too: a flurry of activity at the edge of town. A score of vehicles were racing across the snowy fields from the military installation, hurrying out of town in their general direction. He glanced to the other side of their plane.

Below lay the end of the Trans-Alaska Pipeline. The giant buildings of Gathering Station 1 and Pump Station 1 were lit up behind Cyclone fencing. Here the North Slope oil was cooled, water removed, gas bled off, and the oil began its six-day, eight-hundred-mile journey to the tankers on Prince William Sound.

As they crossed near Pump Station 1, Matt noted a section of the Cyclone fencing had been knocked down. He glanced back to the racing military vehicles. Foreboding lanced through him.

"Get us out of here!" Matt snapped.

"What—?"

The explosion ripped away any further words. The building that housed Gathering Station 1 burst apart in a fiery blast. A ball of flame rolled skyward. The sudden hot thermals and blast wave threw their plane up on end. Jenny fought the controls, struggling to keep them from flipping completely over.

Yells arose from the backseats, accompanied by Bane's barking.

Swearing under her breath, Jenny rolled the Otter away from the conflagration. Flaming debris rained down around them, crashing into the snowy fields, into buildings. New fires erupted. Pump Station 1 blew its roof off next, adding a second ball of rolling flame. The four-foot-diameter pipe that led into the building tore itself apart, blasting up along its length. Burning oil jetted in all directions. It didn't stop until it reached the first of the sixty-two gate valves, halting the destruction from escalating up the pipeline.

In a matter of seconds, the wintry calm of the slumbering township became a fiery hell. Rivers of flame flowed toward the sea, steaming and writhing. Buildings burned. Smaller, secondary explosions burst from gas mains and holding tanks. People and vehicles raced in all directions.

"Jesus Christ!" Craig exclaimed behind them, his face pressed to the glass.

A new voice crackled from the radio, full of static, coming from the general channel. "Clear all airspace immediately! Any attempt to land will be met with deadly force."

"They're locking the place down!" Jenny exclaimed, and banked away from the fires. She headed out over the frozen sea.

Her father stared back to the coast. "What happened?"

"I don't know," Matt mumbled, watching the coastline burn. "Accident, sabotage . . . whatever it was it seemed timed to our arrival."

"Surely it can't have anything to do with us," Craig said.

Matt pictured the downed section of Cyclone fencing, the racing vehicles from the military installation. Someone had broken in, setting off alarms. And after the last two days, he could not dismiss the possibility that it was somehow connected to them. Disaster seemed to be dogging them ever since the reporter's plane crashed. Someone sure as hell did not want the political reporter for the *Seattle Times* to reach that SCICEX station out on the ice.

"Where can we go now?" Craig asked.

"I'm running low on fuel," Jenny cautioned, tapping an instrument gauge as if this would miraculously move the pointer.

"Kaktovik," John said gruffly.

Jenny nodded at her father's suggestion.

"Kaktovik?" Craig asked.

Matt answered, "It's a fishing village on Barter Island, near the Canadian border. About a hundred and twenty miles from here." He turned to Jenny as she banked the Otter westward. "Do you have enough fuel?"

She lifted one eyebrow. "You may have to get out and push us the last few miles."

Great, he thought.

Craig's face had grown more pale and drawn. He had already experienced one plane crash. The reporter was surely getting sick of Alaskan air travel.

"Don't worry," Matt assured him. "If we run out of fuel, the Otter can land on its ski skids on any flat snow."

"Then what?" Craig asked sourly, crossing his arms.

"Then we do what the lady here says . . . we push!"

"Quit it, Matt," Jenny warned. She glanced back to the reporter. "We'll get to Kaktovik. And if not, I've an emergency reserve tank stored below. We can manually refill the main tank if needed."

Craig nodded, relaxing slightly.

Matt stared out at the burning coastline as it retreated behind them. He noted Jenny's father doing the same. They briefly made eye contact. He read the suspicion in the other's eyes. The sudden explosions were too coincidental to be mere chance.

"What do you think?" John muttered.

"Sabotage."

"But why? To what end? Just because of us?"

Matt shook his head. Even if someone wanted to stop or divert them, this response was like killing a fly with a crate of TNT.

Craig overheard them. His voice trembled. "It's a calculated act of distraction and misdirection."

"What do you mean?" Matt studied the reporter's face. It remained tight, unreadable. He began to worry about their passenger. He had witnessed post-traumatic stress disorder before.

But Craig swallowed hard, then spoke slowly. Clearly he sought to center himself by working through this problem. "We passed on word about our attackers to Prudhoe Bay. Someone was going to investigate tomorrow. I wager now that will be delayed. The limited investigative resources up here—military and civilian—will have their hands full for weeks. More than enough time for our attackers to cover their tracks."

"So it was all done so someone could clean up the mess in the mountains?"

Craig waved this away. "No. Such a large-scale affront would need more of a reason to justify it. Otherwise, it's overkill."

Matt heard his own thoughts from a moment ago echoed.

Craig ticked off items aloud. "The explosions will delay any investigation in the mountains. It will also divert us and offer up a new, more exciting story for us to follow. The burning of Prudhoe Bay will be headlines for days. What reporter would want to miss such a story? To be here firsthand. To have witnessed it." The tired man shook his head. "First the bastards try to kill me, now they try to bribe me with a more tantalizing and promising story. They throw it right in my damn lap."

"Distraction and misdirection," Matt mumbled.

Craig nodded. "And not just directed at us. We're small potatoes. I would bet my own left nut that this attack had been preplanned all along. That we're only a secondary distraction. It's the larger world the saboteurs really want to distract. After this attack, everyone will be looking at Prudhoe Bay, discussing it, investigating it. CNN will have reporters here by tomorrow."

"But why?"

Craig met his gaze. Matt was surprised to see the tempered steel in Craig's eyes. He recalled him pulling the flare gun on him. Even under stress, the reporter thought quickly. Despite his scared demeanor, there were hidden depths to this man. Matt's respect for the reporter continued to grow.

"Why?" Craig parroted. "It's like I said. Distraction and misdirection. Let the whole world look over here at the fireworks"—he waggled his fingers in the air—"while the real damage is done out of sight." The reporter pointed to the north. "They don't want us to look over there."

"The drift station," Matt said.

Craig's voice dropped to a mumble. "Something's going to

happen out there. Something no one wants the world to know about. Something that justifies setting fire to Prudhoe Bay."

Matt now knew why Craig had been sent north by his editor. The reporter had tried to blame the assignment on a tryst with the editor's niece, a punishment for a transgression. But Matt didn't buy it. The man knew his business. He had a calculating mind and a keen sense of political maneuvering.

"So what do we do now?" Matt asked.

Craig's eyes flicked to him. "We fly to Kaktovik. What else can we do?"

Matt crinkled his brow.

"If you think I'm going out to that friggin' drift station," Craig said with a snort, "you're nuts. I'm staying the hell away."

"But if you're right—?"

"I've pretty much grown a liking for my skin. The bastards' fiery show may not have fooled me, but that doesn't mean I can't take a hint."

"Then we tell someone."

"Be my guest. No one will hear you above the sound bites for days. By the time you can get someone to listen, to go check, it'll all be over."

"So we have no choice. Someone has to go out there."

Craig shook his head. "Or someone could just hide in that little fishing village and wait for all this to blow over."

Matt considered the persistence of their pursuers, the explosion of Prudhoe Bay. "Do you really think they'd leave us alone out there? If they're buying time to clean up their mess, that might include getting rid of us. They know our plane."

Craig's determined expression sickened.

"And we'd be sitting ducks in Kaktovik."

Craig closed his eyes. "I hate Alaska . . . I really do."

Matt sank back into his own seat. He looked at Jenny. She had heard it all. "Well?" he asked.

Jenny glanced over her gauges. "I'll still need to refuel if we're going to travel so far."

"Bennie's place at Kaktovik."

"We can be there in an hour. And away in another."

He nodded and stared north. Craig's words echoed in his head: *Something's going to happen out there. Something no one wants the world to know about.*

But what the hell could it be?

11:02 P.M.
USS *POLAR SENTINEL*

"We've been ordered to readiness, but not to deploy." Perry stood atop the periscope stand. His officers had gathered in the control room. Groans met his words. They were Navy men, career submariners. They had all heard of the attack on Prudhoe Bay four hundred miles away. They were anxious to act.

Word had reached them half an hour ago through the snail-paced ELF transmission, sound waves passing with mile-long amplitudes through the ocean waters, emitting one slow letter at a time. The real-time communication net of NAVSAT's satellites or UHF were currently under electrical bombardment by a solar storm.

His men had hoped to deploy to the Alaskan coast, to join in the investigation and help in the cleanup. Baby-sitting a bunch of scientists at such a time was intolerable. With a crisis on hand, practically in their own backyard, all had hoped for a call to action.

The latest orders from COMSUBPAC had arrived five minutes ago. Perry shared his officers' disappointment.

"Any word on the cause of the explosions?" Commander Bratt asked. His words were clipped with frustration.

Perry shook his head. "Too early. Right now they're still trying to put out the fires."

But among his own crew, varying theories were already being debated: ecoterrorists bent on saving the Alaskan wilderness from further exploration and drilling, Arabs with an interest in cutting off Alaska's oil production, Texans for the same reason. And the Chinese and Russians got their fair share of the blame, too. More sober minds considered the possibility of a simple industrial accident—but that was not as entertaining.

"So we simply sit on our frozen asses out here," Bratt said gruffly.

Perry stood straighter. He would not let morale sour any further. "Commander, until we hear otherwise, we'll perform our duties as ordered." He hardened his voice. "We'll keep this boat at full readiness. But we won't neglect our current assignments. The Russian delegation is due to arrive in three days to retrieve the bodies of their countrymen. Would you rather we leave the scientists here alone to deal with the Russian admiral and his men?"

"No, sir." Bratt stared down at his shoes. He was one of the few men aboard the *Polar Sentinel* who knew what lay hidden on Level Four of Ice Station Grendel.

Their conversation was interrupted as the radioman of the watch pushed into the conn. He held a clipboard in his hand. "Captain Perry, I have an urgent message from COMSUB-PAC. Flash traffic. Marked for your eyes only."

He waved the lieutenant forward and retrieved the clipboard and top-secret log. "Flash traffic? Are we hooked back into NAVSAT?"

The lieutenant nodded. "We were lucky to retrieve the broadcast intact. They must have been continuously broadcasting to slip through one of the breaks in the solar storm. The message is being repeated more slowly over VLF."

Broadcasting on all channels. What could be so important?

The radioman stepped back. "I was able to send out confirmation that the message was received."

"Very good, Lieutenant." Perry turned his back on the curious faces of his officers and opened the clipboard. It was from Admiral Reynolds. As Perry read the message, an icy finger of dread traced his spine.

FLASH***FLASH***FLASH***FLASH***FLASH***FLASH
384749ZAPR

FM   COMSUBPAC PEARL HARBOR HI//N475//
TO   *POLAR SENTINEL* SSN-777
//BT//
REF   COMSUBPAC OPORD 37-6722A DATED 08 APR
SUBJ   GUESTS ARRIVING EARLY

SCI/TOP SECRET—OMEGA
PERSONAL FOR C.O.
RMKS/
(1) POLAR SATELLITE CONFIRMS RUSSIAN AKULA II CLASS SUBMARINE SURFACED WITH ANTENNA UP AT 14:25 AT COORDINATES ALPHA FIVE TWO DECIMAL EIGHT TACK THREE SEVEN DECIMAL ONE.
(2) UNIT DESIGNATED AS *DRAKON*, RUSSIAN FLAG SUBMARINE. ADMIRAL VICTOR PETKOV ABOARD.
(3) RUSSIAN GUESTS MAY BE ARRIVING EARLY. INTELLIGENCE REMAINS SCANT ON REASON FOR THE ACCELERATED TIMETABLE. WITH RECENT EVENTS AT PRUDHOE, SUSPICIONS REMAIN HIGH ACROSS ALL BOARDS. SABOTAGE CONFIRMED. SUSPECTS STILL UNKNOWN.
(4) *POLAR SENTINEL* TO REMAIN AT ALERT STATUS AND TO PATROL WITH MAXIMUM EARS UP.
(5) GUESTS TO BE TREATED AS FRIENDLY UNTIL OTHERWISE DISCERNED.
(6) PROTECTION OF UNITED STATES INTERESTS BOTH AT OMEGA DRIFT STATION AND ICE STATION GRENDEL REMAINS PRIORITY MISSION FOR *POLAR SENTINEL.*
(7) TO SUPPORT SUCH INTERESTS, DELTA FORCE TEAMS HAVE BEEN ORGANIZED AND ROUTED TO THE ARCTIC. OPERATIONAL CONTROLLER, SENT BY LR, HAS BEEN SPEARHEADED IN ADVANCE TO AREA. INFORMATION TO FOLLOW.

(8) GOOD LUCK AND KEEP YOUR TAP SHOES POLISHED, GREG.

(9) ADM K. REYNOLDS SENDS.

   BT

   NNNN

Perry shut the clipboard, closed his eyes, and ran the notes through his head.

The admiral had coded his own message into the encryption. *LR* was short for "Langley Reconnaissance," which meant the Central Intelligence Agency was involved. So the Delta Teams were being deployed under CIA leadership? Not a good thing. Such an organizational platform led to one hand being unaware of what the other was doing. It also stank of black ops maneuvering. *Information to follow* meant that even Pacific Submarine Command was cut out of the loop. A bad sign.

And at the end: *Keep your tap shoes polished, Greg.* Again the informality in the use of his first name was as good as a long line of exclamation marks. During one of the Navy's formal dinner parties, Admiral Reynolds had used that same phrase when the faction representing COMSUB-LANT, the Atlantic Submarine Command staff, had arrived at the hall. The Pacific and Atlantic submarine teams were fiercely competitive with each other, leading to challenges, war games, and rivalries that stretched across careers. *Keep your tap shoes polished* was shorthand for "get ready because the shit's about to hit the fan."

Perry turned to his XO. "Commander, clear the boat of civilians. Get them back to Omega and rally the men still on shore leave."

"Yes, sir."

"Once the *Sentinel* is secured, ready her to dive on my command."

The chief of the watch spoke up from his station. "So we're heading to Prudhoe Bay?"

Perry searched the hopeful faces of his bridge crew. He

knew there was no need to head to Prudhoe Bay to get into the action; his men would realize soon enough.

He rapped the metal clipboard on his thigh. "Just keep your tap shoes polished, men. We've got some fancy footwork ahead of us."

11:32 P.M.
KAKTOVIK, ALASKA

Jenny stalked around the parked Twin Otter, inspecting it with a flashlight. A scatter of bullet holes peppered one wing, but there was no structural damage. Nothing else needed immediate attention, and she could patch the holes with duct tape. She sipped from a coffee cup as she completed her circuit of the aircraft.

They had landed at the darkened snow strip of the tiny Kaktovik airport half an hour ago. Matt and the others had gone inside the nearby hangar, where a makeshift diner had been built in one corner. She could see them through a grease-rimmed window, bent over mugs of coffee and talking to the young Inuit waitress.

Only Bane remained at her side as she tended the refueling and checked her plane. The large wolf had made his own circuit of their parking space, lifting a leg here and there to yellow the snow. He now followed at her heels, tongue lolling, tail wagging.

Ducking around the rear of the plane, she returned to Bennie Haydon's side. The squat fellow leaned against the fuselage, a cigar clamped between his teeth, one hand resting on the fuel hose. Huskily built, he wore a Purolator cap tucked low over his sleepy eyes.

"Should you be smoking out here?" Jenny asked.

He shrugged and spoke around his stogie. "My wife won't let me smoke inside." Wearing half a grin, he nodded to the waitress.

Bennie had been with the sheriff's department, servicing the patrol fleet, until he saved enough to move out here with his wife and start his own repair shop. He also ran a sight-seeing company out of the same hangar and flew folks in ultralights over the nearby Alaskan National Wildlife Reserve. The small nimble aircraft—really no more than a hang glider with lawn-mower engine and propeller—were perfect for traversing the raw country by air, buzzing the caribou herds or flying low over the tundra. At first it had been only the occasional tourist, but after the growing interest in ANWR for oil exploration, he now transported geologists, reporters, government officials, even senators. His single ultralight had quickly grown into a fleet of a dozen.

Bennie glanced to a gauge on the fuel hose. "Topped off," he said, and began to crank the hose and detach it. "Both tanks."

"Thanks, Bennie."

"No problems, Jen." He tugged the hose free and began to drag it away. "So you going to tell me about them bullet holes."

Jenny followed the mechanic back toward the hangar. "It's a long story without any real answers yet."

Bennie made a thoughtful noise at the back of this throat. "Sort of like you and Matt." He nodded toward the window. In the midnight gloom, the bright interior shone like a beacon.

Jenny sighed and patted Bane as the wolf followed beside her.

Bennie glanced over to her, spooling the hose line. "You know he quit drinking."

"Bennie, I don't want to talk about it."

He shrugged again and puffed out a large cloud of cigar smoke. "I'm just saying."

"I know."

The small door to the hangar banged open. Belinda, Bennie's wife, stood in the doorway. "You two coming in out of the cold? I have eggs and caribou strip steaks frying."

"In a second, hon."

Bane didn't have such patience. With his nose in the air at the scent of frying meat, the dog sauntered toward the door, tail wagging furiously.

Belinda let him pass with a pat on the head, then pointed at the glowing tip of Bennie's cigar. "The dog's welcome, that isn't."

"Yes, dear." He gave Jenny a look that said, *See what I have to put up with*. But Jenny also saw the love shining between both of them.

Belinda closed the door with a sorry shake of her head. She was a decade younger than her husband, but her sharp intelligence and world-weary maturity spanned the gap. She was native to Kaktovik, her family going back generations, but she and her parents had moved to Fairbanks when she was a teenager. It had been at the beginning of the black gold rush—a flood of oil, money, jobs, and corruption. Indians and native Inuit, all anxious for their share of the wealth, flocked to the cities, abandoning their homelands and customs. But what they found in Fairbanks was a polluted, blue-collar town of construction workers, dog mushers, Teamsters, and pimps. Unskilled natives were ground under the heels of progress. To support her family, Belinda became a prostitute at the age of sixteen. It was after her arrest that she and Bennie had met. He took her under his wing—literally. He showed her the skies above Fairbanks and another life. They eventually married and moved here with her parents.

Bennie straightened, drew one last drag on his cigar, then dropped and stubbed it into the snow. "Jen, I know what you think of Matt."

"Bennie . . ." Warning entered her tone.

"Hear me out. I know how much you lost . . . both of you." He took off his oil-stained cap and swiped his thinning hair. "But you gotta remember. You're both young. Another child could—"

"Don't." The single word was a bark, a knee-jerk reaction. As soon as she said it, she remembered Matt cutting her off just as abruptly. But she could not hold back her anger. How dare Bennie presume to know how it felt to lose a child? To think another child could replace a lost one!

Bennie stared at her, one eye squinted, judging her. When he spoke next, it was in a calm, measured voice. "Jen, we lost a child, too . . . a baby girl."

The simple statement stunned her. Her anger blew out like a snuffed candle. "My God, Bennie, when?"

"A year ago . . . miscarriage." He stared out into the dark snowy plains. In the distance the few lights of the seaside village flickered. A heavy sigh escaped him. "It nearly crushed Belinda."

Jenny saw it had done the same to the man in front of her.

He cleared his throat. "Afterward we found out she would never be able to bear a child. Something to do with scarring. Docs said it was secondary to—" His voice cracked. He shook his head. "Let's just say, it was secondary to complications from her old job."

"Bennie, I'm so sorry."

He waved away her sympathy. "We move on. That's life."

Through the window, Jenny watched Belinda laughing as she refilled Matt's coffee. Not a sound was heard but the whistle of wind across the tundra.

"But you and Matt," Bennie resumed, "you're both young."

She heard his unspoken words: *You two could still have another child.*

"You were good together," he continued, kicking snow off his boots. "It's high time one of you remembered that."

She stared through the window. Her words were a whisper, more to her own heart than to her companion. "I do remember."

She had met Matt during an investigation of poaching in the Brooks Range. A conflict had arisen between native rights and the federal government over hunting for food in parklands. He had been there representing the state, but after learning of the subsistence level of existence of the local tribes, he became one of their most vocal advocates. Jenny had been impressed by his ability to look beyond the law and see the people involved, a rarity among government types.

While working together to settle the matter and make new law, the two had grown closer. At first, they simply sought work-related reasons to get together. Then, after running out of fabricated excuses, they simply started dating. And within a year, they were married. It took a while for her family to accept a white man into their fold, but Matt's charm, easygoing nature, and dogged patience won them over. Even her father.

Benny cleared his throat. "Then it's not too late, Jen."

She watched a moment longer, then turned from the window. "Sometimes it is. Some things can't be forgiven."

Bennie met her gaze, standing in front of her. "It was an accident, Jen. Somewhere in there you know that."

Her anger, never far from the surface, flared again. She clenched her fingers. "He was drinking."

"But he wasn't drunk, was he?"

"What the hell does that matter! Even a single drop of alcohol . . ." She began to shake. "He was supposed to be watching Tyler. Not drinking! If he hadn't been—"

Bennie cut her off. "Jen, I know what you think of alcohol. Hell, I worked with you long enough in Fairbanks. I know what it's done to your people . . . *to your father*."

His words were like a punch to the belly. "You're crossing the line, Bennie."

"Someone has to. I was there when your father was hauled in, goddamn it! I know! Your mother died in a car accident because your father was drunk."

She turned away, but she couldn't escape his words. She had been only sixteen at the time. *Epidemic alcoholism* was the coined term. It was devastating the Inuit, a curse winding its way down the generations, killing and maiming along the way—through violence, suicides, drownings, spousal abuse, birth defects, and fetal alcohol syndrome. As a native sheriff, she had seen entire villages emptied from no other cause than alcohol. And her own family had not escaped.

First her mother, then her son.

"Your father spent a year in jail," Bennie continued. "He went to AA. He's been on the wagon and found peace by returning to the old ways."

"It doesn't matter. I . . . I can't forgive him."

"Who?" His voice sharpened. "Matt or your father?"

Jenny swung around, fists clenched, ready to swing at him.

Bennie kept his position before the door. "Whether Matt had been stone-cold sober or not, Tyler would still be dead."

The bluntness of his words tore at the thick scarring that had formed in her own body. It wasn't just around her heart, but strung in tight cords through her belly, in her neck, down her legs. The scarring was all that allowed her to survive. It was what the body did when it couldn't heal completely. It scarred. Tears arose from the pain.

Bennie stepped forward and pulled her into his arms. She sagged in his grip. She wanted to dismiss Bennie's words, to lash out, but in her heart, she knew better. Had she ever forgiven her father? How much of that anger had become a part of who she was? She had entered law enforcement in an attempt to find some order in the tragedies and vagaries of life, finding solace in rules, regulations, and procedures, where punishment was meted out in blocks of time—one, five, or ten years—where time could be served and sins forgiven. But matters of the heart were not so easily quantified.

"It's not too late," Bennie repeated in her ear.

She mumbled her answer to his chest, repeating her earlier words. "Sometimes it is." And in her heart, she knew this to be true. Whatever she and Matt had once shared was shattered beyond repair.

The door swung open again, bringing with it the warmth of the diner, the smells of frying oil, and a bit of bright laughter. Matt stood at the threshold. "You two really should get a room."

Jenny pulled out of the embrace and ran a hand through her hair. She hoped the tears were gone from her cheeks. "The plane's all refueled. We can head out as soon as we're done eating."

"And *where* again were you all going?" Bennie asked, clearing his throat.

Matt scowled at him. For everyone's sake, they had decided it best to keep their destination a secret. "Good try, Bennie."

The man shrugged. "Okay, can't blame a guy for trying."

"Actually I can," Matt said, swinging around. "Hey, Belinda, did you know your husband was making out with my ex-wife on the porch?"

"Tell Jenny she can keep him!"

Matt turned back and gave them a thumbs-up. "You two kids are in the clear." He closed the door on them. "Have fun!"

Standing in the dark, Jenny shook her head. "And you want me to make up with him?"

Bennie shrugged again. "I'm just a mechanic. What the hell do I know?"

11:56 P.M.
ABOARD THE *DRAKON*

Admiral Viktor Petkov watched through the video monitors in the control station. The solid plane of ice spread in a black blanket overhead, lit from below by the *Drakon*'s exterior lights. The four thermal-suited divers had spent the last half hour securing a titanium sphere in place. The procedure involved screwing meter-long anchoring bolts into the underside of the ice cap, then positioning the device's clamps to the bolts so the titanium sphere hung below the ice.

It was the last of five identical devices. Each titanium sphere was positioned a hundred kilometers from the ice island, encircling the lost Russian ice station, marking the points of a star. The sites of insertion were pinpointed to exact coordinates. All that remained was to establish the master trigger. It had to be positioned in the exact center of the star.

Viktor gazed past the divers to the dark waters beyond. He pictured the huge ice island and the station inside it. He couldn't have asked for a better place to trigger the device.

Moscow had ordered him to retrieve his father's work and lay waste to all behind it. But Viktor had larger plans.

Out in the water, one of the divers thumbed the pressure button on the bottom of the device and a line of blue lights flared along the equator of the sphere, drawing Viktor's attention. The last of the five devices was now activated. In the soft blue glow, the Cyrillic lettering could be seen clearly across the sphere's surface, marking the initials for the Arctic and Antarctic Research Institute.

"And these are just scientific sensors?" Captain Mikovsky asked, standing at the admiral's side. The doubt was plain in his voice.

Viktor answered softly. "The latest in bathymetry technology, designed to measure sea-level changes, currents, salinity, and ice densities."

The *Drakon*'s captain shook his head. He was no naive recruit. Upon leaving the docks of the Severomorsk Naval Complex, Mikovsky had been given their mission parameters: to escort the admiral on a diplomatic mission out to the site of a lost Russian ice station. But the captain had to know that more was planned. He had seen the equipment and weapons brought aboard back at Severomorsk. And he surely knew of the coded message from FSB, if not the content.

"These underwater devices have no military application?" Mikovsky pressed. "Like listening in on the Americans?"

Viktor simply glanced over and shrugged. He allowed the captain to misread his silence. It was sometimes best to allow someone's suspicions to run to the most obvious conclusion.

"Ah . . ." Mikovsky nodded, eyeing the sphere with more respect, believing he understood the intrigues here.

Viktor turned his own attention back to the monitors. Over the years, the young captain might learn that there were deeper levels to the games played by those in power.

A decade ago, Viktor had employed a handpicked team of scientists from AARI and began a covert project out of Severomorsk Naval Complex. Such a venture was not unique. Many polar research projects were run out of Severomorsk. But what was unusual about this particular project, titled Shockwave, was that it was under the direct supervision of then-captain Viktor Petkov. The researchers answered directly to him. And in the hinterlands of the northern coastlands, far from prying eyes, it was easy to bury one project among the many others. No one questioned this work, not even when the six researchers on the project had all died in an airplane crash. With their deaths two years ago, so had died Project Shockwave.

Or so it appeared.

No one but Viktor knew the research had already been completed. He stared out as the divers retreated from the sphere of titanium.

It had all started with a simple research paper published in 1979, tying carbon dioxide to the gradual warming of the globe. Fears of melting polar ice caps created horrible scenarios of rising ocean levels and devastating worldwide flooding. Of course, the Arctic and Antarctic Research Institute in St. Petersburg was the central agency in Russia as-

signed to investigate such threats. It accumulated one of the
world's largest databases on global ice. It was eventually
discerned that while the melting of the ice found atop
Greenland and the continent of Antarctica could potentially
raise the world's oceans by a dramatic two hundred feet, the
northern polar ice cap did not pose such a risk. Since its ice
was already *floating* atop an ocean, it displaced as much
water as it would produce if it melted. Like cubes of ice in a
full glass of water, the melt of the polar cap would not lead
to a rise in ocean levels. It was simply no threat.

But in 1989, one of the AARI researchers realized a
greater danger posed if the polar ice cap should suddenly
vanish from the top of the world. The ice cap, if gone, would
no longer act as an insulator for the Arctic Ocean. Without
its ability to reflect the sun's energy, the ocean would evap-
orate more rapidly, pouring vast amounts of new water into
the atmosphere, which would lead in turn to massive
amounts of precipitation in the form of rain, snow, and sleet.
The AARI report concluded that such a change in world cli-
mate would wreak havoc on weather systems and ocean currents, resulting in flooding, agricultural destruction,
ecosystem disintegration, and worldwide environmental col-
lapse. It would devastate countries and world economies.

The hard truth of this prediction was seen in 1997 when a
simple shift in currents in the Pacific Ocean, known as El
Niño, occurred. According to UN agencies, the cost to the
world was over $90 billion and led to the death of over fifty
thousand people—and this was a single shift in currents over
the course of one year. The loss of the northern polar ice cap
would stretch over decades and reverberate over all oceans,
not just the Pacific. It would be a disaster unlike any seen
during mankind's history.

So, of course, such a report led to the investigation of any
possible military applications. Could one destroy the polar
ice cap? Studies quickly showed that the power needed to
melt the vast ice sheet was beyond the grasp of even current

nuclear technology. It seemed such a possibility would remain theoretical.

But one of the scientists at AARI had come up with an intriguing theory. One didn't need to melt the cap—only to
destabilize it. If the cap were partially melted and the rest of
the solid ice sheet shattered, a single Arctic summer could
do the rest. With the cap turned into an Arctic slush pile, the
sun's energy would have greater access to a larger surface
area of the Arctic Ocean, warming the waters around the
fragmented ice, thus leading to the meltdown of the remaining ice pack. One didn't need man-made nuclear energy to
destroy the cap—not when the sun itself was available. If the
polar ice cap could be shattered in the late spring, by the end
of summer it would be gone.

But how did one destabilize the ice cap? That answer
came in 1998 when another scientist from AARI, studying
the crystallization of ice in the Arctic ice pack and the relation of ocean currents to pressure ridge formation, came up
with his theory of harmonics. That ice was like any other
crystalline structure, especially under extreme pressure, and
at the right pitch in vibration, its structure could be shattered
like a crystal goblet.

It was this study that became the basis for Project Shockwave: to artificially create the right set of harmonic waves
and heat signatures to blast apart the polar ice cap.

On the monitor, the titanium sphere glowed out in the
dark waters as the sub's exterior lights dimmed. Viktor
checked his thick wrist monitor. The plasma screen depicted
a five-pointed star. Each point glowed. In the center, the
master trigger awaited deployment.

It wouldn't be long.

Victor stared at the glowing points on the wrist monitor.

The dead scientists had named this configuration the Polaris Array, after the Polyarnaya Zvezda, the North Star. But
the nuclear-powered master trigger went by a more technical designation: *a subsonic disrupter engine.* When it was

activated, its effect was twofold. First, it would act as a conventional weapon, blasting a crater a mile wide. But next, rather than sending out an EM pulse like a regular nuclear weapon, this engine would transmit a harmonic wave through the ice. The wave front would strike the five spheres simultaneously and trigger them to explode, propagating and amplifying the harmonics in all directions with enough energy and force to shatter the entire polar ice cap.

Viktor cleaned a smudge off the screen of the monitor. Tucked away in the corner of the screen was a small red heart that flashed in sync with his pulse.

Soon . . .

For now, he would spend the rest of the night running diagnostics on the project, making sure all was in order.

He had waited sixty years . . . he could wait another day.

In fact, after the completion of Project Shockwave, he had held off implementing his plan for two years. He had found a certain peace of mind in simply having Polaris at his command. Now he believed it had been fate that held his hand. Ice Station Grendel had been rediscovered, the very tomb of his father. Surely this was a sign. He would retrieve his father's body, collect the prize buried within the heart of the station, and then detonate Polaris, changing the world forever.

Viktor stared as the exterior lights of the *Drakon* were extinguished. The titanium sphere of Polaris glowed in the dark, becoming a true North Star in the Arctic night.

There was a reason he had started Project Shockwave a decade ago, picked this particular project to exact his retribution. It was in the final words of the 1989 report, a cautionary warning. The scientist had predicted another danger posed by the destruction of the polar ice cap, more than just the short-term effect of flooding and climatic upheaval.

There was a more ominous long-term threat.

As the Arctic Ocean evaporated, its waters would pour over landmasses in the form of precipitation—in the northern lands, as snow and sleet. As the years marched on, this snow and sleet would turn into ice, building into huge glaciers, expanding those already present and forming new ones. Over the succeeding years, glaciers would spread and pile in vast sheets, driving south across all the northern lands.

After fifty thousand years, a new ice age would begin!

Viktor appreciated the symmetry as he stared at the glow of Polaris in the midnight waters of the Arctic.

His father had died, frozen in ice—now so would the world.

6

Icebound

ᓯᑯᒥ ᐊᔪᖅᓯᑦᑐᖅ

APRIL 9, 5:43 A.M.
AIRBORNE OVER THE POLAR ICE CAP

From the Twin Otter's copilot seat, Matt watched the sun climb over the top of the world. Light glanced achingly over the curve of ice, searing the back of his eyeballs. Jenny wore aviator sunglasses, but Matt simply stared at the beauty of dawn in the polar region. At this latitude, there were only another ten or so sunrises, then the cold orb would stay in the sky for four solid months. So, up here, one learned to appreciate each sunrise and sunset.

This particular morning was spectacular. A steady southeasterly headwind had managed to sheer away the ubiquitous fogs and mists that usually clung to the cap. Below, and in all directions, lay a pristine world of crenellated white ice, jagged crystalline peaks, and sky-blue melt ponds.

From the horizon, sunlight streamed in a rosy tide, stretching toward their flight path. Hues of orange and crimson rippled across the blue skies.

"A storm's coming," a gruff voice said behind him. Jenny's father had awakened with a yawn.

Matt turned. "Why do you say that, John?"

Before he could answer, Craig made a small sound of complaint from where he lolled sleepily in his seat. Clearly the reporter had no interest in the meteorological assessment of the elder Inuit. From behind Craig, Bane lifted his muzzled face and stretched with a jaw-breaking yawn. The wolf seemed as bothered as the reporter at being awakened.

Ignoring them both, John leaned forward and pointed toward the northern skies. Twilight still clung to that section of the world. Near the horizon, it looked like smoke was billowing up. It swirled and churned.

"Ice fog," the Inuit said. "Temperature's dropping even though the sun is rising."

Matt agreed. "Weather pattern's shifting."

Storms up here were seldom mild. It was either clear and calm, like now, or a damnable blizzard. And while snowfall was seldom significant at these latitudes, the winds were dangerous, stirring up squalls of ice and surface snow that achieved blinding whiteout conditions.

He swung to Jenny. "Can we make the drift station before it hits?"

"Should."

It was the first word she had spoken since leaving Kaktovik. Something had upset her over at Bennie's place, but she had refused to talk about it. She had eaten her meal as methodically as a backhoe chewing through a stubborn hillside. Afterward, she had disappeared into the hangar's office for a short catnap. No more than half an hour. But when she returned from the back room, her eyes were red. It didn't look like she had slept at all.

Her father glanced to Matt, catching his eyes for a moment, almost studying him. When Jenny and Matt had been married, he and his father-in-law had grown as close as brothers. They had camped, hunted, and fished regularly. But like Jenny, after the loss of his only grandson, the man had hardened toward him.

Yet, at the time of Tyler's death, Matt had sensed no blame from the elderly Inuit. John, more than anyone, knew the severity of life in the Alaskan backcountry, the risk of sudden death. While growing up, he had been raised in a small seaside village along Kotzebue Sound near the Bering Strait. His full Inuit name was Junaquaat, shortened to John after he moved inland. His own seaside village had succumbed to starvation during the freeze of '75, vanishing in a single winter. He had lost all his relatives—and such a fate was not uncommon. Resources in the frozen north were always scarce. Survival balanced on a razor's edge.

Though John did not blame Matt for Tyler's drowning, he did harbor resentment for the ugly period that followed. Matt had not been kind to his daughter. He had been hollowed out by guilt and grief. To survive, he had gone deeper into the bottle, shutting her out, unable to face the blame in her eyes, the accusations. They had said things during that time that could never be unspoken. Finally, it had grown to be too much. Broken, beaten, unhealed, they had splintered—falling apart.

John placed a hand on Matt's shoulder now. His fingers squeezed ever so softly. In that gesture, Matt found a level of peace and acceptance. It was not only death that the Inuit people learned to survive, but grief also. John patted his shoulder and sat back.

Matt stared, unblinking, at the icy glare of morning, more unsure of his heart than he had been in years. It was an uncomfortable feeling, as if something heavy had shifted loose inside him, disturbing his center of balance.

Jenny spoke, checking her heading and speed with a finger. "We should be at the coordinates Craig gave in another half hour."

Matt kept his gaze fixed forward. "Should we radio the base in advance? Let them know we're coming?"

She shook her head. "Until we know what's going on over

there, the less forewarning the better. Besides, radio communication is still shoddy."

En route, they had been receiving bursts of communication across open channels. Word of the explosions at Prudhoe Bay had spread immediately. As Craig had predicted, news agencies were scurrying, and speculation was rampant.

Craig grumpily sat straighter. "If we just drop in, how are we going to explain our sudden appearance at the base? Are we going to storm in as officers of the law? Investigative journalists? Fleeing refugees seeking asylum?"

"Forget about storming in with any authority," Jenny answered. "I have no jurisdiction up there. I say we explain all we know and warn those in charge. Whoever attacked us might not be far behind."

Craig studied the empty skies, clearly searching for any signs of pursuers. "Will the base be able to protect us?"

Matt turned to Craig. "You know more about this Omega base than any of us, Mr. Reporter. What sort of Navy contingent is stationed there?"

Craig shook his head. "I wasn't given any specifics about my destination . . . just told to pack my bag, then shoved on the first Alaska Airlines flight leaving Seattle."

Matt frowned. There had to be at least a sub and a crew. Hopefully more personnel were stationed at the research base itself. "Well, whoever's there," he decided aloud, "with the storm coming, they'll have to take us in. After that, we'll make them listen to us. Whether they believe us or not, that's a whole other can of worms. After the explosions at Prudhoe, suspicions will be high."

Jenny nodded. "Okay, we'll play it that way. At least until we get a better handle on the situation."

John spoke up from where he was peering out the side window. "I see something off to the north a couple degrees. Red buildings."

Jenny adjusted course.

"Is it the drift station?" Craig asked.

"I'm not sure," Jenny said. "Those structures are about six miles from the coordinates you gave me."

"That's the data my editor gave me."

"It's the currents," Matt said. "They don't call it a *drift* station for nothing. I'm surprised the station is even *that* close to the coordinates. Craig's information has to be almost a week old by now."

Jenny buzzed toward the spread of red buildings.

As they approached, details emerged. There was a wide polynya lake a short distance from the base. Steel bollards had been drilled into the ice surrounding the open water. Submarine docking bollards, Matt realized. Though presently the lake was empty. Beyond the polynya, he counted fifteen red buildings. He recognized them as Jamesway huts from his military days, the cold-weather version of the old Quonset huts. In the middle of the small village, an American flag fluttered atop a tall pole.

"At least it's a U.S. base," Craig mumbled as Jenny banked over the site.

"This has to be the place," Matt muttered.

A few vehicles were lined up on one side. Clear tracks led from the polynya to the cluster of Jamesway huts. But another track led straight out from the base, well trundled and beaten. Where did it lead? Before he could get a good look, Jenny circled around and prepared to land.

Below, a few figures appeared from some of the buildings. All wore parkas and stared skyward. The plane's engine must have been heard. Visitors were surely rare out here in the remote ZCI zone of the polar ice cap. Matt was relieved to see that the gawkers wore parkas of vibrant colors: greens, blues, yellows, and reds. Such colors were meant to be seen, to help find a mate lost in a storm.

Thankfully there was not a single *white* parka among them.

Jenny set the plane's skis and dropped the flaps. She began a smooth descent to the tabletop ice field just north of the base. "Everyone buckle in," she warned.

The Twin Otter fell toward the ice. Matt gripped his seat arms. The plane swooped down, leveled off sharply, then skidded over the ice. The vibration of the skis over the slightly uneven surface rattled every bolt in the plane and the metal fillings in Matt's back molars.

But once she had touched down, Jenny quickly cut power and raised the flaps to brake. The plane slowed, and the vibration died down to a gentle bumping.

Craig let out a sigh of relief.

"Welcome to the middle of the Arctic Ocean," Jenny said, and angled the plane around. She taxied back toward the base, now a short distance away.

"The Arctic Ocean," Craig echoed, eyeing out the windows suspiciously.

Matt could relate to his misgivings. Since three years ago, he distrusted ice. Though the footing under you might look solid, it wasn't. It was never a constant. It was an illusion of solidness, a false sense of security that betrayed when one least expected. You just had to turn your back for a second . . . a moment's distraction . . .

Matt continued to grip his chair arms as if he were still falling from the skies. He stared out at the world of ice around him. Here was his personal hell—not fiery flames, but endless ice.

"It looks like we've stirred up a welcoming party," Jenny said as she cut her engines and the twin props slowly rotated down.

Matt swung his attention back to the base. A group of six snowmobiles rumbled out toward them. They were manned by men in matching blue parkas. He spotted the Navy insignia.

Base security.

One of the men stood up in his snowmobile and lifted a bullhorn in his hand. "Vacate the aircraft now! Keep your hands empty and in plain sight! Any attempt to leave or any hostile action will be met with deadly force!"

Matt sighed. "The Welcome Wagon sure has gone to hell these days."

6:34 A.M.
ICE STATION GRENDEL

Amanda stared at the chaos, amazed at the amount of work that had been done in a single night. Not that day or night really had much meaning in the station, especially in the dark ice tunnels of the Crawl Space. In the detached isolation of her silent world, she watched the drama play out.

"Careful with that!" Dr. Henry Ogden barked across the frozen lake. Even from here, Amanda could read his lips and exaggerated expression.

Under his supervision, a pair of graduate students struggled to raise a light pole. It was the fourth to illuminate the cliff face. Nearby, the generator, which was running the lights and other assorted equipment, trembled in bad humor atop its rubber footpads. Power cords and conduits snaked across the ice lake's surface.

Small red flags marked off sites on the lake. The rocky cliff face itself was no less assaulted. Steel ladders leaned against it. More flags checkered its surface.

Sites of specimens, Amanda imagined. She stared at the sections of the lake cordoned off with string and flags. She knew what *specimens* lay frozen under those spots. The *grendels* . . . as they had come to be called.

News of the discovery had spread quickly. While Amanda was sure Dr. Ogden had not divulged the information himself, such a secret could not be kept long among a group of isolated scientists. Someone had clearly talked.

All around the huge cavern, research students and senior members of the biology staff labored together. But Amanda also spotted several scientists from other disciplines, including her dear friend Dr. Oskar Willig. The Swedish oceanographer was the elder statesman of the entire Omega group. His accomplishments and credentials were numerous and well-known, including the Nobel Prize in 1972. His unruly gray hair was equally as distinguishable, making him easy to spot.

She crossed toward him, stepping around the piles of sample bottles and boxes. At least someone had sanded the floor and strewn a few rubber mats over some of the busier work areas. Dr. Willig knelt on one of these mats, staring down into the ice.

He glanced to her as she walked up. "Amanda." He grinned and sat back on his heels. "Come to see the mascot of the station, have you?"

She returned his smile. "I caught the creature feature last night."

He climbed to his feet with an ease that belied his age. He was a wiry, fit seventy-year-old. "It's a tremendous discovery."

"The legendary Grendel itself."

"*Ambulocetus natans*," Dr. Willig corrected. "Or if you are to believe our notable colleague from Harvard, *Ambulocetus natans arctos*."

She shook her head. Arctic subspecies . . . it seemed Dr. Ogden was not wasting time staking his claim. "So what do you think about his assertions?"

"Intriguing theory. Polar adaptation of the prehistoric species. But Henry has a long way to go between theory and proof."

She nodded. "Well, he has enough specimens to work with."

"Yes, indeed. He should be able to thaw—" Dr. Willig started and peered over a shoulder.

Amanda followed his gaze. He had heard something. It didn't take long to spot the commotion that drew his attention and interrupted their conversation.

Henry Ogden and Connor MacFerran were nose to nose.

The brawny Scottish geologist loomed over the shorter biologist. But Henry was not about to give ground. He stood with his hands on his hips, leaning forward, an angry Chihuahua before a pitbull.

Dr. Willig turned back to her so she could read his lips. "Here we go again. This is the third head butting since I came down here an hour ago."

"I'd better see what's going on," Amanda decided reluctantly.

"Always the diplomat."

"No, always the *baby-sitter*." She left Dr. Willig and crossed to the warring researchers. They barely noted her arrival, continuing their argument.

". . . not until all the specimens are collected. We've not even begun the photographs." Henry had his face almost pressed against the geologist's.

"You can't hog all the friggin' research time down here. That cliff is volcanic basalt with pure carboniferous intrusions. All I need to do is core a few samples."

"How few?"

"No more than twenty."

The biologist's face darkened. "Are you mad? You'll tear the whole thing down. Ruin who knows how much sensitive data."

Amanda barely followed their discourse, missing much as she read their lips, but she gained as much information from the gestures and body postures. A fistfight was about to break out. She could smell the territorial bloom of testosterone.

"Boys," she said calmly.

They glanced to her, to her crossed arms, to her stern expression. Each took a step back.

"What's this all about?" she asked slowly.

Connor MacFerran answered first. His lips were harder to read because of his thick black beard. "We've been patient with the biology team. But we have just as much right to sample this discovery. An inclusion of this magnitude"—he waved to the cliff face—"is not the sole ownership of Dr. Ogden."

Henry stated his case. "We've only had the one night to prep the site. Our collection is more delicate than the bulldozing techniques of the geologists. It's a simple case of priority. My sampling won't harm his specimens, but his sampling could irreparably damage mine."

"That's not true!" Though Amanda could not hear Connor's voice rise, she caught it from the color of his cheeks and the way his chest puffed. "A couple cores in areas free of your damn molds and lichens won't harm anything."

"The dust . . . the noise . . . it could ruin everything." Henry turned his full attention to Amanda. "I thought we had decided all this last night."

She finally nodded. "Connor, Henry's right. This cliff face has been here for fifty thousand years. I think it could last another couple of days for the biology team to collect their samples."

"I need at least ten days," Henry cut in.

"You have three." She faced the broad-shouldered Scotsman, who wore a sloppy grin of satisfaction. "Then you can start collecting cores—but only where Henry says you can."

The large man's grin faded. "But—"

She turned away. It was the easiest way to cut someone off when you were deaf. You simply stopped looking at them. She faced Henry now. "And you, Henry . . . I suggest you concentrate on clearing out a section of cliff face within three days. Because I will authorize drilling in here by that time."

"But—"

She turned her back on both of them and saw Dr. Willig grinning broadly at her. MacFerran stalked off in one direction, heading toward the tunnel exit. Henry marched off in the other, ready to harangue his underlings. That bit of détente should buy her at least twenty-four hours of strained peace between the biologists and geologists.

Dr. Willig crossed to her. "For a moment, I thought you were going to spank them."

"They'd have enjoyed it too much."

"Come." The elderly Swede motioned. "You should see what Dr. Ogden is really protecting."

He took her hand, like a father might a daughter. He led her toward a familiar cleft in the volcanic rock face. Her feet began to drag. "I've been in there already."

"Yes, but have you seen what our argumentative scientist is doing?"

Curiosity kept her feet moving. The pair reached the opening in the cliff. This morning, Amanda had changed out of her thermal sailing suit and simply wore jeans, boots, wool sweater, and a borrowed Gore-Tex parka for her journey into the icy Crawl Space. As they reached the tunnel entrance, she finally noted how warm it was. A steady flow of humid air rolled from the mouth of the cleft.

Dr. Willig led the way, still holding her hand. "It is really quite amazing."

"What is?" The warmth distracted her . . . as did the slightly rank odor carried on the damp flow of air. Water sluiced in small trickles over the rock under her boots. It dripped from the ceiling, too.

Within six steps, they reached the cave beyond the cleft. Like the greater cavern outside, this space had been invaded by modern technology. A second generator vibrated in a corner. Space heaters lined both walls, facing inward. Two light poles blazed in the center, illuminating the space in too great detail.

Yesterday evening, with only the single flashlight, the chamber had been spooky and lost in time. But now, under the glare of the halogen spots, the place had a clinical aspect.

As before, the dissected creature lay sprawled and staked across the room's center. But rather than being frosted in ice, appearing old, it now glistened and dripped. The exposed organs wept in trickles and shone like fresh meat on a butcher's block. It looked like the dissection had started only yesterday, rather than sixty years ago.

Beyond the carcass, through the sheen and flow of melt-water over their surfaces, the six large blocks of ice had become clear crystal. At the heart of each block lay a curled pale beast, nose tucked in the center, long, sinuous body wrapped around the head, then its thick tail around again.

"Does their sleeping shape remind you of anything?" Dr. Willig asked.

Amanda searched her nightmares and found no answers. She shook her head.

"Maybe it's because of my Nordic heritage. It reminds me of some of the old Norse carvings of dragons. The great wyrms curled in on themselves. Noses touching tails. A symbol of the eternal circle."

Amanda ran along the logic track of her friend. "You think some Vikings might have found these frozen beasts before. These . . . grendels?"

He shrugged. "They were the first polar explorers, crossing the North Atlantic to Iceland and glacier-shrouded Greenland. If there's a clutch of these creatures here, who's to say there are not others scattered throughout the frozen northlands."

"I suppose that's possible."

"Just an idle thought." He stared over at the melting blocks. "But it does raise some misgivings in my mind. Especially with all the death found here in the station."

She glanced at him. Dr. Willig knew nothing about Level Four.

He continued, clarifying his point: "All those Russian scientists and staff personnel. It's a tragedy. It makes you wonder what happened sixty years ago. Why the station was lost."

Amanda sighed. She remembered her first cold steps into the tomb. All the bodies—some skeletal, as if starved; some clear suicides; others had met more violent ends. She could only imagine the madness that must have set in here.

"Remember," she said, "the base was lost in the forties. Before the time of satellite communication. Before submarines had reached the North Pole, and before the tangle of Arctic currents was ever mapped. All it would've taken is a fierce summer storm, or a communication breakdown, or a mechanical failure in the base, or even a single, lost, resupply ship. Any of these mishaps could've resulted in the station's loss. Back in the 1930s, the Arctic reaches were as remote as Mars is today."

"It's a tragedy, nonetheless."

She nodded. "We may have more answers when the Russian delegation arrives in a few more days. If they're cooperative, we might have a more complete story." But Amanda knew of one detail the Russians would never be fully forthcoming about. How could they? There was no explanation to justify what had been found on Level Four.

She noted the oceanographer's eyes focused on the curled grendels and remembered he had never finished his last thought. "You mentioned some misgivings. Something about the old Norse symbol of the curled dragons."

"Yes." He rubbed his chin, making it slightly harder to read his lips. When he saw her squinting, he lowered his hand. "Like I was saying, the symbol signifies the circle of eternal life, but it also has a darker, more ominous significance. And with all the tragedy found here . . . the fate of the base . . ." He shook his head.

"What else does the symbol represent?"

He faced her fully so she could read his lips. "It means the end of the world."

7:05 A.M.

Lacy Devlin crouched elsewhere in the Crawl Space. As a junior research assistant with the geology department, her shift under Connor MacFerran did not begin for another two hours. Then again she had already spent most of last night *under* Connor in his makeshift room here at the base. He had a wife back in California, but that didn't mean the man didn't have needs.

She smiled at the memory as she laced her skates.

All set, she stood and stared down the long, slightly curved ice tunnel. She did a few stretches, working loose the knots in her thighs and calves. Her legs were her trademark. Long and smoothly muscular, swelling to powerful hips. She had been a speed skater with the U.S. Olympic team back in 2000, but a torn anterior cruciate ligament in her knee had benched her career. She had eventually finished her undergraduate work and moved to graduate school in Stanford. That was where she had met Connor MacFerran.

Lacy took a few steps in her short-track skates. They were ankle-high, composed of graphite and Kevlar molded to the shape of her feet. When worn, they were as much a part of her body as her own fingers and toes. She also wore an in-sulated skin suit—striped red, white, and blue—over thermal underwear. And of course a helmet. In this case, not her usual plastic racing headgear, but one of the geologists' mining helmets, equipped with a light on its brim.

She started down the tunnel. She had skated many times across the surface of the polar ice cap, but the tunnels were more challenging. The swooping water-melt channels were a delight to fly through.

She pushed with her legs, extending fully, still feeling a bit of that deep ache from last night with Connor. It added to her exhilaration and excitement. Last night, for the first time, he had said he loved her, whispering it urgently in her ear, panting each word as he thrust into her. The memory warming her now, she barely felt the cold.

As she began her run, the tunnel slanted in a short decline, increasing her speed. She had a set course that she ran each morning since the discovery of the Crawl Space. It was out of the geology team's way. There were no interesting inclusions to sample, so the passages in this section were not sanded. Two months ago, she had first walked the course to sight any obstacles and memorize which turns made a complete circuit, ending where she started.

Lacy sped around the first bend, sweeping up the curved ice wall. The wind of her speed whistled in her ears. She crouched as she came around the corner. Ahead lay a series of switchbacks, a crazy S-shaped twist of tunnel. It was her favorite part of the circuit.

Balancing herself, she kept her left arm tucked behind her back and swung her right arm in sync with her stride. Back and forth, she pushed with her legs, accelerating into the switchbacks. She hit the twisted section of tunnel with a shout of glee. With each cutback, she flew high up the walls, momentum keeping her riding in perfect balance.

Then she was out of the switchbacks and into a section that required more attention. Tunnels crisscrossed in a funhouse maze. She braked a bit, slowing to catch the spray-painted markers on the ice. She had memorized the turns, but she knew better than to make a mistake.

She swung her helmet lamp, which cast its single beam far down the dark tunnel, giving the ice a translucent glow. The markers—orange arrows—were easy to pick out. They seemed to shine with their own light.

She shot into the first of the arrow-painted passages, passing by dead ends and tunnels that led out to dangerous terrain. As she passed one of these unmarked tunnels, shadows shifted deep inside, but her speed was too fast to get a look. As she shot past, she risked a glance behind her. *No luck.* She was already too far down the tunnel. The angle was wrong for the beam of her helmet lamp to penetrate the rapidly retreating tunnel mouth.

She faced forward. At such speeds, her attention needed to stay focused ahead of her. Still, her nerves were now jangled, like someone had drenched her with ice water. She had gone from easy contentment and joy to a hard-edged anxiety.

She tried to dismiss it. "Just the shadows playing tricks," she said aloud, hoping her own voice would comfort her. But the echoes of her words spooked her. They sounded unnaturally loud.

She was now acutely aware of how alone she was down here.

A small noise caught up to her. Probably a bit of ice sliding and scraping down the tunnel. Still, the *scritch*ing tightened her jaw. Twisting her neck, she glanced behind her again. The beam of light revealed only empty passage, but the length of view was only twenty yards as the tunnel twisted away behind her.

She turned back around, almost missing one of the orange markers. She had to brake and kick out with her left leg to make the sharp turn into the correct passage.

As Lacy shot into the proper tunnel, her legs trembled under her. Fear fatigued her muscles. She realized she should have taken the tunnel just before this one. She had marked *this* passage because it led outward into a long half-mile single loop. The *other* was a shortcut, too short for her usual fourmile run. Now she just wanted to get the hell out of these passages and back to other people, back to Connor's arms.

As she raced down the loop, she increased her speed, seeking to put some distance between her and the shifting shadows. After a full minute with nothing but her own thoughts, she realized how foolish she was being. There were no more suspicious shadows or noises—just the clean hiss of her blades over the ice.

She began the climb out of the loop. The passage slanted up and required work to keep moving forward. But her momentum and the smooth ice helped. Shoving with her legs, falling into her familiar rhythm, she raced back out of the loop—heading toward home again.

A small laugh escaped her. What was she so afraid of? What could be down here? She studied her reaction. Maybe her night with Connor had awakened some deep misgiving in her after all. Maybe this was an echo of guilt. She had met Connor's wife many times at university functions. Linda was a sweet, gentle woman with an easy, welcoming manner. She didn't deserve to be so—

The noise returned. The slippery sound of ice on ice.

Now it came from *ahead* of her.

She braked. Far down the passage, near the end of the loop, shadows shifted. Her light could not reach that far. She slowed but didn't stop. She wasn't sure. She wanted to see if there was truly anything to fear. Her light bled ahead as she advanced.

"Hello!" Lacy called out. Maybe it was another of the researchers, off to explore on his own.

No answer. Whatever movement she had noted had now stopped. The shadows had settled to their usual stillness.

"Hello!" she repeated. "Is anyone there?"

She crept forward, gliding on her skate blades. She followed the glow of her light as it stretched down the passage.

Ahead, the loop came to an end, reentering the funhouse maze of passages again. Her throat had gone dry and tight from the cold, as if someone were choking her. *I only have to get through the maze . . . then it's a straight shot back to civilization.*

Despite her momentary flare of guilt, she wanted nothing at this moment but to see Connor. Just the thought of the towering man with his strong hands and broad shoulders quickened her legs. Once she was back in his embrace, she would be safe.

She climbed out of the loop and into the maze. Nothing was here. "Just tricks," she whispered to her own heart, "just ice, light, and shadow."

She followed the orange markers, like beacons in the night. Twisting one way, then another. Then, from far down in the dark well, her light reflected back at her. Two red spots glowed.

Lacy knew what she was seeing.

Eyes, unblinking, large—dead of emotion.

She braked to a stop, kicking up ice.

Fear shook through her. She felt her bladder give way a little, the trickle hot in her skin suit.

She backed a single step, then another. Legs trembled. She wanted to turn and run, but she feared turning her back on those eyes. She continued her halting retreat.

Then in a blink, the eyes vanished—whether because her light had pulled back or the presence was gone, she didn't know. Free from their paralyzing stare, she twisted around and fled on her blades.

She raced, fueled by terror. Her arms flailed, her legs kicked, digging out chunks of ice in her panic. She fled blindly into the maze of passages. Her markers were all designed for a counterclockwise circuit, orange arrows pointing the safe way. Now, as she ran backward through her course, the markers were meaningless. They all pointed back toward the creature behind her.

In a matter of moments, she was lost.

She raced down a narrow passage, one she had never been in before, more a crack in the ice than a true tunnel. Her breathing choked into ragged gasps. Blood pounded in her ears. But her own heartbeat was not loud enough to drown out the skitter on the ice.

Crying, tears flowing and freezing on her cheeks, she scrabbled with her blades. The tunnel widened a bit, allowing her more room to push and kick. She only had to get away . . . keep moving. A low moan flowed out from her. It didn't sound like her. But she couldn't stop it either.

She craned around, shining the light over her shoulder. Through the pinch in the tunnel behind her, something was shoving toward her. It was huge. Eyes glowed from its bulk, an albino whiteness, a rolling snowbank.

Polar bear, her mind screamed.

She remembered the whispers of something picked up on the DeepEye sonar. Movement on the scope.

She cried out and raced away.

As she fled around a sharp corner, the floor vanished a few yards in front of her. The bright ice ended at darkness. As a geology student, she knew the name for this: *ice shear*. Like any crystal, when ice was exposed to stress, it broke in clean planes. On glaciers, this led to ice-shear cliffs. But the same features could be found inside glaciers, too . . . or inside ice islands.

Lacy dug in her blades, but her momentum and the downward tilt of the tunnel betrayed her. She flew over the cliff edge and into empty space. A scream, sharp enough to shatter ice, burst from her. She tumbled into the chute, dropping away into darkness.

The shear pit was not a deep one, no more than fifteen feet, and she struck the ice floor with her blades. The impact was too much. Despite the Kevlar ankle guard, one ankle cracked. Her other knee struck so hard that she felt it in her shoulder. She crumpled to the floor in a heap.

Pain drove away her fear, traveling out to all her nerve endings.

She looked upward, to the cliff's edge.

Her light rose in a beacon.

At the precipice, the beast hesitated. It peered down at her with those dead eyes, glowing red in the reflection of her light. Claws dug into the ice. Shoulders bunched as it leaned over the edge. Rapid huffs of mist curled from each slitted nostril as a deep rumble flowed from it, seeming to vibrate the very air.

Staring up, Lacy knew she had been mistaken a moment ago. With this realization, terror drove sanity to the edges of her consciousness.

It was half a ton in mass, its skin smooth, shining oily, more like a dolphin's skin. Adding to this appearance, its head was sleek, earless, but domed high, sweeping down to an elongated muzzle, giving it a stretched appearance. The slitted nostrils rose too high on its face, almost above its wide-spaced eyes.

Lacy stared numbly. It was too large, too muscular, too primeval for the modern world. Even in her madness, she recognized what she was seeing: *something prehistoric, saurian . . . yet still mammalian.*

The beast studied her in turn, its lips rippling back from its long snout to reveal rows of jagged teeth as bright as broken bone against pink gums. Razored claws sank into the ice.

Some primitive part of her responded to the age-old instincts of predator and prey. A small mewling whimper escaped Lacy's throat.

The beast began its slow climb into the pit.

7:48 A.M.
OMEGA DRIFT STATION

Matt was tired of having guns pointed at him. An hour ago, he and the others had been corralled into a mess hall and were now seated at one of the four tables in the room. A small kitchenette occupied the back half of the space. Empty and cold. Breakfast must have already been served.

They had been offered leftover coffee—and though it was as thick as Mississippi mud, it was hot and welcome. Craig hunched over his mug, clutching it with both hands as if it was all that stood between him and a slow, painful death.

Jenny sat beside her father on the other side of the table. Her initial scowl at being forced from her plane had not subsided. If anything, her frown lines had deepened. Her sheriff's badge and papers had done nothing to dissuade the Navy security team from leading them at gunpoint into this makeshift holding cell.

As Matt had suspected, after the attack on Prudhoe, no one was taking any chances. The chain of command had to be followed. Matt knew this only too well from his own military days.

He stared over at the two guards—from their uniforms, a petty officer and a seaman. Each bore a rifle across his chest and a holstered pistol on his belt. Jenny's weapon had been taken from her, along with the service shotgun stored in the back of the Otter.

"What is taking them so long?" Jenny finally whispered under her breath, teeth clenched.

"Communication is still bad," Matt said. The head of the security team had left twenty minutes ago to verify their identification. But that meant reaching someone on the coast, who, in turn, would surely need to reach Fairbanks. They could be here all morning.

"Well, who the hell is in charge here?" she continued.

Matt knew what she meant. The entire security team seemed to consist of the six men who had escorted them to the station. Where were the other Navy personnel? Matt remembered the empty polynya and the docking bollards hammered into the ice. "Those in charge must be out in the submarine."

"What submarine?" Craig asked, perking up from his mug.

Matt explained what he saw from the air. "The old SCI-CEX stations were serviced by Navy subs. This is surely no exception, especially as deep as we are into the polar pack. I'd bet my eyeteeth that the senior Navy personnel are aboard the submarine on some mission. Perhaps off to help at Prudhoe."

"What about the head of the research team?" Craig asked. "There has to be a chain of command among the civilians. If we could get someone to listen . . ."

Since their arrival, a handful of men and women had drifted through to gawk at the newcomers. Their faces were a blend of scientific curiosity and raw need for news of the outside world. One of the men, a researcher with a NASA group, had to be forcibly escorted away by one of the guards.

"I don't know who's in charge of the civilian researchers, but I'd wager that person is gone, too." Matt nodded to their guards. "I'm sure the civilian head of the drift station would've barged right past these two."

As if hearing him, the door burst open—but it wasn't the head of the base. It was Lieutenant Commander Paul Sewell, head of the security team. He strode over to the table.

Bane rose from where he lay, but Matt placed a hand on the wolf. The dog settled to his haunches, remaining alert.

The Navy leader placed Jenny's badge and identification on the table. "Your credentials checked out," he said, and eyed the others. "But your superiors in Fairbanks seemed to know nothing about what you're doing up here. They said you were on vacation."

He passed out the other pieces of identification: Matt's Fish and Game badge, John's driver's license, and Craig's press credentials.

Jenny gathered her badge and ID. "What about my sidearm and shotgun?"

"They're in lockup until the captain returns." His tone brooked no argument. Matt respected Lieutenant Commander Sewell's civil but no-nonsense manner.

Jenny did not. Her scowl grew darker. She did not like being unarmed.

"Sir," Craig said, "we didn't come here to start trouble. We heard about your discovery of an abandoned ice base."

This drew a startled response from the lieutenant commander. "The Russian base?"

Matt practically spit out his coffee. *Russian* . . . Jenny's eyes widened in surprise. John settled his own mug of coffee very slowly to the table.

Only Craig kept his face still and unresponsive. He didn't miss a beat as he continued: "Yes, exactly. I was sent by my paper to report on the discovery. These folks agreed to escort me after I ran into some . . . um, problems in Alaska."

Matt regained his composure and nodded. "Someone tried to kill him."

Now it was the lieutenant commander's turn to raise an eyebrow.

Matt continued: "A group of paramilitary commandos sabotaged his plane and brought it down. Paratroopers dropped in to finish the job. We barely escaped to reach . . . Sheriff Aratuk." He pointed to Jenny.

She nodded. "We've been pursued ever since. We even think the explosions over at Prudhoe Bay are somehow conncctcd to all this . . . to the discovery here."

"How . . . ?" Sewell's brow built into ridges. "Wait! Who even told you about the Russian ice station?"

"My sources are confidential," Craig said, facing the stern lieutenant commander. "I'll only speak further to someone with authority here. Someone who can act."

A frown that matched Jenny's formed on the Navy man's face. As head of security, he was clearly suspicious of the newcomers. Matt noted Craig eyeing the man, too, trying to read him.

"Before anything can be decided, I'll need to consult with Captain Perry when he returns," Sewell finally said.

Passing the buck up the command chain, Matt thought.

"And when is he due back?" Craig asked.

Sewell just stared at him and didn't answer.

"Then who's in charge of the station in the meantime?" Jenny asked. "Where's the head of the research team? Someone we can talk to?"

The lieutenant commander sighed, clearly straining to straddle the line between civility and authority. "That would be Dr. Amanda Reynolds. She's . . . she's out for the moment."

"Then what about us?" Jenny demanded. "You can't hold us here."

"I'm afraid I can, ma'am." He turned from the table and left. The guards remained at the door.

"Well, that got us nowhere," Matt said after a long stretch of awkward silence.

"On the contrary." Craig leaned closer to the table and kept his voice low. "A Russian ice base. No wonder I was called out here. Something must've been found over there. A political hot potato." He ticked off points on his fingers. "The Navy clamps down the drift station. A gag order silences the scientists. And someone must have learned of my itinerary. Tried to stop me from getting here." Craig glanced around the table.

"The Russians?" Jenny asked.

Craig nodded. "If it was our own government, they could've stopped me through a thousand legal channels. Whoever was after us was keeping their noses low to the ground, trying to go under the radar."

Matt nodded. "Craig could be right. The commandos certainly had a military background. It could have been a small strike team sent to execute a surgical attack."

"But why target me?" Craig mumbled. "I'm just a reporter."

Matt shook his head. "You may be the only one outside this base or a need-to-know chain of command in government who has any inkling of the discovery out here." He silently ran over the scenario in his head. Something didn't add up here. What was so important to require such a deadly response?

He stared over at the Navy guards. They stood stiffly, not with the usual casual attentiveness of someone baby-sitting civilians. He had seen soldiers acting the same way prior to a battle. And Sewell's silence when he asked when the submarine and its captain might return . . . it jangled Matt's nerves with warning. If the crew had headed out to Prudhoe Bay to help in salvage and rescue, they'd be gone days. Sewell would've arranged rooms for them. The fact that they were still here meant the captain was expected back soon. And if this was true, why *wasn't* the sub called to help at

Prudhoe Bay? This was a disaster in their own backyard. Why had the submarine remained? Why did it *need* to stay here?

Craig spoke up, stating the obvious. "We need to find out what's going on."

"I'm open to any ideas," Matt said.

Jenny met Matt's gaze. "First we have to devise some way to get over to that Russian ice station. Whatever triggered all this started there."

"But how?" Matt asked. "We can hardly just walk over there. And they've got the plane under guard."

No one had any answers, but from each person's worried expression, everyone knew time was running out.

Matt sensed forces larger than any of them swirling down upon this frozen acre of ice. Russians . . . Americans . . . a lost base hiding some secret . . .

What clandestine war had they gotten themselves into?

7

Running Silent

ᐊᖅᐸᑦᖅᑐᖅ   ᓂᐊᑦᖅᕆᒪᐊᑎᖅ

APRIL 9, 8:38 a.m.
ABOARD THE *DRAKON*

Viktor Petkov smelled the impatience wafting from the young captain. They had been at all stop for the past hour, engines quiet, resting two meters from the surface. The ice was even closer, less than a meter. An hour ago, they had found a small lead in the frozen cap, too narrow to surface through, really no more than a crack. But it was enough to roll their radio antenna up into the open air.

As instructed, they awaited the *molniya* go-code from Colonel General Chenko of FSB, but the burst transmission from Lubyanka was late. Viktor's own patience was running thin. He checked his watch again.

"I don't understand," Captain Mikovsky said. "We're due to arrive at the U.S. research station in two days. What are we waiting for now? Another exercise? To plant more *meteorological* equipment?" He emphasized this last, not hiding his sarcasm. The captain still believed the Polaris array was a mere listening post to spy upon the Americans.

So be it.

Across the bridge, the entire crew remained edgy. They had all learned of the past night's attack on the U.S. oil station in Alaska. None knew what it meant, but they all knew the U.S. forces in the area would be at heightened alert. The waters around here had gotten much warmer, even for a diplomatic mission.

Viktor checked his other arm. The Polaris monitor lay heavy on his wrist. The plasma screen continued to depict the five-pointed star. Each point glowed, awaiting the master trigger.

All was in order.

Overnight, the diagnostic testing of Polaris had gone without mishap, requiring only a bit of calibration. He studied the wrist monitor. The nuclear-powered array utilized the latest sonic technology, capable of shattering the entire polar cap. But when in quiet mode, it also acted as a sensitive receiver. The five points of the star comprised a radar array, a giant ice dish spanning a hundred kilometers. Like ELF systems used in subs, no matter where in the world Admiral Petkov was, his monitor could communicate with the array.

At the corner of the screen, a tiny red heart symbol continued its steady flash in sync with his own pulse.

He raised his eyes just as the officer of the deck burst from the communication shack. "We've received a flash message! Marked for Admiral Petkov."

The clipboard was passed to Captain Mikovsky, who in turn passed it to Viktor.

He took the board a few steps away and opened it. He read down the brief remarks. A cold smile formed on his lips.

URGENT	URGENT	URGENT	URGENT
FM	FEDERAL'NAYA SLUZHBA BEZOPASNOSTI (FSB)		
TO	*DRAKON*		
//BT//			
REF	LUBYANKA 76-454A DATED 9 APR		
SUBJ	OPERATION CONFIRMATION		

TOP SECRET   TOP SECRET   TOP SECRET

PERSONAL FOR FLEET COMMANDER

RMKS/

(1) LEOPARD OPS SUCCESSFUL AT PB. EYES LOOKING ELSEWHERE.

(2) GO-CODE AUTHORIZED FOR TARGET ONE, DESIGNATED OMEGA.

(3) PROCEED TO TARGET TWO ONCE SECURE, DESIGNATED GRENDEL.

(4) PRIMARY OBJECTIVE REMAINS THE COLLECTION OF DATA AND MA-
TERIALS FOR THE RUSSIAN REPUBLIC.

(5) SECONDARY OBJECTIVE REMAINS TO CLEAN SITE.

(6) BE WARNED THAT A US DELTA FORCE TEAM HAS BEEN DEPLOYED.
INTEL REPORTS IDENTICAL OBJECTIVES ESTABLISHED FOR HOSTILE
TEAM. OPERATIONAL CONTROLLER STILL AT LARGE. DELTA MIS-
SION MARKED BLACK BY NSA. REPEAT BLACK.

(7) CHANNELS CONFIRM INTENT ON BOTH SIDES.

(8) DATA MUST NOT FALL INTO HOSTILE HANDS. ALL ACTIONS TO PRE-
VENT THIS ARE AUTHORIZED.

(9) COL. GEN. CHENKO SENDS.

    BT

    NNNN

Viktor closed the binder. He reviewed Chenko's remarks.
*Mission marked black by NSA . . . Channels confirm intent
on both sides.* He shook his head. It was the usual semantics
of covert operations. Fancy words for the tacit agreement on
both sides to the private war that was about to be fought out
here. Both governments would wage this war, but neither
side would acknowledge it ever happened.

And Vickor knew why.

There was a dark secret both governments wanted forever
silenced, and an even darker prize that went with it. Neither
side would ever acknowledge its existence, but neither could
they leave it untouched. The stakes were too high. The prize,
the fruit of his father's labor, was a discovery that could revolutionize the world.

But who would ultimately possess it?

Viktor knew only one thing for certain: it was *his* father's legacy. The Americans would never have it. This he swore.

And after that . . . other matters could be settled.

He glanced again to the Polaris monitor. With the go-code in hand, it was now time to start his own gambit. He pressed the silver button on the side of the wrist monitor, holding it for a full thirty seconds. He was careful not to touch the neighboring *red* button—at least not yet.

Viktor stared at the monitor. He had these thirty seconds to reconsider his decision. Once Polaris was activated, there was no turning back, no retreat. He continued to hold the button, unwavering in his determination.

During the course of his sixty-four years, he had seen Russia change: from a czarist country of kings and palaces, to a Communist state of Stalin and Khrushchev, then into a broken landscape of independent states, warring, poor, and on the brink of ruin. Each transition weakened his country, his people.

And the world at large was no better. Century-old hatreds locked the world into strife and terror: Northern Ireland, the Balkans, Israel and the Arab states. It was a pattern that was repeated over and over without end, without resolution, without hope.

Viktor kept the button pressed.

It was time a new world arose, where old patterns would be shattered forever, where nations would be forced to work together in order to survive and rebuild. A new world would be born out of ice and chaos.

It would be his legacy, in the memory of his father, his mother.

The center trigger remained dark, but the smaller lights at the points of the star began to blink in sequence, winding around and around.

Viktor released the button.

It was done.

Polaris was now activated. It only awaited the master trigger engine to be deployed at the station. Project Shockwave was about to go from theory to reality. Viktor stared at the flashing lights marking the five-pointed star, winding around and around, awaiting his final command.

After that, there would be no abort code.

No fail-safe.

Mikovsky stepped over to him. "Admiral?"

Viktor barely heard him. The captain seemed exceptionally young at the moment. So naive. His world had already ended, and he didn't even know it. Viktor sighed. He had never felt so free.

Unfettered of the future, Viktor had only one goal now: to retrieve his father's body, to collect the heritage that belonged to his family.

At the end of the world, nothing else mattered.

"Admiral?" Mikovsky repeated. "Sir?"

Viktor faced the captain and cleared his throat. "The *Drakon* has new orders."

9:02 A.M.
USS *POLAR SENTINEL*

Perry stood in the control station, his eyes fixed to the number one periscope. They had risen to periscope depth in an open lead ten minutes ago, slowly rising between pressure ridges. Through the scope, he stared out at the expanse of ice fields. The winds had picked up, scouring the frozen plains. Overhead, the skies had gone white. A big storm was coming in. But Perry didn't need to check the weather outside to know this.

All night long, they had been patrolling the waters around the drift station and the Russian base, watching for any sign of the *Drakon,* as ordered. But the midnight waters had remained empty. There was no sonar contact, except for a pod of beluga whales passing at the edge of their range. The *Polar Sentinel* seemed to be alone out here.

Still, tension remained high among his men. They were warriors in a boat without teeth, hunting for an Akula II class fast-attack submarine. Perry had read the intel on the armaments aboard the *Drakon*. Russian for "dragon." A fitting name. It was equipped not only with the usual array of torpedoes, but also rocket-propelled weapons: the lightning-fast Shkval torpedoes and SS-N-16 antisubmarine missiles. It was a formidable opponent even against the best of the American fleet . . . and if pitted against the tiny *Polar Sentinel,* it would be like a match between a tadpole and a sea dragon.

The radioman of the watch stepped into the control station. "Sir, I've raised the commander at Deadhorse. But I don't know how long I'll be able to maintain contact."

"Very good." Perry folded the periscope grips and sent the pole diving back down on its hydraulics. He followed the ensign to the radio room.

"I was able to bounce the UHF off the ionosphere," he said as he led the way into the room. "But I can't promise that it'll last."

Perry nodded and crossed to the radio receiver. They had gone to periscope depth to raise their antennas and send out their report for the past night, but Perry had asked the radioman to attempt to reach Prudhoe Bay. The men were anxious for an update.

Perry unhooked and lifted the receiver. "Captain Perry here."

"Commander Tracy," a ghostly voice whispered in his ear. It sounded like it was coming from the moon, faint, fading in and out. "I'm glad you were able to contact us."

"How is the search-and-rescue going?"

"Still a circus out here, but the fires are finally contained. And we may have our first real lead on the saboteurs."

"Really? Any idea who they are?"

A long pause. "I was hoping you could answer that."

Perry crinkled his brow. "Me?"

"I was trying to raise Omega just as you called. An hour ago, someone anonymous sent in footage of a small aircraft flying over Gathering Station Number One just before it blew. It's grainy, black-and-white . . . as if taken with a night-shot camera."

"What does this have to do with Omega?"

"Your base security contacted the Fairbanks Sheriff's Department and inquired about one of their planes and the identity of one of their sheriffs. We learned of this when we traced the call signs seen from the video footage and contacted Fairbanks ourselves. They're the same plane."

"And where's this airplane now?" Perry suspected the answer. The confirmation came a moment later.

"It landed this morning at your base."

Perry closed his eyes. So much for trying to catch an hour or two of sleep in his cabin after an interminable night.

"I've sent a request to your superiors for those in the plane to be transported back to Deadhorse for questioning."

"Do you think they blew up the pump station?"

"That's what we intend to find out. Either way, whoever they are, they must be kept under guard."

Perry sighed. He could not argue against the wisdom of that. But if they were the saboteurs, what were they doing at the base? And if they weren't, the chain of coincidences was far too spectacular to be blamed on chance alone. First, the explosions at Prudhoe Bay, then the suspicious behavior of the Russians, and now the sudden arrival of these mysterious guests. Without a doubt, they were somehow involved in all of this. But how?

"I'll have to confer with COMSUBPAC," Perry finished, "before I transport the detainees. Until then, I'll keep them safe and sound."

"Very good, Captain. Good hunting." Commander Tracy signed off.

Perry replaced the receiver and turned to the radioman. "I need to reach Admiral Reynolds as soon as we return to Omega."

"Yes, sir, I'll do my best."

Perry stepped out into the hall and ducked back into the conn.

Commander Bratt eyed him from the diving station. "What's the word from Prudhoe?"

"It seems the key to the whole mess has landed in our laps."

"What do you mean, sir?"

"I mean we're heading back to the drift station. We have some new guests to entertain."

"The Russians?"

Perry shook his head slowly. "Just get us back to the station."

"Aye, Captain." Bratt readied the boat to dive.

Perry tried to put the pieces of the puzzle together in his head. But too many pieces were still missing. He finally gave up. Perhaps he could catch a nap before they reached the drift station. He sensed he'd soon need to be at his most alert.

He opened his mouth, ready to pass command over to Bratt, when the sonar watch supervisor announced, "Officer of the Deck, we have a Sierra One contact!"

Instantly, everyone went alert. *Sonar contact.*

Commander Bratt moved over to the BSY-1 sonar suite, joining the supervisor and electronic technicians. Perry joined him and eyed the monitors with their green waterfalls of sonar data flowing over them.

The supervisor turned to Perry. "It's another sub, sir. A big one."

Perry stared at the screens. "The *Drakon.*"

"A good bet, Captain," Bratt said from the nearby fire control station, reading target course and speed. "It's heading directly for Omega."

9:15 A.M.
ICE STATION GRENDEL

Amanda shed her parka as she left the ice tunnels of the
Crawl Space and reentered the main station. The heated in-
terior was welcome after the freeze of the ice island's heart,
but it was still a damp warmth, bordering on the sweltering.
She hung the parka on a hook by the door to the Crawl
Space.

Dr. Willig kept his coat on, but as a concession to the heat,
he unzipped it and threw back the parka's hood. He also
pulled off his mittens, pocketed them, and rubbed his palms.
The seventy-year-old oceanographer sighed, appreciating
the warmth. "What are you going to do now?" he asked.

Amanda headed down the hall. "A big storm's coming. If
I want to return to Omega, I'll have to set off now. Otherwise
I'll be stuck here for another day or two until the storm
breaks."

"And I know you don't want that."

She noted the smile hovering at the edge of his lips.

"Captain Perry should be returning to Omega," he said,
and nodded to the single guard posted at the door. They had
reduced the number of Navy men here, drawing personnel
back to the sub for an exercise. "You wouldn't want to miss
that."

"Oskar," Amanda warned, but she couldn't keep a smile
from her own lips. Was she so easy to read?

"It's okay, my dear. I miss my Helena, too. It's hard to be
apart."

Amanda took her mentor's hand and squeezed it. His wife
had died two years ago, Hodgkin's disease.

"Go back to Omega," Dr. Willig told her. "Don't squander
time when you could be together." By now they had drawn
abreast of the Navy seaman guarding Level Four. Oskar
glanced to him, then back to Amanda. "Still don't want to
tell me about what's in there?"

"You truly don't want to know."

He shrugged. "A scientist is used to hard truths . . . especially one as old as this base."

Amanda continued past the door with Dr. Willig. "The truth will come out eventually."

"After the Russians arrive . . ."

She shrugged, but could not keep a bitter edge from her voice. "It's all politics." She hated to keep secrets from her own researchers, but even more she knew the world had a right to know what had transpired here sixty years ago. Someone had to be held accountable. The delay in releasing the news was surely just a way to buy time, to blunt the impact, possibly even to cover it up. A deep well of anger burned in her gut.

She reached the inner spiral staircase and climbed the steps. The plates vibrated underfoot. Movement drew her eye to the central shaft around which the stairs wound. A steel cage rose from below and passed their spot, climbing toward the upper levels. She turned to Dr. Willig. "They got the elevator working!"

He nodded. "Lee Bentley and his NASA team are having a field day with all this old machinery and gear. Boys and their toys."

Amanda shook her head. What was once defunct and frozen in ice was now thawing and returning to life. They wound their way up in silence.

Once they reached the top level, she said good-bye to her friend and crossed to the temporary room she had used the previous night. She gathered her pack and changed into her thermal racing suit. With the dispute between the biologists and geologists settled for the next couple of days, she was free to return to Omega.

As she headed out, a blue-uniformed woman crossed the common area, an arm raised to catch her attention. Lieutenant Serina Washburn was the only female among the Navy crew stationed up here, a part of the base team. She was tall, ebony-skinned, her hair shorn in a crew cut. Looking at her, one couldn't help but think of the old Amazons of mythology, women warriors of grace and strength. Her demeanor was always serious, her manner quiet. She stepped before Amanda, half at attention, respectful.

"Dr. Reynolds. I have a message relayed from Omega."

She sighed. What was wrong now? "Yes?"

"A group of civilians landed at Omega this morning and are being held by the security team."

She startled. "Who are they?"

"There are four of them, including a sheriff, a Fish and Game, and a reporter. Their identities have been checked and confirmed."

"Then why are they being held?"

Washburn shifted her feet. "With the sabotage at Prudhoe Bay . . ." She shrugged.

No one was taking any chances. "Do we know why they're here?"

"They know about this station."

"How?"

The lieutenant shrugged. "All they'll claim is that some danger is heading our way. Something perhaps tied to the explosions at the oil fields. They refuse to say more until they can speak to someone in authority. And we've been unable to raise Captain Perry."

Amanda nodded. As the base leader, she would have to look into it. "I was about to head back to Omega anyway. I'll check into the matter once I'm there."

She stepped away, but the lieutenant stopped her with a hand. "There's one other thing."

"What's that?"

"The reporter and the others are adamant about coming here. They're raising a real stink about it."

Amanda considered refusing such a visit, but then remembered her frustration a moment ago with all the secrecy and politicking surrounding the discovery on Level Four. *If*

a reporter was here, someone to document everything . . .
and a sheriff, too . . .

She weighed her options. If she returned to interview
these strangers, the coming storm would trap them all at
Omega. And once Captain Perry was back, he'd block the
reporter from coming here. He'd have no choice, tied as he
was by the commands of his superior. But Amanda was
under no such constraint. She took a deep breath. It was a
narrow window in which perhaps to break this political
stalemate and allow a little truth to shine before the awful
discovery was clouded in rhetoric and lies.

Amanda faced the stern lieutenant. "Have the civilians
brought here."

"Pardon?"

"I'll interview them here."

Washburn's only reaction was to lift one eyebrow. "I don't
believe Lieutenant Commander Sewell will agree with that
decision."

"They can be secured here just as readily as over there. If
the commander wants them under guard, I have no objection. He can send as many men with them as he would like.
But I want them brought over here before the storm hits."

Washburn paused a moment, then nodded. "Yes, ma'am."
She turned and headed back across the central common area,
aiming for the cabin that housed the station's shortwave
hookup to Omega.

Amanda glanced around the station. Finally someone
from the outside world would learn what was hidden here, a
small bit of assurance that at least some of the truth *would*
come out.

Still a twinge of unease crept through her. Before she could
trace the sudden anxiety, a tall shadow fell over her, startling
her. It was one of the things she hated most about being deaf.
She could never hear anyone approaching from behind.

She turned to find Connor MacFerran looming over her, a
bewildered expression on his face. "Have you seen Lacy?"

"Ms. Devlin?"

He nodded.

She scrunched her nose in thought. "I saw her when I entered the Crawl Space. She was carrying her skates." Amanda and the geology student shared a common interest in ice racing and had chatted for a bit.

Connor checked his watch. "She should've been back from her run an hour ago. We were to meet . . . to . . . um, to go over some data."

"I haven't seen her since we separated in the ice tunnels."

The Scotsman's face grew concerned.

"You don't think she could've gotten lost down there?" Amanda asked.

"I'd better go check. I know the course she runs." He left, stalking away like a giant black bear.

"Take some others with you!" she called to him. "Let me know when you find her."

He lifted an arm, either acknowledging or dismissing her.

Amanda stared after him. Anxiety grew to worry. She hoped the young woman hadn't injured herself. She headed back toward her cabin, zipping down her thermal suit. She spotted Dr. Willig at one of the tables.

He waved a hand, motioning her over. "I thought you'd be gone already," he said as she strode up.

"Change in plans."

"Well, I was talking to Dr. Gustof." Oskar motioned to the Canadian meteorologist, also seated at the table. Erik Gustof was recognizable by his Norwegian heritage. He wiped his clipped beard of sandwich crumbs and nodded to her. "He has been analyzing some of the data from his outlying arrays. The storm coming is building into a true blizzard. He's registering winds in excess of seventy miles an hour."

Erik nodded. "A true barnbuster, eh? We'll be locked down but good."

Amanda sighed. She remembered the warning of the newcomers: *Danger is headed our way*. It seemed these strangers knew what they were talking about, but she sensed it wasn't the weather that was the real threat.

"Are you all right?" Dr. Willig asked.

"For now," she answered numbly. "For now."

**10:05 A.M.
OMEGA DRIFT STATION**

Jenny pulled on her parka, eyeing their guards. Around her, the others also donned cold-weather gear, some supplied by the base personnel: mittens, scarves, sweaters. Matt tugged on a borrowed wool cap, since his patched green Army jacket had no hood. With his usual stubbornness, he had refused to exchange it for one of the Navy men's parkas. Jenny knew her ex-husband would never part with this tattered bit of his past.

"You'll all need sunglasses, too," Lieutenant Commander Sewell ordered.

"I don't have any," Craig said, hiking his pack of cameras and personal gear higher on his shoulder. One of the Navy petty officers had gone earlier to the Twin Otter to fetch it.

Half an hour ago, Sewell had returned with new instructions. He had been able to reach Omega's civilian head, apparently the daughter of the admiral who commanded the Navy crew stationed here. A nice bit of nepotism, it seemed. Still, Jenny hadn't complained. Dr. Reynolds had granted them permission to cross to the Russian base.

Sewell passed Craig a pair of sunglasses from his own pocket. The commander would be staying here—as would one member of their own team.

Jenny knelt and gave Bane a big hug. The wolf wagged his tail and nibbled her ear. Sewell had refused to allow the dog to accompany them. "You be a good boy," she said.

Thump . . . thump . . . thump . . .

Matt stepped to her side and gave Bane a scratch behind an ear. "We'll be back tomorrow, big guy."

Jenny looked askance at Matt. Bane was the last tie between them. A bit of love shared. When Matt caught her looking at him, they matched gazes, but it quickly grew awkward. He was the first to turn away.

"I'll take good care of your dog," a Navy ensign said as Jenny stood. He held Bane's leash.

"You'd better," Matt countered.

The twenty-year-old lad nodded. "My dad has a husky team back home."

Surprised, Jenny studied the young ensign more closely. He was olive-complexioned, eyes bright with a blend of innocence, youth, and exuberance. He appeared to be native Indian, Aleut perhaps. She read his embroidered name patch. "Tom Pomautuk." Her eyes widened with recognition. "You're not Snow Eagle's son, by any chance? Jimmy Pomautuk's son?"

His gaze flicked up to her with surprise. "You know my da'."

"He ran the Iditarod back in ninety-nine. Placed third."

A proud smile broke over his face. "That's right."

"I ran that race. He helped me when I snagged up my team and turned my sled." Jenny felt more confident leaving Bane in the hands of Snow Eagle's son. "How's Nanook?"

His smile broadened more fully, if not a trace sadly. "He's getting old now. He only helps dad on his tour runs. His days of leading the team are over. But we do have one of his pups in training back on Fox Island."

Sewell interrupted them. "You all need to set out if you're going to miss this storm."

Jenny gave Bane another pat. "You mind Tom." She stepped away.

"I don't like leaving Bane with a stranger," Matt grumbled beside her.

"You're welcome to stay here with him," Jenny said, skirting past Matt and heading with the others toward the door.

Matt followed, a sullen shadow at her back.

The group pushed out into the deep freeze, leaving behind the fluorescent interior lighting for the gloom of the overcast day. The sun was a dull glow, an eternal gloaming, trapped between day and night. Since this morning, the horizons had closed in around the station, socked by the ice fog. This is how Jenny always pictured Purgatory: an endless white gloom.

With her first breath, the cold reached inside Jenny's chest. It was ice water filling her lungs. She coughed reflexively. The temperature had already dropped. In such cold, any exposed bit of skin was in immediate risk of frostbite. Each nostril hair became an icy bristle. Even tears froze in their ducts. It was an impossible place to survive.

Once she cleared the lee of the Jamesway hut, winds gusted and tore at her clothing, seeking warm skin. Upon the sharp breezes, Jenny could smell the storm in the air.

As a group, they hunched off toward the two parked Sno-Cats.

A distant *boom* echoed and rolled over the ice.

Craig glanced around him. "What was that?"

"Fracturing ice floes," Jenny answered. "The storm is stirring up the ice." Other crackling booms erupted, like thunder from over the horizon. She could feel it through her boots. It was going to be a hell of a storm.

Once they reached the vehicles, two Navy seamen led Jenny and her father toward one vehicle. Craig and Matt headed to the other with their own armed escort. Despite the cooperation evidenced by allowing them to visit the Russian ice base, Sewell was hedging his bet, splitting them up, assigning guards to them at all times.

One of the guards stepped to the first Sno-Cat and pulled open the door. "Ma'am, you and your father will take this one."

Ducking her head, Jenny climbed into the cabin of the second idling Sno-Cat, grateful to get out of the wind.

The driver, uniformed in a blue parka, was already in his

seat. He nodded as she slid beside him on the bench seat. "Ma'am."

She frowned back at him. If one more person called her ma'am today . . .

Her father took the spot on the other side of her. The two guards hauled themselves into the backseat.

"Sorry we can't run the heater," the driver said to them all. "To cover the thirty miles, we're gonna have to conserve."

Once everyone was settled, the driver started the tread-wheeled vehicle across the ice. He followed the trundled track of the other Cat as they headed out from the base. Once under way, the driver tapped a button, and a rockabilly tune twanged from the tiny speakers.

A groan rose from the seaman in the backseat. "Trash this hayseed shit. Don't you have any hip-hop?"

"Who's driving this rig? I could put in the Backstreet Boys." The threat was clear in the driver's voice.

"No, no . . . that's all right," the other conceded, and slumped back in his seat.

They continued away from the base, all lost to their own thoughts. Snow crunched under the treads.

As the driver hummed to the music, Jenny glanced behind. After a quarter mile, the red buildings of the base had grown ghostly in the morning fog, swirling into and out of focus with the winds. Snow was beginning to squall up, too.

She began to twist back around when motion caught her attention—not from the base, but out farther. A dark shadow rose through the whiteness, like some breaching whale. She stared a moment longer, unsure what she was seeing out there on the ice.

Then the winds swept the fog clear for a moment. She watched a black conning tower rise past a jagged line of pressure ridges. Its surface steamed in the subzero air like a living creature. From its sides, small spots shone. Tinier red pinpoints of light dazzled and traced over the ice and through the fog. Vague figures scrambled along the ice ridge.

"Is that your submarine?" Jenny asked.

Both seamen swung around. The music critic, the one with the best view, jolted up from his seat. "Fuck!" He tore open the back door. "It's the goddamn Russians!"

Winds whipped into the cabin. The driver braked the Sno-Cat. Jenny saw the other Cat continuing into the ice fog. They must not have seen the submarine.

She turned to her father. He was staring back at the base, too. "They're wearing white parkas," he said calmly.

Jenny noticed, too.

The guard, assault rifle in hand, hopped out the door as their Sno-Cat growled to a stop.

"Keep going," Jenny suddenly urged the driver. She was ignored.

The guard outside lifted his weapon. He studied the sub and men racing over the ice ridge.

Laser sights glowed in the fog, casting about. Then a fiery flash burst from the top of the Russian submarine. A missile jetted through the air in a tight arc and smashed into one of the smaller outbuildings.

The explosion shattered the hut, blowing it into a hail of flaming fragments. A ten-foot-wide hole was punched through the ice.

"They took out the satellite array," the seaman in the backseat moaned. He leaned farther out the open door.

Jenny saw a single red laser pointer squiggle across the ice in their direction. It found the Sno-Cat. She swung around. "Move!" she yelled.

When the driver didn't respond, she punched her foot on the accelerator. The vehicle was still in gear and jolted forward.

"What are you doing?" the driver shouted, and knocked her leg aside.

"They blasted your communication!" Jenny yelled back. "You think they're gonna let us leave!"

Punctuating her words, gunfire erupted outside. The guard was down on one knee, firing. "Go!" he hollered at them.

The driver hesitated half a breath, then jammed the accelerator himself. "Hang on!"

"C'mon, Fernandez!" the seaman in the backseat yelled to his buddy.

Out on the ice, the guard rose to his feet and backed up. His rifle barrel steamed. More laser sights zeroed in on the fleeing Sno-Cat. He turned and ran for the cab. But when he was within a couple steps, he tripped. His right leg flew out from under him. He hit the ice and slid, leaving a red trail behind him.

"Fernandez!" The seaman leaped from the cab. He raced over to his partner, grabbed his collar, and hauled him after the Sno-Cat.

The driver slowed enough for the pair to catch up.

Jenny rolled into the backseat and helped grab the injured man.

Once both men were hauled inside, Fernandez yelled at the driver. "Kick this piece of crap in the ass!" He seemed more angry at being shot than scared. He pounded a fist on the seat.

The other man kept pressure with both gloved hands on his buddy's thigh. Blood welled between his fingers.

The Sno-Cat churned across the ice. Jenny stared ahead. The lead vehicle had disappeared into the ice fog. If only they could do the same . . .

Rockabilly continued to blare from the speakers. Snow crunched. Then a sharp whistling cut through everything.

"Shit," the driver swore.

The blast erupted just ahead of them, spattering the Sno-Cat with chunks of ice. The windshield cracked with spiderwebs. They were momentarily blinded.

Instinctively, the driver ripped the wheel around. The top-heavy Sno-Cat tilted up on one tread, skidding. Through the smoke, Jenny saw what the driver had been attempting to avoid.

A hole lay blasted through the ice. Ten feet down, water and ice sloshed. Steam roiled up from the edges of the blasted pit.

The Sno-Cat continued its icy slide toward the deadly pit, still up on one tread, fishtailing. Jenny was sure they'd never avoid the fall. Still the driver fought the wheel.

No one breathed.

But miraculously, impossibly, the stubborn vehicle stopped just at the edge of the hole's shattered lip.

The driver swore—half in relief, half in restrained panic.

The tilted Sno-Cat slammed back down onto both treads, rattling Jenny's teeth. A booming *crack* resounded with the impact.

Jenny's heart clenched. "Out!" she choked, reaching for a door handle—but it was already too late.

Like a glacier calving from a coastline, the section of ice under them fell away. The Sno-Cat followed, rockabilly blaring, and toppled end over end into the icy ocean.

10:38 A.M.
USS *POLAR SENTINEL*

Perry stood in the control bridge. The entire crew held their breaths. All eyes were on the monitors and equipment. Perry leaned beside one screen. The image was a digital feed from one of the exterior cameras. Half a mile away, the shadow of the *Drakon* floated, limned within a pillar of light shining through the open polynya. The enemy sub showed no indication that it sensed its smaller shadow.

"Captain." Commander Bratt spoke from the fire control station, whispering. He wore a pair of headphones. "We're picking up weapon fire on the hydrophones."

"Damn it!" Perry grumbled under his breath. A fist formed.

Bratt made eye contact with Perry. "Orders?"

From first sonar contact, the *Polar Sentinel* had followed the Akula-class submarine as it bore down upon Omega, running silent and fast. Without armaments, they had no way of defending themselves or mounting an offense against the larger, armed vessel. And without surfacing, they had no way to warn the drift station. So they had played ghost with the other boat.

"I'm detecting a missile launch!" the sonar supervisor hissed.

On the screen, a section of the ice roof suddenly blew downward with a bright flash, as if a meteor had punched through from above. They didn't need the hydrophones to hear the blast echo through the waters.

A moment of stunned silence followed.

"I think that was the satellite shack," Bratt whispered, one finger resting on a vectored map of the Omega station.

They're isolating the station, Perry realized. The station's satellite transmitters and receivers were its only link to the outside world—except for the *Polar Sentinel*.

"What do we do?" Bratt asked.

"We need to get our mouths above water," Perry answered, raising his voice. "Commander, order the boat back to the Russian ice station. We'll broadcast the situation from there while we evacuate the civilians. That will surely be the Russians' next target."

"Aye, sir."

Bratt began issuing hushed orders to the diving crew. The helmsman and planesman trimmed the boat and brought it about. They glided the sub silently away.

Explosions still echoed, ringing down through the ice. The noise helped cover their retreat. Though, in truth, they could've escaped even if it had been dead quiet. Designed with the newest silent propulsion system and a thicker sonar-absorbing anechoic coating, the *Sentinel* was all but invisible to most means of detection. She slid away without any outward sign that the *Drakon* even knew she was there.

As they left, Perry watched the video screen. The column of light faded behind them until there was just darkness.

Bratt called over to him from the boat's diving station. "ETA to the Russian base is thirty-two minutes."

Perry nodded and stared around the bridge. Every face was grim, angry. They were running away from a fight, but it was a battle they couldn't win. The *Polar Sentinel* was the only means to evacuate the station.

Still, as he stood in the center of the sub's control bridge, an overriding fear turned his insides to ice. *Amanda* . . . She had left yesterday for the ice station, to settle some dispute between the geologists and biologists, but she had been scheduled to return to Omega this morning. Had she already returned? Or was she still at the ice station?

Bratt stepped over to him. "The Russians aren't going to need much time to lock Omega down, especially considering the lack of defenses there. After that, they'll be hauling ass over to their station."

His XO was right. It wouldn't leave them much of a window in which to evacuate the civilians. He cleared his throat. "Commander, assemble a quick-response team. Under your lead. Have them suited up and ready to offload as soon as we surface. We need everyone out of there ASAP."

"Will do, Captain. Do you have a timetable for the evac?"

Perry considered the question, judging the speed of the other sub and the meager defenses of Omega. He needed as much time as possible, but he couldn't risk having his boat caught on the surface.

"Fifteen minutes," he said. "I want us diving again in exactly fifteen minutes."

"That's not much time."

"I don't care if you have to yank folks naked from the showers. Get their asses into the *Sentinel*. Don't worry about equipment, supplies, nothing. Just get everyone on board."

"It'll be done." Bratt turned sharply, already shouting orders.

Perry stared after him. Around the bridge, everyone busied themselves at their stations. Alone with his own thoughts, his worries for Amanda grew. *Where was she?*

Deep in the Crawl Space of the station, Amanda followed Connor MacFerran's broad back. After arranging for the transfer of the reporter and his group to the station, Amanda had found herself full of nervous energy. By bringing these newcomers out here, she knew she was violating the intent of the Navy's gag order, if not the letter. Word of the discovery on Level Four was not to be broadcast to the outside world—but that didn't mean she couldn't reveal it to folks already here. The sheriff, the reporter, and the others . . . as long as they were at the station, they were under the umbrella of the gag order, not outside it.

Still, Amanda knew she was skating on thin ice. Greg . . . Captain Perry . . . would not be pleased. He was Navy, like her father. Bending rules was not something they tolerated easily. But Amanda had to be true to her own heart. The facts had to get out. They needed an impartial party to document it all, like the reporter.

With her decision made, she was too edgy to sit for the two or so hours it would take to make the transfer. So after getting confirmation from Washburn, she had headed down to the Crawl Space to see if there was any news on Lacy Devlin.

It was lucky she had decided to check.

She had found Connor MacFerran stamping a set of ice crampons onto the bottom of his boots. They were spiked like golf shoes, meant to keep one's footing stable on the slick surface. Clearly he had been about to head out on his own, ignoring her order to take others with him. "Everyone is busy," he had complained, then patted his down vest. "Besides I have a walkie-talkie."

Of course, Amanda refused to let him go alone, and since she was still wearing her thermal racing suit, she had only to don a pair of crampons herself.

Ahead of her now, Connor halted at a crisscrossing of ice tunnels. He wore a mining helmet and shone its light down the various chutes. He cupped his mouth. His chest heaved. His lips were hidden, but Amanda knew he was yelling out Lacy's name.

Amanda waited, deaf to any response. She carried a flashlight in one hand and a coil of poly-line over one shoulder. They were in an unmapped section of the Crawl Space. It was a maze of tunnels, cracks, and caves.

Connor touched an orange spray-painted arrow on the wall. Amanda had been told it marked the skating course Lacy followed. But Amanda didn't need the markers to track the woman. The floor was scored with old runner marks, a cryptic script of steel across ice.

Connor continued down the marked tunnel, raising his hand to his lips, calling out. But from his steady pace, there seemed no response.

They continued for another twenty minutes, winding down and around a long looping ice chute, then back into the tangle of cracks and tunnels. Connor continued to call out and follow the orange markers.

He was so intent on listening, searching for the next marker, that he missed the scoring of ice that led off the main track and headed down a long crack.

"Connor!" Amanda called to him.

He jumped at her yell. Maybe it had been too loud.

He turned to her. "What?"

She pointed to the one set of tracks leading away. "She went this way." She bent and rubbed the scored ice. It was hard to say how old the marks were. But it was something worth investigating. She glanced up to the geologist.

He nodded and moved into the crack.

She followed with her flashlight.

They moved down the chute, digging in their crampons to keep traction. The tunnel narrowed, but the track kept going.

Connor stopped ahead of her, glancing back—not at her, but back down the tunnel. His brow was crinkled.

"What's wrong?" she asked.

"I thought I heard something." He stood and listened for another few breaths, then shrugged heavily. He turned and continued down the tunnel.

After another ten steps, the path plunged over an ice cliff.

Connor reached the edge first, bending over to shine his helmet light down. He suddenly stiffened and dropped to his knees.

Amanda squeezed up next to him. It was tight. The pit ended about fifteen feet down. The splash of red on the ice was a raw slash. One boot lay in the middle of the stain. Also a mining helmet, the lamp smashed.

Connor turned to her. "Lacy's."

There was no sign of a body, but the bloody track led off to the side. Out of their line of vision.

"I have to go down there," Connor insisted. "There might be another way out that we can't see. If Lacy tried to drag herself . . ."

Amanda stared at the amount of blood on the floor. It seemed hopeless, but she shrugged the coil of poly-line to the floor. "I'm lighter. You brace me, and I'll go down and look."

Connor looked like he was going to leap down there himself. But he only nodded.

Amanda tossed a length of rope to the bottom. Connor braced himself, seated on the ice a couple feet from the edge, legs apart, crampons dug into the walls. He passed a loop of poly-line around his back, under his armpits. He shook it, testing it.

"You ready?" she asked.

"I won't drop a little slip of a girl like you," he groused. "Just find Lacy."

Amanda nodded. She pocketed her flashlight, grabbed the rope, and began to rappel down into the ice pit. She lowered herself, hand over hand, spiked feet against the wall. She quickly reached the bottom.

"Off rope!" she called up as her toes hit the floor.

The line jiggled as the large man unbraced himself and crawled over to the edge. He still wore the loop of poly-line around his chest. He stared anxiously down at her and mouthed something, but with his thick beard and the glare of his helmet lamp, she could not make out what he was saying.

Rather than admit her ignorance, she simply waved to him. She pulled out her flashlight.

As she swung her light, her nose curled. The smell was rank. It seemed to hover at the bottom of the pit like bad air in a cavern, heavy, thick, suffocating. She swallowed hard. One summer, while going to Stanford, she had worked in the kennel of an animal research facility. The stench here brought her back: blood, feces, and urine. It was a smell that she had come to equate with fear.

She followed the blood trail with her flashlight. It led past the cliff to an opening in the ice wall. It was a horizontal slot, even with the floor, similar to a street drain that led into a city's underground sewers. It was no higher than her knee, but almost as long as the length of her body.

A *big* sewer drain.

She crossed toward it and called out, "Lacy!"

Deaf, she glanced up to Connor to see if he registered any response. He still knelt up at the cliff's edge, but he was staring back down the tunnel rather than into the pit.

Her toe hit something on the floor, drawing her gaze back down. It was Lacy's boot. It spun from her kick. She instinctively followed it with her flashlight. It hit the wall and stopped. From this angle, her light shone down into the boot.

It wasn't empty. Bright bone, splintered at the end, stuck out of the boot.

She screamed. But no noise came out. Or maybe it did. She had no way of telling. She scrambled backward on the ice, crampons now acting like ice skates.

She craned up to the cliff's edge.

No one was there.

"Connor!"

She could see his light up there, deeper in the tunnel. But it jittered all around, like he was doing some Scottish jig up there. Even the rope snaking down the cliff wall whipped and flailed.

"Connor!"

Then the light stopped its dance, as if hearing her. It settled still, pointing toward the top of the tunnel. The dancing rope went slack.

Amanda backed across the ice, trying to get some distance, trying to see farther down the mouth of the tunnel. She pointed her flashlight up. Her throat constricted into a knot, and blood pounded in her useless ears. She didn't bother calling out again.

Something moved over the geologist's headlamp, casting a shadow over the ceiling. Something large, hunched . . .

She now held her flashlight with both hands, pointing it like a weapon. It was surely just Connor. But being deaf, she had no way of knowing for sure. Maybe he was calling out to her . . .

Terror tightened her belly.

The shadow drew closer.

Amanda didn't wait.

She bolted across the ice, fleeing along Lacy's bloody track, aiming for the only means of escape. She dove belly first onto the ice. The wind was knocked out of her. She didn't care. She slid toward the dark sewer drain, flashlight pointed forward.

Then she was gone.

The slot swallowed her away.

The momentum of her slide carried her several feet down the drain. Illuminated by her flashlight, the low ceiling drew upward. She scrambled up to her knees as she slowed, spinning slightly on the ice.

The sloped floor dumped into a hollow space. She sat up. The roof here was high enough to stand if she ducked her head, but she remained seated. Her flashlight waved around the room.

It was a dead end . . . in *every* sense of the word.

Across the bowled floor of the hollow, bones lay everywhere: cracked, splintered, some bleached white, some yellowed. Empty skulls, human and animal, gleamed. Femurs, ribs, scapulas.

One word rang in her head.

Nest . . .

In a back corner lay a crumpled form, bent and broken, unmoving, festooned in a red, white, and blue Thinsulate outfit. Frozen blood pooled around the shape.

She had found Lacy.

10:47 A.M.
ON THE ICE . . .

Matt fought the two guards who flanked him in the backseat of the Sno-Cat. "We have to go back!" he yelled.

An elbow struck him across the bridge of the nose. Stars and pain blinded him, knocking him back into his seat. "Stay seated, or we'll handcuff you." Lieutenant Mitchell Greer grimaced and rubbed his elbow.

The other guard, a bullnecked seaman by the name of Doug Pearlson, had drawn his pistol. It was presently pointed at the roof of the Cat, but the threat was plain.

"Matt, calm down," Craig said from the front seat.

"We have our orders," the driver, a petty officer, said.

A minute ago, Lieutenant Commander Sewell had radioed their vehicle. He had ordered them to continue to the Russian ice station immediately. The commander had been unable to raise the station himself, and warning of the Russian ambush had to be relayed.

Then an explosion had cut off communication. It was a close hit, sounding at their heels. The ice shook under the Cat's treads. All eyes searched behind. Gunfire sounded in the distance.

But the threatening storm had rolled in early, squalling up snow in a ground blizzard. All attempts to raise the other Sno-Cat failed. Fear for Jenny and her father had driven Matt to attempt to commandeer their vehicle, but he was outmanned and outgunned.

There was still no sign of the trailing vehicle.

"Try them again then!" Matt snapped, blinking back tears from the pain of his bruised nose. He could taste blood in the back of his mouth.

The driver shook his head and unhooked the radio. "Cat Two, this is Cat One. Respond. Over." He held the receiver up.

No answer.

"It could just be a local blind spot," the driver said. "We see that up here. Sometimes you can communicate with someone halfway across the globe, but not in your own backyard." He shrugged, bouncing slightly as the Cat rode over a series of ice ridges.

Matt didn't believe a word of it. Jenny was in trouble. He knew it down to the soles of his feet. But by now, they were a couple miles ahead of her Sno-Cat. Even if he broke out of here, he wasn't sure he could make it to her in time to help.

"I'm sure she's okay," Craig said, trying to meet his eyes.

Matt held back his retort.

The Sno-Cat trundled straight through the blizzard, heading farther and farther from the woman he once loved. Maybe still loved.

Jenny must have blacked out. One moment the Sno-Cat was toppling around her; the next ice water burned through her jeans, startling her to full alert. She shoved up and quickly took in her surroundings.

The Cat was upside down. Water filled the lower foot of the cabin. The motor still grumbled, vibrating the upended vehicle. The roof light glowed in the waters below her, grimly illuminating the tableau.

Her father was rising from the floor, cradling his wrist.

"Papa?" She shuffled across the roof toward him.

"Mmm, okay," he mumbled. "Jammed my hand."

His eyes glanced to the driver. The man lay facedown in the water. His head bent unnaturally backward. "Neck's broken," her father said.

The other two guards were fighting the door.

Fernandez slammed his shoulder against the handle. It didn't budge. The pressure outside the half-submerged Cat held the doors shut. "Fuck!" He limped back on one foot, blood from the gunshot wound trailing through the waters around him.

"Try to find something to smash a window," Fernandez barked. The whites of his eyes glowed in the watery light.

Jenny stepped toward them. "How about this?" She reached behind the other guard's back and slipped out his sidearm. Turning, she thumbed the safety and fired into the Cat's windshield, crackling the Arctic safety glass and tearing it partly away.

"Yeah," Fernandez said, nodding. "That'll do."

The guard retrieved his gun and holstered it, scowling at her.

"Don't take offense at Kowalski here," Fernandez said, and waved them forward. "Joe doesn't like folks touching his things."

They ducked under the seats.

Kowalski kicked out the remaining glass.

The open water churned and frothed inside the pit. Ice blocks and cakes bobbed in the mix.

"Out of the frying pan . . ." Fernandez mumbled.

"Make for that crack in the wall," Jenny said, pointing to a crumbled section that looked climbable.

"Ladies first," Kowalski offered.

They were now thigh-deep in the water. Jenny pushed out on numb legs. The searing cold cut through her as she fell into the sea. She fought her body's natural reflex to curl against the frigid water. Seawater froze at 28.6 degrees F. This felt a million degrees colder, so cold it burned. She kicked and pawed chunks of ice out of the way. Slowly she swam across the few yards to the ice slope and pulled herself into the crack, numb fingers scrabbling for purchase.

Once out of the water, she glanced back. The others followed. Kowalski tried to help Fernandez, but he was shoved away.

Behind them, the idling Sno-Cat tipped nose first, then sank into the blue depths. Its lights trailed down into the darkness. For a moment, Jenny saw the pale face of the driver pressed against the glass. Then the Sno-Cat and its lone passenger disappeared.

Jenny helped her father climb from the water into the cracked section of the wall. The slot was jagged with blocks and dagger-sharp protrusions, but the obstacles offered a natural ladder to climb out of the pit.

As a group, they worked their way up. It was a cold, sodden climb. Wet clothes turned to ice. Hair froze to skin. Limbs shook with petit mal seizures in a futile attempt to keep warm.

They all pushed free, one after the other, beaching themselves up onto the ice. It was not exhaustion that immobilized them, but the cold. It held them all as surely as any vise. It was inescapable.

The wind had kicked up. Snow and ice spun dizzily around her.

Her father somehow crawled to her, wrapping her in his arms, cradling her. It had been ages since he had held her like this. She had been only sixteen when she had lost her mother. For the next two years, an aunt and uncle had fostered Jenny while her father was in jail, then probational recovery. Afterward, she had barely spoken to him. But Inuit life was built around social gatherings: birthday parties, baby showers, weddings, and funerals. She had been forced to make an uneasy peace with her father, but it was far from close.

Especially not this close.

Tears flowed and froze on her cheeks. Something finally broke inside her. "Papa . . . I'm sorry."

Arms tightened around her. "Hush, conserve your energy."

"For what?" she mumbled, but she wasn't sure she had even spoken aloud.

Hunter/Killer

ᖅᐊᖄᒍᐅᕐᐊᖅᑎᕤᐃᓄᐊᖅᑎ

APRIL 9, 11:12 A.M.
USS *POLAR SENTINEL*

"Skylight ahead!" the chief of the watch yelled. "Forty degrees to port!"

"Thank God," Perry whispered to the periscope's optical piece. He walked off the degrees, turning the scope. They had spent five minutes searching for the man-made polynya near the ice island. The storm surge through the area had shifted the surface ice by several degrees. Nothing was constant up here, he thought. *Nothing but the danger.*

Through the scope, the ceiling of the world was black ice, but off to port, where the chief had indicated, he spotted an unnaturally square opening in the roof. It shone a brilliant aquamarine, lighting the waters under it to the pale blue of a Bahamian sea. He eyed his goal with a tight smile. "It's the polynya! Port ahead one-third, starboard back one-third, right full rudder. Get us under that skylight!"

The term *skylight* had been used by submariners since first venturing under the polar ice cap. An opening in the ice.

Somewhere to surface. There was no better sight, especially with the press of time upon them.

His orders were relayed and a slight tremor vibrated the deck plates as the sub hoved around and aimed for their goal. He watched through the scope. "All ahead slow."

As they neared the opening in the thick ice, he spoke without taking his eyes from the periscope. "Chief, what's the ice reading above?"

"Looks good. The opening's frozen over a bit." The chief peered closer at the video monitor of the top-sounding sonar. "Across the skylight, I read no more than six inches of ice, but no less than three."

Perry sighed with relief. It should be thin enough to surface through. He studied the dark ice surrounding the aquamarine lake, jagged and menacing, like the teeth of a shark.

"We're under the skylight," Bratt reported from the diving station.

"All stop. Rudder amidships." As his orders were obeyed, he walked the periscope around, checking to make sure there was plenty of room for the sub to surface without brushing against the dragon-toothed walls of the canyon. Once satisfied, he straightened and folded the periscope grips. The stainless-steel pole descended below. "Stand by to surface." He swung to Bratt. "Bring her up slowly."

The soft chug of a pump sounded as seawater ballast was forced out of tanks inside the boat. Slowly the sub began to rise.

Bratt turned to him. "That Russian boat will surely hear us blowing ballast."

"There's no helping it." Perry stepped down from the periscope deck. "Is the evac team ready to debark to the station?"

"Aye, sir. They're suited up. We'll empty that place in under ten minutes."

"Make sure you get everyone out of there." Perry's thoughts turned to Amanda for the hundredth time.

Bratt seemed to read his mind, staring intently at him. "We won't miss anyone, sir. That's for damn certain."

Perry nodded.

"Ready for ice!" the chief bellowed.

Overhead, the reinforced bridge crashed through the frozen crust, shuddering the boat. A moment later, the bulk of the submarine followed, cracking through to the surface. All around, valves were opened or closed, dials checked. Reports echoed from throughout the boat.

"Open the hatches!" Bratt yelled. "Ready shore team!"

The locking dogs were undone, and men in parkas gathered, rifles shouldered. One held out a blue parka for Bratt.

Bratt yanked into it. "We'll be right back."

Perry glanced to his watch. The Russians were surely already under way by now. "Fifteen minutes. No longer."

"Plenty of time." Bratt led his men out.

Perry stared as they climbed away. Cold air, fresh and damp, blew down from above. Once the last man was gone, the hatch slammed shut. Perry paced the length of the periscope stand. He wanted to be out there with Bratt, but he knew his place was here.

Finally, he could stand it no longer. "Chief, you have the conn. I'm going to watch from Cyclops. Patch any communication from the shore team to the intercom there."

"Aye, sir."

Perry left the bridge and headed toward the nose of the submarine. He climbed through the hatches and past the empty research suites. He opened the last hatch and entered the naturally illuminated chamber beyond.

He crossed under the arch of clear Lexan. The water sluicing over the glass splintered out in jagged lines of ice, growing visibly into complex fractal designs over the Lexan surface. Beyond the sub, the view was poor. Steam rose off the submarine's carbon-plate hide, and flurries of snow swirled down in frosted strokes from the heights of the mountainous ice ridges.

Perry stared toward the cavernous opening that led down into the Russian station. He made out the vague shapes of men, trudging, bent against the wind. Bratt's team. They disappeared into the mouth of the tunnel.

The intercom buzzed. A tinny voice spoke. "Captain, bridge here."

He crossed and pressed the button. "What is it, Chief?"

"The watch radioman reports no reception from NAVSAT. We're blanketed under another solar storm, leaving us deaf and dumb for the moment."

He swore under his breath. With the satellites down, he needed word to reach the outside world. He jabbed the intercom button. "Any ETA on how long we'll be out of satellite communication?"

"It's anyone's guess. Radioman says he expects short bursts of open air, but he can't say when. Best guess is that the current bevy of solar storms will quit sometime after sunset." Another long pause. "He's going to try an ionosphere bounce with the UHF, but there's no guarantee anyone'll hear us in this weather. With a bit of luck, we might raise Prudhoe Bay."

"Roger that, bridge. Have him keep trying as long as we're surfaced. But I also want a SLOT configured and hidden out on the ice." A SLOT, or Submarine-Launched One-Way Transmitter, was a communication buoy that could be deployed and set with a time delay to burst a transmitted satellite report. "Set the SLOT to transmit well after sunset." This should help ensure their message got out after the solar storm passed and reopened satellite communication.

"Aye, sir."

Perry checked his watch. Five minutes had passed. He stepped back under the Lexan arch. Visibility was mere yards now. He could just make out the line of pressure ridges, but no details. He kept his vigil. After another interminable minute, ghostly shapes pushed through the snow. It was the first of the evacuees.

Through the hollow of the boat, he could hear the outside hatch clang open. He imagined the whistle of wind. More and more shapes appeared out of the squall. He tried to count them, but the swirling snow confounded all efforts to tell one from another, man from woman.

His jaw ached from clenching his teeth.

The intercom buzzed. "Captain, bridge again. Patching through Commander Bratt."

The next words were scratchy with static. "Captain? We've hauled through all the levels. I have two men with bullhorns running the occupied areas of the Crawl Space."

Perry had to resist interrupting his XO and demanding to know Amanda's fate.

The answer came anyway. "We learned Dr. Reynolds is still here."

Perry let out a deep sigh of relief. She hadn't returned to the drift station and been caught in the attack. She was safe. She was here.

The next words, though, were disquieting. "But, sir, no one has seen her in the last hour or so. She and one of the geologists went searching for an AWOL student in the ice tunnels."

He hit the button. "Commander, I don't want *anyone* left behind."

"Roger that, sir."

Perry checked his watch. "You have seven minutes."

Before any acknowledgment could be transmitted, the control station cut in again. "Bridge to Captain. For the past few minutes, we've stopped picking up any evidence of weapon fire from the hydrophones. Sonar also reports suspicious echoes that could be a sub diving. Air venting, mechanicals . . ."

It could only be the *Drakon*. The Russian hunter/killer was on the move. Time had run out. Perry knew he couldn't risk the lives here. He spoke into the intercom. "Patch me back to Bratt."

"Aye, Captain."

A moment later, his XO's voice scratched out of the speaker. "Bratt here."

"Commander, company is on the way. We need everyone out of there now!"

"Sir, we haven't even cleared all of the Crawl Space yet."

"You have exactly three minutes to empty that station."

"Roger that. Out."

Perry closed his eyes and took a deep breath. Glancing over his shoulder, he took one last look out Cyclops, then ducked out of the room. He climbed back through the sub and assumed command of the bridge again.

Men milled in ordered confusion, helping wide-eyed civilians down ladders and into the living spaces beyond the control station. The interior of the sub had already dropped a good twenty degrees, open to the blizzard above.

Dr. Willig suddenly appeared at Perry's side. "I know you're busy, Captain," the Swedish oceanographer said breathlessly, snow melting in his hair.

"What is it, sir?"

"Amanda . . . she's still down in the Crawl Space."

"Yes. We know." He kept his voice clipped, tight. He couldn't let his own panic show. He had to be leader here.

"Surely we're going to make sure everyone is out of there before leaving."

"We'll do our best."

His answer did little to fade the fear in the old man's eyes. Amanda was like a daughter to him.

The chief waved from his station. "We've got Commander Bratt on the line again, Captain."

Perry checked his watch, then glanced to the open hatch. The ladder was empty. Where was his XO? He crossed to the boat's radio. "Commander, time's run out. Get your ass over here now."

The answer was faint. The entire bridge had hushed. "Still missing a handful of civilians. In the Crawl Space now with

Lieutenant Washburn. Request permission to stay behind. To offer protection for those still here. We'll find them . . . then find a good hiding place."

Perry clenched a fist. A new voice spoke at his side. It was Lee Bentley, one of the NASA crew. "I left the commander my schematics of the station. Detailing the access tunnels and old construction shafts."

Beyond the scientist, all eyes focused on Perry. Dr. Willig had never looked paler. They awaited his decision.

Perry hit the radio's transmit. "Commander . . ." He held the button. Fear for Amanda hollowed his heart, but he had a boatload of crew and civilians to protect. "Commander, we can wait no longer."

"Understood."

"Find the others . . . keep them safe."

"Roger that. Out."

Perry closed his eyes.

Dr. Willig spoke into the heavy silence, his voice rich with disbelief. "You're just going to leave them behind?"

With a deep breath, Perry turned and faced the chief of the watch. "Take us down."

11:22 A.M.
ICE STATION GRENDEL

Blood pounding in her ears, Amanda crouched in the nest of bones. The smell of bowel and blood filled the small space. Lacy's corpse looked like some broken mannequin, unreal. Something had torn the geology student apart. Something large.

Amanda panted through clenched teeth.

The girl's body lay on its back, limbs broken, face smashed, like she had been shaken and slammed repeatedly against the ice.

Amanda kept her eyes away from the corpse's belly. It had been ripped open. Frozen blood trailed from the open cavity. Out in the wild, wolves always ate the soft abdominal organs of their prey, burrowing into the bellies first, feasting on the rich meal inside.

Without a doubt, such a predator was down here now. But what was it? *Not a wolf . . . not so far north.* And she saw no evidence of the usual king of the Arctic wilds, the polar bear. No droppings. No piles of white hairs.

So what the hell was down here?

Amanda took a post by the only exit and quickly pieced a few things together in her head. She recalled the movement recorded on the DeepEye sonar she was testing. She knew for certain now it had been no sonar ghost.

Amanda's mind, panicked, ran along impossible channels. Whatever was down here had sensed the passage of the sonar scan, fled from it, back to its nest in the core of the ice island. But what could do that? What animals could sense sonar? Having studied sonar in depth for her own research with the DeepEye, she knew the common answers: bats, dolphins . . . and *whales*.

She glanced fleetingly over to the sprawled, gutted corpse. It reminded her of another body spread and cut open on the ice.

Dr. Ogden's dissected *Ambulocetus* specimen.

According to the biologists, the *Ambulocetus* species were the forefathers of the modern whale. The thought chilled her further.

Could it be possible? Could there be living specimens down here, not just frozen ones?

A terrified shudder passed through her. It seemed ridiculous, but nothing else made sense. Not a wolf, nor a polar bear. And here, alone, nightmares gained flesh and bone. The impossible seemed possible.

She cupped her hand over her flashlight. Beyond the tunnel, the shine of Connor's helmet lamp still reflected in the outer cavern. She studied as best she could the only way out of here. Everything lay still. There was no sign of movement, no way of knowing if the predator was still out there or if it was returning even now.

She was trapped—not just in the cave, but also in a cocoon of silence. Without her hearing, she was cut off from any telltale sign of approach: a growl, a scrape of claw on ice, the hiss of breath.

She feared going back out.

But how could she stay?

Glancing back, she sought someplace to hide within the nest. The walls had a few cracks and blocky tumbles of ice-fall. But none was deep enough to nestle away safely.

She turned again to the tunnel.

A heavy shadow shifted past the reflected light.

Startled, she rolled back, scrabbling through bones. She flicked off the flashlight. Now the only illumination came from beyond the nest, flowing down the throat of the slotted tunnel. Something crouched out there at the entrance, like a boulder in a river of light.

Then it began to roll slowly toward her.

She fled to one of the cracks in the wall. Her mind raced, struggling against panic. She flicked her flashlight back on and tossed it near Lacy's corpse, hoping its brightness would attract the creature's attention. This last thought sparked others. How did it really see in the dark? Body heat? Vibrations? Echolocation?

She had to assume all.

She pulled up her suit's hood and jammed herself sideways into the crack, barely able to press her body away. She rubbed the ice walls with one hand, then slathered her face. If it was body heat, her insulated suit should keep her hidden, leaving only her face exposed. She cooled her skin with ice water as best she could.

Crammed into the crack, she hoped she offered no direct silhouette to any possible echolocation. She covered her mouth and held her breath, fearing even her own heated exhalation could give her away.

She willed herself to dead stillness and waited.

It didn't take long.

Amanda stared in disbelief as the creature crawled into the cave and crouched across from her now.

A *living* grendel.

It shoved its head into the cave first. Hot breath steamed from two slitted nostrils high on its domed head. Its long white muzzle dripped fresh blood and gore.

Connor . . .

Lips growled back to reveal razored teeth. It shambled into its nest, snout raised, sniffing. It was large, half a ton, slung low to the ground. It measured ten feet from muzzle to the tip of its thick tail.

As it entered its nest, it circled around the cavern's edge, wary. It moved like an otter, sinuous and lithe, but this creature was white-skinned and hairless, sleek. It looked like a creature built to move smoothly through water or to slide down tight tunnels. Black eyes narrowed as it shied from the brightness of her discarded flashlight.

It passed by Amanda's hiding spot, its attention focused on the pool of brightness. Almost at her toes, it stopped and bunched up as it stared into the flashlight's glare. Shoulders muscled into ridged peaks, haunches rose. Rear claws dug into the ice floor as its tail lashed violently, sweeping the floor of old bones.

Then it leaped as quick as any lion, pouncing at the light. It landed atop Lacy's corpse, sending the flashlight flying. It tore and ripped, using teeth and claws, blindingly fast. Then it spun away, chasing after the light, batting the metal tool around the cavern. Finally the flashlight smashed against a block of ice and extinguished.

Amanda continued to hold her breath.

The entire attack had transpired in dead silence.

The sudden darkness blinded Amanda for a heartbeat. Then the glow from the outside cavern filtered in. In the dimness, the grendel was a ghostly shadow.

It circled around the cavern. *Once, twice.* It still seemed oblivious to her presence. It settled to the center of its nest, head craning, checking all walls. For a moment, whether it was her own fright or some ultrasonic sonar, Amanda felt the tiny hairs on the back of her neck quiver.

A trickle of sweat rolled down her brow.

The grendel swung back toward her, sniffing, huffing. It seemed to stare right at her.

Amanda tried not to scream.

It didn't matter.

The grendel rose to its feet, lips curled in menace, and slunk toward her hiding place.

11:35 A.M.
OUT ON THE ICE . . .

Jenny still lived. Somehow . . .

She lay with her father atop the ice, but he had long since stopped responding, though his cold arms remained locked around her, holding her. She didn't have the strength to move, to check on him. Already their clothes had frozen together, fusing father to daughter. The blizzard blew around the pair, isolating them. She had lost sight of the two Navy men: Fernandez and Kowalski.

She tried to shift, but she could no longer feel her limbs. Her shivering had stopped, too, as her body gave up feeding blood to her extremities. Her systems were in pure survival mode, expending all resources to keep the core alive.

Even the cold had vanished, replaced with a deadly sense of calm. She found it hard to stay awake, but in sleep lay only death.

Papa . . . She could not speak. Her lips would not move. Another name arose, unbidden, unwelcome: *Matt* . . .

Her heart ached, thudding leadenly.

She would have cried then, but her tear ducts had frozen

over. She didn't want to die this way. For the past three years, she had trudged through life, going through the motions of living. Now she wanted to live. She cursed the time lost, the half-life she had lived. But nature was immune to wishes and dreams. It simply killed with the determined heart of any predator.

Her eyelids drifted closed. They were too painful to keep open.

As the world faded away, flares bloomed through the swirling snow. *One, two, three, four* . . . They were hazy glows through the blizzard, flying back and forth, sailing through the air. *Snow angels* . . .

She squinted, struggling to hold her eyes open. They grew brighter, and after another few breaths, a growling whine accompanied them, piercing angrily through the wail of winds. *Not angels* . . .

From the snow, strange vehicles rode forth. They looked like snowmobiles, but they moved too fast, skimming over the ice with a gracefulness and speed that belied ordinary Ski-Doos. They reminded her instead of jet skis, flying over the ice.

But the vehicles here were neither snowmobiles nor jet skis. As they grew from illusion to solid reality, the machines glided over the ice, not deigning to touch the surface of the world. Jenny had seen such craft before, at shows, experimental models.

Hovercraft.

But these were small, no larger than two-man jet skis, open on top, ridden like a motorcycle. The windshield of each bubbled back to protect the driver and passenger. And like jet skis, the underside of each bore ski runners, but the machines seemed only to need them as they banked and slowed. Each craft settled with skill to the ice, landing on their runners and sliding to a stop a few yards away.

Men unmounted. All dressed in white parkas. Rifles were leveled.

Jenny heard Russian being spoken, but the world remained blurry, lit only by the headlamps of the personal hovercraft.

The soldiers wore face masks, storm troopers. They approached with caution, then with a bit of urgency. Some checked the blasted ice pit. Others came forward. One knelt before Jenny. He barked something in Russian.

All she could manage was a groan.

He reached for her. She blacked out a moment. It had taken all her strength to utter even that small sound. When next she awoke, she found herself strapped into a bucket seat, harnessed in place with shoulder and belt straps. The world was a blur around her. She was flying.

Then enough awareness cut through the haze for her to recognize that she rode behind a soldier. He didn't wear a parka, only a thick gray sweater. She realized she was wearing his coat. The fur-lined hood pulled almost over her head.

They were heading back to the drift station. A fire burned from the cratered ruins of an outbuilding.

It made no sense, so she simply passed out again.

She woke next to a world of pain. It flared over every inch of her body. It was as if someone were flaying her alive, as if acid streamed over every inch of her body, agonizing, stripping away her skin. She screamed, but no sound came out. She thrashed against the arms that held her.

"It's all right, Miss Aratuk," a gruff voice said behind her. "You're safe." The same voice spoke to someone else holding her. "Turn the water slightly warmer."

Jenny snapped a bit more fully into awareness. She was naked in a shower, being held under the stream. She managed to free her tongue. "It . . . it burns."

"The water's only lukewarm. Blood is just returning to your skin. You have some patches of mild frostbite." Something jabbed her arm. "We've given you a bit of morphine to dull the pain."

She finally glanced back to the speaker. It was Lieutenant

Commander Sewell. She sat on the fiberglass floor of a communal shower. A handful of Navy men were in the room, busy. Other showers steamed.

After a few moments, her agony dulled to simple torture. Tears flowed down her face, mixing with the shower's water. Slowly her temperature rose. Her body began to shiver uncontrollably.

"M . . . mm . . . my father," she chattered out.

"He's being taken care of," Sewell said. "He's actually faring better than you. Already into towels. Tough old bastard, that one. Only a little frostbite on his nose. He must be made of ice."

This raised a smile. *Papa . . .*

She allowed her body to shake and quake. Her core body temperature slowly struggled to normalcy. Sensory feeling awakened with a million pinpricks in her hands and feet. It was slow crucifixion.

Finally she was allowed to stand. She even warmed up enough to feel slightly ashamed by her nakedness. There were uniformed men all around. She was led out of the showers, passing by Kowalski, bare-assed and shivering under his own stream of water.

As hot towels were wrapped around her, she asked, "Fernandez?"

Sewell shook his head. "He was dead by the time the Russians reached you."

Her heart heavy, she was walked over to chairs in front of space heaters. Her father was already there. He sipped from a mug of hot coffee. The morphine wobbled her feet, but she managed to reach the chairs.

"Jen," her father said. "Welcome back to the living."

"You call this living?" she asked dourly. As she sat there, she pictured Fernandez's quirked smile. It was hard to believe someone so alive was now dead. Still, a dull buzz of relief seeped through her, perhaps partly due to the morphine, but mostly rising from her own heart.

She was alive.

As the space heater blew humid air in her face, a mug of coffee was pushed into her trembling hands.

"Drink it," Sewell said. "We have to warm up your insides as much as your outsides. And caffeine's a good stimulant, too."

"You don't have to sell me on the coffee, Commander." She took a burning sip. She felt it slide all the way down. A shudder—half pleasure, half pain—shook through her.

With coffee warming her hands and belly, she glanced around. She was in some large dormitory room. Cots lined both walls. Tables and chairs in the center. Most here were civilians, scientists . . . but a few Navy personnel were mixed in.

She turned back to Sewell. "Tell me what happened."

He eyed her. "The Russians. They commandeered the base."

"I sort of figured that on my own. Why?"

He shook his head. "It has something to do with that Russian ice station we found. Something hidden over there. They've been systematically interviewing key personnel to see what we know. It was why you were rescued from the ice. They thought you might be escaping with something or someone, so they had you hauled back. I informed them of your noncom status."

"What are they searching for?"

"I don't know. Whatever is over at that other base is being kept under wraps. NTK only."

"NTK?"

"Need-to-know." His voice hardened. "And apparently I'm not one of those who needs to know."

"So what now?"

"There's not much we can do. We only had a small security force." He waved an arm around the room. "The bastards killed five of my men. We were quickly subdued and corralled in here. So were the civilian personnel. They're keeping us all under guard. We were told as long as we didn't make any trouble that we'd be freed in forty-eight hours."

Her father spoke from his wrap of blankets. "What about the other Sno-Cat? The one with Matt and Craig?"

Jenny found herself tensing, fearing the worst.

"As far as I know, they're okay. I was able to contact them before being caught. I told them when they reached the ice station to raise the alarm."

Jenny sipped from her coffee. Her hands trembled worse. For some reason, she had to fight back tears. "Everyone else is here?"

"Everyone still living."

She glanced around the room, searching for a specific face. She didn't find him. "Where's Ensign Pomautuk?"

Sewell shook his head. "Not here. He's among the missing, along with a handful of civilians. But I can't say for sure. The Russians took some of the critically injured to the hospital wing. Maybe he's over there. Details are still sketchy."

Jenny stared over to her father. The tip of his nose was ashen, frost-nipped. His eyes read her fear. One hand slipped from his wrap and sought her own. She took his fingers. They were rough with old calluses, but still strong. He had faced so many hardships in his life and survived. Absorbing his strength, she faced Sewell again. "This forty-eight-hour deadline? Do you believe they'll let us go?"

"I don't know."

Jenny sighed. "In other words, *no*."

He shrugged. "At the moment, it doesn't matter whether we believe them or not. The occupying force outnumbers us two to one. And they've got all the guns."

"What about your captain and your submarine?"

"The *Polar Sentinel* might be out there somewhere, but they have no armaments. Hopefully they're hauling ass out of here, heading for help. That is, if they're still alive."

"What now? Do we simply wait? Trust the Russians' word about our safety?"

By now, Kowalski had joined them, wrapped head to toe in towels. He plopped down heavily into a chair. "Fuck no," he answered her question.

Silence followed his assertion. No one argued.

"Then we need a plan," Jenny said finally.

11:45 A.M.
ICE STATION GRENDEL

Hadn't they gone this way already?

Lieutenant Commander Roberto Bratt was lost, which didn't help his temper. He always blamed his short fuse on his heritage: his mother was Mexican, his father Cuban. Both had been loud and volatile, always fighting. But these damn tunnels would have confounded even Gandhi's patience. Everything looked the same: ice and more ice.

Ahead, his junior lieutenant hurried down another tunnel. He followed, his boots grinding on the sand-covered floors. "Washburn!" he called out. "Do you know where the hell you're going?"

Lieutenant Serina Washburn slowed her steady trot and pointed her flashlight back to a purple blaze spray-painted on the wall. "Sir, this marks the only place we haven't searched yet. After this, we'll need a paint can to trail our way into the unmarked areas."

He waved her on. *Great . . . just great . . .*

During the chaos of the evacuation, Bratt's team had used bullhorns to sound the alarm through the tunnels. Word had spread quickly. People had poured out of the ice tunnels. But with the Russians breathing down their necks, they didn't have time to do a complete sweep of the Crawl Space on foot.

As such, when the dust settled, people turned up missing—including the head of Omega, Dr. Amanda Reynolds.

With folks unaccounted for, Bratt had felt compelled to stay behind, but he had been surprised when Lieutenant Washburn had *insisted* on joining him. The station had been under her guardianship. She wasn't about to abandon it until every damn one of her charges was cleared out of here.

As they continued deeper, Bratt appraised his partner. Washburn was actually a couple of inches taller than him, tall for a woman, but lean and muscular. She looked like a track runner. Her hair was worn in a crew cut, giving her a stark look that somehow didn't lessen her femininity. Her skin was smooth coffee, her eyes large and deep. But for the moment, she was all business.

And so was he. He switched his focus to the ice tunnels. He had a mission: find any civilian strays and keep them safe.

Lifting the bullhorn to his lips, he squeezed the trigger. His words blasted from the horn, echoing down the tunnels. "This is Lieutenant Commander Bratt! If anyone can hear this, please sound off!"

He lowered the bullhorn. His ears rang. It took a moment for him to be able to listen for any response. He expected no answer. They had been searching and shouting for a half hour without even a whisper of a response. So when someone finally did call out, he wasn't sure if it was real or not.

Washburn glanced back to him, one eyebrow cocked.

Then the shout repeated, faint, but ringing clear through the ice tunnels: "Over here!"

It came from ahead of them.

Together, they hurried forward. Bratt shrugged his rifle higher on his shoulder. His field jacket and parka were heavy with ammunition, gleaned from his own men as they evacuated back to the sub. Washburn was similarly loaded down, but she sped ahead of him.

The tunnel emptied into a large ice cavern, full of idling generators, lamp poles, and equipment. The air here was noticeably warmer, humid. The back half of the cavern was a wall of pocked volcanic rock.

"Christ," he swore under his breath.

A short, bald man, bundled in an unzipped parka, came slipping across the ice lake that floored the room. It was one of the base scientists. He was flanked by two younger men.

"Dr. Ogden?" Washburn said, identifying the lead man. "What are you still doing here? Didn't you hear the call to evacuate?"

"Yes, yes," he said as he reached them, out of breath, "but my work has nothing to do with politics. This is science. I don't care who controls the station as long as my specimens are protected. Danger or not, I could not leave them. Especially at this critical juncture. The thawing is near completion."

"Specimens?" Bratt asked. "Thawing? What the hell are you talking about?"

"They must be protected," the scientist insisted. "You have to understand. I could not risk the data's corruption."

Bratt noted the shifting feet and wringing hands of the man's younger associates—postgrads by the look of them. They were not so convinced.

"You have to see!" Dr. Ogden said. "We're picking up EEG activity!" He hurried back the way he had come, back to the volcanic cliff face.

Washburn followed. "Is Dr. Reynolds here, too?"

Bratt dogged after them to hear the answer. *If all the missing personnel were here . . .*

But the doctor's response dashed such hopes. "Amanda? No, I don't know where she is." He glanced back, eyebrows tucked together. "Why?"

"She's here somewhere," Washburn answered. "Supposedly off with Dr. MacFerran, looking for a missing colleague."

Ogden rubbed at his frozen mustache. "I don't know anything about it. I've been here all night with the biology team."

As they reached the wall, Bratt noted water splashing underfoot, flowing from a crevice in the cliff face. The biologist led the way into the cavern. But after a few steps, a new form came splashing from deeper inside, running headlong into them.

It was another student, a young woman in her early twenties. Bratt caught her as she slipped in her panic. *How many fools were down here still?*

"Professor! S-something's happening!" she stammered.

"What?"

She pointed back down the cleft. She tried to speak, but her eyes were wild.

Ogden fled forward. "Is something wrong?"

They all followed after him. In another ten steps, the way opened into a space the size of a two-car garage. It was a bubble in the rock. More lamp poles glowed. Equipment was stacked all around.

Bratt gasped at both the sight and the smell. He had worked one summer at a fish plant in Monterey. The heat, the reek of rotting fish guts, the stench of blood. It was the same here—but it was not fish that caused this smell.

Rolled to one side was the flayed and gutted body of some pale white creature. It looked like it might be a beluga whale, but this thing had legs. This creature was not the only one here. Another six specimens, fresher and intact, lay curled on the floor. Crusts and chunks of ice still clung to their pale flesh. Two had colored leads taped to their forms, running to machines with video screens. Small sine waves flowed across the tiny monitors.

Ogden searched around the room. "I don't understand." He turned to the panicked postgrad student. "What's the matter?"

She pointed to one of the curled specimens, the one closest to its gutted brethren. "It . . . it moved . . ."

Ogden scowled at her and waved a dismissive hand. "Preposterous. It's just the shadows in here. One of the light poles simply shifted."

The girl hugged her arms around her chest. She didn't look convinced. This was one seriously spooked girl.

Ogden turned back to Bratt and Washburn. "It's the EEG readings. It's disturbed some of our less experienced team members."

"EEG? Like brain waves?" Bratt asked, staring over to the run of electronic waves across the monitoring screen.

"Yes," Ogden said. "We've recorded some activity from the thawing specimens."

"You're kidding. These things are alive?"

"No, of course not. They're fifty thousand years old. But such a phenomenon is seen sometimes when living specimens are frozen rapidly, then warmed again slowly. Though the subject is dead, the chemicals in the brain begin to thaw and flow. And chemistry is chemistry. Certain neurochemical functions will begin anew. But over time, without circulation, the effect fades away. That's why it was so important that I stay and collect the data before it disappears. We're looking at activity that hasn't been seen in fifty thousand years!"

"Whatever," Bratt said. "As long as these things stay dead."

As if hearing him, one of the bodies spasmed. A tail lashed out of its curled position and struck a light pole, sending it crashing.

Everyone jumped back—except Dr. Ogden, who stared in disbelief.

The body unrolled further, twisting in savage S-curves. Then it began to flop and jerk on the floor like a hooked marlin. Violent tremors flowed through its frame in waves of convulsions.

The biologist stepped closer, one arm stretching out in amazement, as if he needed to touch it to make it real. "It's reviving."

"Doctor . . ." Bratt warned.

The beast flopped toward Ogden. Its maw split wide, revealing a shark's jagged dentition. It snapped blindly at the biologist, coming within inches of his fingers. Ogden danced back, cradling his hand as if it had actually been bitten.

Bratt had had enough. He reached forward and yanked Ogden back, then shoved everyone behind him, rifle appearing in his hands.

The doctor stumbled next to him. "It's amazing!"

Bratt opened his mouth, but he felt a sharp buzzing behind his ears. His jaw vibrated like a tuning fork. It was a familiar feeling. Working on a sub, he had been exposed to intense sonar. He knew what he was feeling.

Others felt it, too, rubbing at their ears.

Ultrasonics . . .

"Look!" one of the students said, pointing to the EEG machines.

Bratt glanced over. The slow sine waves were now spiking and racing. The two specimens attached to the lead were now beginning to tremble. Another tail whipped from its frozen curl.

They all fled to the crevice opening.

"I can't believe it," Ogden said, digging one finger in an ear. "I think the first beast is calling to the others."

"With sonar," Bratt said, jaw buzzing.

"Early whale song," the biologist corrected. "The *Ambulocetus* is a progenitor of the modern cetacean species. The ultrasonics must act as a biological trigger, waking others of its pod. Perhaps even calling others to it. A defense mechanism. The better to protect each another."

The thrashings spread. Equipment crashed. The ultrasonic keening grew worse.

Off to the side, the first creature lay panting, gulping air through its gaped jaws. It then rolled to its belly, unstable, shaking, cold.

"Someone shoot the damn things!" the girl urged in a high-pitched voice.

Bratt hefted his weapon up.

The biologist stared from the gun to the wobbly creature. "Are you crazy? This is the discovery of the century . . . and you want to kill it? We need to protect them!"

Bratt kept his tone civil but firm. "Sir, this ain't no *Free Willy* situation going on here. Right now, I'm more worried about protecting *us*." He grabbed the smaller doctor by the elbow and shoved him down the cleft. "And in case you hadn't noticed, these things look more like great whites, than plankton-munching humpbacks. I think they can protect themselves just fine."

Ogden began to protest, but Bratt turned away and faced Washburn. "Move 'em out, Lieutenant."

She nodded, one eye on the thrashing monsters.

Bratt herded everyone behind him as they retreated. Once clear of the cliff, they hurried across the ice lake.

"The Russians must have known about this," Odgen droned. "It must be why they are trying to commandeer the station. They want the glory for themselves."

Bratt knew the doctor was wrong. He was one of the few who knew what lay hidden within the lab on Level Four. It was *not* glory the Russians sought, but silence and cover-up.

As they reached the far side, Washburn shouted from a few steps back. "Commander! We've got company!"

He swung around.

From the cleft in the cliff face, one of the creatures slid out onto the ice. Another followed it . . . then another . . .

They wobbled on their feet, shaky but determined. And after fifty thousand years, they were probably damn hungry, too.

"They're waking up fast," Ogden said, respect clear in his voice.

Bratt waved toward the exit. "Out!" he yelled. "Everyone get moving!"

Across the ice lake, three heads swiveled toward the sound of his voice. He again felt the buzzing surge sweep over him. The goddamn things were pinging him with their sonar.

"Shit," he swore, raising his rifle as he retreated. They were being hunted!

Two more creatures slipped from the cliff.

"Washburn, get everyone moving down the tunnel. *Now!* You know the way. I'll keep any of these beasties from getting too close."

He lifted his rifle.

"Don't!" Ogden begged.

"Professor, this time it ain't up for debate."

11:58 A.M.
OUT ON THE ICE . . .

Matt's spine felt like jelly. For well over an hour, the driver of the Sno-Cat, a petty officer named Frank O'Donnell, had been racing the treaded vehicle at top speed, oblivious to the rough terrain. It was like riding a paint shaker. Every bone in his body felt rattled and bruised.

He stared out at the blowing snow. Winds battered the vehicle. He had long given up any hope of dissuading the Navy men from their goal of reaching the Russian ice station. His only concession was that the driver had tried to raise the other Sno-Cat every five minutes.

Nobody answered.

They had also tried to raise someone at the base on the short band, but their luck wasn't any better there. It was as if they were alone out here.

Matt's fear for Jenny had developed into a grapefruit-sized stone in his gut. He found it hard to concentrate on his own situation.

"There's the station!" O'Donnell called back to them, and pointed straight ahead. Relief cheered his voice. "Looks like they left the goddamn light on at least."

Matt leaned forward, glad for the distraction from his worries. Craig glanced to him, eyes bright.

Ahead, a wall of ice rose in mountainous pressure ridges. Snow blasted horizontally across the landscape, obscuring any details. But near the base of one peak, a glow cut through the midday gloom.

"I don't see any station," Craig said.

"It's all underground," the driver explained "The entire facility."

The Sno-Cat aimed for the glowing beacon, bouncing over ridged ice. Matt spotted other vehicles, half covered in snow, sheltered in ravines between ridges. There was even a sailboat anchored with its sails snugged down. The Cat passed them all, continuing straight for the glowing opening.

"Fuck!" Lieutenant Greer's outburst startled everyone.

Eyes turned to where he had his face pressed to the side window. Out in the blizzard, Matt saw something impossible. Crashing through the ice, a submarine conning tower climbed from the depths, steaming and sluicing water.

"The Russians!" Pearlson hissed. "They beat us here!"

Matt noted the polynya through which the submarine surfaced. It was small, too small for the large Russian sub. Little room for more than the conning tower.

"What are we going to do?" Matt asked.

"I'm almost out of gas," O'Donnell said.

Greer was senior officer here. He didn't hesitate, thinking quickly. "Make for the station!"

Matt nodded, silently agreeing. They needed cover. It was death to stay out here. Surely the submarine's hydrophones had heard their Cat trundling over the ice. The Russians would know they were here.

O'Donnell kicked the slowing Sno-Cat back up to full speed. Matt bounced to the ceiling as the vehicle struck a particularly sharp ridge.

"Hang on!" O'Donnell yelled.

Matt rubbed his head and sat back. *Now he tells me.*

Greer clutched the seat back in front of him. "O'Donnell . . ."

"I see them, sir!"

Matt glanced over to the sub. Men in white parkas climbed to the top of the sub's flying bridge. Arms pointed toward them.

The Sno-Cat made a sharp turn, racing toward the base's opening.

"Slow down!" Craig yelled from the front seat, arms braced against the dashboard.

Matt's eyes widened as he realized what the driver intended. "You've got to be kidding . . ."

O'Donnell jammed the Sno-Cat forward. It flew straight at the tunnel.

Gunfire suddenly erupted. Slugs tore into the back end of the Cat, sounding as if someone had tossed a flaming bundle of firecrackers into their trunk. The noise deafened. Glass shattered out of the rear window.

Matt might have shouted, but it was hard to tell.

Then the Cat hit the tunnel.

O'Donnell downshifted and slammed the brakes hard. But the Cat's momentum was unimpressed by his efforts. It shot down the stairs, rear end flying high, bouncing off the ice ceiling. The back of the cabin crumpled under the collision—then the Cat rebounded to the stairs with a squeal of treads.

The passengers became a tangle of flailing limbs. More glass showered upon them.

Matt caught a glimpse of steel doors in the headlamps ahead.

Then they struck with an impact that slammed everyone forward. Matt flew over the front seat, striking the windshield with his shoulder. The window popped from its frame. He rolled out onto the hood, half draped in safety glass. He slid all the way to the floor beyond, landing in a graceless heap in front.

At least they had stopped.

"Are you all right?" Craig asked as Matt pushed to his feet. The reporter leaned forward out the cab. His scalp injury had reopened. Blood trailed over his face.

"Better than you," Matt answered, testing his limbs to make sure he wasn't lying.

O'Donnell groaned, cradling his side. He must have hit the steering wheel hard, bruising some ribs. In the backseat, Greer and Pearlson were already up, staring out the shattered back window, watching for the Russians.

Matt surveyed the state of their transportation. The Sno-Cat was jammed in the doorway, a plug in a storm drain. "Nothing like door-to-door service."

"Everybody out!" Greer ordered from the backseat, retrieving his weapon from the floor. He pointed toward Matt and the station.

The doors were pinned by the station's frame, but with the windshield gone, they had a ready-made exit. Matt helped them clamber over the hood.

"Move deeper down!" Greer yelled as he climbed through last, waving them ahead. "The Sno-Cat's wreckage will slow the Russians, but who knows for how long."

As a group, they hurried down the passage. Greer caught up with Matt. He shoved a 9mm Beretta pistol at him. "Do you know how to use this?"

"I served in the Green Berets."

Greer glanced harder at him, judging him anew, then slapped the gun into his hand. "Good, then you won't shoot your goddamn foot off."

Matt hefted the weapon. "Not unless it would get me out of this mess."

Within a few more yards, the entrance tunnel emptied into a large circular space with rooms opening off it. Tables and chairs were spread around a central staircase. Half-eaten meals dotted some of the tabletops. They searched the space as they crossed it, weapons ready.

It was empty.

"Where is everyone?" Matt asked.

Running, Greer led them down the stairs. The second level was just as empty.

"They're gone," Pearlson said, shocked.

"Evacuated," Greer corrected. "The *Polar Sentinel* must have gotten wind of the attack and come directly here. Cleared the base."

"Great," Matt said. "We came all the way out here to warn them, and they've already rolled up shop."

"What are we going to do?" Craig asked, half his face bloody, the other half ashen.

Greer continued taking them deeper. "There's an old weapons locker on the third level. Grenades, old rifles. We'll grab as much as we can carry."

"Then what?"

"We hide. We survive."

"I like the last part of your plan," Matt said.

As they reached the third level, gunfire suddenly sounded, echoing to them. It didn't come from above them—but *below*.

"Someone's still here," Craig said, eyes wide.

"It sounds like it came from the level just under us," Pearlson said.

"Let's go!" Greer led the way.

As they set off, an explosion blasted from above. Everyone froze again.

"The Russians," Matt said.

"Hurry!" Greer ordered and continued down the stairs.

Voices called out above them. Orders shouted in Russian. Footsteps echoed, running.

Craig and Matt fled down the steps after Greer. Pearlson and O'Donnell maintained their rear guard. They hit the fourth level. Here, instead of a common open area like the tiers above, the stairs opened onto a long hall.

It was empty, too. But a set of double doors blocked the far end.

"The Crawl Space," Pearlson said behind them.

"It's a good place to hide," Greer said. "A fucking maze. C'mon!"

"But who was shooting?" Craig asked as they ran.

Matt wanted to know, too.

Greer frowned and growled, "Pray it's *our* guys."

Matt took the lieutenant's suggestion to heart. They needed reinforcements. But this, of course, begged another question.

If it was the good guys, what were they shooting at?

Dead End

ᐅᒥᖅᕹᒪᕐᖄ ᓄᖃᒍᐊᓂ

In the gloom of the bone nest, the massive creature crept toward Amanda's hiding place, hunched, suspicious, unsure. Its maw gaped open, teeth bloody. Claws still trailed shredded bits of Lacy's racing suit.

Pressing deeper into the crack in the ice, Amanda sensed an ultrasonic wailing from the grendel, which she felt in her jawbone, the roots of her teeth, the hairs on the back of her neck. It kept her frozen, like a rabbit in headlights.

Go away, she begged with all her heart. She had been holding her breath for so long, stars began to glow across her vision. She dared not exhale. Small rivulets of cold sweat ran down her exposed face.

Please . . .

The grendel approached within a foot of her niche. Silhouetted against the glow from the outer cavern, the beast's features were shadowed. Only its two eyes still captured some of the light reflected off the ice walls.

Crimson . . . bloody . . . emotionless and as cold as the press of ice overhead.

Amanda met that gaze, knowing she would die.

Then the beast whipped its head around, back toward the exit tunnel. The creature's sudden movement drew a startled breath from Amanda. She couldn't hold it any longer. She tensed, fearing she had given herself away.

But the beast ignored her and shambled fully around, facing the tunnel now. It cocked its head, one way then the other, plainly listening.

Amanda had no way of knowing what it heard. Was someone coming? Was Connor still alive, screaming for help?

Whatever it was, the grendel lashed its tail a few times, then dashed toward the tunnel, shooting its low form up and away.

Amanda remained in her niche for one long, trembling shake, then fell out. She stumbled over to the tunnel on weak legs. Stars continued to dance across her vision, more from fear than anoxia. She hunched by the tunnel in time to see the shadowed bulk of the beast lope away, aiming toward the cliff.

Fearing the silent unknown more than the beast, Amanda climbed up the slotted passage. She used her crampons for purchase on the slippery slope, ducking as the ceiling lowered. When she reached the end, she poked her head out.

To the side, the grendel scaled the ice cliff, racing like a gecko up a stucco wall. It vanished over the edge, moving fast, clearly on the hunt.

Amanda's eyes settled on the blue poly-line still draped over the cliff's edge.

She stared at the rope.

It was her only hope.

Amanda rolled out of the slot and to her feet. She rushed to the cliff, praying the rope was still attached to whatever was left of Connor. The last she had seen, the geologist had the poly-line wrapped around his chest.

She reached the cliff and wrapped her gloved fingers around the rope.

Please, God . . .

She tugged on the rope. It seemed to hold. She leaned out, testing her weight. It still held.

Tears welled in her eyes as she mounted the wall. She climbed, hand over hand, crampons dug deep into the ice. Fear fueled her muscles. Fatigue was impossible. She clawed and kicked her way to the top.

Reaching the edge, she heaved herself over and landed only inches from the macerated form of Connor MacFerran. His helmet lamp shone toward the ceiling, a beacon in the dark tunnels.

Amanda twisted away. She crawled to her feet, trying to keep her eyes away from the ravaged wreckage. Like Lacy, his belly had been ripped open. Blood pooled around him, a frozen stain on the ice. It was this last that had allowed Amanda to scale the cliff. During her hour down below, the ruin of Connor's body had frozen to the ice, becoming a bloody anchor for her escape.

With a hand over her mouth and a prayer of forgiveness on her lips, she bent down and undid the geologist's helmet. She needed his light. Working the chin strap, she could not look away from Connor. His left eye and nose were torn away, raked by a claw. His throat had been ripped out just at the collarbone. His beard was a frozen matt of blood.

She finally freed the helmet, sobbing now.

Then she stood and put the helmet on. It was too big. It hung crooked, but she snugged the chin strap. She faced down the long tunnel. There was no sign of the grendel.

As she stepped away, a glint caught her eye. She turned. A small ice ax lay on the ground. It was Connor's. He had worn it at his belt. He must have tried to use it to protect himself.

She hurried and collected it. Though it was just a hand tool, it gave her a measure of relief.

She returned to the tunnel, girding herself for the terrifying journey ahead. But as she fingered the handle to the ice ax, another memory was triggered. Earlier, when she had confronted Connor about searching for Lacy by himself, he had waved off her concern. Everyone was too busy, he had claimed. But then he had said something else. The words returned to her now.

Besides, I have a walkie-talkie.

Amanda spun around.

She dropped back to Connor's body. She searched his ripped goose-down vest, leaking feathers and stuffing, and found the small handheld radio.

Kneeling, she twisted the dial. A small red battery light glowed. She pressed the walkie-talkie to her lips. "This is Amanda Reynolds." She struggled to modulate her voice, trying to whisper, but fearing no one would hear her if she were too faint. "If anyone can hear me, I'm trapped in the Crawl Space. There is a large predator hunting the tunnels. It killed Lacy Devlin and Connor MacFerran. It is loose now, off somewhere . . . I don't know where. I'm going to attempt to reach the upper levels. Please . . . please, if you read this, bring weapons. I will broadcast my location as soon as I can reach any of the marked tunnels."

She placed her fingers over the radio's speaker. *Please, someone be listening.* She waited, trying to feel any vibration in the speaker, some sign that someone was communicating with her, but there was nothing.

She stood again and faced the dark tunnel. The beam from her helmet lamp pierced ahead. She held the radio in one hand, the ice pick in the other.

She had to get out of the Crawl Space.

Then she'd be safe.

12:15 P.M.
ABOARD THE *DRAKON*

His men had performed flawlessly.

Captain First Rank Anton Mikovsky stood watch atop the submarine's periscope stand, hands behind his back. He wore his underway uniform: green tunic and pants, cuffs tucked into boots. Reports continued to flow from battle stations.

All areas remained green.

He was taking no chances. Word from the shore team confirmed that Ice Station Grendel had been secured. The Americans who had crashed through the station's doors in a Sno-Cat were still missing. The group—five men—had holed away like frightened rabbits, vanishing into the depths of the station. But they would be found. It was only a matter of time. The rest of the station was empty, cleared out by the submarine they had heard taking on ballast less than an hour ago.

Mikovsky knew his opponent. A United States research sub. The USS *Polar Sentinel*. It was no threat. It was an experimental model, unarmed. Surely by now it was fleeing with its evacuees. He was under orders not to pursue.

His primary mission was to occupy the base, secure it, set up a communication station, then dive to patrol the waters against the real threat. In the Arctic, the enemy was the fast-attack subs that constantly patrolled under the polar cap.

Their window on this mission was exactly twelve hours. *Vhodi, vidi.* Get in, get out. The confusion over at Prudhoe Bay would slow his opponents.

"Captain." The radioman of the watch strode over to him. "I was able to raise Omega base."

"Very good." He climbed from the periscope stand and crossed to the communication shack. The radioman passed him the handset. "Captain Mikovsky here. I must speak to Admiral Petkov."

Through the static, words cut in and out. "Right away, Captain. The admiral has been awaiting your call."

On hold, Mikovsky planned his words. Admiral Petkov had remained behind at Omega, to interrogate the prisoners and search the U.S. base. Petkov wanted to make certain that whatever the Russian government sought inside Ice Station Grendel hadn't already been transferred to the U.S. science labs at the research base.

Mikovsky had never seen a man so driven, yet so calm at the same time. It was disquieting. There were currents that ran through the man that were icier than anything found out here in the arctic. Petkov's nickname—*Beliy Prizrak,* the White Ghost—was disturbingly fitting. A week ago, when Mikovsky had first been granted this mission to captain a flagship alongside an admiral from the Northern Fleet, he had been thrilled and honored. He had basked in the envy of his fellow ranked officers. But now . . . now he was happy the admiral was off his boat.

As if he heard him from afar, Petkov's voice came on the line, stolid and emotionless. "Captain, what is your status?"

He swallowed hard, caught off guard. "Grendel is secure, sir. The station was evacuated just as you suspected, but there are five hostiles unaccounted." He quickly recounted the crash of the Sno-Cat into the station. "I've doubled the strike team to twenty men. They will perform a level-by-level sweep. I will forward the all clear for your arrival."

"I'm heading out there now. Has the nuclear charge been offloaded to the station?"

"Y-yes, sir." Mikovsky pictured the meter-wide titanium sphere. As ordered, it had been bolted to the floor on the deepest level of the station. "But, Admiral, there's no need for you to come here until we're entirely secure. Procedure—"

"I don't care if you find these Americans or not. Lock down the base, especially Level Four. I'm heading out with the hovercraft teams. Take your boat down immediately.

Maintain deep patrol. Rendezvous scheduled at Grendel at sixteen hundred."

"Yes, sir." He checked his watch. *Less than three hours.* "*Drakon* will surface-at-ice here again at exactly sixteen hundred."

"Very good." The static went silent as the Ghost vanished into the ether.

Mikovsky turned to the radioman. "Get me the strike-team leader."

"Yes, sir."

A commotion drew his attention to the sonar team. They were bent over the various arrays, arguing.

He crossed to them. "What's wrong?"

The sonar chief snapped up. "We've picked up an anomaly. But it makes no sense."

"What sort of anomaly?"

"Multiple active sonar signals. Very weak."

"Coming from where?" Mikovsky's mind instantly ran through possible sources: the U.S. research sub, the approach of a fast-attack submarine, perhaps even surface ships beyond the cap. The answer was even more disturbing.

The chief looked up at him. "The signals originate from *inside* the station."

12:22 A.M.
ICE STATION GRENDEL

Pistol in hand, Matt followed Lieutenant Greer through the double doors, leaving behind the organized structure of the ice station for the free-form flow of ice tunnels, chutes, sudden cliffs, and caves. Craig stuck to his side, trailed by stone-eyed Pearlson and a wincing O'Donnell. They ran down into the depths of the maze.

Greer had the only flashlight, found near the entrance. His light danced over the walls as he ran, igniting the dark ice to a shimmering blue. It was like racing through the bowels of an ice sculpture.

"Do you know where you're going?" Craig asked.

"Someone's down here," Greer said. "We need to hook up with them."

"How big is this Crawl Space?" Matt asked.

"Big" was the only response.

They continued to run, knowing the Russians weren't far behind. Distance was more important than direction.

Zigzagging down the tunnels, they fled deeper into the depths of the ice island. As they reached a crossing of passages, gunfire erupted again. Automatic fire, from up ahead. But which tunnel?

They all stopped.

"Which way?" Pearlson asked.

The answer came a moment later. Light bloomed down to the right. Frantic and bobbling. More shots. Loud and deafening in the close spaces.

"Here comes trouble," Matt said, pointing his Beretta down the tunnel.

Shouts could be heard now.

The Navy patrol raised their weapons.

Around a bend in the tunnel, the light bloomed brighter, illuminating a running figure. A young man stumbled into view, slipping and sliding despite the sandy floors. He scrambled, arms out, as if grasping for help. He was clearly not military, evident from his shoulder-length brown hair, North Face parka, and Thinsulate dry pants.

He fell toward them. Matt expected the man would beg for help. Instead he ran right through them. "Run!" he yelled in passing.

More figures appeared, racing at full tilt: an older bald man, a twentysomething girl, and another young man. A tall, striking black woman in military blue led this group.

"Washburn!" O'Donnell called out when she came into sight.

"Pick up your balls and get moving!" she barked back at him.

More gunfire blazed behind the group. Muzzle fire framed the last figure, another sailor. He dropped to one knee, firing a barrage behind him. Lit by a flashlight's beam, the distant tunnel glowed like a blue snake winding deep into the ice.

"What's the matter?" Greer asked.

Beyond the kneeling gunman, Matt spotted a darkness flowing up the tunnel.

What the hell?

Washburn led her charges to them. She screamed to be heard over the gunfire. "We have to get out of these tunnels . . . *now!*"

"We can't," Greer said as Washburn pounded to them. "The Russians—"

"Fuck the Russians!" Washburn said, panting hard. "We've got a hell of a lot worse on *our* asses!" She waved the others ahead of her.

The gunfire died. The other sailor was on his feet and sprinting toward them. He fumbled to replace his rifle's spent magazine. "Go, go, go!"

Greer jabbed a finger at O'Donnell and Pearlson. "You and you. Take the civilians back up."

O'Donnell nodded. He grabbed Craig by the elbow and took off with the panicked folk. Matt shook off Pearlson's attempt to do the same.

The seaman shrugged and headed up on his own, but he called over his shoulder back to his lieutenant. "What about the Russians, sir?"

Fuck the Russians. Matt was still stunned by the woman's response.

Greer's reply was more useful. "Take them as far as the Crawl Space exit. Then wait for us!"

The only acknowledgment was a quick turn on a heel, and the group continued their headlong flight up the tunnel.

The last Navy man reached them.

"Commander Bratt," Greer said, sounding surprised.

"Prepare to lay down cover fire!" Urgently, Bratt spun around, dropping to a knee. He ripped a fresh magazine from his coat and slapped it home.

Greer joined his senior officer, standing behind him, rifle pointed over Bratt's shoulder. He passed his flashlight into Matt's free hand.

Matt glanced between the retreating party and the two stationary gunmen. He debated which was best—to stay or go. His only other choice was to flee blindly down some side tunnel and get lost. No option seemed wiser than another, so he simply stood his ground.

He stepped to Bratt's other shoulder.

Bratt glanced up at him, then away. "Who the hell are you?"

Matt raised his pistol, pointing it past the officer. "Right now, I'm a guy covering your ass."

"Then welcome to the party," Bratt grumbled back.

"What's coming?" Greer asked on the other side.

"Your worst goddamn nightmare."

From beyond the reach of the flashlight, red eyes reflected back at them. Matt's head began to buzz oddly, like mosquitoes whirling in his skull.

"Here they come!" Bratt said, sucking in a breath.

A massive snowy-skinned creature striped in red . . . no, *blood* . . . thundered into view. It filled the tunnel, weeping red from multiple gunshot wounds. Gouged tracks furrowed its sides. The side of its face was raw hamburger. But it kept coming.

What the hell was it?

Other shadows could be seen in brief glimpses behind it.

The lead beast charged toward them. Claws tore at the ice.

The buzzing grew louder in Matt's skull.

Then a barrage of rifle fire erupted, startling Matt to react. He aimed the 9mm pistol, but he knew the gun was useless.

No more than the Alaskan grizzly, such a meager weapon would never bring down this creature. Several of the fresh wounds had been direct strikes between the monster's eyes.

And still the beast ripped toward them, keeping its domed forehead low, charging like a bull, using its thick rubbery skin and insulating blubber as a bulletproof shield, a natural battering ram.

Matt pulled his trigger, more in blind fear than with any real hope for a kill shot.

"Damn things won't die!" Bratt confirmed.

Matt continued to fire, squeezing round after round, until the pistol's slide locked open.

Out of bullets.

Greer noticed. "Go!" he ordered, tossing his head in the direction of the retreating party, now vanished. His voice vibrated from his own rifle's recoil as he passed a radio at Matt. "Channel four."

Matt took the radio, ready to flee.

Then the lead beast crashed to the ice, as if slipping, legs going limp. It slid farther on the ice, nose dragging, then stopped. Its eyes remained staring at them, still reflecting red in the flashlight. But there was no longer life behind them.

Dead.

The buzzing in Matt's head faded to a nagging itch behind his ears.

Bratt regained his feet. "Pull back."

The beast's bulk blocked the remaining creatures, but the animals still could be seen moving behind the mound of macerated flesh.

Matt and the two Navy men retreated to the next intersection of tunnels. Rifles continued to point at the dead bulk plugging the tunnel.

"That should hold them for now," Greer said.

The bull's body jolted forward, sliding toward them, shouldering over slightly. Then it stopped again.

"You had to say that," Matt muttered, backing away.

Greer sneered. "What the fuck?"

The bulk began sliding again.

"The others are pushing from behind!" Bratt said, amazed more than terrified. "Shit!"

The buzzing in Matt's head, dulled a moment ago, flared anew. But he sensed it came from a new direction, like someone looking over his shoulder. Matt swung toward the neighboring cross tunnel.

As his flashlight turned, a pair of red eyes glowed back at him.

Only ten yards away.

Matt jerked his pistol up, pure reflex, as the creature charged.

From the corner of his eye, he spotted the still open slide on his weapon.

Nope, still out of bullets.

12:49 P.M.

Unable to determine what drew the grendel away, Amanda had no clue as to its whereabouts now. Connor's mining helmet hung crooked on her head, casting a slanting beam of light down the tunnel, hitting an orange spray-painted marker on the wall.

Lacy Devlin's trail marker.

Amanda searched farther down the wall. *Please . . .*

Another painted spot appeared against the blue ice: a green diamond. Lacy's path had finally crossed another. A sob escaped Amanda. She had reached the mapped areas of the Crawl Space at last.

She raised the handheld radio and pressed the transmit button. "If anyone's listening, I've found another trail. Green diamonds. I'm following it up. I've seen no sign of the beast for the past hour. But please help me."

She clicked the radio off, preserving the battery, and prayed. If only someone *was* listening . . .

In dead silence, she increased her pace.

As she followed one diamond to the next, she judged she must be close to the inhabited areas of the ice cavern system. Taking a chance, she reached up and twisted her helmet lamp, extinguishing her sole source of light.

Darkness closed around her, close and claustrophobic.

She was now deaf *and* blind.

After half a minute, her eyes adjusted to the press of black ice. She scanned around, first with her eyes, then slowly swiveling her head.

She found what she had been seeking.

Overhead, a faint star glowed deep in the ice, a pool of brightness. Someone was down here with flashlights.

As she stared, standing stationary, the glow suddenly split into two tinier stars, fainter but distinct. Each glow flew quickly away from the other.

One rose higher and away, a fading star, waning, then gone.

The other shot in her direction. Growing brighter, moving fast.

Searchers . . . someone had surely heard her.

She feared calling out, especially knowing what else lurked in these dark tunnels. Her best chance was to shorten the distance between the moving glow and herself. She twisted her helmet lamp back on.

In the glare of her small bulb, the other glow disappeared. She hated to extinguish the only sign of hope, but it was too dangerous to traverse the ice maze in the dark—and she dared not lose the trail of green diamonds. If her rescuers had heard her, it was this path they would search to find her.

She hurried forward, stopping every other minute to turn off her light and check her bearings in relation to the rescue party.

And she did one other thing at each stop.

12:52 P.M.

"I'm still following the trail of green diamonds. But please be careful. The predator that killed Lacy and Connor is still loose somewhere in these tunnels."

In Matt's pocket, the radio passed to him by Greer continued to relay this lost woman's saga. He had already tried to raise her, but she either couldn't pick up the signal or had some malfunction with her radio. Whatever the reason, Matt had his own problems.

He continued his mad flight down the ice tunnel, empty pistol in hand, flashlight in the other.

Five minutes ago, the solitary hunter had charged into the crossroads, separating Matt from the two Navy men, filling the passage. The pair had opened fire, trying to buy Matt time to flee.

It hadn't worked.

After a moment's hesitation, the beast gave chase—a lioness running down the lone gazelle.

With nothing but an empty pistol in hand, Matt ran headlong down the tunnel, slipping and sliding down steep traverses. He barely kept his footing. His shoulders struck with bruising force against walls and outcroppings. But he refused to slow down. He had already seen how fast a bullet-riddled monster moved. He feared the speed of a healthy, undamaged specimen.

For a few long minutes, he had seen no evidence of the monster. Maybe it had slipped away. Even the fuzzy feeling in his head had quieted. It was as if something emanated from them, something outside the wavelength of ordinary hearing.

Now it had vanished.

Dare he hope the beast was gone with it?

The radio crackled again. *"Please . . . if you can hear this, bring help. Bring guns! I'm still on the green diamond trail."*

What the hell did that mean? *Green diamond trail.* It sounded like a Lucky Charms cereal advertisement.

"I've not seen any sign of the grendel now for the past forty-five minutes. It seems to have disappeared. Maybe it fled."

Matt scrunched his brow. *Grendel?* Was that what had attacked them? If so, it seemed this woman knew more about what was down here than anyone else did.

He raced around a corner, skidding on his heels, spinning to make the turn. Ahead the tunnel diverged into two passages. The beam of his flashlight caught a flash of odd color against the ice. A blue circle was painted at the threshold to the right, a green diamond on the left.

Trail markers

Understanding dawned. He chose the left tunnel and continued running, still watching his back, but now also searching for the next green diamond.

Hell, if I'm running, I might as well run toward someone who knows what the hell is going on down here.

Matt continued, winding this way and that. Gravity and the slick slope pulled him deeper and deeper—and still there was no sign of the woman on the radio. It was endless dark ice, and he moved in a glowing blue grotto, lit by his lone flashlight.

"Hello!" The call this time did not come through the radio. It came from ahead of him.

Matt skated around another bend, one hand against the ice wall to balance himself. His flashlight beam rounded the corner and illuminated a strange sight: a tall and shapely woman, naked, painted blue, like some Inuit goddess.

He skidded toward her, realizing that she wasn't naked but instead wore some skintight pale blue unitard, its hood pulled up. She also wore a mining helmet crooked on her head. Its lamp shone in his eyes.

"Thank God!" she cried, hurrying toward him.

Her features became clear when she switched off her lamp. The confusion in her eyes spread over her face.

"Who are you?" She glanced past him. "Where are the others?"

"If you're looking for a rescue party, you'll have to settle for me." He lifted the useless pistol in his hand. "Though I'm not sure I'm going to do you much good."

"And you are?" she asked again. Her words were slightly slurred, her voice unusually loud. Was she drunk?

"Matthew Pike, Alaskan Fish and Game."

"Fish and Game?" Her confusion deepened. "Could you lower your flashlight? I . . . I'm deaf, and I'm having trouble reading your lips against the glare."

He lowered his light. "Sorry. I'm one of the group being shuttled from Omega."

She nodded, understanding. But suspicion also glinted. "What's going on? Where's everyone else?"

"The station's been evacuated. The Russians attacked Omega."

"My God . . . I don't understand."

"And they're now in the process of commandeering the facility here, too. But what about you? Who are you? Why are you down here alone?"

She moved closer, but her eyes flickered between him and the tunnel behind him. "I'm Dr. Amanda Reynolds. Head of Omega Drift Station." She told him an abbreviated, hurried story of missing scientists and the sudden attack by the giant ice predator.

"You called them grendels over the walkie-talkie," he said as she finished her bloody tale. "Like you knew about them."

"We found frozen remains here. Down in some ice cavern. They were supposed to be fifty thousand years old, dating back to the last ice age. Some type of extinct species."

Extinct, my ass, he thought. Aloud he related his own experiences since the Russian attack, keeping a watch on the tunnels with his flashlight.

"So there's more than one grendel . . ." she mumbled, her voice a whisper. "Of course, there must be. But how have they remained hidden for so long?"

"They're not hiding now. If this is some frozen nest, it's

too dangerous to remain down here. Do you know another trail to the surface? With what was on my scent, maybe we'd better get off this green diamond trail. Try another."

She pointed forward. "This trail should lead to others. But I'm not that familiar with the Crawl Space. My guess is that they all end eventually at the exit."

"Let's hope so. C'mon." Matt headed out, going slowly now, cautious, backtracking up. "We need to watch for any sign of the grendels: spoor, scratched marks in the ice. Avoid those areas."

She nodded. He had to respect this woman. She had faced one of these beasts alone and survived. And now she sought to escape with nothing but a walkie-talkie and a small ice ax. All the while deaf to what might be out there.

"With a bit of luck," she said, "we won't run into any more of them."

Matt turned just as a wave of buzzing cut through his skull, rattling the tiny bones in his ears.

He felt a frantic clutch on his elbow. Amanda pulled beside him. Even deaf, she must have felt the reverberation. And from the way her fingers cut into his right biceps, she knew its implication.

Their luck had just run out.

Blood on the Ice

ᐊᒍᐃᖃᑕᐅᖅ ᓯᑯᒥ

After an hour in front of the space heater, Jenny felt almost thawed—and oddly reenergized. Maybe it was the caffeine, maybe it was the morphine, maybe it was the stupidity of their plan.

Moments ago, word had reached them that the Russian submarine had left. This news came from a seaman who had been found hiding in one of the research shacks by the Russian forces and tossed into the barracks to join the rest of the captives. The seaman had witnessed the sub's departure.

"Do you have any estimate of how many Russians are still here?" Lieutenant Sewell asked him, kneeling beside the newly arrived sailor.

The man shivered in his seat, his hands soaking in a bowl of warm water. His teeth chattered as he answered. "Not for certain, sir. I spotted some ten men, but there have to be more I didn't see."

"So, more than ten," Sewell said, his lips thin with worry.

The seaman glanced to his senior officer, eyes wide. "Th-

they shot Jenkins. He tried to bolt across the ice. He was going to bug out to the NASA station. Try to use their crawler to get away. They shot him in the back."

Sewell patted the man's shoulder. They had all heard similar reports. It was clear the Russians were under strict orders to lock down this station. One by one, all of the officers and a few of the scientists had been dragged away at gunpoint. But they were returned unharmed, except for one lieutenant who came back with a broken nose.

Interrogation, Sewell had told Jenny. The Russians were clearly searching for something, something that once lay hidden at the lost ice station. They hadn't found it. Yet.

Jenny had caught a glimpse of their interrogator as he stood in the doorway: a tall, stately Russian with a shock of white hair, and a face even paler.

Sewell began to rise from his knee, but the shivering seaman stopped him again, pulling a wet hand from the bath. "Sir, I also saw two Russians dropping a canister into a hole in the ice. Other holes were being drilled."

"Describe the canisters."

"They were the size of minikegs." The seaman shaped them with his dripping hands. "Solid black with bright orange end caps."

"Shit."

Jenny had been leaning over, tying on dry boots. She straightened. "What are they?"

"Russian incendiary charges. V-class explosives." Sewell closed his eyes as he stood up. "They must be planning on melting this entire base into the ocean."

To the side, Kowalski had finished dressing and stood in front of the heater. He held his hands toward the warmth. His fingernails were still tinged slightly blue. "So do we go ahead with our plan?"

"We have no choice. It's becoming clearer and clearer that the Russians' mission here is a plunder-and-purge. They intend to grab what they can and burn everything behind them.

Whatever is over at the Grendel base, the Russians are determined to take it and leave no one to tell the tale."

Kowalski sighed. "Then, as long as they don't find what they're looking for, we live. Once they do, we die."

Sewell didn't even bother responding to the man's statement. He turned instead to Jenny. "Our plan. Still think you can pull off your end?"

Jenny's father placed a hand on her shoulder. She covered it with her own. He didn't want her to go. "I'll make it."

Sewell stared at her a moment, clearly trying to weigh her resolve. She met his hard gaze. He finally nodded. "Let's go."

Kowalski stepped to her side. He towered over her, a gorilla with only slightly less body hair. "You'll need to keep up with me."

She rolled her eyes.

Sewell led them both over to where a pair of sailors had pulled away a section of ceiling and cut through the insulation of the Jamesway hut with plastic knives. Their work was hidden out of direct sight of the guarded doorway. Luckily the Russians mostly kept out of the room, confident about their imprisonment—and rightly so. Where could the captives escape to even if they could get out of the barracks? The prison hut was well patrolled, and beyond the camp lay only a prolonged freezing death.

Their parkas had been confiscated. Only a fool would risk the freezing storm with nothing but the shirt on his back.

To escape here meant certain death.

This grim thought plagued Jenny as she watched the pair of sweating sailors labor overhead. They worked within the gap in the fiberglass insulation, unscrewing an exterior plate in the hut's roof. It was difficult work with only plastic utensils, but they were managing.

A screw fell to the floor from above.

Sewell pointed up. "Normally there's a skylight installed there. One of three. But in the Arctic, where it's dark half the year and continually sunny the other, windows were found to be more of a nuisance, especially as a source of heat loss. So they were plated and sealed."

"One more to go," one of the men grunted overhead.

"Dim the lights." Sewell signaled. The lamps around the immediate area were extinguished.

Jenny pulled a spare blanket around her shoulders and knotted it to form a crude hooded poncho. It was too large for her slight frame, but it was better than nothing. Anything to cut the wind.

The last screw fell. A plate dropped next into the waiting hands of one of the workers. It was followed by a blast of cold air.

Wind whistled inside. Much too noisy. Sewell pointed to a petty officer, who turned up his CD player. The band U2 wailed over the howl of the blizzard outside.

"You'll have to hurry," Sewell said to Kowalski and Jenny. "If anyone chances in here, we'll be discovered. We'll have to reseal the opening ASAP."

Jenny nodded. A bunk bed had been shoved under the opening to use as a makeshift ladder. Jenny scrambled up. She met her father's eyes for a moment, read the worry in them. But he remained silent. They had no choice. She was the best pilot here.

Standing atop the bunk, Jenny reached up through the hole in the ceiling. She gripped the icy edge of the roof. Without gloves, her fingertips immediately froze to the metal, burning. She ignored the cold.

Helped by the two sailors shoving her hips, she pulled up and poked her head into the blizzard. She was immediately blinded by the winds and blowing ice.

She donned her goggles and dropped belly first to the curved roof of the hut and slithered out. She moved carefully, her nose inches from the corrugated exterior. The winds threatened to kite her off the roof. Worse, the Jamesway huts had barrel-shaped roofs, like the older Quonset huts. The roof sloped steeply to the snowy ground on either side.

Jenny straddled the top, clinging as best she could to the ice-coated surface. She carefully crabbed around to see Kowalski miraculously squeeze his bulk through the dimly lit hole, like Jonah squeezing from the blowhole of a metal whale.

He grunted a bit, then signaled her, jabbing a finger toward the windward side of the hut. The pair shimmied and slid on their butts to where the sloping roof went straight down toward the ground. The ice threatened to take them over the edge against their will.

On this side of the Jamesway, snow had built up into a large bank, a frozen wave permanently breaking against the hut, reaching almost to the roof. Kowalski searched from his perch for any Russian guards. Jenny joined him. It looked clear for the moment, but visibility was mere feet in the ground blizzard.

He glanced over to her.

She nodded.

Kowalski led the way. Sliding feetfirst over the edge, he dropped down onto the snowbank, then rolled skillfully down its icy slope. He vanished out of view.

Readying herself, Jenny glanced back to the hole. It had already been closed. There was no turning back. She slid on her cold rear over the icy edge of the roof and fell to the snow.

Now to escape.

She rolled artlessly down the snowbank, losing control of her tumble and landing atop Kowalski. It was like hitting a buried boulder. The collision knocked the wind out of her.

She gasped silently.

Rather than helping her, Kowalski pushed her farther down into the snow. He pointed with his arm.

Beyond the edge of a neighboring hut, a group of shadowy figures hunched against the wind. They were only discernible because of the pool of light cast about them from idling hovercraft bikes.

The pair stayed hidden.

The shadowy group soon mounted their hovercraft. The engines must have been idling because the headlamps immediately rose, swaying in the gusts, then turned away. The wall of winds covered the sound of the engines, giving an eerie quality to the sight.

The vehicles vanished into the empty ice plains. The two remaining guards stalked away and disappeared into the next building.

Jenny watched the glow of the last hovercraft fade out. They could be going to only one place: the Russian ice station. Her thoughts turned to the other Sno-Cat that had vanished, heading in the same direction, carrying Matt and the Seattle reporter.

For the first time in years, Jenny prayed for Matt's safety. She wished she could have spoken the words that bitterness and anger had locked inside her all this time. It seemed so pointless now, so many years wasted in despair.

She whispered soft words into the wind.

I'm sorry . . . Matt, I'm so sorry . . .

Gunfire erupted behind them, loud and near.

"Up!" Kowalski yelled in her ear, yanking her to her feet. *"Run!"*

1:12 P.M.
ICE STATION GRENDEL

Amanda fled alongside the tall stranger. The grendel still remained out of sight farther up the maze of passages, but the buzz of its echolocation filled the back of her head with a fuzzy, scratchy feeling.

It was tracking them, slowly, cautiously, driving them deeper into the ice island.

"What is it waiting for?" Matt asked.

"For our luck to run out," she answered, remembering Lacy Devlin's fate. "One of these times, we're going to turn into a dead end. A blocked passage, a cliff. Then we'll be trapped."

"Deadly and smart . . . a great combination."

Together they rounded a curve of smooth tunnel. The crampons on Amanda's boots gave her traction, but Matt slid, skidding around on the ice. She grabbed his arm to help him keep his footing.

Matt turned to her. "We can't keep this up. We're just heading deeper and deeper down, away from where we want to go."

"What else can we do?" She held up the small ice ax she had taken from Connor. "Face it with this?"

"Not a chance."

"Well, you're Fish and Game. I'm geophysical engineering. This is your department."

Matt bunched his brows. "We need something to lure this thing off our scent. Lay a false track for it to follow. If we could slip past it, get above it, then at least we'd be heading toward the exit as we ran."

Amanda struggled for an answer to this riddle, her mind shifting into objective mode. She reviewed what she knew about the beasts. Little to nothing was the answer, but that did not preclude her from extrapolating hypotheses. The grendels hunted by echolocation, but they were also sensitive to light and perhaps even heat. She remembered her experience in the beast's nest. It hadn't been aware of her hiding place until after it destroyed the flashlight and she had begun to sweat.

Light and heat. She sensed an answer here, but what?

They ran past another crisscrossing of tunnel—then she had it!

"Wait!" she called out, and stopped.

Matt slowed, braking on his heels, one hand on the wall. He turned to her.

Amanda backed to the tunnel crossings. *Light and heat.* She tugged the chin strap to her helmet and pulled it off. She twisted on the lamp so it glowed brightly, then reached to her waist where her air-warming mask was belted in place next to its heater. She unhooked it and dialed the heating element to full burn. It quickly grew warm in her hands.

"What are you thinking?" Matt asked.

She hurried back to the crossroads, eyes scanning for any sign of the hunter. "These creatures hone in on light and heat signatures." She flipped over her mining helmet and crammed the air-warming mask and its heater—now hot to the touch—inside the helmet.

She lifted her creation higher.

Matt joined her and nodded. "A lure for a false trail."

"Let's hope this does the trick." She slipped past him, ducked low to the ice, and flung the helmet down the main tunnel. The yellow helmet skated and spun atop its crown, light twirling like an ambulance siren. It bounced off a wall and disappeared around the bend, carrying her air-warming unit with it.

Amanda stood and faced Matt. "Light and heat. The grendel will hopefully follow after the lure, heading deeper. Once past here, we can sneak behind its back and head up."

"Like tossing a stick for a dog." Matt nodded, eyeing her with more respect. He turned off his flashlight. The only illumination now came from the vanished helmet.

In the darkness, they retreated down the side tunnel and hid behind a tumbled fall of ice blocks. Crouched together, they stared back at the main passage. The glow of the helmet was faint, but it was stable. The helmet must have come to a stop somewhere below. Amanda hoped it rested far enough down the shaft to give them a good lead from the beast.

Now to wait, to see if the grendel took the bait.

1:18 P.M.

Matt knelt on one knee. He spied through a peephole that pierced the tumble of ice. Eyes wide, he strained to soak up every photon of light that illuminated the neighboring passage. He struggled to hear any sign of the beast. All that he could sense was the vague, nagging vibration of the hunting beast's sonar. It was dull—but growing.

The woman's fingers in his hand suddenly spasmed tighter.

Matt spotted it, too. Shifting shadows.

A dark bulk pushed into view, soaking up the feeble glow of the abandoned helmet. The creature filled the passage, shouldering up to the crossroads. In the shadows, it looked as black as oil, though Matt knew it was as pale as bleached bone.

It stopped.

Lips rippled back to show the glint of teeth. Its bulky head swayed to either side. The buzz of its sonar swamped over them. It seemed to vibrate the very darkness, searching for prey.

Matt held perfectly still. Though well hidden by the fall of ice, he feared any movement might attract the beast. Could it sense their body heat through the frozen blocks?

He felt the creature's gaze upon him.

He feared even to blink. *Take the bait, damn you!*

The gaze continued to penetrate the tunnel, suspicious, sensing something. It snorted deep in its throat—then it tossed its head around.

It slunk down the passage, slowly but steadily, drawn toward the light and the heat. Whatever it had sensed from them, it ignored and turned toward the stronger lure.

Then it was gone.

Matt waited a full minute, long enough for the beast to move far down the passage and around the bend. Then he carefully stood and moved back to the main corridor. They didn't dare wait too long. Soon the grendel would learn of their ruse and backtrack here. They needed to put as much distance between the beast and themselves as possible.

Amanda kept beside him. He checked the passage. The shadow of the grendel could be seen sliding around the bend as the beast hunted its false prey.

He signaled Amanda.

They reached the main corridor and headed away into the dark, careful of their steps, feeling with their hands as the distant light of the helmet totally waned away.

After a minute, Matt had to risk using his flashlight, praying that the flare of light didn't attract the grendel. He flicked on the lamp but held his palm over it, muting the glow. The light streamed faintly between his fingers, but it was enough. They increased their speed.

Neither spoke.

As they half ran and half skated along, moving upward in the passageways, Matt grew concerned about other grendels that might be down here. Yet so far there had been no telltale brush of sonar.

He finally risked his own walkie-talkie. He passed the flashlight to Amanda, then pressed the radio to his lips. He whispered, afraid to let his voice carry too far. "Lieutenant Greer? Can you read me? Over."

He listened for an answer, racing a step ahead of Amanda.

A voice answered, faint but audible, "This is Lieutenant Commander Bratt. Where are you?"

Matt frowned. "Hell, if I know. Where are you?"

"We're gathered with the others at the exit to the Crawl Space. Can you reach us?"

"I've found Dr. Reynolds. We'll try our damnedest."

Matt turned to Amanda. Beyond her, echoing up to them, a roar suddenly sounded.

From his expression, Amanda must have noted his distress. "What's wrong?"

"I think Little Willy just discovered our ruse."

Amanda glanced over her shoulder. "It'll be back this way. Take off your boots."

"What?"

"You'll have better traction on the ice."

Nodding, he bent and unlaced his pair of moccasin boots and yanked off his wool socks. The ice was cold, but she was right. He gripped the ice better. Tucking the moccasins into his jacket, he set off at a dead run with Amanda.

Matt raised the radio again. "Matthew Pike here. Dr. Reynolds and I are heading up. But we've got company on our tail."

The answer was immediate. "Then haul ass as best you can. We'll do what we can to help, but we have no way of telling where you are."

Matt noted a splash of paint on the wall as he ran past. *Of course* . . . He raised the radio again. "We're following the tunnels marked with green diamonds! Does that mean anything?"

There was a long pause, then the radio squawked again. "Roger that. Green diamonds. Out."

Matt pocketed the radio in his patched Army jacket, praying they could help. Otherwise, he and Amanda were on their own.

They fled up the tunnels, racing through a series of convoluted passages.

Then Matt felt it: the buzz saw of the beast's sonar.

The bastard had found them.

As he reached the end of a particularly long, straight chute, Matt glanced behind him. A pair of red eyes blinked into existence. Across twenty yards, they matched gazes: predator and prey.

A rumbled growl flowed from the grendel.

The challenge was given.

The final chase was on.

1:22 P.M.
OMEGA DRIFT STATION

Jenny fled with Kowalski across the snow. They ducked low
as they ran, limiting their silhouettes. Wind shoved against
their shoulders, trying to force them back. The edges of
Jenny's makeshift woolen poncho flapped and snapped. She
used one hand to clutch the hood around her head, pulling
the corners up over her mouth and nose, leaving only the
goggles exposed.

They trudged on. The winds, the snow, the ice . . . all
made their escape slow and torturous. The exposed inches of
her skin already burned. But she dared not let up the fight.

Behind them, the sounds of gunfire cracked and echoed
through the blizzard—but the shots weren't directed at
them. As planned, Sewell and the others had feigned a
frontal assault, a rush at the barracks doors, intending to
draw attention from the fleeing pair. The Russians would be
forced to call for reinforcements to the barracks.

Jenny prayed no one was killed, but fear for her father
was foremost in her mind.

Especially since their plan was feeble: get aloft, call for
help, and ride the winds to the coast.

They rounded another building. The base's parking lot appeared ahead. Across the ice field, shadowed mounds
marked the resting places of various snow machines, a wintry cemetery of abandoned vehicles.

But there was no sign of the plane. With visibility down
to a few yards, it lay cloaked somewhere deeper out in the
snowstorm.

Crouched in the lee of the hut, Jenny tried to get her bearings. Blinded by the blizzard, they might walk right past the
Otter without even seeing it. And they didn't have the time
to wander around and around. If the Russians didn't kill
them, the weather would.

Now that they had stopped, the cold sank through the layers of Jenny's clothing, seeking the marrow of her bones. Her cheeks felt like they'd been scrubbed with a wire brush. She rubbed circulation into them with her palms. Her fingers felt swollen, like numb sausages.

They waited for the winds to let up for a single breath, hoping for the briefest glimpse of their target out on the ice field. But the winds didn't cooperate. They continued to blow steady and strong, as sure as any ocean current.

Finally Kowalski's patience wore thin. "Let's go!" he hissed in her ear. "We can't wait any longer."

Behind them, the gunfire had died away. Sewell's feigned insurrection had already been shut down. If the Russians performed a head count, they would come up with two short, and a search would start. They had to be gone before that happened.

Kowalski shouldered his way back into the full force of the wind. Jenny followed, using his broad back as a windbreak. They crossed through the parking lot and out into the scoured ice fields.

After ten steps, Jenny glanced over a shoulder.

The base had already vanished into the storm. Even the lights seemed more mirage than real.

They continued into the ice field. Jenny sought any sign of her aircraft. But they moved inside a white bubble, a snow globe continually shaken and swirled. They moved slowly, placing one foot in front of the other, aiming as straight as they could.

Minutes passed. Jenny grew concerned. *Surely we should have reached the Otter by now.*

Then a flickering light appeared. Kowalski swore. It had to be one of the base's peripheral lamp poles, run off the generators. Disoriented, they had somehow circled back. But it made no sense. The wind was still in their faces.

A shadow suddenly darted through the weak glow. Dark and low to the ground . . . coming at them.

Jenny and Kowalski froze.

It moved too fast to discern any details.

Out of the storm, the dark beast lunged.

Kowalski bent to take the brunt of the charge, a bear about to take on a lion.

Then in a blink, the snow swirled, transforming shadowy beast into heartfelt companion.

"Bane!" Jenny dove around the Navy seaman and stepped into the wolf's lunge. The huge canine knocked her back onto her rear. A hot tongue sought her cold skin.

The wolf could not push any closer to her, trying to merge his form with hers, scrambling, whining.

The light, borne aloft, approached. It was not a lamp pole, but a figure bearing a burning flare in hand. The shape, obscured by a thick parka, stepped toward them.

Jenny noted one thing immediately. It was a *blue* parka—not white.

U.S. Navy.

"I knew it had to be either you or your husband," the newcomer said. Relief rang in his voice. It was Tom Pomautuk, the ensign left in charge of Bane. "Bane started whining, then suddenly ripped out of his lead."

Kowalski gained his feet. "Where have you been hiding?"

The young ensign pointed his flare. "Sheriff Aratuk's airplane. When the first explosion hit, Bane bolted out here."

Going for the familiar, Jenny thought, *heading to the only piece of home he knows out here.*

"I had to follow," Tom continued. "The dog was my responsibility. And once I realized what was happening, I thought I could use the radio to transmit a Mayday."

"Did you reach anyone?"

Tom shook his head. "I didn't have much time to try. I had to hide from the patrols, cram myself and the dog into the cargo space. But after the blizzard struck, I doubted anyone would risk coming out here. So I tried again. As a matter of fact, I was outside the plane, burning ice from the antennas with the flare, when Bane started to whine and tug in your direction."

Jenny gave Bane a final pat. "Let's get out of this wind."

"Amen to that," Kowalski said, a shiver trembling through his frame.

"What's the plan?" Tom asked, leading them across the ice. The ghostly shape of the Twin Otter grew out of the white background.

Jenny answered, "First let's pray the engines turn over. Under the cover of the storm, we should be able to start the engines with no one hearing. But it'll still take a few minutes to warm them up."

"You want to take off?" Tom asked, turning back to her. "Fly—in this weather?"

"I've flown in whiteout conditions before," Jenny assured him. But this was no ice fog, she added to herself. The blizzard would challenge all her skill.

They reached the plane, undid the storm ties, and yanked away the frozen chocks. Once ready, they climbed inside. Insulated from the wind, the cabin seemed fifty degrees warmer. Jenny climbed over to her pilot's seat. Kowalski took the copilot's chair. Tom and Bane shared the row behind them.

The plane's keys were still where she had left them. She switched on main power and ran a quick systems check. All seemed in order. She flipped toggles, disengaging the engine-block heaters from the auxiliary battery.

"Here goes nothing," Jenny said, powering up the twin engines. The familiar vibrato of power trembled through her seat cushion.

The engine noise was lost somewhat on the winds, but Jenny could still discern the whine of the twin motors. How far did the sound carry? Were the Russians coming even now?

She glanced to Kowalski. He shrugged as if reading her mind. *What did it matter?*

She throttled up slowly, letting the engines warm. Beyond the windows, she could vaguely make out the props stirring up the blowing snow.

After a full minute, she asked, "Ready?"

No one answered.

"Here we go," she said, barely loud enough to be heard. It sounded, even to her, more like a prayer. She pushed the engines, the props chopped into the winds, and the Twin Otter broke from its spot on the ice. The plane slid on its skids, moving out.

Jenny worked the controls to angle them away from the base. Her plan was to taxi into the wind, using the force of the storm to help her get aloft. It would still be a hell of a ride.

"Hang on," she began to say, but was cut off.

"We've got company," Kowalski said. He had craned around and was staring behind them.

Jenny checked. Two glows, like a car's headlights, shone behind them. Then the two lights split apart, sailing away from one another, but arcing toward the Otter.

Hovercrafts.

Jenny throttled up, generating a roar from the props. The plane sped ahead, but it was slow with the headwind pounding at the windshield. Normally a fierce headwind was perfect for a quick takeoff, but these winds gusted, battering the plane. "The Russians must have heard us."

"Or they posted infrared scopes and spotted the engines heating up out here."

A blast of rifle fire suddenly cut through the engine noise, sounding distant in the blanket of the storm. A few slugs struck the fleeing plane with sharp pings. But the tail assembly and storage spaces shielded the cabin.

Jenny fought to increase their speed into the wind.

"They're coming around!" Tom called from the backseat.

Jenny glanced to the right and left. Two glows could be seen, swinging up to get clear shots at the cabin.

Damn, those bikes flew fast.

She stared out into the storm breaking over her windshield, pressing against her, holding her back. This would never work. They didn't have the time to fight the winds. She needed a new angle of attack—and there was only one other option.

"Hold on!" she called out.

She throttled down the port engine while kicking up the starboard. At the same time, she worked the flaps, one up, the other down. The Otter spun on its runners, like a hydroplaning car. It skidded on the ice, coming full around, pointing back the way they had come.

"What are you doing?" Kowalski yelled, pushing off the window he had been pressed against.

Jenny jammed both engines to full power. Props churned snow into a blur. The Otter leaped ahead, racing again over the ice.

With the wind at their backs, the plane accelerated rapidly.

Kowalski realized where they were heading. Back toward the base. "You don't have the clearance. You'll never get the lift you need."

"I know."

The pair of hovercraft whirled out and back, spinning around to give chase. A single bullet pinged against the Otter's tail.

"We'll never make it," Tom whispered.

Jenny ignored them all. She raced ahead, watching her gauges, especially her speed. *C'mon . . .*

From the corner of her eye, she saw the lights of the base appear ahead. Darker shadows marked the village of Jamesway huts.

The Otter sped toward them.

The vibrations of the runners over the ice lessened as the plane began to lift. Jenny held her breath. She didn't have enough speed yet. The momentary lift was only from the storm winds. She was right. The runners hit again, shaking the plane as the skids rode across the uneven ice field.

"Pull around!" Kowalski yelled. "We can't make it!"

Jenny hummed under her breath and aimed directly for

one of the dark buildings, a shadow in the glow of the base's lamp poles. She prayed it was aligned like the barracks from which she and Kowalski had escaped.

The plane sped toward it. Jenny held back just a pinch of power. She would need it.

"What are you—?" Kowalski began, then finished with *"Oh, shit!"*

Like the barracks, a snowbank had blown against the windward side of the Jamesway hut, a frozen wave banking almost to the roof.

The Otter struck the icy slope, nose popping up. Jenny kicked the engines with the last bit of power. The runners rode up the bank, then shot skyward.

The skids brushed against the corrugated roof of the building with a rasp of metal on metal—then they were away, airborne into the teeth of the storm.

For the next few stomach-rolling minutes, Jenny fought for control of her craft. The plane bobbled, a kite in a storm. But while the winds were blowing fiercely, they were also steady. Jenny turned into the storm, using the wind's rush over her wings to propel her upward. She eventually found her wings, and the Otter stabilized.

Sighing, she checked her gauges: altitude, airspeed, compass. In these whiteout conditions, the instruments were all she had to go by. Beyond the windshield, there was no discernible way of telling sky from ice.

"You're fucking awesome!" Kowalski said, wearing a shaggy grin.

Jenny wished she could share his enthusiasm. Still watching her instruments, she felt her gut tighten. The gauge on the reserve fuel tank was draining away. The dial swept from full, to half, to quarter. One of the stray bullets must have torn a line. She was blowing fuel behind her. She checked her main tank.

It was holding fine—if you could call a mere eighth of a tank *fine*.

"What's wrong?" Tom asked.

"We're almost out of fuel."

"What?" Kowalski asked. "How?"

Jenny pointed and explained.

Kowalski swore fiercely once she was done.

"How far can we get before we have to land?" Tom asked.

Jenny shook her head. "Not far. Maybe fifty miles."

"Great . . ." Kowalski groaned. "Just far enough to land in the middle of bumfuck nowhere."

Jenny understood his anger. Out here, lost, without food or warm clothes, they would not survive long in the freezing cold.

"What can we do?" Tom asked.

No one answered.

Jenny continued to fly. It was all she could do for now.

1:29 P.M.
ICE STATION GRENDEL

With no more tricks to play, Matt and Amanda had only one course left, the most basic means of defense. "Run!" Matt yelled, giving Amanda a rough push.

She let out a gasp, then leaped away like a startled doe.

Matt did his best to keep up with her, but barefoot, it was like running with two freezer-burned steaks tied around his feet.

They fled up the tunnels, but with every few steps, Matt was losing ground.

"I know . . . I know this place!" Amanda yelled. "We're not far from the exit!"

Matt glanced over a shoulder.

The grendel flew down the tunnel toward them—only ten yards away now. It loped after them, sinuous and lethal, claws casting up spats of ice. It must have sensed that its prey was close to escaping. All caution gone.

"Get down!" This new shout came from the tunnel ahead of them, cutting through the constant buzz.

Matt swung around to see a bristle of weapons pointed his way.

The Navy team!

Amanda disappeared among them. Matt was too far behind. There was no way he could make it. He dove onto his belly, arms outstretched, ax held in both hands.

The passage erupted with gunfire. Bullets whistled over his head. Ice chipped from the walls and ceilings, pelting him from stray shots and ricochets.

Matt rolled to his back, staring back between his legs.

The grendel crouched only a yard away, head bulled down. It clawed toward him, determined to reach its prize. A bellow rumbled through its chest. Steam puffed from its buried nostrils. Blood spilled over its sleek features as flesh was macerated by bullets.

Matt backpedaled away, pushing with his bare feet.

Under fire from three automatic weapons, the beast still fought toward him. One claw lashed out and snatched Matt's pant leg, pinning it to the ice. Matt tugged, but it wouldn't budge. For a heartbeat, he met the hunter's eye.

Matt read the fire in there.

The grendel's lips snarled back. It might die, but it would take him with it.

Matt swung his ice ax—not at the beast but over his head, as far as his arm could reach. The pick end jammed into the ice. With his other hand, he unbuckled his pants and ripped loose the top button. Using the ax as an anchor, he hauled himself out of his pants and rolled from the beast.

Stripped to his thermals, he crawled away. The beast roared behind him, a haunted sound that crossed all spectrums, eerie and forlorn.

Matt reached the row of men.

Hands grabbed him, hauled him to his feet.

He looked back at the beast. It had also rolled around, half climbing the walls to turn. It fled away from the stinging attack and vanished around the far bend.

Matt joined Amanda, and together they approached the others: a cluster of scientists and a handful of Navy personnel.

Craig gaped at him. "I thought you were dead for sure."

"We're not out of this yet."

Bratt organized his command: Greer, O'Donnell, Pearlson, and Washburn. He explained their situation.

Amanda stared hard at Bratt. "The *Polar Sentinel* left?"

"Captain Perry had no choice."

Amanda seemed to shrink back, stunned. "What are we going to do?"

Bratt answered, "We can't stay down here. We're running low on ammunition. We're going to have to take our chances with the Russians."

"Sir, I know a few places we could hide on Level Three," the tall black lieutenant said. She nodded back up the tunnels. "There are service shafts and storage spaces. Also an old weapons locker. If we could make it there without being seen . . ."

"Anywhere's better than these fuckin' tunnels," Greer said.

Bratt nodded. "We'll have to be careful."

Matt would be happy to be out of these ice passages himself. The nagging buzz was beginning to ache his ears.

He suddenly jolted.

Oh, God . . .

He swung around. His ears had been ringing from the close-quarter rifle fire. Only now that it had faded did he feel it.

The creature had been driven off—but the buzzing continued.

He saw the look of recognition in Amanda's eyes.

"We're not alone!" Matt yelled.

Flashlights suddenly shot up, poking down other tunnel openings. Pair after pair of red eyes reflected back at them.

"They're the thawed group from the caves!" Bratt called out, waving everyone back. "They finally got around that damned carcass."

"The rifle fire must have drawn them!" the biologist yelled in terror, pulling back.

"Out!" Bratt yelled. "We don't have the firepower to hold off this many!"

Together, they ran up the tunnel in a mad rush.

The sudden movement drew the beasts, like cats after fleeing mice.

"This way!" Amanda screamed.

The double doors to the station appeared ahead.

In a mad rush, they hit the doors. Matt held the way open and waved the civilians through. "Move, move, move!"

The Navy personnel kept up a rear guard, then quickly followed into the station.

As the doors were slammed shut, a shot rang out ahead of them. Matt ducked from a ricochet off the metal wall.

It seemed their gunfire had drawn more than just grendels.

"Halt!" a soldier in a white parka barked at them in heavily accented English. He and four others had a post at the other end of the hall. Assault rifles were trained on them. "Drop weapons! Now!"

No one moved for a breath.

Amanda had been continuing forward, deaf to the command, but Matt grabbed her elbow. She glanced to him.

Matt shook his head. "Stay with me," he mouthed.

"Do as they say," Bratt ordered, tossing aside his rifle as example. Other weapons clattered. "Keep moving forward. Get away from the doors."

"Keep hands in air!" the Russian yelled at them. "Move in single line to here!"

With a nod from Bratt, they followed their captor's instructions.

Quickly forming a line, they hurried down the long hall. They hadn't taken more than ten steps when something huge hit the double doors behind them. The metal doors buckled.

Everyone froze.

"Down," Bratt ordered.

They dropped to hands and knees. Matt pulled Amanda down with him.

A single shot fired, perhaps in startled reflex. But the aim was good. O'Donnell was a moment too slow in dropping with the others. The back of his head exploded, showering bone and blood. Then his body toppled backward, limbs flung out.

A flurry of Russian commands followed, yelling at each other.

"Goddamn it," Bratt swore on the floor, his face purpling with rage.

Matt glanced between the trigger-happy Russians and the buckled door. Neither choice was good.

The Russian in charge stepped forward. "What trick—?"

Something again charged the door, hitting it like a runaway train. Hinges ripped clean, and both doors flew into the hall.

Accompanying the doors, a grendel barreled into the hall. Others followed.

Chaos ensued as everyone surged forward on the floor.

Shots rang out, wild with fear.

"Stay down!" Bratt yelled. "Crawl forward."

They would never make it. If they didn't catch a stray bullet like O'Donnell, they'd be ravaged by the beasts.

"Over here!" Amanda yelled. She had rolled to the wall and reached up to a door handle above her head. A bullet came close to shaving off a finger, but she managed to yank the handle. Using her other hand, she hauled the door open. The thick steel hatch now acted as a shield against the bullets. "Inside!"

They all tumbled after her.

Greer was last, diving through, a grendel at his heels.

Amanda slammed the door shut behind him as the beast struck. The concussion knocked her into Matt. He steadied her, but she shoved to the door.

In the dark, Matt heard a metal bar slide home.

Muffled as they were by the thick hatch, the echo of the gun battle still reached them. Occasional heavy bodies collided with the walls and door.

As the battle waged in the hallway, they all lay panting on the floor, huddled in a mass just inside the doorway. Matt took a moment to pull out his moosehide boots and cram them over his aching, frozen feet.

"We should be safe for the moment." Amanda spoke from the darkness. "This door is solid plate steel."

"Where are we?" Matt asked, lacing his boots.

"The heart of the station," Bratt answered. "Its main research lab."

A light switch was flipped and bare bulbs flickered to life.

Matt stared around the clean and orderly lab. Steel tables were aligned with military precision. Glass-fronted cabinets housed beakers and polished tools. Refrigeration units lined one wall. Other smaller rooms opened off the main lab, but they were too dark to see into.

As Matt's gaze circled the room, another chain of lights flickered into existence. Each bulb flared, one after the other, illuminating a curving concourse that arced away into the distance. The corridor seemed to follow the outer wall, probably circled the entire level.

Matt bore witness to what each bulb illuminated. "Oh, dear God . . ."

Act Three

FEEDING FRENZY

ᐊᒥᖅᑲᒃᓯᓯᑐᓂ ᑯᑯᓪᓚᑕᑐᖅᑉ

Timeless

ᗄᑫᒃᑐᓚᐃᑦᑐᖅ

APRIL 9, 1:42 P.M.
OUT ON THE ICE . . .

Bundled in a white parka, Viktor Petkov rode through the heart of a blizzard. His hands were encased in heated mittens, his face protected from the winds by the furred edge of his hood, a thick wool scarf, and a pair of polarized goggles.

But no amount of clothing could keep the cold from his heart. He was heading to the gravestone of his father, a frozen crypt buried in the ice.

He straddled the backseat of the hovercraft bike, harnessed in place. The skilled driver, a young officer under Mikovsky, handled the vehicle with a reckless confidence that could only come from youth. The craft flew over the ice, no more than a handspan above the surface, a rocket against the wind.

The storm continued its attempt to blow them off course, but the driver compensated, maintaining a direct line toward the lost station using the bike's gyroscopic guidance system.

Viktor stared out at the snow-blasted landscape. Around him lay nothing but a wasteland, a desert of ice. With the sun blanketed by clouds and snow, the world had dissolved into a wan twilight. It sapped one's will and strength. Here, hopelessness and despair took on physical dimensions. With winds wailing in his ears, the eternal desolation sank into his bones.

Here is where my father spent his last days, alone, exiled, forgotten.

The craft swung in a slow arc, following the shadow of a pressure ridge, the spines of a sleeping dragon. Then, out of the continual gloom, a misty light grew.

"Destination ahead, Admiral!" the driver called back to him.

The hovercraft adjusted course under him. Flanking the lead bike, the other two craft matched the maneuver like a squadron of MiG fighters in formation. The trio raced toward the light.

Details emerged through the blowing snow. A mountain range of ice, a black pool, square, man-made, and at the base of one peak, a shaft of light shone like a beacon in the storm.

They rounded the polynya and swept toward the opening to the base. Engines throttled down. The three hovercraft lowered to their titanium skis, touching down again, skidding across the ice. They slid to a stop near the entrance, parking in the lee of a ridge to protect the vehicles from the worst of the storm.

The driver hopped off while Viktor struggled with his harness's buckle. Bound as he was in mittens, his dexterity was compromised, but even bare-knuckled, he would still have had difficulty. His hands shook. His eyes were fixed to the ragged shaft—blasted, hacked, and melted down to the tomb below. He had seen ancient burial sites ripped into like this by grave robbers in Egypt. That is what they all were—the Americans and the Russians—filthy grave robbers, fighting over bones and shiny artifacts.

He stared, unblinking.

I am the only one who belongs here.

"Sir?" The driver offered to help, reaching toward his harness.

Viktor snapped back to the moment, unbuckled on his own, and dismounted. On his feet now, he yanked off and pocketed the heated mittens. The cold immediately burned his exposed flesh, like Death's handshake, welcoming him to his father's crypt.

He stalked past his men, heading toward the entrance. He found a lone guard inside the shaft. The fellow snapped out of his shivering hunch.

"Admiral!" he said.

Viktor recognized the man as one of the senior officers of the *Drakon*. What was he doing standing guard duty? He was instantly alert. "What's wrong, Lieutenant?"

The man fought his tongue. He seemed to be struggling to find the right words. "Sir, we've run into a couple of problems. One here, one back at Omega. Captain Mikovsky is awaiting your call on the UQC."

Viktor frowned, glancing back at the empty polynya. A black line, almost buried in the snow, trailed from the lake and disappeared down the shaft. It was a UQC line, an underwater telephone, a type of active sonar that transmitted voices instead of pings. Such communication spanned only short distances, so the *Drakon* had to still be patrolling the local waters.

He waved the guard to proceed.

The half-frozen party headed down the tunnels, slipping past the blasted ruin of a Sno-Cat near the door. The guard continued to speak rapidly. "The problem here, sir, is that a handful of military men and civilians have barricaded themselves on Level Four. We couldn't get to them because of some strange beasts that attacked our men."

"Beasts?"

"White-skinned. Massive. The size of bulls. I didn't see them myself. The creatures disappeared back into the ice caves by the time reinforcements arrived. We lost one man, dragged away by one of the creatures. The hall is under guard now."

Viktor's legs grew numb under him at the description. Before leaving, he had read his father's secret reports in Moscow.

Grendels . . . could it be them? Could a few still be alive?

They were soon inside the main station. The black vulcanized line ended at a small radio unit. The radioman stood rapidly at the appearance of the admiral.

"Sir! Captain Mikovsky is holding for—"

"I heard." He strode to the UQC phone, picked up the handset, and spoke into the receiver. "Admiral Petkov here."

"Admiral, I have an urgent report from our forces at Omega." The words echoed hollowly, like someone was speaking through a long pipe, but it was clearly Captain Mikovsky. "I wanted you updated immediately."

"Go ahead."

"There's been a security breach. A female prisoner and a U.S. seaman escaped the barracks internment and reached a small aircraft."

A fist tightened. How could this happen?

"They escaped, sir. With the storm, we have no way of tracking them. Most likely they're heading to the Alaskan coast to raise the alarm."

Fury built inside Viktor's chest. Such a mistake should never have been allowed to happen. The mission called for no eyewitnesses to the war here. It had all been carefully timed. Under the cover of both blizzard and solar storm, the United States' reconnaissance satellites would have been able to discern only vague infrared signatures at best. And while echoes of the prior battles would be recorded by patrolling subs and ships, without living eyewitnesses, there was a level of plausible deniability on the part of the Russian government. Even the U.S. research sub, the *Polar Sentinel,* had been allowed to leave unmolested with its evacuees. While the sub might have spotted the *Drakon* in these waters, they couldn't visually verify what happened above the ice.

Plausible deniability. It was the new catchphrase of modern battle.

But now two prisoners had escaped, two eyewitnesses who could place him, a Russian admiral, on-site.

Viktor forced himself to take a deep calming breath. He stanched his anger, snuffing it out. His initial reaction had been reflexive, purely military. Ultimately it didn't matter. He placed a hand over the Polaris wrist monitor, reminding himself of the larger picture.

Viktor found his calm center again. Besides, both governments had authorized this secret war, what was coyly termed in political circles as a skirmish. Such clandestine battles occurred regularly between foreign powers, including the United States. They were waged in hidden corners of the world: the waters off North Korea, the deserts of Iraq, the hinterlands of China, and more than once even here in the lonely wilds of the polar seas. The chains of command understood these skirmishes, but the details never reached the radar screens of the public at large.

Out of sight, out of mind.

"Admiral," Mikovsky continued, "what are your orders?"

Viktor reviewed the current situation. It was unfortunate but salvageable—yet he could take no further chances. Omega and its prisoners were no longer an asset. The prize was plainly not over there. He kept his voice stoic and firm. "Captain, take the *Drakon* to Omega."

"Sir?"

"Once there, draw back our men from the base and retreat."

"And Omega . . . the prisoners?"

"Once our men are clear, ignite the buried charges. Melt the entire base into the ocean."

A long pause. It was a death sentence for those innocents left behind. The captain's words returned faintly. "Yes, sir."

"Afterward, return here. Our mission is almost complete."
Viktor replaced the handset to its cradle. He turned to the men
gathered around him. "Now to the other problem at hand."

1:55 P.M.
ICE STATION GRENDEL

Matt gaped, horrified, along with the others. A long curving
hall stretched out from the main lab room. Lit by bare bulbs,
the passage followed the outer wall of this level, circling and
vanishing around the curve of this tier. Inset into the back
wall every couple of feet were steel tanks standing on end,
taller than Matt by a foot. Thick rubber hoses and twisted
conduits ran along both floor and ceilings, connecting tank
to tank. Though the fronts of the tanks were windowed in
thick glass, the details inside remained murky because of the
thick frost over the clear surface.

But a dozen of the closest tanks had the frost recently
scraped from them. The glow of the overhead bulbs shone
plainly upon the sight inside. The interior of each tank was
filled with solid ice, a perfect blue clarity.

And like an insect trapped in amber, a shape was embedded in the heart of each tank. Naked. Human. Each face contorted in a rictus of agony. Palms pressed against the glass,
fingers blue and clawing. Men. Women. Even children.

Matt stared down the long tunnel. Tank after tank. How
many were there? He turned his back on the macabre sight.
He saw the shocked looks on the others' faces.

Two members of the group, though, looked more embar-
rassed than horrified.

He walked back to the main room and faced them: Lieutenant Bratt and Amanda Reynolds. "What is all this?" He
waved an arm down the hall.

Craig appeared at his side. Washburn and the civilian scientists gathered with him.

"It's what the Russians are trying to cover up," Amanda said. "A secret lab dating back to World War Two. Used for human experimentation."

Matt studied the barred door. Greer and Pearlson stood guard there. For the moment, the Russians had given up on trying to get the door open. They were probably wary of the return of the grendels after chasing them back into the Crawl Space with gunfire. But that fear wouldn't keep them out forever.

"What were the bastards trying to do here?" Washburn asked, looking the most shaken, her stoic demeanor shattered.

Amanda shook her head. "We don't know. We locked down the lab as soon as we discovered what was hidden here." She pointed to a glass cabinet that contained a neat row of journals, covering two shelves. "The answers are probably there. But they're all coded in some strange script. We couldn't read them."

Craig approached and cracked the door open. He leaned over, studying the bindings. "There are numbers here. Dates, it looks like. He ran a finger down the journals. "If I'm reading this right, from January 1933 . . . to May 1945." He pulled the last one out and flipped through it.

"Twelve years," Bratt said. "It's hard to believe this operation ran for so long without anyone knowing."

Amanda answered, "Back then, communication up here was scant. Travel rare. It wouldn't be hard to hide such a place."

"Or lose it when you wanted to," Matt added. "What the hell happened here?"

The biologist, Dr. Ogden, spoke from the hallway. He straightened from one tank. "I may have an idea."

Everyone turned to him.

"What?" Bratt asked brusquely.

"The grendels," he said to the lieutenant commander. "You saw what happened. The specimens came to life after being frozen for centuries."

Amanda's eyes widened. "That's impossible."

Bratt turned to her. "No, ma'am. Dr. Ogden is right. I saw it happen with my own eyes."

Dr. Ogden continued: "Such a miraculous resurrection is not unheard of in the natural world. Certain turtles hibernate in frozen mud over an entire winter, then rise again with the spring thaw."

"But frozen solid?" Amanda asked.

"Yes. Arctic wood frogs freeze as hard as stone during the winter. Their hearts don't beat. When frozen, you can cut them in half, and they don't bleed. All EEG activity ceases. In fact, there's no cellular activity at all. For all intents and purposes, they're dead. But come spring, they thaw, and within fifteen minutes, their hearts are beating, blood pumping, and they're jumping around."

Matt nodded when Amanda glanced at him. "It's true. I've read about those frogs."

"How can that be?" Amanda argued. "When a body freezes, ice expands in the cells and destroys them. Like frostbite. How do the frogs survive that?"

"The answer is quite simple," Ogden said.

Amanda raised an eyebrow.

"Sugar."

"What?"

"Glucose specifically. There's a Canadian researcher, Dr. Ken Storey, who has been studying Arctic wood frogs for the past decade. What he's discovered is that when ice starts forming on a frog's rubbery skin, its body starts filling each cell with sugary glucose. Increasing the osmalality of the cell to the point that life-killing ice can't form inside it."

"But you said the frogs do freeze?"

"Exactly, but it is only the water *outside* the cells that ices up. The glucose *inside* the cell acts as a cryoprotectant, a type of antifreeze, preserving the cell until thawed. Dr. Storey determined that this evolutionary process is governed by a set of twenty genes that convert glycogen to glucose.

The trigger for what suddenly turns these specific genes on or off is still unknown, but a hormonal theory is most advocated, something released by the frog's glandular skin. The odd thing, though, is that these twenty genes are found in *all* vertebrate species."

Amanda took a deep breath. "Including the *Ambulocetus* . . . the grendels."

He nodded. "Remember I told you that I would classify this new species as *Ambulocetus natans arctos*. An *Arctic*-adapted subspecies of the original amphibious whale. The gigantism, the depigmentation . . . are all common Arctic adaptations. So why not this one, too? If it made its home here—in a land ruled *not* by the sun, but by cycles of freezing and thawing—then its body might adapt to this rhythm, too."

Bratt added. "Besides, we *saw* it happen with the monsters. We know they can do this."

Ogden nodded and continued: "It's a form of suspended animation. Can you imagine its potential uses? Even now university researchers are using the Arctic frogs as a model to attempt freezing human organs. This would be a boon to the world. Donated organs could be frozen and preserved until needed."

Matt's gaze had returned to the line of tanks. "What about these folk? Do you think that's what's going on here? Some type of sick organ bank? A massive storage facility for spare parts?"

Ogden turned to him. "Oh, no, I don't think that at all."

Matt faced him. "Then what?"

"I wager the Russians were attempting something grander here. Remember when I said the twenty genes that orchestrate the wood frog's suspended animation are found in *all* vertebrate species. Well, that includes humans."

Matt's eyes widened.

"I believe that these people were guinea pigs in a suspended animation program. That the Russians were trying to instill the grendels' ability to survive freezing into humans, seeking a means of practical suspended animation. They sought the Holy Grail of all sciences." Ogden faced the questioning looks around him. *"Immortality."*

Matt swung to face the contorted, pained figures in the ice. "Are you saying that these people are still alive?"

Before anyone could answer, a pounding sounded from the door, determined, stolid. Everyone went silent.

A hard voice called out to them. "Open the door immediately . . . if we have to cut our way through, you will suffer for our troubles."

From the dead tone of the other's voice, it was no idle threat.

The wolf was at their door.

2:04 P.M.
AIRBORNE OVER THE POLAR CAP

Jenny fought the gale pounding at her windshield. It blew steady, but sudden gusts and churning winds kept her fingers tight on her controls, eyes glued to her instruments. She had not even bothered to glance out the windshield for the past ten minutes. What was the use?

Though she couldn't see anything, she still wore her snow goggles. Even with the blizzard, the midday glare shot through the windshield. It made her want to close her eyes. How long had it been since she'd slept?

She pushed these thoughts away and watched her airspeed. *Too slow.* The headwind was eating her speed. She tried to ignore the fuel gauge. The needle pointed to a large red *E*. A yellow warning light glowed. *Empty.* They were flying on fumes into a blizzard.

"Are we sure about this?" Kowalski said. The seaman had given up trying to raise anyone on the radio.

"I don't see we have much other choice," Jenny said. "We

don't have enough fuel to reach the coast. We'd be forced to land anyway. I'd rather land somewhere where we had some chance of living."

"How far out are we?" Tom asked from the backseat. Bane lay curled on the seat beside him, tail tucked around his body.

"If the coordinates you gave me are correct, we've another ten miles."

Kowalski stared out the windshield. "I can't believe we're doing this."

Jenny ignored him. They had already debated it. It *was* their only choice. She struggled to eke out a bit more speed, taking every lull in the wind to surge ahead, lunging in spurts toward their goal. The controls had grown more sluggish as ice built on the wings and crusted on the windshield. They were slowly becoming a flying ice cube.

They traveled in silence for another five minutes. Jenny barely breathed, waiting for the props to choke out as her greedy engines consumed the last of her fuel.

"There!" Tom suddenly blurted, jamming an arm between Jenny and Kowalski. Bane lifted his head.

Jenny tried to follow where the ensign pointed. "I don't see—"

"Ten degrees to starboard! Wait for the wind to let up!"

Jenny concentrated on where he indicated. Then, as the snow eddied out in a wild twist, she spotted a light ahead, glowing up at them. "Are you sure that's the place?"

Tom nodded.

"Ice Station Grendel," Kowalski moaned.

Jenny began her descent, studying her altimeter. Without fuel, they needed a place to land. They couldn't go back to Omega and to touch down in the wasteland of the polar cap was certain death. There was only one other place that offered adequate shelter. The ice station.

It was risky, but not totally foolhardy. The Russians would not be expecting them. If they could land out of direct sight,

Tom Pomautuk knew the layout of the station well enough to possibly get them into one of the exterior ventilation shafts that brought fresh air down to the buried station. They could hole up there until the Russians left.

And besides, their dwindling fuel situation left them little other choice.

The Otter lurched as the portside engine coughed. The prop skipped a beat, fluttering. In a heartbeat, the Twin Otter became a *Single* Otter. Flying on one engine, Jenny fought to hold the plane even while dropping her flaps. She dove steeply. "Hold tight!"

Kowalski had a death grip on both armrests. "I got that covered."

There was no sight line to the ice fields below. Jenny watched her altimeter wheel down. The winds continued to fight, grabbing the plane, trying to hold it aloft.

Jenny bit her lower lip, concentrating. She tried to fix the position of the station's beacon light, now gone again, in her mind's eye. A map formed in her head, fed by data from her instruments and her own instinct.

As the altimeter dropped under the two-hundred-foot ceiling, she focused on her trim, fighting both the wind and the dead engine to hold herself level. The snow became thicker, not just from the sky but now blowing up at her from the ice plain below.

She intended to descend from here as gradually as possible. It was the only safe way to land blind. Slow and even . . . as long as the last engine held. She watched the altimeter drop under a hundred . . . then seventy . . . then—

"Watch out!" Tom called from the backseat.

Her gaze flicked up from her focus on her instruments. Out of the storm ahead, the winds parted in places to reveal a wall of ice ahead of them, broken and thrust up into jagged teeth, misted with blowing snow. It lay less than a hundred yards ahead. She thought quickly, weighing options in a heartbeat. She plainly didn't have the engines to make it over them.

Beside her, Kowalski swore a constant string, his version of a prayer.

Jenny gnashed her teeth, then jammed her stick forward, diving more steeply. *Screw it,* she thought, *I'm sticking this landing.* She dropped the plane the last fifty feet, sweeping out of the sky, plunging toward the peaks of ice.

The ground was nowhere in sight.

Kowalski's prayer became more heartfelt, finishing with "I really, really hate you!"

Jenny ignored him. She concentrated on her instruments, trusting them. They promised the ground was down there somewhere. She completely dropped her flaps; the plane dipped savagely.

It was too much for her last engine. The motor gasped, choked, and died. In that moment, they became a frozen rock with wings, hurtling earthward.

"Fuuuucccckkkk!" Kowalski cried, hands now pressed to the side window and dash.

Jenny hummed. The momentum of the glide continued to hold —barely. The needle on the altimeter slipped lower and lower, then settled to zero. There was still no sign of the ground.

Then her skis hit the ice, soft and even.

She punched up her flaps to brake their speed. They had landed at speeds much faster than she liked.

As the Otter continued to race over the slick surface, side winds threatened to topple it over on a wing, attempting to cartwheel them off to oblivion. But Jenny worked her flaps, plied the Otter with skill, and adjusted their course to keep the wings up.

"Ice!" Tom called from the backseat.

The peaks were rushing at them. The plane's speed had hardly slowed. With skis for landing gear, the Otter had no hydraulic brakes—just flaps and friction. She had plenty of the former, little of the latter.

Still, after a decade of mushing in a dog sled, Jenny knew the delicate physics of ice and steel runners.

The Otter continued to skate toward the towering cliffs, sliding toward a certain crash. Jenny had already recognized the inevitable.

She was going to lose her plane.

"This is going to hurt," she mumbled.

As the plane swept toward the cliff face, she prayed the ice remained slick. Everything depended on her flaps—and timing.

She watched the cliffs grow in front of her. She counted in her head, then at the last moment, she dropped the flaps on the starboard side and continued to brake with the other. The nimble plane fishtailed, spinning around like an Olympic figure skater.

The tail assembly swept backward and struck the cliff, absorbing a fair amount of the impact and tearing away in the process. Jenny jerked in her seat harness as the plane jarred. The wing glanced next, taking more of the impact, crumpling up and away. Then the cabin hit, striking the cliff broadside—but since the worst of the impact had already been absorbed by the tail and wing, their collision was no more than a fender bender.

Everyone was shaken but alive.

Bane climbed back into his seat from the floor, looking none too pleased by the whole experience. Jenny turned to Kowalski. He reached out with both hands, grabbed her cheeks, and kissed her full on the mouth.

"Let's never fight again," he said.

Outside, the engine on the crumpled wing broke away and hit the ice.

"We'd better get out of here," Tom said.

They hauled out of the plane. Before climbing free, Jenny removed some supplies from the emergency locker: a flashlight, a pair of extra parkas and mittens, a large coil of poly-line rope, a flare gun, and a pocketful of extra flares. She glanced to the empty hooks that normally held her service shotgun and silently cursed Sewell for confiscating it.

She exited the broken plane and tossed one of the spare parkas to Kowalski.

"Looks like Christmas came early," he muttered as he pulled into it. It was too small for his large frame. The sleeves rode four inches up his forearm, but he didn't complain.

Jenny quaked in the winds, but at least she was sheltered by the cliffs, the worst of the storm blunted. She quickly donned her parka.

Bane trotted around the wreckage, then lifted his leg. His yellow stream misted steamily in the frigid cold.

Kowalski stared a moment. "Damn smart dog. If I had to go, I'd be doing the same thing, too. Remind me from here on out never to get into anything smaller than a 747."

"Be respectful. She gave all she had to get you here." Jenny stared at the wreckage, feeling a surprisingly deep pang of regret at the loss.

Tom tugged his parka tighter around his boyish shoulders. "Where now?"

"Off to where we're not welcome," Kowalski answered. He pointed to the mountain range. "Let's see if we can sneak in the back door."

As they headed off, Jenny asked, "Where does this supposed hidden ventilation shaft lead?"

Tom explained the base's air circulation system. It functioned without pumps. Shafts were simply drilled from the surface to the deepest levels of the station—even below the station. The colder surface air, being heavier than the warmer air below would sink into these shafts and displace the warmer stagnant air. "This creates a passive circulation system," Tom finished. "The fresh air is pocketed in a cavern system that wraps around the station. A reservoir of clean air, so to speak. It is then heated through baffles and used to service the station."

"So the ventilation shaft empties into this cavern system?" Jenny asked.

Kowalski nodded. "We should be safe once we get there." Tom agreed. "We call it the Crawl Space."

2:13 P.M.
ICE STATION GRENDEL

Matt fled with the others down the circular hall as it wound the circumference of this research level. To his right, he marched past the gruesome tanks, one after the other. Matt found himself counting. He was up to twenty-two.

He forced himself to stop. The tanks continued around the bend. There had to be fifty at least. He turned to the other wall of plate steel. It was interrupted by a few windows into offices, some sealed doors, and a few open hatches. He peered through one of these and spotted a hall of small barred cells. And in another, a larger barracks facility.

Here is where they must've housed the prisoners, Matt thought. He could only imagine the terror of these folk. *Did they know their eventual fate?*

Dr. Ogden trailed at Matt's heels, while Amanda strode ahead of him. The biologist would occasionally rub at the frosted glass of a tank with the cuff of his sleeve, peer inside, and mutter.

Matt shook his head. He hadn't the stomach for further scientific curiosity. He only wanted to get the hell out of here, back to the Alaskan backcountry, where all you had to fear was a hungry grizzly.

Behind him, a loud clang echoed from the main lab. The Russians were breaking in. After the threat from that icy voice, the group had fled, heading farther into this level.

Bratt led them. "It should be another ten yards or so." He clutched a set of folded station plans in his hand.

Craig kept peering over the commander's shoulder at the papers. The schematics came from a material sciences researcher from the NASA group. The scientist had mapped the entire physical plant of the station. Matt prayed the man knew his business.

Greer yelled. He was farther down the hall, scouting ahead. "Over here!" The lieutenant had dropped to one knee. A hatch lay between two tanks. Conduits and piping led out from it and spread to either side, trailing out along floorboards and ceiling to service the awful experiment.

Pearlson indicated a diagram plated to the wall above the hatch. It was the layout of this level. He tapped a large red X on the map. "You are here," he muttered.

Matt studied the map, then glanced forward and back. They were at the midpoint of the storage hall. Halfway around this level.

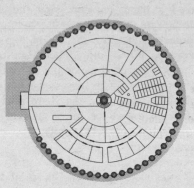

Pearlson and Greer set to work unscrewing the panel, using steel scalpels. Around them, everyone carried pilfered weapons found in the labs before they fled: additional scalpels, bone saws, steel hammers, even a pair of meat hooks wielded by Washburn. Matt did not want to speculate on the surgical use of those wicked tools. He himself carried a yard-long length of steel pipe.

Matt studied their party as the sailors worked on the hatch. They had all reverted to a pack of stone-age hunter/gatherers . . . armed with expertly crafted surgical weapons. A strange sight.

Ogden was again rubbing at a nearby tank. The squeaking of wool on glass drew Matt's attention. He had to resist clubbing the man with his pipe. *Leave them be,* he wanted to scream.

As if reading his mind, Ogden turned to him, eyes pinched. "They're all indigenous," he muttered. The man's voice cracked slightly. Matt finally realized the tension wearing at the biologist, close to breaking him. He was trying to hold himself together by keeping his mind occupied. "Every one of them."

Despite his previous objection, Matt stepped closer, brows bunched together. "Indigenous."

"Inuit. Aleut. Eskimo. Whatever you want to call them." Ogden waved a hand, encompassing the arc of tanks. "They're all the same. Maybe even the same tribe."

Matt approached the last tank the biologist had wiped. This one appeared at first empty. Then Matt looked down.

A small boy sat frozen in ice on the bottom of the tank.

Dr. Ogden was correct in his assessment. The lad was clearly Inuit. The black hair, the sharp almond eyes, the round cheekbones, even the color of his skin—though now tinged blue—all made his heritage plain.

Inuit. Jenny's people.

Matt sank to one knee.

The boy's eyes were closed as if in slumber, but his tiny hands were raised, pressing against the walls of his frozen prison.

Matt placed his own palm on the glass, covering the boy's hand. Matt's other hand clenched on the pipe he carried. What monsters could do this to a boy? The lad could be no older than eight.

A sudden flash of recognition.

He was the same age as Tyler when he died.

Matt found himself staring into that still face, but another ghost intruded: Tyler, lying on the pine table in the family cabin. His son had died in ice, too. His lips had been blue, eyes closed.

Just sleeping.

The pain of that moment ached through him. He was glad Jenny wasn't here to see this. He prayed she was safe, but she should never see this . . . any of this.

"I'm sorry," he whispered, apologizing to both boys. Tears welled in his eyes.

A hand touched his shoulder. It was Amanda. "We'll let the world know," she said thickly, her pronunciation further garbled by her own sorrow.

"How could this . . . he was only a boy. Who was watching after him?"

But Matt's face was turned to the glass. Still, her fingers squeezed in sympathy.

Ogden stood on his other side. Eyes haggard, he was half bent studying a panel of buttons and levers. One finger traced some writing. "This is odd."

"What?" Matt asked.

Ogden reached to a lever and pulled it down with a bit of effort. The snap was loud in the quiet hall. The panel buttons bloomed with light. The glass of the tank vibrated as some old motor caught, tripped, then began to hum.

"What did you do?" Matt blurted, offended, anger flaring.

Ogden stepped back, glancing between Matt and Amanda. "My God, it's still operational. I didn't think—"

A loud crash reverberated down the hall, echoing to them.

"The Russians," Bratt said. "They're through."

"So are we," Greer said with a grimace. "Almost." Pearlson struggled with the last quarter-twist screw.

Craig stood at their backs, eyes wide and unblinking, staring between their hurried labor and the hall. The reporter held a foot-long steel bone pin, a surgical ice pick, clutched to his chest. "C'mon, already," he moaned.

Shouts could now be heard. Footsteps on steel plate, cautious still.

"Got it!" Greer spat. He and Pearlson lifted the service hatch free.

"Everyone out!" Bratt ordered.

Craig, the closest, dove first. The others followed, flowing through the opening.

Matt, suddenly weak and tired, still knelt by the frozen boy. His hand on the glass ached from the cold of the ice inside. He felt the vibration in the glass from the buried machinery.

Amanda stepped away. "Hurry, Matt."

He looked one more time at the boy. He felt like he was abandoning the child as he stood. His fingers lingered an extra moment, then he turned away.

Greer helped Amanda through, then waved to Matt.

He shoved over and ducked under the hatch.

Washburn was crouched on the far side. She pointed one of her steel hooks, like some Amazonian pirate, down the crawlway.

Matt followed Amanda on hands and knees, pipe under one arm. Bratt led the party, followed by Craig and the biology group. Matt hurried, making room for the others behind him: Pearlson, Greer, and Washburn.

The tunnel was a mere shaft bored through the ice. Rubber mats lined the floor to aid in climbing through it. Conduits shared the space, running along both walls.

After five yards, the tunnel suddenly darkened. Matt peered over his shoulder. Greer had pulled the hatch in place, hopefully hiding their retreat or at least delaying its discovery. This fourth level was large and broken into many compartments. The Russians would lose time, hunting through the level; hopefully they'd miss the loose hatch for a while.

The way became darker—and colder.

Finally the chute dumped into some old service cubbyhole. It was merely a cube cut out of the ice. A few pieces of wooden furniture crowded the space, along with spools of conduit and copper wire, stacks of spare metal plates, a thick rubber hose, and a tool trunk.

A ladder, just wood rungs pounded into one of the ice walls, climbed to another shaft twenty feet above.

Bratt pointed the rolled sheaf of his schematics. He kept his voice low. "That should lead to the third level. They stairstep up, one level at a time."

Washburn studied the next tunnel. "We might be able to make it to the old weapons locker on the third level. It's in the main section of the station, but if the Russians' attention were distracted for a moment, a small team might be able to reach it."

Bratt nodded. "Up," he ordered.

Surgical tools were pocketed in order to free hands. The group mounted the ladder in the same order as before. Matt followed Amanda. He reached the top and pulled himself into the next service shaft.

A shout sounded behind him. Russian. It came from down the tunnel to the lab on Level Four.

"Damn it," Greer growled.

The Russians had already found their rabbit hole.

A shot rang out. The slug ricocheted down the shaft and rebounded into the cubbyhole. Ice blasted as the bullet struck the wall, inches from where Washburn climbed the ladder.

Matt reached down and helped haul her up. Nimble as a cat, Washburn slipped past him. "Get the others moving faster," he urged her.

No further prompting was needed. Everyone in the chute had frozen at the rifle blast, but now they hurried away, Bratt in the lead.

A new commotion echoed down to them. Mumbled orders in Russian. They were hard to discern. Matt's ears were still ringing, but he didn't like the furtive tone of this new speech.

Matt leaned over the tunnel opening. "Get your asses up here!" he hissed down to the last two men. They had both splayed themselves against the walls to either side, wary of further gunshots.

Greer leaped to the ladder first, flying up like a monkey. Pearlson was at his heels, practically crawling up his partner's legs.

Matt grabbed the loose hood of Greer's parka and dragged the man to him, then shoved him after the others.

Pearlson had one hand on the lip of the service shaft. Matt turned to help him next. Over the seaman's shoulder, he saw a black object bounce into the room below.

Matt's eyes widened with horror. It looked like a matte-black pineapple.

Pearlson must have been looking at Matt's face at that moment. "What . . . ?" He glanced back over his own shoulder.

The black object danced on the ice, striking the wall at the base of the ladder.

"Shit!" Pearlson said, staring up at Matt.

Matt lunged out and grabbed the seaman's hood.

Pearlson knocked his arm away and leaped up, covering the shaft's opening with his own torso. "Go!" he wailed in grim terror.

Matt fell back as the grenade exploded. The concussion knocked him farther back. The flash of brightness blinded him. He felt a wash of heat over his face and neck. He surely screamed, but was deaf to it.

The flash died away immediately, but not the heat—it grew more intense.

The source became horribly clear as Matt's vision blinked back.

Pearlson still blocked the exit, but his clothes were on fire. No, not his clothes—his entire body.

It had been no ordinary grenade, but an incendiary device, exploding with liquid fire.

Pearlson's body tumbled backward as the end of the shaft melted toward Matt, the rubber matting bubbling. He backpedaled away. His face and neck felt sunburned. If Pearlson hadn't shielded the chute, they all would've been parboiled inside. The residual heat still felt like an open oven. The ice turned to water, dripping all around.

The Russians must have known they ran a good chance of losing the escapees in the warren of service tunnels and chutes. Their ploy had been brutal and swift. The grenade would either kill them or flush them out.

A hand grabbed Matt's shoulder.

It was Greer. The lieutenant stared unblinking toward the melted ruins. "Move it."

Matt's ears still throbbed. He barely heard the man, but he nodded.

Together they crawled after the others.

But where could they go? Death lay either way. The only question remaining was the method of their demise. Matt stared ahead, then behind.

Ice or fire.

12

Raiding Parties

ᓂᖕᑲᕈᒻᒪᕐᑐᑦ ᓴᕚᒡᓴᖅᑲᐅᑦ

APRIL 9, 2:15 P.M.
USS *POLAR SENTINEL*

The group of men and women awaited Captain Perry's order. The *Polar Sentinel* hung at periscope depth under an open lead between two ice floes. Winds wailed just feet overhead, blasting at sixty miles per hour across the open plains, but here, submerged, it was deadly quiet.

Perry turned to the radioman, a freckle-faced petty officer, who looked as pale as the white sheaves of paper in his hand. "And there remains no expectation of satellite contact?" Perry asked.

The twenty-two-year-old radioman swallowed hard, but he bore the heavy weight of the group's gazes. "No, sir. The magnetic storm is fiercer than the blizzard above. I've tried every trick I could think of."

Perry nodded. They were still on their own. The decision could not be put off any longer. Half an hour ago, the same radioman had rushed into the conn. He had picked up a message in Russian over the UQC. The underwater phones, while convenient for communicating short distances, offered no privacy, especially to a boat equipped like the *Sentinel*. The small submarine was not only fast and silent, but it had the best ears of any vessel in the sea.

Sailing twenty miles away, they had intercepted the vague sonar communication between the Russian team's leader and the captain of the *Drakon*. Their shipboard translator had made short work of the brief exchange. Perry had listened to the recording himself, heard the cold, hollow voice issue the order.

Ignite the buried charges. Melt the entire base into the ocean.

The Russians intended to lay waste to everything. The civilians, the remaining soldiers . . . all would be sacrificed, burned off the ice cap.

Upon hearing this, Perry had immediately ordered the helm to find someplace to raise their antenna. Even though it was doubtful anyone could still respond in time, an emergency Mayday had to be sounded. The timetable was too short.

But even this feeble effort had met with failure. Fifteen minutes ago, they had surfaced in a thin lead, hummocked by snowbanks on either side. The antenna array had been sent up into the topside blizzard, and the radioman went to work. But it was no use. Communications were still down.

Dr. Willig stepped forward now. The Swedish oceanographer had become the spokesman for the civilians aboard. "Those are our people over there, our colleagues, our friends, even family. We understand the risk involved."

Perry studied the faces around him. His crew, manning their respective stations, wore expressions just as determined. He turned and climbed the step up to the periscope stand. He took a moment to weigh his own motivations. *Amanda was over there . . . somewhere.* How much of his judgment now was skewed because of his feelings for her? How much was he willing to risk: the crew, the civilians under his protection, even the boat?

He read the determination in the others, but it was ultimately his responsibility. He could either continue their flight to the Alaskan coast, or he could head back to Omega and do what he could to rescue the personnel.

But what challenge could the *Sentinel* offer the larger, fully armed Russian hunter/killer? They had only three weapons at hand: *speed, stealth,* and *cunning.*

Perry took a deep breath and turned to the waiting radioman. "We can't wait any longer. Float a SLOT in the lead here. Set it for continual broadcast to NAVSAT, looped with the recorded Russian message."

"Aye, sir." The man fled back to his shack.

Perry glanced at Dr. Willig, then faced his second-in-command. "Diving Officer, make your depth eight-five feet, thirty-degree down angle . . ."

Everyone held his or her breath, awaiting his decision. Where would they go from here: forward or back?

His next order answered this question. "And rig the boat for ultraquiet."

2:35 P.M.
ABOARD THE *DRAKON*

Captain Mikovsky stood watch over the helmsman and planesman as the two men guided the surfacing submarine up into the polynya. His diving officer, Gregor Yanovich, watched the depth gauge, sounding their rise.

All was steady.

Gregor turned to him. The officer's eyes were haunted by worry. The man had been his XO for almost a full year. The two men had grown to know each other's moods, even thoughts. Mikovsky read his officer's internal wrangling now: *Are we really going to do this?*

Mikovsky merely sighed. They had their orders. After the prisoners' escape, the drift station had become more of a risk than an asset to their mission.

"All vents shut," the chief called out, glancing to his captain. "Ready to surface."

"Surface," Mikovksy ordered. "Keep her trim and steady."

Switches were engaged. Pumps chugged, and the *Drakon* rose, surfacing quickly and smoothly. Reports echoed up from the sub. *All clear.*

"Open the hatch," he called out.

Gregor relayed the order with a wave to the sailor stationed by the locking dogs. As the crewman set to work, the XO strode up to Mikovsky. "The shore team is ready to debark." The man's words were stilted, stiffly spoken, forced professionalism because of the grim task before them. "Orders?"

Mikovsky checked his watch. "Secure the prisoners. Double-check that the incendiaries are deployed as instructed. Then I want all men back aboard in fifteen minutes. Once the last man is aboard, we'll flood immediately and take her deep."

Gregor still stood, eyes no longer looking at Mikovsky, but off toward some imagined distance where what they were about to do could be fathomed and forgiven. But no one had eyesight that stretched that far.

Mikovsky gave the final order. "As soon as the deck is awash, blow the V-class series. There must be no trace of the drift station."

2:50 P.M.
ICE STATION GRENDEL

As Jenny climbed the next ice ridge, clawing her way up, she was glad her father had stayed behind at Omega. The terrain here was brutal. Her mittens already bore cuts from the knife-sharp ice. Her fingers ached, and the calves of her legs burned. The rest of her was chilled to the marrow.

With a gasp that was more of a moan, she pulled herself up to the lip of the ridge.

Already straddling the ridgeline, Kowalski helped her over, and together they slid on their butts and hands down the far side. "You okay?" he asked, pulling her to her feet.

She nodded, taking deep breaths of the frigid air, and turned as Bane and Ensign Pomautuk cleared the ridge next. The young man had to push the wolf's rear to get him over the edge. Then they both slid and trotted down the far side.

"How much farther?" Jenny asked.

Tom checked his watch with a built-in compass. He pointed an arm. "Another hundred yards."

Jenny stared where he indicated. It seemed impassable. It had taken them an hour, and they had barely crawled into the outer fringe of the mountainous pressure ridges that topped the buried station. Ahead, the land was folded, cracked, uplifted, and shattered. It was like hiking through a jumbled pile of broken glass.

But they had no choice.

They trudged onward. Winds crashed overhead, sounding like waves breaking against a stony shore. Snow frothed and foamed in billows and currents.

Jenny continued to use Kowalski's bulk as a windbreak. The brawny seaman was like some clay golem, marching steadily through the snow and ice. She focused on his shoulders, his backside, matching him step for step.

Then Kowalski suddenly tilted, tumbling down to a knee, arms flying out as he fell. "Fuck!"

His boot had shattered through a pocket of thin ice, revealing a small pool, no larger than a manhole cover. He sank to his thigh before catching himself on the edge. He rolled away, swearing a litany as he hauled his soaked leg from the freezing depths. "Fucking great! I can't seem to stop falling in the goddamn water."

Despite his bravado, Jenny noted the glimmer of true fear in his eyes. She and Tom helped him up. "Just keep moving," she said. "Your body heat and movement should keep you from icing up."

He shook free of their arms. "Where is this goddamn ventilation shaft?"

"Not far!" Tom led the way from here, Bane trotting at his side. Kowalski followed, grumbling under his breath.

Jenny, a step behind, heard a slight sloshing sound behind her. She glanced over a shoulder. The broken chunks of ice bobbled up and down, disturbed from below. *Just the currents.*

She continued after the others.

After another five minutes of hiking, Ensign Pomautuk's assessment proved true. They rounded a pinnacle of ice and found a true mountain of a peak blocking their way.

"We've reached the outer edge of the submerged ice island," Tom said.

Jenny stared underfoot. It was hard to believe she was walking on top of an iceberg, a monster extending a mile deep.

"Where's this ventilation shaft?" Kowalski asked, teeth chattering.

"Over there," Tom said, pointing to a black tunnel opening near the base of the mountain. It was too square to be natural, about a yard on each side. A brass grate had once locked it closed, but it had been peeled open, half buried in snow.

Polar bears, Jenny thought, *hunting for a den.* She approached warily.

Tom crossed without fear and dropped to his hands and knees. "We have to be careful. It's fairly steep. Forty-five degrees. We should rope up for safety."

Jenny fished the Maglite flashlight from her pocket and passed it to the ensign. He flicked it on and shone it down the tunnel.

"It looks like it makes an abrupt right turn about ten yards down," Tom said, pointing the flashlight. He slipped the coil of rope from around his shoulder. "Like one of the entrances to our snow houses."

Jenny leaned closer. It was typical of Inuit architecture to build one or two sharp turns in the entrance shaft of an "igloo." The turns blocked the snow-laden winds from a direct path into the home.

"Fuck it! Let's just get the hell inside." Kowalski shivered beside Jenny.

As Jenny straightened, the tiny hairs on the back of her neck suddenly quivered. As a sheriff, she had developed keen senses, a survival trait. *They were not alone.* She swung around, startling Kowalski with her sudden movement.

"What—?" he began, turning with her.

From around the pinnacle, something sloshed into view. It was heavy, with a bullet-shaped head, black eyes, claws digging in the ice. It lifted its muzzle and scented the air toward them.

Jenny stared, frozen. What the hell was it?

Bane jammed forward, barking a warning. His shoulders bunched, hackles bristled, head bent low.

The creature crouched at the threat. Blubbery lips rippled back to reveal the jaws of a great white.

That was enough for Jenny. Having grown up in Alaska, she knew that if it had teeth, it was going to try to eat you.

"Get inside!" she yelled, and grabbed Bane by his scruff. "Go!"

Tom didn't have to be told twice. He knew how to jump at orders and demonstrated his skill now. He dove down the shaft, belly first, sliding on the slick ice.

Jenny backed to the shaft's opening, dragging Bane.

Kowalski waved her inside. She lost her hold on Bane as she turned. The wolf trotted a few steps away and began to bark again. She reached for him, but she was blocked.

"Leave the dog!" Kowalski growled, manhandling her inside. He followed at her heels, leaving her no choice.

She slid down the steep ice chute.

"Bane," she shouted sharply back. *"Heel!"*

She glanced over her shoulder, but her view was blocked

by Kowalski's bulk. The momentum of their slide slowed as they neared the sharp turn in the tunnel.

"Crawl! Move it!" he urged her.

The shaft suddenly darkened behind them.

"Shit! It's following us!"

Jenny reached the sharp turn in the tunnel and glanced back. The creature clawed its way down the passage, scooting and undulating on its smooth belly, moving fast.

Bane raced only a few steps ahead of it, bounding down the shaft.

"Move!" Kowalski yelled, and tried to shove her around the corner.

But this time she held her spot, struggling with her parka. She ripped the emergency flare gun free from her pocket. "Get down!" She pointed it up the shaft.

The seaman flattened himself.

Jenny aimed past the wolf's ear and fired. The flare flamed across the distance, earning a startled yip from Bane as it sailed past him, and exploded against the muzzle of the beast.

The beast roared as light burst around it, blinding all its senses. It pawed at its stung face.

As Bane leaped to their side, Jenny rolled away. Crawling and sliding, she headed after the vanished ensign with the flashlight.

Kowalski kept a watch behind them until they rounded the corner. "It looks like it's heading back out." He faced Jenny. "Found you too damn spicy for its liking."

The way quickly became steeper. They were soon sliding headlong down the chute. Jenny did her best to brake herself with boots and hands, but the walls were slick.

After a minute, Tom called out to them, his voice echoing, "I've reached the end! It's not much farther."

He was right.

The light brightened, and Jenny found herself dumped out of the shaft into a large ice tunnel. Kowalski followed, landing almost on top of her, then Bane. Jenny rolled out of the way and stood, rubbing her hands. She stared around her. How far down into the ice island were they?

Tom stood by one wall. His finger traced a green diamond painted on the wall. "I think I know where we are . . . but . . ." He swung his flashlight back to the floor. Someone had spilled red paint.

Bane, his hackles still raised, sniffed at the marking.

Jenny climbed to her feet. Not paint . . . *blood.*

It was still fresh.

Kowalski shook his head. "We should've never left that damn drift station."

No one argued with him.

2:53 P.M.
OUTSIDE OMEGA DRIFT STATION

Master Sergeant Ted Kanter lay in the snowdrift, half buried, dressed in a polar-white storm suit, covered from head to foot. He stared through infrared binoculars toward the U.S. research base. He had watched the Russian submarine surface fifteen minutes ago, steaming into the blizzard gale.

He lay only a hundred yards from the station. His only communication to the outside world was the General Dynamic acoustic earpiece clipped in place. He wore a subvocal microphone taped to his larynx. He had made his report and continued his watch.

He had been ordered to remain at alert but to make no move.

Such had been his orders since arriving.

A quarter mile away, two white tents bivouacked the remainder of the Delta Force advance team, minus his partner, who lay hidden in a snow mound a couple yards away. The six-man team had been stationed here for the past sixteen hours, flown in and dropped in the dead of night.

His team leader, Command Sergeant Major Wilson, designated Delta One for this mission, was with the rest of the assault team at Rally Point Alpha, four miles away. Their two helicopters were covered with Arctic camouflage, hidden away until the go-order was given.

In position this morning, Kanter's team had watched from close quarters as the Russian submarine had arrived with the dawn. He monitored as the soldiers swamped the drift station and commandeered it. He had watched men killed, one shot only forty yards from his position. But he could not react. He had his orders: watch, observe, record.

Not *act,* not yet.

The mission's operational controller had left standing orders to advance only once the go-code was transmitted. Matters had to be arranged, both political and strategic. In addition, the mission objective, nicknamed the "football," had to be discovered and secured. Only then could they move. Until that moment came, Kanter followed his orders.

Fifteen minutes ago, he had watched the Russians leave the boat. He had counted the shore party, then added that number to the complement of hostiles previously stationed here, keeping track of the Russian forces.

Now men were returning. He squinted through his scopes and began counting down as the men returned to the sub and vanished through hatches. His lips tightened.

The pattern was clear.

He pressed a finger to his transmitter. "Delta One, respond."

The answer was immediate, whispering in his ear. "Report, Delta Four."

"Sir, I believe the Russians are clearing out of the base." Kanter continued to subtract forces as additional men climbed over the nearby pressure ridge and headed to the docked sub.

"Understood. We have new orders, Delta Four."

Kanter tensed.

"The go-code has been activated by the controller. Ready your men to move out on my order."

"Roger that, Delta One."

Kanter rolled back from his hiding spot.

Now the true battle began.

2:54 P.M.
USS *POLAR SENTINEL*

Perry paced the control bridge of his submarine as it raced under the ice. No one spoke. The crew knew the urgency of their mission, the risk. The plan was almost impossible to fathom. He knew that even if he succeeded, it could cost him his captain's bars. He didn't care. He knew right from wrong, blind duty from personal responsibility. Still another question nagged: Did he know bravery from simple stupidity?

While en route to Omega, he had come close a hundred times to calling the *Polar Sentinel* back around, ordering it to return to the safety of the distant Alaskan coast. But he never did. He simply watched the distance to their destination grow smaller and smaller. Had captains of the past been plagued by such doubts? He had never felt so unfit to lead.

But there was no one else.

"Captain," his chief whispered to him. The *Polar Sentinel* was baffled and soundproofed, but no one dared speak too loudly lest the dragon in the waters should hear them. "Position confirmed. The *Drakon* is already surfaced at Omega."

Perry crossed to the man. He checked their distance to Omega. Still another five nautical miles. "How long have they been there?"

The chief shook his head. Up until now, details had been sketchy. Without going active with their sonar, staying in passive mode, the exact whereabouts and location of the

Drakon had been fuzzy. At least they had found the other sub. Still, that narrowed their own window considerably. The Russians must already be evacuating the station. According to the intercepted UQC communication, the captain of the *Drakon* would blow the base once he began his descent. The Russian captain wouldn't risk damaging his own boat during the conflagration.

But what was the time frame?

His diving officer, Lieutenant Liang, stepped to his side. His features were tight with worry. "Sir, I've run the proposed scenario over with the helm crew. We've wrangled various options."

"And what's the time estimate for the maneuver?"

"I can position us in under three minutes, but we'll need another two to rise safely."

"Five minutes . . ." *And we still have to get there.*

Perry glanced to their speed. *Forty-two knots.* It was blistering for a sub running silent, but that was the *Sentinel's* advantage. Still, they dared go no faster. If the *Drakon* picked up the cavitation of their propellers or any other telltale sign of their approach, they were doomed.

He calculated in his head the time to reach Omega, to get in position, to orchestrate the rescue . . . and escape. They didn't have the time. He stared at his chief. If only the *Drakon* hadn't already been in position, weren't already evacuating Russian forces . . .

Liang stood quietly. He knew the same. They all did. Once again, he prepared to call their boat around. They had made a run for it, but it was hopeless. The Russians had beaten them.

But he pictured Amanda's smile, the crinkles at the corners of her eyes when she laughed, the way her lips parted under his own, softly, sweetly . . .

"Chief," Perry said, "we need to delay the *Drakon's* departure."

"Yes, sir."

"I want you to ping the other boat with active sonar."

"Sir?"

Perry turned to his men. "We need to let the *Drakon* know someone shares their waters. That someone is watching." He paced, running out his plan aloud. "They expected us long gone. That no one would be around to witness what is going to happen. By pinging them, it will force their captain to confer with his commander, delay a bit longer. Perhaps buy us the time we need."

"But they'll be on full alert with all their ears up," Liang said. "As it is, we'll be hard-pressed to sneak under their nose and perform the rescue maneuver."

"I'm aware of that. We were sent north to run the *Polar Sentinel* through its paces. To prove its capacity in speed and stealth. That's just what I intend to do."

Liang took a deep, shuddering breath. "Aye, sir."

Perry nodded to the chief. "One ping . . . then we go dead silent."

"Aye to that, sir." The chief shifted over to the sonar suite and began conferring.

Perry turned to his diving officer. "As soon as we ping, I want the helm to heel the boat away at forty-five degrees from our present course. I don't want them to get a fix on us. We run fast and silent."

"As a ghost, sir." Liang turned on a heel and retreated to his station.

One of the sonar techs suddenly jumped to his feet. "Sir! I'm picking up venting! Coming from the *Drakon*!"

Perry swore. The Russian sub was preparing to dive, taking on ballast, venting air. They were too late. The evacuation had already been completed.

The chief stared over at him. His face was plain to read: *Continue as planned or abort?*

Perry met the other's gaze, unflinching. "Ring their doorbell."

The chief spun around and placed a hand on the sonar supervisor. Switches were flipped and a button punched.

The chief nodded to him.

It was done. They had just given themselves away. Now to observe the reaction. A long moment stretched even longer. The *Sentinel* swung under their feet, deck plates tilting as the sub adjusted to a new trajectory.

Perry stood with clenched fists.

"Venting stopped, sir," the technician whispered.

Their call had been heard.

"Sir!" Another sonar tech was on his feet, hissing urgently for attention. The tech wore headphones. "I'm picking up another contact. Noise on the hydrophones." He pointed to his earpiece.

Another contact? Perry hurried to him. "Coming from where?"

The tech's eyes flicked upward. "Directly on top of us, sir."

Perry waved for the phones. The technician passed them to him, and he pressed an earpiece to his head. Through the phone, he heard what sounded like drums, beating slowly . . . more than one . . . their cadence picked up rapidly.

Perry had once been a sonar tech. He knew what he heard drumming through the ice from above. "Rotor wash," he whispered.

The technician nodded. "There are two birds in the air."

2:56 P.M.
ABOARD THE *DRAKON*

Mikovsky was getting the same information from his sonar crew. A moment ago, their boat had been pinged, deliberately and precisely. Clearly someone was in the waters below—and now another party was in the skies above.

The *Drakon* was pinned down, trapped.

If the other sub had pinged them, then they certainly had

a weapons lock. He could almost sense the torpedo aimed at his ass. The fact that no fish was already in the water suggested the ping had only been a warning.

Don't move or we'll blast your boat out of the water.

And he could not argue. He had no defense. Trapped in the polynya, the *Drakon* had no way to maneuver, no way to escape an enemy attack. Surrounded on all sides by ice, he couldn't even get a decent sonar sweep. While surfaced here, he was half blind.

Still, that wasn't the greatest danger.

He stared over the shoulder of his XO and studied the radar screen. The snowstorm and wavering magnetic fluxes in the region wreaked havoc with the readings. Two helicopters sped toward him, low over the ice, making contact difficult and target locks impossible, especially in the blowing whiteout surrounding the boat.

"They're coming in shallow, hugging ridgelines," Gregor warned.

"I'm detecting a missile launch!" another sonar man yelled.

"Damn it!" Mikovsky glanced to the monitors feeding from exterior cameras. He could make out vague outlines of the pressure ridges surrounding the lake. The rest of the world was solid white. "Aerial countermeasures. Blow chaff!"

There was no weaker position for a sub than surfaced. He'd rather be lying on the bottom of a deep ocean trench than where he was now. And that was where he was going . . . to hell with whoever had pinged them. He'd rather take his chances below.

"Flood negative!" he shouted to Gregor. "Sound emergency dive!"

"Flooding negative." A klaxon blared down the length of the boat. The submarine rumbled as ballast tanks were swamped.

"Continue blowing chaff until sail is awash!" Mikovsky

swung to the crew at the fire control station. "I want to know who's down here with us. Weapons Officer, I need a lock and solution as soon as we clear the ice."

Nods met his orders.

Mikovsky's attention flicked back to the video monitor. From the deck of his boat, a cloud of shredded foil belched into the air. The chaff was intended to distract the incoming missile from its true target. But the blizzard winds tore the foil away as soon as it exited from the sub, stripping the boat, leaving it exposed.

As the dive tanks flooded, the *Drakon* dropped like a stone—but not before Mikovsky noted movement on the monitor.

A spiral of snow . . . coming right at them.

A Sidewinder missile.

They would not escape.

Then the sea swelled over the exterior cameras, taking away the sight.

The explosion followed next, deafening. The *Drakon* jolted as if struck by a giant hammer. The sub rolled, carrying the video camera back to the surface. The streaming feed on the monitor showed the back half of the polynya. Its edge was cratered away, a blasted cove. The docking bollards sailed skyward. Fire spread over ice and water.

The missile had missed! A near miss, but a miss nonetheless. A lucky blow of chaff must have pulled the weapon a few degrees off course.

But from the force of the concussion through the water, the sinking *Drakon* had been shoved to the side and forced slightly back to the surface, exposing itself again. But not for long. The sub rocked stable and recommenced its stony plunge. The outside decks slipped under the sloshing water.

Mikovsky thanked all the gods of sea and men and turned away.

Then something caught his attention. On another video monitor. This camera, submerged a yard underwater, was aimed back toward the surface. The image was watery, but through the blue clarity of the polar sea, the image remained strangely vivid, limned by the flaming explosion of the Sidewinder.

On the video monitor, a soldier, dressed in polar camouflage, climbed into view on the opposite ridge. He bore a length of black tube on one shoulder, aimed square at the camera.

Rocket launcher.

A spat of fire flamed from the far end of the weapon.

Mikovsky screamed. "Ready for impact!"

He didn't even finish his shout when the *Drakon* shuddered from the rocket strike. This time it was no miss.

Mikovsky's ears popped as the rocket pierced somewhere aft, exploding a hole through the plating. *An armor-piercing shell.*

They were flooding. Smoke billowed into the conn. The *Drakon,* already heavy with water in the ballast tanks, yawed as the seawater pounded into the stern, lifting the nose. His planesman fought his controls to hold them level. Gregor leaned over him, yelling.

Mikovsky's ears rang. He could not hear his words.

The sub continued to tilt. A clanging hammered through the captain's temporary deafness. Additional hatches were being closed, manually and electronically, as the flooding sections of the boat were further isolated.

Mikovsky leaned against the thirty-degree tilt in the floor.

From the video monitor, he watched the nose of the *Drakon* break the water's surface, tilting high in the air like a breaching whale, while the stern, heavy with the flood, dragged downward.

They were exposed again on the surface.

Mikovsky searched quickly for the lone warrior who had fired the rocket—then spotted him. The parka-clad man ran along the ice ridge, diving down the far side, running full tilt.

Why was he fleeing?

The answer appeared out of the blowing snow a moment later. Two helicopters, both painted as white as the blizzard, a Sikorsky Seahawk and a Sikorsky H-92 helibus. From the bus, ropes tumbled out open doors as the craft slowed. Men immediately slid down the whipping lines, weapons on backs. The helibus then swung out in a wide arc, dropping soldiers behind it, aiming for the drift station.

Mikovsky could guess the identity of the new arrivals. He had been briefed by the White Ghost.

United States Delta Force.

The other helicopter, the Seahawk, flew over the listing submarine, buzzing it like a fly over a dying bull's nose. Mikovsky stared, sensing his doom. Under him, the *Drakon* sank into the sea, stern first. The best its captain could hope for was leniency for his crew, mercy from his captors.

As he prepared the order to abandon ship, the Seahawk flew right over the exterior camera. Mikovsky squinted at the monitor. Something was strange about the undercarriage of the aircraft. It took a full breath for Mikovsky to recognize what he was seeing.

Drums . . . a score of gray drums were attached to the Seahawk's belly, like a clutch of steel eggs.

He recognized them on sight. All sub commanders did.

Depth charges.

He watched the first drum drop free from the Seahawk's undercarriage, tumbling end over end toward the foundering sub.

Mikovsky had his answer to the fate of his crew.

There would be no mercy.

3:02 P.M.
USS *POLAR SENTINEL*

Perry stood in the Cyclops chamber, surrounded by the open Arctic Ocean. The *Sentinel* had retreated a safe distance away from the fighting, remaining silent in the waters. Even their motors were stilled as they floated.

Upon the first missile strike on the surface, Perry had ordered the *Sentinel* to dive deep. The *Drakon* was clearly under attack from the surface. This was confirmed a moment later when his sonar chief had reported a successful rocket attack. Listening from a half mile away, they had heard the explosion and the resulting *bubbling* of a ruptured submarine.

"It looks like the cavalry finally arrived," Lieutenant Liang had said, grimly relieved, voicing everyone's opinion.

The XO was probably right. The attackers had to be the Delta Force team noted in Admiral Reynolds's last message.

Still, Perry had wanted confirmation before letting anyone know of their presence in these waters. The timing of this attack was too perfect. How had the Delta Force team crossed the blizzard to arrive so opportunely? And why hadn't the two helicopters been heard before now? Had they been flying too high and were only picked up by the hydrophones as they made their bombing dive toward the surface?

Perry didn't like questions he couldn't answer—and in a submarine, paranoia was a survival trait. It kept you alive in dangerous waters.

As such, Perry stood in the forward chamber, watching the battle through the *Sentinel*'s window. He had wanted to see with his own eyes what was happening. He had tried to use the exterior cameras from the control bridge, but they didn't have the zoom capability to cross the distance.

So Perry had improvised. Standing now in the Cyclops chamber, he used a set of ordinary binoculars to watch the battle.

Half a mile away, the *Drakon* was nose up in the waters, silhouetted in the storm light beaming through the open lake above. She listed at close to sixty degrees, almost vertical in the water.

Perry watched, knowing that his counterpart on the other sub must be sounding the evacuation alarm. The battle was already over. The Russian crew had only one chance here: to abandon ship.

Then through the binoculars, a bright flash ignited the waters, freezing the image upon Perry's retina before temporarily blinding him. He blinked away the dazzle as the dull explosion roared to him. It sounded exactly like a rumble of thunder, followed by the rattling of deck plates from the distant concussion.

Perry's vision cleared. The *Drakon* was fully upright, surrounded in a whirlpool of bubbles. Chunks of ice, blown down from above, rattled back up out of the depths.

The room intercom buzzed. "Captain, Conn. We're reading a depth charge!"

Perry hurried away, tapping the intercom as he passed. "Pull us out of here!" he called out, then ducked through the hatch and ran back toward the bridge.

Another explosion shuddered through the boat, rocking the *Sentinel.*

These icy waters were about to get too damn hot.

3:03 P.M.
OMEGA DRIFT STATION

John Aratuk accepted death. He had seen entire villages, including his own, meet brutal and harsh ends. He had held his wife's hand as she lay dying, trapped in the wreckage of his drunken accident. Death was a constant in his life. So as others around him shouted or cried, he sat quietly, his hands bound with plastic ties behind his back.

Another explosion shook the barracks building, setting the hanging lamps to swinging. The ice under the buildings bowed and rattled from the forces of the nearby explosions, threatening to shatter the entire area.

Around John, the military men were struggling to get free of their bonds, using whatever sharp edge they could find to saw through the tough plastic.

The Russians had bound them after Jenny and the seaman had escaped, keeping them under constant armed guard. Then a few moments ago, the Russians had fled. It was clear from their hurried departure and frantic grab for supplies that they were abandoning the base.

But why? Had they discovered what they came to find? And what was to be their own fate? These questions had been bandied about, mostly among the civilian scientists. But John had seen the answer in Lieutenant Commander Sewell's eyes. He had overheard the conversation about the V-class incendiary bombs planted throughout the drift station. There was no doubt what was going to happen, what the Russians intended.

Then the blasts had started, rocking the ice, deafening even the storm.

"Everyone stay calm!" Sewell yelled in a firm authoritative voice. His attempt at assuredness was weakened as he almost lost his footing with another rattle of ice. He caught himself on one of the bed frames. "Panic will not help us escape!"

John continued to sit, unconcerned. Jenny had escaped. He had heard the Twin Otter buzz by overhead. John positioned his feet closer to the space heater.

At least he'd die warm.

3:04 P.M.
OUTSIDE OMEGA DRIFT STATION

Master Sergeant Kanter lay on the far side of a steep pressure ridge. The rocket launcher he had used to pierce the sub was propped beside him, but it was no longer needed. His ears ached from the concussion blows of the depth charges. Even though he was half shielded by the ridgeline, the explosions felt like punches to his solar plexus. Each one pounded at him.

He watched drum after drum drop into the sea, sink the preset ten feet, and blow. Water ballooned up, then exploded skyward, casting a funnel of water and ice high into the air. The float ice under Kanter bucked with each blow.

The wide lake of the polynya had turned into a roiling and hellish pool. Fires burned onshore. The edges of the lake were shattered. Steam flowed into the snowy blizzard, masking and shrouding the bulk of the sinking submarine. It foundered in the lake, vertical in the water, only its nose visible—and even this was sinking rapidly.

Kanter spotted a pair of Russian sailors bob up in the lake, struggling to keep their heads above water. They wore orange float suits. Evacuees, attempting to escape. It did them no good. A depth charge landed a yard from them. It blew, casting their shattered and broken forms through the air to smash against both ice and their own boat.

There would be no escape.

Farther out, the Sikorsky helibus circled the hovering Seahawk. It had dropped the remaining team members and awaited further orders. Somewhere Delta One was organizing ground forces to retake the U.S. research base.

But Kanter's attention remained on the polynya.

The majesty of the attack was breathtaking, a symphony of ice, fire, water, and smoke. He felt each explosion down to his bones, becoming a physical part of the attack himself.

Kanter had never been prouder than at this moment.

Then he spotted movement on the flank of the dying sub.

3:06 P.M.
ABOARD THE *DRAKON*

Mikovsky was strapped in a seat, as were most of the key bridge crew, trying to keep some semblance of order. Their boat was dead: compartments crushed, flooding everywhere, engines almost gone. Smoke choked through the bridge, making it difficult to think, to see. The explosions deafened them. The bridge crew wore emergency air-breathing masks, but such meager safety devices would not save them—only allow them one last act of revenge.

"Message relayed through digital shortwave!" the radioman yelled from the neighboring communication shack, half his face burned by an electrical fire he had managed to put out. His words sounded as if they came from down a long tunnel, hollow and whispery.

Mikovsky glanced to his weapons officer. He got the nod he wanted. They could not carry on proper protocol, but communication was still intact. His weapons officer confirmed the fire control solution and target fix—one unlike any calculated before.

Their vessel might be doomed, but they weren't dead.

The *Drakon* carried a full complement of two-hundred-knot Shkval torpedoes, SS-N-16 antisubmarine missiles, and one pair of UGST rocket torpedoes. This last pair were the latest in Russian design, powered by a liquid monopropellant with its own oxidizer. They were mounted in special flank tubes that deployed by pushing out from the sides of the boat. It had been an accident in such a deployment that had led to the *Kursk* tragedy back in 2000, a mishandling that led to the loss of all aboard.

There was no mishandling today.

He got the nod that the starboard UGST rocket tube was flooded and ready, target locked. All that remained was one word from him.

The last word he would ever speak.

"Fire!"

3:07 P.M.
USS *POLAR SENTINEL*

"I'm reading a weapons launch!" the sonar chief yelled, jerking to his feet. "Torpedo in the water!"

Perry started toward the man. "Target?"

The *Polar Sentinel* was in full retreat from the hot zone. The bombardment of depth charges threatened his own boat. The cap of ice overhead trapped the concussive waves from the explosions, radiating them outward under the ice. Like dropping a cherry bomb down a toilet.

But as the *Sentinel* fled, Perry kept tabs on the Russian sub. He was taking no chances.

"Target does not appear to be us," the sonar chief said.

"Then who?"

3:07 P.M.
OUTSIDE OMEGA DRIFT STATION

Frantic, Master Sergeant Kanter tried to raise Delta One. He needed to get the warning out.

"Delta One, here."

Kanter still wore his subvocal microphone—where the barest whisper could be heard—but now he yelled. "Sir, you have to tell the Seahawk—"

He was too late. From his vantage on top of the ice ridge, Kanter saw a blast of fire ignite below the churning waterline of the foundering submarine. From the flank side of its drowned bulk, a lance of gray metal burst out of the water, leaping into the air.

The missile rocketed skyward, aimed dead center on the Seahawk helicopter hovering overhead. It was impossible for the craft to get out of the way in time.

"Christ!" Delta One screamed in his ear, spotting the danger.

The torpedo struck the helicopter. It seemed for a moment

to spear completely through the Seahawk, an arrow piercing its target.

Kanter held his breath.

Then the rotors slammed into the thrusted tip of the torpedo rocket. The blast—accentuated by the two remaining depth-charge drums still attached to the helicopter's undercarriage—shattered outward in a ball of metal and flame.

Kanter dove behind his ridgeline, seeking shelter from the rain of oil and steel, covering his head. Through the noise of the explosion, he heard the telltale *whup-whup* of another chopper.

He glanced back over a shoulder.

The remaining helicopter, the Sikorsky helibus, raced overhead. Kanter saw it pelted with flaming debris, cutting right through the craft. A section of the Seahawk's broken rotor flipped end over end and crashed into the forward crew cabin. The helibus lurched over on its side, its blades chopping vertically at the air.

Kanter struggled to his feet, but the slick ice and blowing winds betrayed him. He fell. He fought again, fingers digging at the sharp ice. The toes of his boots fought for purchase.

He snapped a look up. The helibus plummeted toward him, spinning toward the crash, whipping around and around.

It was impossible to get out of the way in time.

Kanter simply rolled to his back. Staring skyward, he faced his death. *"Shit . . ."* He had nothing more profound to say and that bothered him more than anything.

3:14 P.M.
USS *POLAR SENTINEL*

Perry listened as stations reported their status.

He hardly heard, his mind still on what had just happened.

Moments ago, the *Drakon* had sunk away and rolled into the deep ocean trench below, fading beyond crush depth. Perry had listened himself to the final bubbling as the Russian submarine gasped its last breath and was gone.

But it had not died alone.

Float ice is a great drum, transmitting sound to the waters below. Perry had heard it all happen. Then a helicopter had jammed into the cap, shattering through it. It had been visible through the periscope. The wreckage hung for a stretch, lit by the fires of its own oil and fuel. Then the surrounding ice melted from the heat of the conflagration and released its hold. The twisted wreckage sank into the sea, chasing the *Drakon* down into the depths.

Now all had gone dead quiet.

Perry kept his own boat running silent, patrolling the waters.

What the hell was going on? Cut off from the world, he was unsure what to do next. Should they surface and attempt to contact those who'd taken out the Russians? Was it indeed a Delta Force team or could it be a third combatant? And what about the Russian ice station? Was it still commandeered by a team of Russian ground forces?

"Sir?" Lieutenant Liang was staring at him. "Do we prepare to surface?"

That was the most logical next step—but Perry held off.

A submarine was at its most effective when no one knew it was there, and he wasn't ready to give up that advantage. He slowly shook his head. "Not yet, Lieutenant, not yet . . ."

3:22 P.M.
PACIFIC SUBMARINE COMMAND
PEARL HARBOR, HAWAII

Admiral Kent Reynolds strode through the foot-thick steel blast doors of the command's flag plot room. Already in the cavernous room were his handpicked team, experts in their fields called in last night, most buzzed from their beds and set to work here.

The heavy door shut behind him, the locks engaging.

In the center of the room stretched a long conference table, constructed of polished native koa wood, a true Hawaiian treasure in rich, dark hues—not that any of the table's handsome surface could be seen through the piles of loose papers, books, folders, charts, and laptop computers.

Around the table, his team of communication, intelligence, and Russian experts worked singly and in small groups. Their voices were hushed, keeping private their conversations from one another. Even here, secrets were shared reluctantly among the factions gathered.

A tall, gangly fellow stepped away from one of the backlit wall maps. He wore an Armani suit minus the jacket, shirtsleeves rolled up. It was Charles Landley of NRO, the National Reconnaissance Office. A good family friend, he was married to one of Reynolds's nieces. He had been poring over a chart of the Arctic region, a map looking directly down upon the North Pole.

He turned now, wearing a tired expression, no welcoming smile. "Admiral Reynolds, thank you for coming so quickly."

"What is it, Charlie?"

Five minutes ago, Admiral Reynolds had been interrupted from a conference call with COMSUBLANT, his counterpart on the Atlantic coast, but Charles Landley wouldn't have summoned him away unless it was urgent.

"SOSUS has picked up a series of explosions."

"Where?" SOSUS was an ocean-based listening system of linked hydrophones. It could pick up a whale's fart anywhere in the seven seas.

Charlie stepped to the wall and tapped a spot on the map. "We believe with eighty-five percent probability that it was at the coordinates of the Omega Drift Station."

Admiral Reynolds had to take a deep breath. Fear for his daughter, Amanda, always present these last hours, flared to an ache behind his sternum. "Analysis?"

"We believe it was a series of depth charges. We also detected signature bubbling of an imploding submarine." Charlie lifted one eyebrow. "Prior to these strong detects, we also picked up what sounded like helicopter bell beats . . . but they were too weak to say for certain."

"A strike team?"

Charlie nodded. "That is what current intel believes. Without pictures from the Big Bird recon satellite, we're blind to what's going on."

"How long until the spy platform is clear of the solar storm?"

"At least another two hours. In fact, I believe that is why the Russians dragged their feet for two weeks after being leaked news of the Arctic discovery. They were waiting for this blackout window to open so they could proceed free of spying eyes."

"And the strike team that sank the sub?"

"We're still working on that data. It could be either a *second* Russian assault team—in which case, it was the *Polar Sentinel* that was sunk. Or it's our Delta Force team, and the *Drakon* has been scuttled."

Admiral Reynolds allowed himself a moment of hope. "It has to be the Delta Force team. The word I've gleaned from Special Forces is that the Delta teams were deployed in advance of the Russian attack."

Charlie stared at him, eyes pinched, pained. The admiral braced himself for his friend's next words. Something was wrong.

"I've learned something else." These words were spoken in hushed tones.

Admiral Reynolds's gaze flicked to the team gathering and collating data. Charlie had not shared whatever he had discovered with these others. The admiral sensed the next bit of news was the true reason he had been so urgently summoned. The throbbing behind his ribs grew more lancing.

Charlie led him over to a side table under one of the maps. A titanium laptop rested atop it, floating the NRO icon over its flat-screen monitor. Charlie booted the laptop and typed in his security code. Once it was up and running, he opened a file that required him to place his thumb over a glowing print-reader to open.

Stepping away, Charlie waved him forward.

Admiral Reynolds leaned toward the screen. It was a Pentagon memo stamped top secret. It was dated over a week ago. The heading was in bold type: GRENDEL OP.

Charlie shouldn't have been able to access this file, but NRO moved within its own channels. Its organization had its fingers and eyes everywhere. His friend deliberately concentrated on the wall map of Asia. It had nothing to do with the current situation, but he kept his attention focused there anyway.

Slipping a pair of reading glasses from a pocket, Admiral Reynolds leaned closer and read the message. It was three pages. The first section detailed what was known about the history of the Russian ice station. As he read, Admiral Reynolds found his vision blurring, as if his body were physically trying to deny what it was seeing. But there could be no doubt. The dates, the names, were all there.

His gaze settled on the words *human experimentation*. It took him back to his father's war stories, of the liberation of Nazi concentration camps, of the atrocities committed within those dark halls.

How could they . . . ?

Sickened, he continued to read. The last part of the report detailed the U.S. military's response: the purpose, the objectives, the endgame scenarios. He read what was hidden at the ice station and the ultimate mission statement of Grendel ops.

Charlie reached a hand to his shoulder as he straightened,

steadying him, knowing he would need it. "I thought you deserved to know."

Admiral Reynolds suddenly found it hard to breathe. *Amanda* . . . The pain behind his sternum stabbed outward, lancing down his left arm. Bands of steel wrapped around his chest and squeezed.

"Admiral . . . ?"

The hand tightened on his shoulder, catching him as his legs weakened. Through a haze, he noted others in the room slowly turning their way.

Somehow he was on the floor, on his knees.

"Get help!" Charlie shouted, half cradling him.

Admiral Reynolds reached up and clutched at Charlie's arm. "I . . . I need to reach Captain Perry."

Charlie stared down at him, his eyes bright with worry and sorrow. "It's too late."

13

Run of the Station

⊲⊳ᶜᴸˢ∩ᒃᶜ ∆ᵇ⊲σ

Matt shivered as he leaned over the station schematics. The map was unfolded and spread on the floor of the cramped cubbyhole, another of the old service rooms carved out of the ice. He knelt on one side of the paper, flanked by Craig and Amanda. On the far side crouched Washburn, Greer, and Lieutenant Commander Bratt.

Off to the side, the group of biologists kept to themselves. Dr. Ogden stood, leaning on one wall, eyes glazed. His lips moved silently as if he were talking to himself, going over something in his head. His three grad students—Magdalene, Antony, and Zane—huddled together, wearing matching expressions of misery and fear.

A full half hour had passed since the fiery death of Petty Officer Pearlson. Racing on pure adrenaline, the remaining group had fled here to one of the service sheds on Level Three.

Since then, they had weighed several different strategies: from staying put and holing up, to dividing their numbers and fleeing throughout the warren of service passages to lessen the risk of the entire group's capture, even to trying to escape to the surface and make for the parked Sno-Cats and Ski-Doos. But as the pros and cons of each were discussed, one fact became clear. In each scenario, they would have a better chance of survival if they had additional firepower.

So before any decision about where to go next was made, they needed to reach the armory. Washburn had inventoried the WWII weapons locker. It held several boxes of Russian grenades, a trio of German-made flamethrowers, and a wall of oiled and sealskin-wrapped Russian rifles.

"They still work," Washburn said. "I test fired a pair last week. The ammunition is boxed in straw-filled crates. Here and here." She jabbed the end of her steel meat hook at two corners of the armory marked on the map.

Matt leaned closer, studying the layout. He had to shift the weight on his knees. Having lost his pants to Little Willy, he was left with only his long underwear. And kneeling on the ice was testing the limits of the garment's thermal capability.

Washburn continued: "We should be able to get in and out in under a minute. The problem is getting there."

Bratt nodded. Greer had returned a moment ago from scouting the service tunnel that led back to the station base. On this floor, the service hatch opened into the generator room and battery compartment. Unfortunately, the armory lay on the far side of the level, clear across the open central space.

Matt squinted, trying to force his brain to thaw and think. *There has to be a way . . .* Along with the others, he pored over the map.

The generator room had a side door that led to a neighboring electrical room, but from there, they would have to cross the open central space. Without a doubt, it would be guarded. And with the pilfered medical supplies as their only weapons, they would be hard-pressed to subdue the guards without rousing the rest of the base.

Matt sat back, lifting his knees from the ice and rubbing them. "And there's no other access into this level? We have to enter through the generator and electrical rooms."

Bratt shrugged. "As far as we know. We have only these plans to go by."

Craig spoke up. "Well, the obvious distraction would be to switch off the generators, black out the station, and make a run for the armory."

Greer shook his head. "We have to assume that the Russians know where the main generators are. If we knock out the power grid, they'll be swarming right where we don't want them." He tapped the map. "Level Three."

Amanda had been studying the lieutenant as he spoke, reading his lips. "Besides," she added, "even if we turn off the generators, the batteries will retain enough power to keep most of the lights on. They've been charging since the generators were first overhauled by the material sciences team."

Matt considered all sides of the discussion. "What if we leave the generators running"—he rested his finger on the designated room, then shifted it to the neighboring electrical suite—"but cut only the circuits to the top level of the station? If Lieutenant Greer is correct, such a blackout would draw the Russians' attention to that level, away from us."

Greer nodded to Bratt. "He's right, sir. I'd wager the Russians already have most of their forces up top. They'd be on heightened guard, believing we might make a break for the surface. Cut off the power to just that level and the whole occupying force will be rushing up there."

"Well, let's just hope that includes the guards stationed on our level," Bratt grumbled. He stared at the map, considering this option.

"Whatever we do," Amanda said, "we'd better act fast. At some point, the Russians are going to start sending search parties into these service tunnels."

"Or simply lob more incendiary grenades down here," Craig said dourly. The reporter crouched on his heels, arms

wrapped around his chest. His gaze flicked to the three tunnels that left the small room, clearly watching for Russian
commandos to storm through or for another of the black
pineapples to bounce in and incinerate the lot of them.

Bratt nodded and straightened. "Okay. Let's scout out the
electrical room. See if it's even possible and do a head count
on the Russians on this tier." He eyed the group. "Greer and
Washburn are with me."

"I'm coming, too," Matt said. He was not about to be left
behind.

Greer supported Matt's decision. "The man was Green
Beret, sir. And we sure as hell could use an extra body if we
have to take out any guards."

Bratt eyed Matt up and down, then nodded. "The rest will
stay here."

Matt raised his hand. "We should also have someone on
watch in the generator room. In case we get in trouble, they
could haul ass back here and get everyone else moving up
higher."

"Very good," Bratt acknowledged.

"I'll do it," Craig said, but he looked like the words had to
be choked out of him.

"Then let's get this done." Bratt folded up the schematic
and passed it to Amanda. He quickly reviewed the plan. "We
hit the lights. Use the distraction to take out any soldiers that
remain here. Then make a dash-and-grab on the weapons
locker."

Matt picked up the length of sharpened pipe from the
floor. He met Amanda's worried gaze and offered a smile
that he hoped looked reassuring.

"Be careful," she said.

He nodded and followed the Navy trio into the service
duct. Craig crawled on hands and knees behind him. The
generator room was only sixty feet down the tunnel. They
reached the end, and Washburn used her meat hooks to work
the vent free.

They crawled into the room. The reek of diesel oil and exhaust gases hung heavy in the humid, heated air. The generators rattled in their stanchions, plenty of noise to cover their invasion.

As they gathered, Matt noted the stacks of batteries against the left wall; each was the size of a standard air-conditioning unit. As he eyed the power storage units, a glint on the neighboring wall caught his eye. The corners of his mouth lifted with pleasure.

He dropped his pipe and crossed to the wall. He removed the heavy fire ax from its wall pegs.

"Oh, man," Greer griped, lifting the foot-long steel bone pins in his hands. "I wish I had seen that first."

"Finders keepers," Matt said, hefting the ax to his shoulder.

Bratt led them to the neighboring room. All four walls were covered with electrical panels. As they searched for the controls to Level One, Matt saw the difficulty immediately. Everything was coded in Russian Cyrillic.

"Here," Washburn whispered. She pointed to a set of hotdog-sized glass-and-lead fuses. "These are the relays for the first level."

"Are you sure?" Matt asked.

"My father was an electrician with Oakland PG&E," she said.

"And she reads Russian," Greer said. "My sort of woman."

"The main switch is corroded in place," she said. "I'll have to pull the fuses."

"Wait." Bratt crossed and posted himself at the door that led to the main room. A small window in the door allowed him to spy into the central open space. He pointed to his eyes with two fingers, then splayed four fingers up in the air.

He spotted four guards.

Bratt turned to them. "Mr. Teague," he whispered tersely, pointing to Craig. "Close the generator door. We don't want the noise to alert the guards when we open the main door."

The reporter nodded, closing the door and keeping guard in front of it.

Bratt turned to the others. "On my count," he whispered tersely. "Pull the fuses, then be ready to bolt." He lifted his hand, all fingers up. He counted down, lowering one finger at a time.

Five . . . four . . . three . . .

3:28 P.M.

Admiral Viktor Petkov stood in the entrance room to Level Four's research labs. The steel door lay on the floor behind him, the hinges and security bar cut away. Across the door's surface, letters were scored in Russian Cyrillic:

ГРЕНДЕЛ

It was the name of the laboratory, the name of the base, the name of the monsters that nested in the neighboring ice caves.

Grendel.

His father's project.

Viktor stood in front of an open cabinet. It contained dated journals, coded and stored, written in his father's own handwriting. Viktor didn't touch anything. He simply noted the missing volumes. Three of them. Whoever had been here knew what they had been looking for. A fist clenched. He could guess the identity of the thief—especially considering the news just related to him.

The young lieutenant who had relayed the update still stood stiffly at his shoulder, awaiting his response. Viktor had yet to acknowledge the man's hurried report.

A moment ago, the lieutenant had rushed in, insisting on speaking to the admiral immediately. The radio operator manning the UQC underwater phone had picked up some disturbing noises over the unit's hydrophone. He reported hearing distant blasts echoing under the ice shelf: multiple explosions.

"Depth charges," the lieutenant had related. "The radioman believes he was hearing the concussion of depth charges."

But that wasn't the worst of the news. Amid the explosions, a weak static-chewed message had been transmitted on shortwave. A Mayday from the *Drakon*. Their submarine was under attack.

It had to be the U.S. Delta Force team, finally having arrived on the playing field. Late, but making up for its tardiness with deadly efficiency.

The lieutenant had then finished his message, barely keeping the panic from his voice. "The radioman reported definite bubbling, marking a sub implosion."

Viktor fixed his gaze on the gaps in the shelf of journals. There was no doubt who had stolen the volumes: the same person who called the attack down upon the *Drakon*, the Delta Force controller, the leader sent in advance to covertly obtain his father's research, to secure it before calling in the clean-up crew. Now with the prize in hand, the Delta Forces had been mobilized.

"Sir?" the lieutenant mumbled.

Viktor turned. "No one else must know about the *Drakon*."

"Sir . . . ?" There was a long pause as the admiral fixed the man with his steel-gray eyes, then a strained response: "Yes, sir."

"We will hold this station, Lieutenant. We will find the Americans who were here earlier." He continued to clench a fist. "We will not fail in this mission."

"No, sir."

"I have new orders to pass on to the men."

The lieutenant stood straighter, ready to accept his assignment. Viktor told him what he wanted done. The Polaris engine had been unpacked and bolted to the floor on Level

Five. By now, all the crew had been briefed with the mission assignment: to retrieve the research here, then erase all signs of the base. And while the crew certainly knew the destructive nature of the explosive device on Level Five—believing it to be a mere Z-class nuclear incendiary device—none knew its true purpose.

The lieutenant paled as Viktor gave him the code to prime the Polaris device. "We will not let the Americans steal the prize here," he finished. "Even if it costs all our lives, that must not happen."

"Yes, sir . . . no, sir," the young man stammered. "My men will find them, Admiral."

"Don't fail, Lieutenant. Dismissed."

The lieutenant fled away. There was no threat like one's own death to motivate a crew. The Americans would be found, and the prize recaptured, or no one would be leaving this base alive—not the Americans, not the Russians, not even himself.

Viktor studied his wrist monitor as he listened to the lieutenant's footsteps retreating below. On the monitor, the Polaris star glowed brightly, marking his continued contact with the array. The center trigger remained dark.

He waited.

Before detonating Polaris, he had first hoped to return to Russia with his father's research in hand, to clear his family name. But now matters had changed.

Viktor had risen through the ranks to become admiral of the Northern Fleet because of his ability to mold strategies to circumstances, to keep the larger picture in mind at all times. He did so now as he stared at the tiny red heart-shaped icon in the lower corner of the wrist monitor, slipping back to another time.

He was eighteen, entering his apartment, full of pride, clutching his admission papers to the Russian Naval Academy. He smelled the urine first. Then the gusty breeze through the open door set his mother's body to swinging from her broken neck. He rushed forward, the admission papers fluttering from his fingers and landing under his mother's heels.

He closed his eyes. He had come full circle now, leaving his mother's body and ending here at his father's crypt.

From one death to another.

It was now time to complete the cycle.

Vengeance weighed far heavier on his heart than honor.

That was the bigger picture.

He opened his eyes and found the monitor had changed—subtly but significantly. The five points of the star continued their sequential flashing, winding around the dial, and the small heart icon still blinked with each pulse beat in his wrist. But now a new glow lit the monitor, a crimson diamond in the center of the star.

The lieutenant had followed orders.

The Polaris engine had been primed.

All was in readiness, requiring only one last act.

Viktor reached to the one button he had held off touching until now. He depressed the red bezel on the side of the wrist monitor, holding it for the required minute.

Seconds counted away—then the central trigger light on the wrist monitor began to flash. *Activated.*

He studied the blinking. The trigger marker flashed in sync with the heart icon in the corner of the screen. Only then did he let go.

It was done.

The detonation of the Polaris device was now tied to his own heartbeat, to his own pulse. If his heartbeat ceased for a minute's time, the device would blow automatically. It was an extra bit of insurance, a fallback plan in case all should turn against him.

Victor lowered his arm.

He was now a living trigger for the array. There was no abort code, no fail-safe. Once it was initiated, nothing could stop Polaris.

With its detonation, the old world would end, and a new

one would begin, forged in ice and blood. His revenge would be exacted on all: the Russians, the Americans, the world. Viktor's only regret in such a scenario was that he would not be around to see it happen.

But he knew how to live with regret . . . he had done it his entire life.

As he began to turn away, a sailor ran up to him, coming from the hall that held the frozen tanks. "Sir! Admiral Petkov, sir!"

He paused. "What is it?"

"S-something . . ." He motioned back to the hall. "Something is happening down there."

"What? Is it the Americans?" Viktor had left a group of guards by the service vent. They were to wait until the caustic blast from the incendiary grenade cooled, then proceed and hunt down any survivors.

"No, not the Americans!" The sailor was breathless, eyes wide with horror. "You must see for yourself!"

3:29 P.M.

. . . two . . . one . . .

From his post beside the electrical panel, Matt watched as Bratt finished his silent count, ticking down with his fingers, ending with a clenched fist in the air.

. . . *zero . . . go!*

Washburn began yanking at the fuses that powered Level One, but the old glass tubes were stubborn, corroded in place. She was going too slow.

Matt motioned her aside and used the butt of his fire ax to smash the line of fuses. The tinkling cascade of shards blew outward. A wisp of electrical smoke followed, snaking into the air.

The effect was immediate. Distant shouts echoed to the group.

Bratt waved them all to the door. Through the window, Matt saw a handful of men in white parkas rush toward the central spiral staircase. Rifles were at the ready. More shouting followed, interspersed with barked orders.

Two of the four men mounted the stairs and fled upward. Two remained on guard.

"A couple birds aren't leaving the nest," Greer grumbled.

"We'll have to take them out," Bratt said. "We have no other choice. Our hand is played."

The two soldiers, dressed in unzipped parkas, continued to man their posts, but they kept their attention fixed toward the stairs, their backs to the electrical suite.

Bratt pointed to Washburn and Matt. "You take the one on the left. We'll take the other." He nodded to Greer.

Matt readied his ax. He had never killed a man with such a crude weapon. In the Green Berets, he had shot men, even bayoneted one, but never hacked one with an ax. He glanced over to Craig.

The reporter stared, wide-eyed, unblinking at them. He sheltered by the door to the neighboring generator room.

"Watch through this window," Matt said. "If anything goes wrong, you haul ass back to the others. Get them running."

Craig opened his mouth, then closed it and nodded. He hurried over. Something fell out of his coat and clattered against the floor.

Bratt scowled at the noise, but the rumbling generators more than covered it. Matt retrieved the object. A book. He recognized it as one of the journals from down in the lab. He lifted an eyebrow and handed it back to Craig.

"For the story," the reporter said hurriedly, tucking it back away. "If I ever get out of this mess . . ."

Matt had to give the guy credit. He stuck to his guns.

"Ready," Bratt said.

Nods all around.

Bratt reached for the handle. He waited for a flare-up of

shouting from the levels above, then tugged the door open. The four of them ran through, splitting into two teams to cross toward the guards, whose backs still remained toward them.

Matt raced, oblivious to the ache in his feet. He carried the ax in both hands. Washburn flew beside him, outdistancing him in five steps.

But with her speed, she failed to spot the abandoned dinner tray on the floor.

Her foot hit it and skidded out from under her, turning her efficient sprint into a headlong tumble. She tried to catch herself on a table, but only succeeded in taking it down with her at the heels of the two guards.

The crashing noise drew both men around, weapons raised.

Bratt and Greer were close enough. With a flash of silver, Bratt whipped a scalpel at the man. It flew with frightening accuracy, impaling the man's left eye. He fell backward, mouth open, but before he could scream, Greer dove on top of him.

Matt faced his own target, leaping over Washburn's struggling form. "Stay down!"

Still in midair, he swung his ax in a wide arc—but he was too slow, too far away.

Gunfire spat from the end of the Russian's AK-47. It chewed a path over his shoulder, then oddly continued up toward the ceiling.

Only then did Matt notice Washburn below him. She had lashed out with one her meat hooks, impaling the soldier through the calf and ripping him off balance.

Matt landed as the guard fell back, hitting the floor hard. With the detachment that could only come from years of Special Forces training, Matt brought his ax down upon the head of the soldier. The skull gave way like a ripe watermelon.

Matt quickly let go of the handle, rolling away on his knees, as his target convulsed under the embedded ax.

Matt's hands shook. Too many years had passed since he'd been a soldier. He had made the mistake of looking into the eyes of the man he killed—rather, *boy* he had killed. No older than nineteen. He had seen the pain and terror in his victim's eyes.

Bratt was at their side. "Let's go. Someone surely heard that shooting. We can't count on the confusion buying us much time."

Matt choked back bile and climbed to his feet. Sorrow or not, he had to keep moving. He remembered Jenny's Sno-Cat vanishing into the blizzard's gloom amid sounds of gunfire and explosions.

They had not started this war.

A step away, Greer stripped his target's camouflage gear: parka and snow pants. "With all the noise, we'll need someone to act as lookout." He rubbed the bloodstains off the waterproof coat and began to pull it on, ready to stand in for the fallen soldier.

"Let me," Matt said. "You know better what we'll need from the armory."

Greer nodded and tossed the gear at him.

Sitting in a chair, Matt yanked the pants on over his boots. The man had a larger frame, making it easier. Once suited, he pulled the oversized parka over his own Army jacket and retrieved the AK-47 from the floor.

Meanwhile, Washburn and Bratt had dragged the bodies behind two overturned tables while Greer had used the butt of his weapon to shatter a few overhead bulbs, creating deeper shadows.

"Okay, let's move out," Bratt said, and led Washburn and Greer at a dead run toward the armory.

They vanished through the doorway.

Alone now, Matt pulled the parka's hood over his head, hiding his features. He stared down at himself.

If nothing else, at least I'll die with pants on.

He stepped closer to the stairway, placing himself be-

tween the stairs and the smeared pools of blood. So far no
one had come to investigate the short spate of gunfire—but
they would. Bratt was right. The confusion would last only
so long.

Matt prayed it lasted long enough.

His prayer was not answered. Footsteps suddenly
sounded on the stairs, echoing from above, pounding down
toward this level.

Damn it . . .

Matt moved closer, but he kept his head tilted to keep his
features hooded. A line of soldiers appeared, bristling with
weapons, ready for combat. They barked at him in Russian.

Too bad he didn't understand a word of it.

Instead he hurried forward, feigning panic. He kept his
weapon lowered, but his finger remained on the trigger. He
pointed his other arm down, frantically motioning toward
the lower levels. With all the shouting and noise, the soldiers
probably couldn't tell for sure from which level the gunfire
had originated. He tried to indicate it came from farther
below.

To reinforce the act, Matt took a step forward, like he
meant to follow the others down.

The leader of the squad waved him to hold his position,
then motioned his squad down the stairs. They continued
their dash into the depths of the station.

Matt backed away as the last man spiraled away into the
ice. He let out a loud sigh. His ruse would not last long—but
luckily it didn't have to.

Bratt appeared at the armory door, both shoulders loaded
with weapons. "Quick thinking there." He nodded to the
staircase. He must have been watching from the doorway.

Behind Bratt, Washburn and Greer exited, similarly
loaded, lugging a wooden crate between them.

"Grenades," Greer said as he passed, his words bitter.
"Now it's our turn for a surprise or two."

Together the group fled back to the electrical suite, then

into the generator room. Craig was no longer there. He must have retreated back to the others.

With a bit of manhandling, they crawled through the vent, hauling their arsenal, dragging the box of grenades behind them.

Matt led them, carrying the pilfered AK-47 and two additional rifles on his back. His parka pockets were full of ammunition.

Reaching the end, he rolled out of the duct and into the service cubbyhole. He stood up, his eyes darting around the room.

The place was empty. The others were gone.

Washburn came next. Her expression soured. "The reporter must have been spooked by the gunfire. He did what we told him and bugged out with the others."

Matt shook his head as the others crawled inside.

Greer scowled as he eyed the empty room. "I hate this. We go to all the trouble to bring in the party supplies and everyone's already left."

"But where did they go?" Matt asked.

Bratt had been searching the floor. "I don't know, but they took the station schematics with them. Our only map to this damn place."

3:38 P.M.

Admiral Petkov followed the young ensign down the hall. He kept his attention away from the frosted tanks with their frozen sentinels inside. He felt the eyes of the dead upon him, sensing the accusations of those unwilling participants in his father's experiments.

But those were not the only ghosts who laid claim to the lost base. All the researchers stationed here, including his father, had died—entombed in ice as surely as the poor unfortunates in this hall.

Among so many ghosts, it was only fitting that the *Beliy Prizrak,* the White Ghost of the Northern Fleet, should stride these halls now, too.

Ensign Lausevic led him onward, half stumbling as he tried to hurry but did not want to rush his superior. "I'm not sure what it means, but we thought you should see it for yourself."

Viktor waved the man on. "Show me."

The curved hall followed the exterior wall of this level. They were almost halfway around when laughter from up ahead trailed back to Viktor. They rounded the curve and spotted a cluster of five soldiers. They had been lounging, one smoking, until the admiral appeared.

Laughter strangled away, and the group straightened. The cigarette was hastily stamped out.

The group parted for the admiral. They had been clustered around one of the tanks. Unlike the other dark, frosted vessels, this one glowed from within. The frost had melted and wept down the glass front.

Viktor crossed to it. He felt the heat coming from its surface. A small motor could be heard chugging and wheezing behind it, along with a faint gurgling.

"We didn't know what to do," Lausevic said, running a hand through his black hair.

Inside the tank, what was once solid ice was now a bath of warm water, gently bubbling, its ice melted by a triple-layered heating mesh that covered the entire back half of the chamber. The mesh was the source of the light. The outer layers glowed with a ruddy warmth, while the deeper levels shone more intensely, brighter.

"Why wasn't I alerted to this earlier?" Viktor intoned.

"We thought it was a ploy by the Americans to distract us," one of the other men said. "It's right by the duct they fled through." He pointed to a nearby vent. A bit of smoke from the incendiary grenade still wafted through its opening.

"We weren't sure it was important," Lausevic added.

Not important? Viktor stared at the tank. He was unable to take his eyes from the sight.

Within the tank, a small boy floated, suspended within the bubbling water. His eyes were closed as if in slumber. His face looked so peaceful, smooth, olive-skinned, framed in a halo of shoulder-length black hair. His limbs floated at his side, angelic and perfect.

Then his left arm twitched, jerking as if pulled by the strings of an invisible puppeteer.

The young ensign pointed. "It's been doing that for the past few minutes. Starting with just a finger twitch."

The boy's leg kicked, spasming up.

Viktor stepped closer. *Could he still be alive?* He remembered the missing journals. That was the quest here. To retrieve his father's notes. To see if the last report made by his father was true. He had read this final report himself, hearing his father's voice in his head, as if he were speaking directly to his son.

He remembered the final line: *On this day, we've defeated death.*

He watched the boy. *Could it be true?* If so, the stolen notebooks wouldn't matter. Here was proof of his father's success. Viktor glanced to the soldiers. He had witnesses to verify it. Though the exact mechanism and procedure were locked in his father's coded notes, the boy would be living and breathing proof.

"Is there a way to open the tank?" Viktor asked.

Ensign Lausevic pointed to a large lever on one side of the tank. It was locked at the upper end marked CLOSED in Russian. The lower end of the levered slot was lettered in Cyrillic: OPEN.

Viktor nodded to the ensign.

He stepped forward, gripped the heavy handle with both hands, and tugged. It resisted the ensign's efforts for a moment. Then, with a loud *crack,* the lever snapped out. Lausevic used his shoulders to pull the lever and slam it down into the "open" slot.

Immediately a rush of water sounded, not unlike a toilet flushing. From his position, Viktor saw the grated bottom of the tank open. Water flowed down a drain.

Caught in the swirling force of the draining water, the boy's body spun, arms flailed out. His body seemed boneless, limp. He bumped against the glass, the back mesh. Then, as the water drained fully away, he settled in a loose pile on the bottom of the tank, as lifeless as some deep-sea denizen washed up on a beach.

Then with a soft, damp *pop,* the seal on the glass released. The entire front of the tank swung open like a door, blowing out compressed air from within. There was a faint hint of ammonia that came with it.

Lausevic pulled the door aside for the admiral.

Viktor found himself stepping forward, dropping to his knees beside the naked boy. He reached to the boy's arm, draped half out the door.

It was warm, heated by the bubbling bath.

But there appeared to be no life.

His hand slipped from wrist to the small fingers. He tried to will the boy back to life. What stories could he tell? Had he known his father? Did he know what had happened here? Why the base had gone dead quiet so suddenly?

It had been the last years of World War II. The Germans were marching into Russia, laying siege to city after city. Then a remote research station in the Arctic went quiet, late reporting in . . . first one month, then another. But with the war heating up at home, no one had time to investigate. With communication being what it was and travel through the polar region so difficult, there were no resources for a full investigation.

Another full year passed. Nagasaki and Hiroshima were bombed. Nuclear weaponry became the grand technology, hunted and sought by all. Ice Station Grendel and its research project were now antiquated, not worth the cost or manpower to discover its fate. The currents could have taken the station anywhere. The ice island that berthed it might even have broken apart and sunk, something not uncommon with such floating giants.

So more years passed.

The last report of his father, with its wild claims of breaching the barrier between life and death, was dismissed as exaggerated rants and shelved. The only bit of proof was supposedly locked in his journals, lost with the base and its head researcher.

The secret of life and death.

Viktor stared down at the slack face of the boy, so peaceful in slumber. Lips a faint blue, face gray and wet. Viktor wiped the face dry with one hand.

Then small fingers clamped onto his other palm, harder and stronger than Viktor could have imagined.

He gasped in surprise as the boy's body suddenly convulsed inside the tank, legs kicking, head thrown back, spine arched up, contorted.

Water poured from his open mouth, draining down the tank's grating.

"Help me get him out!" Viktor yelled, drawing the boy to him.

Ensign Lausevic squeezed in and grabbed the thrashing legs, getting a good kick to his temple in the process.

Between the two of them, they hauled the boy out to the hall. His body jerked and thrashed. Viktor cradled his head, keeping him from cracking his skull on the hard floor. The boy's eyes twitched behind their lids.

"He's alive!" one of the other soldiers said, backing a step away.

Not alive, Viktor silently corrected, *but not dead either. Somewhere in between.*

As the convulsions continued, the boy's skin grew hot to the touch; perspiration pebbled his skin. Viktor knew that one of the main dangers of epileptic patients during violent or prolonged seizures was hyperthermia, a raising of body temperature from muscle contractions that led to brain damage. Was the boy dying, or was his body fighting to warm life back into it, heating away the last dregs of its frozen state?

Slowly the convulsions faded to vigorous shivering. Viktor continued to hold the boy. Then the boy's chest heaved up, expanding as if something were going to burst out the rib cage. It held that swelled state, back arched from the floor. Blue lips had warmed to pink, skin flushed from the violence of the seizures.

Then the boy's form collapsed in on itself, seeming to cave in, accompanied by a strangled choke. Then he lay still again, back to tired slumber, dead on the floor.

A pang of regret, mixed inexplicably with grief, ran through Viktor.

Perhaps this is the best his father had ever achieved, significant but ultimately not successful.

He studied the boy's face, peaceful in true death.

Then the boy's eyes opened, staring up at him, dazed. His small chest rose and fell. A hand lifted from the floor, then settled back weakly.

Alive . . .

Lips moved. A word was mouthed, groggy, breathless still. *"Otyets."*

It was Russian.

Viktor stared up at the others, but when he gazed back down at the boy, the child's eyes were still on him.

Lips moved again, repeating his earlier word. *"Otyets . . . Papa."*

Before Viktor could respond, the pounding of many boots suddenly echoed to them. A group of soldiers appeared, armed. "Admiral!" the lieutenant in the lead called out as he approached.

Viktor remained kneeling. "What is it?"

The man's eyes flicked to the naked child on the floor, then back to the admiral. "Sir, the Americans . . . power's out on the top level. We think they're trying to escape the station."

Viktor's eyes narrowed. He stayed at the boy's side. "Nonsense."

"Sir?" Confusion crinkled the officer's eyes.

"The Americans are not going anywhere. They're still here."

"What . . . what do you want us to do?"

"Your orders have not changed." Viktor stared into the eyes of the boy, knowing he held the answers to everything. Nothing else mattered. "Hunt them. Kill them."

3:42 P.M.

A level below, Craig crawled down the service tunnel, map crumpled in his hand. The chamber had to be close. The others trailed behind him.

He paused at a crossroads of ductwork. The intersection was tangled with conduit and piping. He pushed his way through and headed left. "This way," he mumbled back to the rest of the party.

"How much farther?" Dr. Ogden asked from the rear of their group.

The answer appeared just ahead. A dim glow rose through a grated vent embedded in the floor of the ice shaft.

Craig hurried forward. Once near enough, he lay on his belly and spied through the grate to the room below. Viewed from above and lit by a single bare bulb, the chamber appeared roughly square, plated in steel like the station proper, but this room was empty, long abandoned and untouched.

It was the best hiding place Craig could think of.

Out of the way and isolated.

He wiggled around so he could use his legs to kick the grate loose. The screws held initially, but desperation was stronger than rusted steel and ice. The vent popped open, swinging down.

Craig stuck his head through to make sure it was clear, then swung his feet around and lowered himself into the room.

It was not a long drop. The room had flooded long ago. The water had risen a yard into the room, then froze. A few crates and fuel drums were visible, half buried in the ice. A shelving unit stacked with tools rose from the ice pool, its first three shelves anchored below.

But the most amazing sight was the pair of giant brass wheels on either far wall. They stood ten feet high with thick hexagonal axles attached to massive motors, embedded in the ice floor. The toothed edges of the wheels connected to the grooves of a monstrous brass wall that encompassed one entire side of the room.

The wheel on the right side lay crooked, broken free from some old blast. Scorch marks were still visible on its brass surface. The dislodged wheel had torn through the neighboring steel wall, cracking through to the ice beyond. Perhaps it was even the source of flooding.

Craig peered through the crack. It was too dark to see very far.

"What is this place?" Amanda asked as she landed in a crouch. She stood, staring at the gigantic gearworks.

Craig turned to her so she could read his lips. "According to the schematics, it's the control room for the station's sea gate." He pointed to a grooved brass wall. "From here, they would lower or raise the gate whenever the Russian submarine docked into the sea cave below."

By now the others—Dr. Ogden and his three students— had dropped into the room. They stared around nervously.

"Will we be safe here?" Magdalene asked.

"Safer," Craig answered. "We had to get out of the service ducts. The Russians will be swarming and incinerating their way through there. We're better off holing up here. This room is isolated well off the main complex. There's a good chance the Russians don't even know this place exists."

Craig crossed to the single door, opposite the sea gate. There was a small window in it. Beyond he could see the narrow hall that led back to the station. It had flooded almost to the roof. No Russians would be coming from that direction.

Amanda had to lean in close to read his lips. "What about Matt and the Navy crew?"

Craig bit his lip. He had a hard time meeting her eye. "I don't know. They'll have to take care of themselves."

Earlier, while watching from the electrical room, he had seen Washburn slip and fall, alerting the two Russian guards. The resulting rifle fire had driven him back to the civilian party. Surely Matt and the others were dead or captured. Either way, he couldn't risk staying around. So he had led their group off—going down rather than up. The gate control room seemed the perfect hiding place.

Dr. Ogden, along with his graduate students, stepped to join them, careful of the icy floor. "So are we just going to hide here, simply wait for the Russians to leave?"

Craig shifted aside a wooden box of empty vodka bottles. The last survivors of Ice Station Grendel must have had a party at the end. The bottles clinked as he moved them. Wishing for a stiff drink himself, he sat on one of the crates. "By now, someone must know what's going on here. Help has to be on its way. All we have to do is survive until then."

Amanda continued to stare hard at him, her gaze penetrating. Craig sensed her deep anger. She had not wanted to flee earlier, not without knowing the exact fate of Matt and the Navy crew. But she had been outvoted.

Craig looked away, unable to face that silent accusation. He needed something to distract himself, something to get all their minds off of their current situation. He reached inside his jacket and pulled out one of the three volumes he had looted from the research laboratory. Here was a puzzle to help them bide their time. Perhaps even one of the scientists might have a clue to deciphering this riddle.

Amanda's eyes widened, recognizing the book. "Did you steal that?"

Craig shrugged. "I took the first volume and the last two." He slipped the other books from his jacket and passed one to Amanda and one to Ogden. "I figured these were the best. The beginning and the end. Who needs to read the middle?"

Amanda and Dr. Ogden opened their copies. The biologist's students peered over their professor's shoulder.

"It's written in gibberish," Zane, the youngest of the trio of grad students, commented, his face screwed up.

"No, it's a code," Amanda corrected, fanning through the pages.

Craig cracked the third volume that still rested in his lap. He stared at the opening line.

ᒐᐅᑎᑕᑭᓂᒡᐤᒎ   ᒍᖅᒡᑯᒡᑎᑊᒎᐣᑕᓐᖕᓯ
ᐅᑎᑊᒎᖕᐃᑎᐸᓐᓂᓐ   (ᑭᑊᖏᖅᑕᒡᑭᑊᒎ

"But what's this script?" Craig asked. "It's clearly not Russian Cyrillic."

Amanda closed her book. "All the journals are like this. It'll take a team of cryptologists to decipher them."

"But why code it at all?" Craig asked. "What were they hiding?"

Amanda shrugged. "You may be reading too much into the code. For centuries, scientists have been paranoid about their discoveries, hiding their notes in arcane manners. Even Leonardo da Vinci wrote all his journals so that they could only be read when reflected in a mirror."

Craig continued to stare at the odd writing, trying to find meaning in the squiggles and marks. But no answer came. He sensed something was missing.

As he sat, a new sound intruded. At first he thought it was his imagination, but the noise grew in volume.

"What is that?" Magdalene asked.

Craig stood up.

Amanda stared around at the others, confused.

Craig followed the noise to its source. It echoed out of the crack, where the broken wheel had shattered through the wall. He crouched, ears cocked.

"I . . . I think . . . it's barking," Zane said as the others crowded around.

"It's definitely a dog," Dr. Ogden said.

Craig corrected the biologist. "No, not dog . . . *wolf*!" Craig recognized the characteristic bark. He had heard it often enough over the past few days. But it made no sense. He could not keep the amazement out of his voice. "It's *Bane*."

Three Blind Mice

ᐱᖁᒍᕆᐊᑦ ᖅᑲᐱᑐᑦ ᐊᕐᖁᒡᓕᐊᐊᑦ

Crouched at an intersection of tunnels, Jenny signaled Bane to be quiet by raising a clenched fist. At her side, the wolf cross growled deep in his throat, pushing tight to her, protective. Matt had trained the dog to respond to hand commands, an especially useful tool while hunting out in the woods.

But in this case, *they* were the prey.

Tom Pomautuk stood behind her, flanked by Kowalski. He pointed to the green spray-painted diamond that marked the tunnel to the left. "That way," he whispered, breathless with terror.

Jenny pointed for Bane to take the lead. The dog trotted ahead, hackles raised, alert. They followed.

For the past half hour, they had caught glimpses of the beasts: massive, sleek, and muscular creatures. But similar to their experience with the first creature, they had found a way to keep them at bay.

Jenny gripped her flare gun. The explosion of light and

heat from a flare blast was enough to disorient the creatures and send them scurrying back—but they continued to dog their trail. And now they were down to two charges, loaded already in the double-barreled gun. After that, they were out of ammunition.

The light around them suddenly flickered, going pitch-dark for a long moment. Tom swore, knocking the flashlight against the wall. The light returned.

Kowalski groaned. "Don't even think about it."

The flashlight, retrieved from the emergency kit in the Twin Otter, was old, original gear that came with the plane. Jenny had never changed its batteries. She cursed her lax maintenance schedule as the flashlight flickered again.

"C'mon, baby," Kowalski moaned.

Tom shook the light, throttling it with both hands now. But no amount of rattling could fan the flashlight back to life. It died.

Darkness fell around them, weighing them all down, pressing them together.

"Bane," Jenny whispered.

She felt the familiar rub on her leg. Her fingers touched fur. She patted the dog's side. A growl rumbled deep in him, silent but felt through his ribs.

"What now?" Tom asked.

"The flares," Kowalski answered. "We can strike one of 'em, carry it. It might last till we find somewhere safe to hole up away from these monsters."

Jenny clutched her flare gun. "I only have two charges left. What'll we use to chase the creatures off?"

"Right now, we need to *see* the creatures if we have any hope of surviving down here."

Jenny couldn't argue with that logic. She cracked open the weapon and fingered one of the charges.

"Wait," Tom whispered. "Look over to the right. Is that light?"

Jenny stared, straining to see anything in the darkness.

Then she noted a vague spot of brightness. Something glowing through the ice. "Is it the station?"

"Can't be," Tom answered. "We should still be a ways off from the base entrance."

"Well, it's still a source of light." Kowalski stirred beside Jenny. "Let's check it out. Light one of the flares."

"No," Jenny said, staring toward the ghostly light. She reseated the flare and closed her gun. "The brightness will blind us to the source."

"What are you saying?" Kowalski grumped.

"We'll have to seek our way in the dark." Jenny pocketed the gun and groped out for Kowalski. "Join hands."

Kowalski took her palm in his. She fumbled and found Tom's hand.

"Heel, Bane," she whispered as they set off, Kowalski in the lead.

Like three blind mice, they crept down the tunnel, making the next turn that headed toward the light source. It was slow going. Jenny felt an odd tension in her jaw, as if she were clenching it, a minute vibration deep behind her molars. It had been with them ever since they entered the tunnels. Perhaps it was a vibration from whatever generators or motors powered the station above them.

But she wasn't convinced. If they were far from the station, why did it seem to be growing stronger?

They made a few more turns, zeroing toward the light.

"It feels like we're heading deeper again," Kowalski said.

In the pitch dark, it was hard to tell if the seaman was correct.

"We have to be well off that marked trail we were following," Tom said. "We could just be getting ourselves lost."

"The light's stronger," Jenny said, though she wasn't sure. Maybe it was just her eyes growing accustomed to the darkness. The inside of her head itched. *What was that?*

"This reminds me of my grandfather's stories of Sedna," Tom whispered.

"Sedna?" Kowalski asked.

"One of our gods," Jenny answered. She knew they probably shouldn't be talking so much, but in the darkness, it was a comfort to hear another's voice. "An Inuit spirit. Like a siren. She is said to lure fishermen into the sea, chasing after her glowing figure until they drowned."

"First monsters, now ghosts . . . I really hate the Arctic." Kowalski squeezed her fingers tighter.

They continued on, sinking into their own thoughts and fears.

Jenny heard Bane padding and panting at her side.

After a full minute, they rounded a curve in the tunnel and the source of the light appeared. It came from an ice cave ahead—or rather from a crumbled section of the back wall. The ice glowed with a sapphire brilliance, piercing after so much darkness.

They let go of one another and edged forward.

Kowalski entered the cave first, searching around. "A dead end."

Tom and Jenny joined him, studying the shattered section of wall. "Where's the light coming from?" Jenny asked.

She was heard.

A voice called out from ahead. *"Hello!"* It was a female voice.

Bane barked in response.

"Tell me that's not Sedna?" Kowalski hissed.

"Not unless she's learned English," Tom replied.

Jenny shushed Bane and returned the shout. "Hello!"

"Who's out there?" another voice called, a man this time. Jenny reacted with shock as she recognized the voice. "Craig?"

A pause. *"Jenny?"*

She hurried forward. The shattered section of wall revealed a vertical crack in the surface. The light streamed out toward them. Through a crack, only two inches wide, faces peered back at her. They were only a yard away. Tears rose in her eyes.

If Craig was here, then surely Matt . . .

"How . . . What are you doing here?" Craig asked.

Before she could answer, Bane began to bark again. Jenny turned to quiet him, but the wolf faced back toward the passage from which they'd come.

At the tunnel mouth, red eyes stared out at them, reflecting the feeble light.

"Shit," Kowalski said.

The creature hunkered into the cavern, wary and snorting, coming toward them. This beast was the largest they'd seen yet.

Jenny yanked out her flare gun, aimed, and fired. A trail of fire arced across the ice cavern and burst between the forefeet of the beast. The exploding flare blinded them all with its flash.

Against the glare, the beast reared up, then slammed down. It backpedaled its bulk down the passage, away from the fiery display.

Tom and Kowalski edged closer. "We can't trust that thing will stay gone for long," the seaman said.

Jenny clenched her gun. "I only have one more flare." She turned to the crack in the wall. "Then we have nothing to chase them off with."

Craig heard her. "They're grendels. They've been hibernating down here for thousands of years."

Jenny pushed such matters aside for now and asked the other question utmost in her mind. "Where's Matt?"

Craig sighed. He took a moment too long in answering. "We got separated. He's somewhere in the station, but I don't know where."

Jenny sensed something unspoken behind his words, but now wasn't the time to question him. "We need to find another way out of here," she continued. "Our flashlight is out, and we're down to one flare to defend ourselves."

"How did you get down here?" he asked.

Jenny waved vaguely behind her. "Through a ventilation shaft back there. It goes to the surface."

"Well, it's not safe anywhere out there. We've some metal tools in here. Maybe we could hack the crack wider. Get you through to us." His voice was full of doubt.

The ice was a yard thick. They'd never make it.

Another voice spoke from behind Craig. A woman, the same one who had called out earlier. "What about the fuel drums for the sea-gate motors? Maybe we could create a gigantic Molotov cocktail. Blow a way through."

Craig's face moved away from the crack. "Hang on, Jen."

She heard muffled words, arguing, as the group beyond sought some solution or consensus. She heard something about the noise alerting the Russians. She glanced over to the flare as it began to fade. She would rather take her chances with the Russians.

Craig again appeared at the crack. "We're going to try something. You'd better stand back."

Something was shoved into the crack. It looked like a hose nozzle. It smelled of kerosene and oil.

Jenny scooted back from the wall. Tom and Kowalski continued to guard the tunnel with Bane at their side.

A flicker of flame dazzled in the crack, then a *whoosh* of fire blasted toward Jenny. She fell backward as a ball of flame rolled past her face. The heat singed her eyebrows.

"Are you okay?" Kowalski asked, stepping toward her.

She waved him back, pushing up. "I don't think I need to worry any longer about that bit of frost nip on my nose."

"You're lucky you still have a nose."

In the crack, a blazing inferno glowed. Flames lapped out into the cavern. Steam sizzled and billowed, instantly precipitating and wetting walls, floors, and bodies. Runnels of fiery oil seeped into their cavern.

It was surreal to see flames dancing atop ice.

"They're trying to melt a path through for us," Jenny realized.

The fiery channels traced across the floor toward them, driving them back.

Kowalski frowned. "Let's hope they don't set us on fire first."

4:12 P.M.

Amanda held the hose nozzle while one of the biology students, Zane, manned the manual pump. "Keep the pressure up," she ordered, yanking the release lever and spraying more fuel onto the fire in the crack, careful not to let the flames leap to the hose. She had to be careful. Strong outward pressure had to be maintained. It was like trying to add lighter fuel to an already burning barbecue.

Craig was on the other side of the crack, shielding his face with his hand. Steam roiled out, along with smoky billows. Underfoot, channels of water ran into the room as the ice blockage melted. Floating oil burned in several patches, washed out with the meltwater. The biology team smothered them with fire blankets found among the supplies on the shelves.

Craig turned to her. "We're about halfway through."

"How wide?" she asked, reading his lips.

"A foot and a half, narrow but enough to squeeze through, I think."

Amanda nodded and continued her deft fueling. It would have to do. They didn't want the melted tunnel too wide or the grendels could follow the other party in here.

But the grendels weren't the only danger.

Magdalene waved from her post by the door, drawing Amanda's attention. "Stop!" she mouthed.

Amanda cut the hose feed.

The biology postgrad had pressed against the wall beside the door. She thumbed toward it. "Soldiers."

Craig crossed to her. He peeked through the door window, then ducked away. He faced Amanda. "They've pried open the far door. The hall out there is flooded and frozen over, but they surely spotted the flickering flames through the window."

"But they can't know it's us," Ogden said, clutching his fire blanket.

Craig shook his head. "They'll have to investigate the fire. Until they're finished here, they won't want the base blowing up under them."

Amanda spoke, careful to modulate her voice to a whisper, "What are we going to do?"

Craig eyed the crack. "Come up with a new plan since this one's screwed."

"What—?"

Craig shook his head, his face going unusually hard. He pulled the drawstring on his parka's hood and pressed it to his ear, then lifted the wind collar of his coat and pressed it against his throat.

Amanda watched his lips.

"Delta One, this is Osprey. Can you read me?"

4:16 P.M.

"Delta One, respond," Craig repeated more urgently.

He listened for any response. The miniature UHF transmitter in the lining of his parka was efficient at bursting out strong signals, capable of penetrating ice. Yet it still required a special receiving dish pointed at his exact coordinates to pick up the signal. The radio dish was established at the Delta team's rendezvous camp about forty miles from here. The unit had been tracking him since he flew in last night.

And while it took only a whisper to communicate *out* to the Delta team under his command, the radio's *reception* was a problem. The anodized thread woven throughout the parka's stitching was a poor receiving antenna through so much ice. He needed to get out of this frozen hole to clear his communication.

Still, faint words finally reached him, cutting in and out. *"Delta . . . receiving."*

"What is your status?"

"The target . . . sunk. Omega secured. Awaiting further orders."

Craig allowed himself a surge of satisfaction. The *Drakon* had been wiped off the chessboard. Perfect. He pressed the throat mike tighter. "Delta One, the security of the football is compromised. Extraction complicated by Russian presence. Any direct hostile action on your part could result in a defensive reaction to destroy the data along with the station. I will attempt to get clear of the ice station. I will radio for evacuation when clear. Only move on my order."

Static answered him, then a scatter of words: *". . . complication . . . two helicopters down . . . men on the ground . . . only one bird still flying."*

Shit. Craig had to forgo trying to ascertain what had happened. There was too much interference, but clearly the Russian submarine had put up a fight. "Are your forces still mobile?"

"Yes, sir."

"Good. Hold Omega secure. Mobilize an evac team only on my all-clear order. I will attempt to reach you."

". . . One . . . roger that."

"Osprey out." Craig yanked the drawstring receiver, and it zipped back into its hood. He found the group, wide-eyed, staring at him.

"Who are you?" Amanda asked.

"My real name is not important. Craig will do for now."

"Then *what* are you?"

He tightened his lips. What was the use of subterfuge now? If he was going to secure the data files, he would need the cooperation of everyone here. He answered the question honestly. "I'm CIA, liaison to the Special Forces groups. Currently in temporary command of a Delta Force unit which has retaken Omega."

"Omega is free?" Amanda asked.

"For the moment." He waved toward the crack. "But that fact will do us no good here. We need to get out of this station."

"How?" Dr. Ogden asked, standing nearby.

Craig waved to the crack in the wall. "They somehow got in here. We'll get out the same way."

"But the grendels . . . ?" Magdalene asked.

Craig crossed to the crate of empty vodka bottles that he had moved earlier, then eyed the entire party. "To survive, we're going to have to work together."

4:17 P.M.

Jenny watched the flames flare up again in the crack, driving her back.

Thank God . . .

A moment ago, as the fires had temporarily died, she had taken a cautious step closer and peered into the heart of the recent conflagration. A foot away, the ice crack had been melted into a true passage, narrow but passable.

They were almost through.

For a moment, she had feared the others were out of fuel. She had heard anxious whispering—then the hose had reappeared, forcing her back.

Now flames again lapped greedily from the tunnel, boring through the remainder of the ice. They were going to make it. Still, Jenny held her breath. She turned to Tom and Kowalski.

The pair, along with Bane, guarded the other tunnel, watching for the approach of any of the creatures.

Tom caught her eye. "It's still down there. I keep seeing shadows moving."

"Bastard's not about to give up on its meal," Kowalski concurred.

"It should stay away as long as the fire keeps going," Jenny said, adding a silent *I hope*.

"In that case," Kowalski grumped, "I want a goddamn flamethrower for my next birthday."

She studied the dark tunnel and tried to understand what lurked out there. She remembered Craig's name for the beast: grendel. But what was it really? There were myths among her people about whale spirits that left the ocean and dragged off young men and women. She had thought such stories just superstitious tales. Now she wasn't so sure.

The fury of the blaze had died down again, drawing back her attention. *What are they doing over there?*

Jenny waited. The fires died to flickers. She stepped forward again, ready to call out. But a dark shape appeared instead, pushing out the narrow crack. It was a figure cloaked in a soggy blanket.

The blanket was tossed back, throwing out light and revealing a tall, slender woman, dressed in a blue thermal unitard. The light came from a mining lantern held in one hand. She lifted it now.

"Amanda . . . Dr. Reynolds!" Tom exclaimed.

Jenny recognized the name, the head of the Omega Drift Station.

"What are you doing?" Kowalski asked. He waved an arm at the crack. Another figure pushed out of the melted passage. "I thought we were joining *you*."

"Change in plans," she said, staring around at them. "Looks like it's safer out here than in there."

To punctuate her statement, a blast of rifle fire echoed from the other side, ringing off metal.

The second figure shook free of the blanket. It was Craig. He helped the next person out of the crack. "Not to sound trite, but the Russians are coming."

Another four people pushed into the cavern: three men and a woman. They wore matching terrified expressions. Bane sniffed at them, weaving among their legs.

The eldest of the new group spoke to Craig. "The Russians are shooting at the door."

"Must be trying to keep us pinned there," Craig said. "More soldiers are probably already on their way through the ducts."

Kowalski pointed back to the crack. "Considering what's out *here,* I'd say let's go back in there and wave the white flag at the Russians."

"It's death either way," Craig answered with a shake of his head. "And here at least we have the firepower to challenge the grendels." He pulled an object out of his pocket. It was a glass vodka bottle, full of a dark yellow liquid and stoppered with a scrap of cloth. "We have ten of them. If your flares kept the grendels back, then these homemade Molotovs should, too."

"What then?" Jenny asked.

"We're going to get out of here," Craig said. "Up that ventilation shaft."

"And I was just getting comfy here," Kowalski said.

Jenny shook her head at such a foolhardy plan. "But we'll just freeze to death hiding up there. The blizzard is still blowing fiercely."

"We're not going to hide," Craig said. "We're going to make for the parked vehicles, then strike out for Omega."

"But the Russians—"

Amanda interrupted. "Omega has been liberated by a Delta Force team. We're going to try to reach an evacuation point."

Jenny was stunned into silence.

Kowalski rolled his eyes. "Fuckin' great. We escape from

that goddamn place just before it's liberated by Special Forces. We've got to work on our damn timing."

Jenny found her tongue. "How do you know all this?"

Amanda pointed a thumb at Craig. "Your friend here is CIA. The controller for the Delta Force team."

"What?" Jenny swung toward Craig.

He met her eyes as more gunfire rang out from beyond the crack. "We need to move out," he said. "Find this ventilation shaft."

Jenny remained frozen in place, her mind too busy trying to assimilate this new information. "What the hell is going on here?"

"I'll explain it all later. Now's not the time." He touched her arm, then added more softly, "I'm truly sorry. I didn't mean to get you pulled into all of this."

He slipped past her, lighting the first Molotov cocktail with a Bic lighter, and headed to the tunnel. Once there, he lobbed the bottle far down the passage.

The explosion of fire was fierce, splattering along the hall. Jenny caught a glimpse of the bull beast fleeing around a bend in the tunnel and away.

"Let's go," Craig said, heading toward the inferno. "We don't have much time."

4:28 P.M.

Loaded down with the pilfered gear from the armory, Matt mounted the wall ladder and climbed behind Greer. At the top of the ladder, Lieutenant Commander Bratt crouched in the chute above, illuminated by a military penlight hanging around his neck. The commander helped Greer off the ladder and into the tunnel.

As he climbed, Matt glanced down. Washburn maintained a watch on the two tunnels that entered the service cubby, rifle raised. The tall woman was taking no chances. The group had reached Level Two and was striking out for Level One.

Matt clambered up the remaining rungs pounded into the ice wall. An arm reached down and grabbed the hood of his white parka, hauling him up.

"Any sign of the civilian group up here?" Matt asked, huffing from the weight of the weapons, every pocket stuffed with grenades.

"No. But they could be anywhere. We'll just have to count on them finding a safe hiding place."

Matt crawled into the tunnel, following after Greer and making room for Washburn. Soon they all were snaking down the ice chute, Greer in the lead, Bratt now bringing up the rear.

None of them spoke. Their plan was simple: keep moving up, find a weak spot in the Russians' defenses, and try to blast their way free of the station. The *Polar Sentinel* had deployed a SLOT buoy, a Submarine-Launched One-Way Transmitter. Bratt knew where it was hidden atop the ice. They hoped to reach it and manually enter a Mayday, then seek shelter among the ice peaks and caves on the surface. Under the cloak of the blizzard, they might be able to play cat and mouse with the Russians long enough for help to arrive.

And in the meantime, they'd be a decoy for the Russians, keeping the enemy's attention away from the civilians still hiding in the station.

The party reached another cubbyhole, somewhere between Level One and Level Two. They entered the space more cautiously now. The Russians would be searching these upper levels, expecting them to make a break for the surface.

Greer entered first and swept his flashlight over the floor, seeking any evidence of fresh footprints. He gave the thumbs-up.

Matt crawled out and stretched his back.

Then the ground shook. A blast echoed to them, muffled but still loud. Matt hunched down. A spatter of rattling gun-shots followed, erratic, like firecrackers.

"What the hell—?" he muttered under his breath.

Ice crystals danced in the air, shaken loose by the concussion. He glanced to the others as they climbed into the cubbyhole. They were wearing smiles. So was Greer.

"So let me in on the joke," Matt said, straightening.

Greer thumbed over his shoulder. "It would seem the Russians finally discovered their dead comrades on Level Three."

"We booby-trapped the armory before leaving," Washburn added, her smile cold and satisfied. "Figured once they found the bodies they'd check there first."

"Payback for Pearlson and all the others," Bratt finished, growing sober again. "And the distraction down there should slow the Russians, make them more wary. They now know we're armed."

Matt nodded, still shaken. So much bloodshed. He took a deep, shuddering breath. For the hundredth time since returning from the armory, he wondered about the fate of Jenny and her father. Fear for them dulled any sympathy for the deaths here. He had to keep going. He would not let anyone stand between him and Jenny. This resolve both frightened him and warmed him. For the past three years, he had allowed grief and old pain to build a wall between them. Now such feelings seemed as thin as the cold air here.

They continued on, working their way upward, aiming for the top level.

After another two ladders and more chute crawling, muffled voices and shouting reached them. They followed toward the source, cautious, silent, communicating with hand signals. Flashlights were turned off.

Ahead, faint light seeped down the tunnel. They headed toward the source: a grate along one wall of the tunnel. With extreme care, they moved forward.

In the lead, Bratt reached the vent first and peered out. After a long moment, he moved past the grate, turned, and pointed to Matt, waving him forward.

Holding his breath, Matt crawled to the grate and bent his head to spy out. The vent opened into a kitchen, the galley for the station. Stoves and ovens lined one wall, while tables and shelves filled most of the free space. A double set of doors opened out to the main room.

A Russian soldier held one of the doors open, flashlight in hand. His back was to them. He was talking to another soldier.

Beyond them, in the darkened main room, flashlights bobbled. Men ran up and down the central staircase, shouting and barking to one another. A soldier covered in blood pounded up the steps. He had a medic's cross on the upper shoulder of his parka. He yelled and more men followed him down.

Finally, the pair of soldiers moved away, allowing the swinging door to close behind them. A square window in the double doors still shone with the lights bobbling in the adjacent room.

Matt stared over to Bratt.

The commander sidled closer, speaking in his ear. "Can you play Russian again?"

"What do you mean?" But even as Matt asked, he already knew the answer. He still wore the stolen white parka.

"We have a short window of opportunity. It's still dark. Everyone's shaken. If you keep your hood up, you should be able to walk among them without them knowing."

"And do what?"

Bratt pointed toward the closed doors. "Be our eyes."

Matt listened to the plan as it was hurriedly related. His heart thudded in his chest, but he found himself nodding.

Bratt finished, "With the current commotion from the booby trap, we might not have a better chance."

"Let's do it," Matt agreed.

Washburn was already using one of her multipurpose meat hooks to free the grate.

Once the vent was open, Bratt touched Matt's arm. "This plan all depends on your acting ability."

"I know." Matt took a deep breath. "I'd better find my motivation for this scene."

"How about survival?" Greer growled behind him.

"Yeah, that'll do." Matt crawled out of the vent and stood up, facing the double doors.

The others followed him, taking up positions in the galley. They moved quickly. Timing was everything.

Bratt gave Matt a questioning stare. *Are you ready?*

4:48 P.M.

Jenny kept Bane beside her as she walked with Craig. Ahead, Kowalski lobbed another fiery charge down the long passage. It burst with a shatter of glass and a splash of flames across floor and walls.

The way was clear.

Not a single grendel had been seen in the last twenty minutes.

Dr. Ogden, the biologist, had offered an explanation. "These creatures live in darkness and ice. And while heat and light might attract them, these bombs are sensory overload. Painful and disorienting to the creatures. So they flee."

So far his assessment had proved valid. They had succeeded in reaching the original marked trail unmolested and unchallenged and were now winding down into the depths of the ice island, heading toward the ventilation shaft. The only disturbance had been when an echoing blast of some distant explosion sounded far above them. The tunnels had rattled, stopping everyone. But with no other repercussions or explosions, they had continued onward.

Behind Jenny, Amanda remained in whispered discussions with the biology team while Tom watched their backs, armed with a pair of Molotovs.

Craig continued his quiet explanation: "I was the advance man, the surgical op for the mission. I was sent in to find the data and secure it. But the Russians must have caught wind of my cover and mission and tried to ambush me in Alaska. If it hadn't been for Matt, they would've succeeded."

"You could have told us."

Craig sighed. "I was under strict orders. A need-to-know basis only. This comes from the highest positions of power. Especially after the attack on Prudhoe Bay. The stakes were too high. I *had* to get here."

"All for some possible research into cryogenics." Jenny tried to picture the tanks with the frozen bodies inside them. It seemed impossible, too monstrous.

Craig shrugged. "I had my orders."

"But you used us." She thought back to his discussions and arguments on the Twin Otter after the explosions at Prudhoe Bay. He had manipulated them. "You played us."

He smiled apologetically. "What can I say? I'm good at what I do." His smile faded, and he sighed. "I had to use the resources at hand. You were the only means for me to get here under the Russians' radar. Again I'm sorry. I didn't think it would get this messy."

Jenny kept her gaze fixed forward as the group edged past the exploded Molotov. She kept one question to herself. Was this man *still* playing them?

Craig continued, but now it sounded more like he was speaking to himself. "All we have to do is get clear of the station. Then the Delta team can come in with full forces and secure this place, too. Then it will all be over."

Jenny nodded. *Over . . . if only it were that easy.* She kept one hand on Bane, needing to feel the simple, uncomplicated loyalty at her side. But it was more than that. And she allowed herself to admit it. Bane also was a physical connection back to Matt. Her fingers rubbed into the dog's ruff, feeling his body heat. Craig had told her about Matt, how he and a group of Navy men had attempted to raid the station's old weapons locker.

No one knew what happened after that.

Bane leaned against her leg, seeming to sense her fear.

"I see the ventilation shaft!" Kowalski called back.

The group headed after the tall seaman, their pace increasing. Jenny guided Bane past the flames of the exploded Molotov. The heat was stifling, reeking of burned hydrocarbons. The ice melted and ran underfoot, slick and treacherous. Streams of fire traced channels across the floor.

Once they were past, the way grew dark again. Kowalski led, the lantern raised above his head.

Ahead a black chute opened on the left wall. The end of the ventilation shaft.

The group gathered in front of it. Jenny pushed forward. From here, it was up to her. The tunnel was too steep to climb with just boots and hands. Tom handed her an ice ax that they had found in the sea-gate control room. She checked the tool's balance, weight, and most importantly, its sharp edge.

Dr. Reynolds sat on the floor and unbuckled her ice crampons, taking them off. "I should be the one doing this," the woman said.

"They fit me, too," Jenny argued. "And I've been ice climbing many times in Alaska." She left unsaid what had already been discussed. The crampons were too small for any of the men, and Amanda's deafness was a handicap if she got into any trouble in the shaft.

Dr. Reynolds passed her the steel crampons.

Jenny quickly snugged them to her boots. The spiked tips and soles would allow her to scale the shaft. The ice ax was both to aid in this and to protect her.

Once she was outfitted, Tom passed her two of the remaining Molotovs. "I dropped the rope right near the entrance when we were . . . were attacked. If you anchor it to the grate above, it should just about reach down here."

Jenny nodded, shoving the firebombs in the pocket of her parka. "No problem. Keep a watch on Bane. The grendels have him wired. Don't let him run off."

"I'll make sure he stays, and I'll follow behind him up the shaft."

"Thanks, Tom."

Kowalski bent a knee and offered a hand to help her up. She climbed him like a ladder, ducking into the shaft and pulling up her feet to kick in with her crampons. They dug deep, the sharp points well maintained.

"Be careful," Kowalski said.

She had no voice to reassure him or herself. She set off up the shaft, practicing what her father had taught her long ago while glacier hiking and climbing: *Keep two points of contact at all times.*

With both feet spiked in place, she reached up with the ice ax and jammed it tight. Once it was secure, she moved one leg up, kicked in, then brought the other up.

It was slow going. *Slow is safe,* her father's old words whispered in her ear.

Working up the shaft, one step at a time, she allowed a small measure of relief to buoy her at the thought of her father. *At least he's safe. Commander Sewell promised to look after him, and now the Delta units have arrived.*

All she had to do was reach them.

But what about Matt?

Her left foot slipped out of its plant, gouging ice. She smacked to her belly on the ice. All her weight was carried on the ice ax until she was able to resecure her feet. Once planted, she still took a moment to suck in large gulps of cold air.

Two points of contact—at all times.

She shoved aside her fears for Matt. It did her no good. She had to focus, to survive. After that, she could worry.

This thought raised an unbidden smile. Matt had once said she could worry a hole through plate steel.

Wishing for a tenth of Matt's composure now, she planted her ax farther up the ventilation shaft and continued onward. Ahead the bend in the shaft appeared. *Almost to the top.* She rounded the corner and spotted the glare of daylight at the end of the shaft. It was open, clear.

With her goal in sight, she hurried upward—but not so fast as to be careless. The two men in her life whispered in her ears.

Slow is safe.

Don't worry.

And lastly, words reached out of her past, from a place deep and locked away. She remembered soft lips brushing her neck, warm breath on her nape, words husky with ardor: *I love you . . . I love you so much, Jen.*

She held these words to her heart and spoke aloud, remembering what had been forgotten and knowing it to be true. "I love you, too, Matt."

4:50 P.M.

Disguised in the Russian parka, Matt pushed out the galley doors and entered the main station. Though the level remained darkened, he kept one arm raised, shielding his face, holding the furred edge of his white hood low over his brow. He carried the AK-47 on one shoulder.

Men continued to bustle, oblivious to his appearance. He kept to the level's outer edge, crossing along the periphery, staying in the dark. Most of the commotion was in the room's center, where soldiers gathered, staring down the spiral steps. From below, smoke billowed up from the explosion of the booby-trapped armory.

A pair of men hauled a heavy form stretched in black plastic wrap.

Body bag.

Another pair of soldiers, laden as grimly as the first, followed. Comrades watched the procession with angered expressions. Shouts continued to echo up from below. Men spoke heatedly all around. Flashlights circled and patrolled.

A beam passed across his form. Matt kept his head turned away. As he maneuvered around the area's tables, he bumped a chair, knocking it over. As it clattered, he hurried on. Someone yelled at him. It sounded like a curse.

He simply gestured vaguely and continued along the room's edge. He finally reached a vantage point where he could see into the hall that led out to the storm. He spotted the wreckage of the Sno-Cat still partially blocking the way, but it had been shoved aside enough to allow a narrow space to pass to the surface. Two men stood by the Cat, but he could see movement behind the crashed vehicle.

From the corner of his eye, he continued to stare into the distance. That was his mission: recon the level and determine how many hostiles stood between them and freedom. If escape looked possible, he was to signal the others, then use the grenade hidden inside his pocket to create a distraction, lobbing it toward the central shaft. The ruckus should cover the Navy crew's rush toward the entrance. Matt was to offer cover fire with his own rifle. But first, he had to decide if escape through the hall was even possible.

He squinted—then jumped when someone barked right at his shoulder. He had not heard the man's approach.

Matt turned partially toward the newcomer, a hulking figure in an unzipped parka. Seven feet, if he was an inch. Matt glanced briefly, looking for some insignia of rank. Though the man's face was rugged and storm-burned, he appeared young. Too young to be of significant rank.

Matt stood a bit straighter as the man continued in Russian, pointing his rifle toward the two bagged bodies as they were sprawled across one of the mess hall tables. His cheeks were red, spittle accumulated at the corners of his lips. He finally finished his tirade, huffing a bit.

Only understanding a few words of Russian, Matt did the one thing everyone did when faced with such a situation. He nodded. *"Da,"* he mumbled grimly. Along with the word *nyet,* it was the extent of his Russian vocabulary. In this case, it was a toss-up which to use: *da* or *nyet.*

Yes or no.

Clearly the man had delivered an impressive rant, and agreement seemed the best response. Besides, he was not about to *disagree* with the giant.

"Da," Matt repeated more emphatically. He might as well commit.

It seemed to work.

A hand as large as a side of beef clapped him on the shoulder, almost driving him to his knees. He caught himself and remained standing as the fellow began to pass.

He had pulled it off.

Then the grenade secreted inside his parka jarred loose and bounced to the floor with a loud clatter. The pin was still in place, so there was no real danger of it exploding.

Still Matt winced as if it had.

The grenade rolled to the toes of the giant.

The man bent to pick it up, his fingers reaching, then pausing. He had to recognize the armament as ancient. Half bent, the fellow glanced up at him, bushy eyebrows pinched as the gears in his brain slowly turned.

Matt was already moving. He swung his assault rifle around from his shoulder and drove its stock into the bridge of the man's nose. He felt bone crush. The soldier's head snapped back, then forward. His body followed.

Not missing a beat, Matt dropped to his knees beside the fellow, pretending to help the guy stand as eyes looked toward them. He laughed hoarsely as if the man had tripped.

Before anyone grew wiser, Matt reached the grenade

under the man, pulled the pin, and bowled it under the tables toward the central shaft. It wouldn't get the distance compared to throwing it, but it would have to do.

Unfortunately, it didn't get far at all. It struck an over-turned chair, the same one he himself had knocked down a moment ago. It bounced back toward him.

Crap . . .

He ducked, shielding himself with the giant's body. The fellow groaned groggily, arms scrabbling blindly.

Matt swore, realizing he had forgotten to signal the others.

Fuck it . . . they'll get the message.

The grenade blew.

A table flew into the air, spinning end over end. Matt barely saw it. The force of the blast drove him and his un-willing partner across the floor. Shrapnel ripped through the soldier's thick neck. Blood spouted in a hot gush over Matt's face.

Ears ringing from the blast, Matt rolled away. He was deaf for the moment to any shouting. He watched men picking themselves up off the floor. Flashlights searched the room, now smoky from the blast.

Movement caught his eye.

Through the double doors to the galley, a trio of figures rushed toward him. Bratt was in the lead. They aimed for him.

Matt, still shell-shocked, couldn't understand why they weren't making for the exit. Still on the ground, he lolled around.

Oh, that's why . . .

He was sprawled right in the entrance to the hall that led out.

The Sno-Cat lay just a few yards away.

Even closer, only five steps from him, two soldiers stood with weapons leveled. They shouted . . . or he assumed so, since their lips were moving. But his ears still rang. He couldn't hear, let alone understand if he could.

They came toward him, weapons firming on shoulders, aiming at his head.

Matt took a gamble. He lifted his arms. *"Nyet!"* It was a fifty-fifty chance. *Da* or *nyet*.

This time he chose wrong.

The closer man fired.

15

Storm Warning

ᐱᖅᓯᖅᑐᖅ ᐳᖅᐸᐅᑎᕐᑦ

From a couple of paces away, Amanda stared toward the ventilation shaft. The sheriff had vanished beyond the reach of the lantern's light. The other members of the party gathered at the opening, anxious, eyes darting all around.

She felt isolated. She had thought herself accustomed to the lack of auditory stimulation, to the way it cut you off from the world more thoroughly even than blindness. Hearing enveloped you, connected you to your surroundings. And though she could see, it was always like she was watching from afar, a wall between her and the rest of the world.

The only time in the past years when she had felt fully connected to the world had been those few moments in Greg's arms. The warmth of his body, the softness of his touch, the taste of his lips, the scent of his skin . . . all wore down that wall that separated her from the world.

But he was gone now. She understood he was a captain first, a man second, that he had to leave with the other civilians, had to rescue those he could. Still, it hurt. She wanted him . . . needed him.

She hugged her arms around herself, trying to squeeze the terror from her own body. The burst of courage she had been riding since seeing a grendel for the first time had waned to a simple will to survive, to continue moving forward.

Tom stirred beside her, petting Bane as he stood watch. Kowalski guarded the opposite side of the hall. The tension kept their faces locked in a stoic expression, eyes staring unblinkingly.

She imagined she appeared the same.

The waiting wore on them all. They kept expecting an attack that never came. *The Russians . . . the grendels . . .*

She followed Tom's blank stare down the hall. She recalled her earlier discussion with Dr. Ogden.

The biologist had developed a theory about the grendels' social structure. He imagined that the species spent a good chunk of their life span in frozen hibernation. A good way to conserve energy in an environment so scant on resources. But to protect the frozen pod, one or two sentinels remained awake, guarding their territory. These few hunted the surrounding waters through sea caves connected to the Crawl Space or scoured the surface through natural or man-made egress points. While exploring down here, Ogden had found spots in the Crawl Space that looked like claws had dug a grendel free from its icy slumber. He had his theory: "The guardians must change shift every few years, slipping into slumber themselves to rest and allowing a new member to take over. It's probably why they've remained hidden for so long. Only one or two remain active, while the rest slumber through the centuries. There's no telling how long these things have been around, occasionally brushing into contact with mankind, leading to myths of dragons and snow monsters."

"Or Beowulf's Grendel," Amanda had added. "But why have they stayed here on this island for so long?"

Ogden had this answer, too. "The island is their nest. I examined some of the smaller caves in the cliff face and found frozen offspring, only a few, but considering the creatures' longevity, I wager few progeny are necessary to maintain their breeding pool. And as with most species with small litters, the social group as a whole will defend their nest tooth and nail."

But where are they now? Amanda wondered. Fire would not hold the grendels at bay forever, not if they were defending their nest.

Tom swung around, clearly attracted by some noise.

She turned and looked. The group by the ventilation shaft stirred. She immediately saw why. A length of red rope snaked from the opening, dangling to the floor. Jenny had made it to the top.

The group gathered closer.

Craig faced them with a hand up. His lips were illuminated by his lantern. "To minimize the load on the rope, we should go up in groups of three. I'll go with the two women." He pointed to Amanda and Magdalene. "Then Dr. Ogden and his two students. Then the Navy pair with the dog."

He stared around, waiting to see if there were any objections.

Amanda glanced around herself. No one seemed to be disagreeing. And she surely wasn't going to. She was with the first group. Without any protests, Craig helped Magdalene up, then offered a hand to her.

She waved for him to go ahead. "I've been climbing all my life."

He nodded and mounted the rope, pulling himself up.

Amanda then followed. The climb was strenuous, but fear drove their party quickly upward, away from the terror below. Amanda had never been happier to see daylight. She scrambled up after the other two, then rolled into open air.

The winds buffeted her as she stood.

Jenny helped steady her. "The blizzard is breaking up," she said, her eyes on the skies.

Amanda frowned at the blowing snow, blind to the surroundings beyond a few yards. The cold already bit into her exposed cheeks. If this storm was breaking up, how bad had it been before?

Craig bent to the hole, clearly calling to those below, then straightened and faced them. "We'll have to hurry. If the storm is letting up, we'll have less cover."

They waited for the next party—the biology group. It didn't take too long. Soon three more figures rolled out of the ventilation shaft. Craig bent again to the shaft.

Amanda felt the tiny hairs on the back of her neck quiver. Deaf to the storm and the chatter around her, she sensed it first. She swung around in a full circle.

Sonar . . .

"Stop!" she yelled. "Grendels . . . !"

Everyone tensed, facing outward.

Craig was still at the hole. He scrambled in his parka for one of the Molotovs. She saw his lips moving. ". . . screaming down the shaft. The creatures are attacking below, too."

Henry Ogden struggled to light his own Molotov, but the wind kept snuffing his lighter. ". . . a coordinated attack. They're using sonar to communicate with one another."

Amanda stared into the whiteout. It was an ambush.

From out of the deep snow, shadowy figures crept toward them, slipping like hulking phantoms from the heart of the storm.

Henry finally got his oily rag burning and tossed his bottle outside, toward the group. It sailed through the snow, landed in a snowbank, and sizzled out. The beasts continued toward them.

Amanda caught movement from around another ice peak to the far right. Another grendel . . . and another.

They were closing in from all sides.

Craig stepped forward, a flaming Molotov in his raised hand.

"Avoid the snow," Amanda warned. "It's fresh, wet."

Craig nodded and threw the fiery charge. It arced through the blowing snow and struck the knifed edge of a pressure ridge. Flame exploded across the path of the largest group.

The beasts flinched, stopping.

Run away, she willed at them.

As answer, Amanda felt the sonar intensify, a grendel roar of frustration. Out in the open, they were less intimidated by the fiery display.

Craig turned to her, to the others. He pointed an arm. "Back down the ventilation shaft!"

Amanda swung around in time to see Bane leap out of the same shaft, snarling and barking, as wild as a full wolf. But Jenny caught her dog, trying to keep him from running at the grendels.

Around them, there was much shouting. Amanda heard none of it. People were too panicked for her to catch what was being said. Why was no one diving into the shaft?

Then she had her answer.

Kowalski scrambled out of the hole, shouting, red-faced. "Get back!" She was able to read his lips as he yelled. "They're right on our tail!"

Tom appeared next, the left arm of his parka singed and smoldering. He rolled out, shoving his arm into the snow. Smoke billowed from the shaft. "The shaft caved in with that last Molotov. It's blocked."

Kowalski stared toward the flames out in the storm, his face sinking. "Shit . . ."

Amanda turned. The fires from Craig's Molotov were foundering in the snowmelt. The beasts, obeying some sonar signal, began to march toward the group again, splashing and stamping through the remaining flames.

As Amanda backed, the party pulled tighter together.

There was no escape.

Standing only a yard away with his AK-47, the Russian fired at Matt's head. Muzzle flash flared from the rifle barrel. Still deafened from the grenade blast, Matt didn't hear the shot— *or the one that took out the shooter*.

Matt fell back, his left ear aflame. He watched, confused, as the right side of the guard's head exploded out in a shower of bone and brain. It was all done in dead silence. Matt struck the ground, landing on his shoulder. Blood trailed down his neck. The shot had nicked his ear. He saw Bratt, Greer, and Washburn running at him. Bratt's rifle still smoked.

In the hallway, the second guard tried to react, swinging his weapon, but Greer and Washburn both fired. A bullet struck the Russian's shoulder, spinning him like a top. Another blasted through the man's neck, spraying blood over the wall.

Sound began to return to Matt. Mostly the louder noises. Yells, more shots. The double doors to the galley suddenly exploded outward, tearing from hinges and blowing across the room; fire and smoke followed. Another booby trap.

Amid the chaos, Matt struggled to stand as the group reached him. Bratt grabbed him by the hood and hauled him up, yelling in his good ear. "Next time I duct-tape that damn grenade to you!"

As a group, they sprinted toward the Sno-Cat.

"More soldiers . . . !" Matt gasped, waving ahead, trying to warn.

Shots fired at them—from beyond the Sno-Cat. They dove down, using the wreckage as a shield. Rifle shots rattled the trashed vehicle.

Matt crouched, his back to the Sno-Cat. He stared back into the main room, cloudy with smoke. They were still exposed. They had to move.

Smoke swirled, and movement near the room's center

caught Matt's eye. A man seemed to be floating up the shaft from below, lit by a couple flashlights. He was tall, white-haired, wearing an open greatcoat. In his arms, he carried a boy wrapped in a blanket. The boy was crying, covering his ears.

It made no sense.

"Get down!" Bratt yelled to Matt, pushing his head lower.

Greer tossed a grenade over the top of the vehicle toward the hidden snipers. Washburn rolled another back toward the main room.

"No!" Matt cried.

The twin explosions snuffed out Matt's hearing again. The Sno-Cat jolted a foot toward them from the blast. Chunks of ice rained down; steamy smoke filled the hall.

Bratt motioned, pointing an arm. They had no choice but to make a run for it. They leaped as a group, having to trust that the grenade took out all the hostiles ahead of them.

The commander took the lead, followed by Washburn and Matt. Greer ran behind them, firing blindly back toward the main room. The shots sounded far away, more like a toy cap gun.

Then Greer shouldered into Matt, trying to get him to hurry, but succeeded in almost knocking him down. He glanced back angrily as he caught his balance.

Greer was down on one knee. He hadn't pushed Matt. He had fallen.

Matt stopped, skidding around on the ice-strewn floor, meaning to go to his aid. The man's face was a mask of fury and pain. He waved Matt onward, shouting soundlessly.

Matt saw why. Blood pooled under Greer, pouring from his leg. The blood pumped in a bright red flow. *Arterial.* Greer slumped to the floor, rifle across his knees.

Washburn grabbed Matt's arm, taking in the scene immediately. She yanked him, making him follow her.

Greer met Matt's gaze, then did the oddest thing. The man simply shrugged, disappointed, like he'd simply lost a bet.

He lifted his rifle, pointed it toward the station, and began to fire again.

Pop . . . pop . . . pop . . .

Matt allowed himself to be dragged away. They fled past the Sno-Cat and headed toward the blasted doorway. Bodies lay in crumpled piles; there was no resistance.

Matt spotted a familiar object resting in a severed hand. He snatched it up in midrun and shoved it into his pocket. It could come in handy.

The trio fled to the surface, out into the storm.

Once Matt was free of the station, the wind seemed to dispel his deafness. He heard the blizzard's howl.

"This way!" Bratt yelled, aiming them toward the parked snow vehicles. They planned to steal a Ski-Doo and head out to the SLOT transmitter, hidden among the peaks.

But first they had to get there.

It was a hundred-yard dash.

Clearing the entrance, they sprinted across the open, heading toward the vehicles half buried in the blowing snow.

It was too much to hope they were unguarded.

Guns fired at them. Ice spat up from the impacts, stinging them.

Bratt and Washburn dropped to their bellies, sheltering behind a shallow ridge of ice. Matt did the same. The snipers were hidden in a valley between two ice peaks. Well protected. Matt spotted orange tents sheltered up there.

"That's where the corpses from the station are kept," Washburn hissed. "I know a back way in, and I have one more grenade. Cover me." She began to crawl away, retreating toward the station's entrance.

Bratt aimed his gun and fired toward the tents. Matt rolled and hauled his AK-47 around. He aimed, searching for snowy shadows. He fired whenever he saw movement.

Off to the side, Washburn reached a narrow crevasse between two peaks, ready to circle behind the snipers.

Then, as was usual for this day, everything went dreadfully wrong.

5:11 P.M.

By the shaft opening, Jenny readied herself along with the others. She held Bane's scruff. The storm winds still blew fiercely, but the snowfall had waned to flurries and gusts.

"On my mark!" Kowalski yelled a few steps away. He and Tom stood in front, bearing flaming Molotovs over their heads.

Five grendels massed ahead of them. The beasts' approach had stopped as explosion after muffled explosion erupted, sounding as if they were coming from just beyond the next peak. The creatures, tuned to vibrations, were disturbed by the concussions.

"It's the station," Tom had said. "Someone's attacking."

Kowalski had agreed, "Sounds like grenades."

The momentary confusion of the beasts had bought them time to light a pair of Molotovs and devise a quick plan.

It wasn't artful. Simply down and dirty.

Kowalski took the lead, stepping toward the nearest grendel and waving his flaming torch at it.

Lips pulled back in response, baring teeth like a dog. The other grendels retreated a step, edgy now, wary. The lead bull kept his spot, not intimidated by the show.

"This one's well fed," Ogden whispered at Jenny's side, crowding her. "It's surely one of the pod's sentinels. Its territoriality will be the most fierce."

That was their hope. Take out the leader and maybe the pack will scatter.

Kowalski took another step. Tom dogged behind him.

In a blur, the grendel suddenly leaped at them, roaring.

"Fuck!" Kowalski screamed, and tossed the Molotov

toward the monster's open jaws. He flew backward, bouncing into Tom. They both fell.

The seaman's aim, though, proved true. The flaming bottle sailed end over end into the creature's maw. The result was spectacular.

An explosion of burning oil burst from the creature's jaws, like some fire-breathing dragon. It howled, spitting and hacking out flaming oil. It spun in agony and blind fury. The others fled from the display, bounding away in all directions.

The smell of burning flesh filled the small ice vale.

"Now!" Kowalski screamed, springing to his feet with Tom.

The young ensign had managed to keep his Molotov out of the snow. He whipped it now with the strength of a major-league ballplayer. It arced past the flailing monster and burst farther down the path, flaming more of the trail ahead, warding away any other grendels.

"Let's go!" Kowalski yelled, taking the lead.

The wounded beast collapsed to the ice, its lungs burned away. Flames still danced from its lips and the two nostrils high on its head. It didn't move.

Kowalski gave it a wide berth just in case. Tom waved for the others to follow. Jenny ran alongside Craig and Dr. Reynolds. Free now, Bane raced ahead, joining Kowalski at the front. Behind them, the biology group kept pace with Tom.

The party fled through fire and ice, running full tilt.

Kowalski had their last Molotovs. He kept a fiery path blazing ahead of them. The grendels scattered out of their way.

Then a scream . . .

Jenny turned and saw Antony down, one leg plunged through a hole in the ice. Tom and Zane helped draw the panicked boy out.

Kowalski had stopped, waiting for them a few yards

down. "Sucks, doesn't it!" They would all have to be careful of such sinkholes. A leg could be easily broken . . . or a neck.

Zane helped his friend to his feet.

"Shit, that's cold," Antony said.

Ice cracked behind him. Up from the hole, a grendel burst forth, battering from below. It lunged and snatched the boy's leg, biting deep. Zane and Tom were thrown backward as the ice shattered outward. The half-ton beast dropped back into the hole, dragging Antony with it.

He didn't even have time to scream before he was gone.

Amid cries and shouts, everyone raced forward haltingly. With the snow covering the ice, it was impossible to discern the thinner patches.

"They're pacing us," Ogden said, panting. "Tracking us under the ice by our footsteps."

"We can't stop," Kowalski said.

No one wanted to. They continued onward, but more slowly. Kowalski bravely took the point. Everyone kept to his footsteps, not wanting to take any unnecessary chances.

Jenny had seen polar bears hunting seals in such a manner, pouncing up from below to nab their unsuspecting prey. The area must be riddled with iced-over breathing holes, permanent cracks in the ice protected by the pressure ridges around here.

They would have to be careful.

Jenny spotted a mound of snow rise as something heavy pushed up from below. She heard the crinkle of breaking ice from beneath it. The grendels were still following them.

"Around the next ridge!" Tom called from the back. "The station's parking lot is just ahead!"

They cautiously increased their pace.

Jenny rounded the bend and saw he was right. The jumble of peaks opened into flat ice. They were almost out of the treacherous pressure ridges.

As they made for the opening, gunfire cracked through

the whine of winds. Kowalski reached the edge and raised his arm, halting them all while he scanned ahead. More gunfire sounded close by, a real firefight.

Tom pulled up next to them. "Someone's fighting the Russians."

"Could it be the Delta team?" Amanda asked Craig.

He shook his head.

Kowalski hissed to them. They all moved forward, gathering together. He pointed an arm. Just ten yards from their hiding place rested a Sno-Cat, with snowmobiles and other vehicles lined up just past it.

Beyond the parking lot, Jenny spotted two figures out on the ice, firing toward the peaks to the left. Gunfire answered them, spattering into the short ridge that sheltered the pair.

It was impossible to tell who was who. Though the snowfall from overhead had died away, the winds continued to blow surface snow in scurfs and eddies, obliterating detail.

Bane suddenly lunged forward, breaking away from the group. He raced between the parked vehicles, heading out toward the open plain.

Jenny made to leap after him, but Kowalski grabbed her elbow and hissed. He pointed an arm.

Beyond the firefight, the glowing entrance to the base shone in the stormy gloom. Figures appeared, limned against the light, pouring out from inside. A major battle was about to begin.

She turned her attention, but Bane was gone, lost among the parked snow craft.

The gunfire grew more intense.

"Now what do we do?" Tom asked.

5:14 P.M.

From his position behind the ice ridge, Matt watched as Washburn was tackled, swamped under three men. She kicked and fought, but it was no use. More soldiers moved out, flanking the entrance. Additional men took up sniping positions within the shelter of the entrance hall.

It wouldn't be long until Matt and Bratt were outflanked and shot. Matt covered the men near the entrance, trying to keep them from edging into a position from which they could shoot directly at his group. Bratt did the same with the group hiding among the tents.

But they were running low on ammunition.

"I'll try to draw their fire," Bratt said. "Make for the vehicles. Try to grab one and head out."

"What about you?"

Bratt shied from the question. "I'll do what I can to hold them off you for as long as possible."

Matt hesitated.

Bratt turned to him, his eyes fierce. "This isn't your war!"

And it isn't yours either, Matt wanted to add, but now was not the time for debate. He simply nodded, acquiescing.

Bratt turned his attention, pulling out a grenade from a pocket. He pointed and signaled his plan. "Ready."

Matt took a deep breath and pushed himself from his belly into a crouch, keeping low. "Go!"

Bratt lobbed the grenade. He didn't have the arm to reach the group in the tents, not against the winds blowing out from the ice mountains. But he did a damn good job anyway. The explosion of ice obliterated the view.

That was Matt's cue. He took off at a full sprint. Behind him, Bratt twisted to fire at the men positioned near the station entrance.

The plan might have worked, except that the Russians by the tents had managed to load their rocket launcher. Matt heard the fizzling blast, followed by the telltale whistle.

He dove and twisted, skidding a few yards on his shoulder. The sharp ice shredded his parka. He watched Bratt turn, ready to leap away, but the distances were too short, the rocket too fast.

Matt covered his face, both to protect himself and not to watch.

The rocket struck with a resounding blast. The ice shuddered under Matt. He lowered his arm and pushed up. Their temporary shelter was now a smoking hole of steam.

There was no sign of Bratt.

Then a boot landed beside him, thudding in the snow, sizzling against the ice.

Horrified, Matt rolled away. He shoved to his feet. Not allowing the man's sacrifice to be in vain, he ran for the vehicles.

5:16 P.M.

Jenny stared at the lone figure running across the ice. He wore a white parka . . . one of the Russians. Then a gust of snow and steam blanketed over him.

"We have to move out now," Craig said beside her, drawing her attention. "Use the distraction to grab what vehicles we can."

"Who can drive a Cat?" Kowalski asked, pointing to the sturdy vehicle. It was only ten yards away. *So close . . .*

Ogden raised his hand. "I can."

Kowalski nodded. "Tom and I'll grab a couple snowmobiles to act as flankers and decoys. The Cat should hold the rest of you. I've got two Molotovs left." He tossed one to Tom. "We'll do what we can to keep the Russians off your asses."

"Let's do it," Craig said.

The group bolted toward the nearby Cat. Tom and Kowalski divided and ran for two Ski-Doos.

Henry reached the Sno-Cat first and yanked the door open. Zane and Magdalene clambered into the front seat while Henry tried the engine. It sputtered, then caught. The noise seemed loud, sure to draw the attention of the Russians now that the firefight had stopped. Hopefully the soldiers were still deafened by the rocket explosion. And if not, there was always the perpetually howling wind to cover the sound.

Jenny searched for any sign that they were heard. But the cloud from the rocket attack continued to mask the area. The winds blew the steamy smoke toward the station's entrance, keeping the view blanketed. But it would not last long.

She heard one Ski-Doo engine wind up, then another. Tom and Kowalski had found their mounts.

"Inside!" Craig urged, pulling open the rear door for Amanda and Jenny.

As Amanda grabbed the edge of the doorframe, sharp barking cut through the engine noise.

Jenny stepped around the rear of the Cat. *Bane . . .*

She searched, then spotted movement. A figure lumbered from the snow fifty yards away. The lone Russian in the white parka. She hissed to Craig.

He came over. Amanda paused in the open door.

Jenny pointed to the armed figure, who seemed unaware of them. He had been close to the explosion. Probably dazed and deaf.

"We'll have to take him out," Craig said.

Then Jenny spotted another figure, dark and low to the ground. It was Bane. The wolf mix leaped at the man, bringing him down.

Craig saw it, too. "It looks like we won't have to deal with the man after all. That is some mutt. A real attack dog."

Jenny watched with a frown. Bane was not that sort of dog.

She watched the man wrestle the dog, then sit up on his knees and hug him, pulling the dog tight. She fell forward two steps. "It's Matt!"

A sob escaped Matt as he clutched Bane. *How had the dog gotten here? All the way from Omega?* It seemed a miracle.

He heard a small cry in the wind, but he couldn't tell from where. He glanced up. Then he heard it again. Someone was calling his name.

Bane dashed a few steps, then turned back to Matt, clearly urging him to follow.

He did, one leg numbly stumbling after the next. He trudged after the dog, not believing his luck.

And he never should have.

Again a characteristic whistling wail pierced the winds.

Another rocket.

The Russians must know his goal. They were going to take out the parking lot, cutting off any means of escape.

Matt stumbled after Bane, meaning to catch the damn dog, drag him down. But the wolf kept running ahead. He raced among the first of the vehicles.

"Bane! No!"

Ever obedient, Bane stopped and spun back to look at him.

Then the rocket hit, blasting Matt back from the force of the concussion. He landed on his back, the wind knocked out of him. He felt the wash of heat from the explosion roll over him.

He cried in his heart and aloud. "No!"

He sat up. The parking lot ahead was gone, a blasted ruin of ice and torn vehicles. At the center gaped a hole clear to the ocean below.

Matt covered his face with his hands.

Jenny must have blacked out for a fraction of a second. One moment, she was standing by the Sno-Cat, calling out to

Matt—the next she was on her back. She sat up, the world spinning slightly.

Her ears ringing, she lay some twenty feet from the Sno-Cat. She remembered the jolt as ice bucked under her, throwing her high. Across the way, the Cat was crashed on its side, toppled over by the force of the explosion.

Matt . . .

She flashed back to seeing him just before the attack. The fear drove away her momentary daze.

Jenny struggled to stand. Craig was doing the same ten feet to her right. Surprisingly, Amanda was already up. She stood by the Sno-Cat, seemingly unfazed.

Beyond them, the ice field was obliterated, swirling in steam. A large hole had been blasted through to the ocean below. Wreckage of vehicles lay all around, thrown and scattered like so many toys. There was no sign of Matt or Bane, but steam still misted thickly.

Closer, Jenny saw Tom sprawled in the snow, pinned under his snowmobile. The young ensign was not moving. A trail of crimson flowed from under him.

Oh God . . .

She spotted Kowalski's vehicle halfway up the neighboring pressure ridge, on its side, motor still chugging. But there was no sign of the seaman.

"We need to help them," Amanda said.

Jenny stumbled over to her.

Amanda turned. Her words were slurred more than usual. "The blast . . ." She shook her head. "It almost fell on top of me."

Jenny placed a hand on her shoulder. It must be terrifying to see that play out without a single sound.

Craig joined them.

Through the Cat's windshield, figures moved. Ogden bore a gash on his forehead. He and Magdalene were trying to calm Zane. He was dazed, flailing, half conscious.

"We have to get them out," Jenny said.

"The door's jammed," Amanda said. "I tried . . . I couldn't . . . maybe all of us together."

Craig stepped away from the toppled Sno-Cat. "We're not going to have the time." He stared out beyond the blasted pit in the ice.

As the winds blew the steaming mist from the blast zone, a line of figures in white parkas were setting out across the ice, weapons ready.

Craig turned to them. "The cleanup squad. We have to get away from here before they spot us."

Jenny stared at the spread of ruined vehicles. "Where?" She pointed to the pressure ridges. "Back into grendel territory."

Craig shook his head, trying to map out some plan. "The Delta team could be here in twenty minutes . . . if we could hole up till then."

Amanda had been following their conversation. "I may know a better way. But we'll have to hurry. Follow me." She turned and started away, heading out from the parking lot.

Jenny stared from the figures in the Sno-Cat to Tom's limp form. She hated abandoning them, but she had no choice. Especially unarmed. Her fingers rested on her empty holster. Frustrated, guilty, she turned away.

As Jenny started after Craig and Amanda, the sound of engines whined into existence behind them. She glanced over her shoulder and spotted a pair of headlamps glowing beyond the fog and mists. They sped off to the side in tandem, circling around the zone of the rocket attack.

Hover-cycles.

She ran faster.

Thirty yards ahead, Amanda vanished around a shelf of ridgeline. Craig followed. As she reached the ridge, Jenny skidded to a stop. She cast one look back at those she was abandoning. Movement drew her eye. Tom, still buried under his bike, weakly lifted an arm.

She gasped, "Tom's still alive!"

Craig yelled to her from the niche in the ice, a naturally sheltered cove. "We don't have time to go back! The Russians will be on us any second!"

Jenny spotted their means of escape. Inside the niche stood a single-masted sailing boat, an iceboat, resting on long titanium runners. Amanda was near the prow of the boat, grasping a small hand ax. She chopped through the ropes that secured the boat.

Jenny hovered at the entrance to the niche and glanced back to Tom. His arm fell back to the snow, motionless again.

She gritted her teeth and made a hard choice. They could not risk capture again. She turned her back on Tom and the others and strode to the iceboat.

"One to each side!" Amanda instructed as she worked quickly, hopping around the boat with her ax. "We'll have to push her out a ways!"

Jenny hurried to obey as the whine of hovercraft echoed over the ice. Craig glanced meaningfully at her. Time had indeed run out. Rescue of the others was truly impossible. They worked faster.

With the boat untethered, Amanda tossed the ax inside, then shoved from the prow. "Back her out ten feet, then I'll let out the sails."

They all pushed, but it was damn heavy. It refused to budge. They would never get it out in time.

"C'mon," Craig mumbled on the starboard side.

Then suddenly the boat broke free. It wasn't heavy. The runners had just been ice-locked in place. They quickly hauled the boat clear of the shelter and out into the stronger winds.

"Everyone aboard, up near the front!" Amanda yelled as she ran around to the stern end. "One person on each side for balance."

Jenny and Craig clambered aboard.

From the stern, Amanda unhitched the sail with the speed

of experience. In moments, sailcloth caught the stiff winds, unfurled, and snapped to the ends of their ties.

The boat immediately sped straight backward, pushing away from the pressure ridges, shoved by the winds blowing down from above.

As they skated in reverse, Jenny spotted the two hover-cycles beyond the boat's prow. They were circling toward the Sno-Cat. She spotted two riders on each vehicle.

Unfortunately the Russians spotted them, too.

The cycles turned toward them.

"Damn it!" Craig swore on the other side.

The passengers on the cycles fired at them, peppering the ice in front and around the boat. A couple rounds punched through the sail but did little damage.

Amanda called from the stern. "Lie flat! Keep your heads down!"

Jenny was already doing that, but Craig pressed lower.

Overhead the sail's boom sprang around, whipping at a speed that would crack a skull. The boat soon followed suit. The craft spun on the ice, lifting up on one runner.

Jenny held her breath, sure they would topple, but then the boat jarred back to the ice. The sails popped like a sonic boom—and they were off.

Winds tore past them.

Jenny risked a peek up and backward. With the boat turned around properly, they raced away from the cycles, their speed escalating. Past Amanda, Jenny watched the two hover-bikes begin to fade back. In this gale, they were no match for the racing boat.

Jenny allowed a bit of hope to warm inside her.

Then she spotted a flash of fire from either side of the lead cycle.

Minirockets!

Matt ran across the ice, staying low, as bullets pelted and ric-ocheted around him. Anger fueled him as he dodged around overturned vehicles and wreckage, seeking whatever shelter he could, but the line of Russian soldiers moved deter-minedly behind him.

Ahead, the blasted pit in the center of the parking lot blocked his path. He would have to circle around it, losing time, but at least the foggy steam rising from the ragged hole was thicker around its edges.

He headed toward the windward side, aiming for where the mists were the most dense. But where could he go after that? He couldn't hide forever in the fog. He had to lose the Russians, get them off his tail.

Movement drew his eye out to the open ice fields. He saw a billow of blue blowing across the ice—an ice racer. It was chased by two hovercraft. Then a large explosion erupted near the boat, casting up ice and fluming water high. A last-moment jag by the boat was all that saved it, but ice rattled down atop it. The bikes closed in on the foundering boat.

Closer, a bullet cracked into the ice by Matt's heel. He danced away, turning his attention to his own predicament. More bullets blasted at him. But as he turned his attention from the ice racer, another sight caught his eye.

Maybe . . .

He tried to judge the distance, then thought, *Fuck it.* He preferred to die trying to save himself rather than simply being shot in the head by the Russians.

Matt changed course. He sprinted directly toward the rocket impact, aiming for the steaming hole. He remained in plain sight, letting the Russians clearly see him. Bullets chased after him, striking closer now.

Reaching the hole, Matt dove over the edge, arms wide.

Below, chunks of ice floated at the bottom of the blast

hole. He wrested his body around to avoid knocking himself out on a chunk, then plunged into the frigid waters.

The cold cut through him immediately, closing like a vise grip, burning rather than freezing. He fought his body's attempt to curl fetally against the affront. His lungs screamed to gasp and choke.

It was death to give in to these reflexes.

Instead, he clamped his chest tight and forced his legs to kick, his arms to pull himself down under the edge of the ice shelf. Exertion helped—as did the triple-layer Gore-Tex parka. He swam out into the dark ocean.

The waters were as black as ink, but he focused toward the target he had glimpsed from the surface. Sixty yards away, murky storm light beamed down into the ocean depths.

It was the man-made lake through which the Russian submarine had surfaced earlier. Matt swam toward it, keeping just under the plane of ice. He kicked against the cold, against the weight of his clothes. He had to make it.

The Russians would believe him dead after his suicidal plunge. They would give up the chase. When able, he would climb free of the polynya and strike out for some ice cave in the peaks. In an inside pocket of his stolen parka were a pack of Russian cigarettes and a lighter. He would find some way to start a fire, keep warm until the Russians left.

It was not the best plan . . . in fact, it had too many faults even to list.

But it was better than being shot in the back.

Matt struggled toward the light. *Just a little farther . . .*

But the shaft of lifesaving light did not seem to be getting any closer. He thrashed and crawled through the waters, kicking against the occasional ice ridge overhead to speed him toward the open water.

His lungs ached, and pinpricks of light swirled across his vision. His limbs quaked from the cold.

Maybe this wasn't the best idea after all . . .

Matt refused to let panic set in. He had been through all manner of training in the Green Berets, in all terrain. He simply continued to kick with his legs and draw with his arms. As long as his heart still pumped, he was alive.

But a deeper terror arose in his heart.

Tyler died this way . . . drowning under ice.

He shoved this thought aside and continued his determined crawl toward the light. But the fear and guilt persisted.

Like father, like son.

A small stream of bubbles escaped his lips as his lungs spasmed. The shaft of light grew dimmer.

Maybe I deserve it . . . I failed Tyler.

But a part of him refused to believe it. His legs continued to thrash. He clawed toward the light. It seemed closer now. For an endless time, he fought toward his salvation—both now and in the past. He would not die. He would not let guilt kill him, not any longer, not like it had been doing to him slowly over the past three years.

Matt kicked into the light, momentum carrying him out under the lake. Brightness bathed down upon him.

He would live.

With the last of his air dying in his chest, he crawled upward, toward light, toward salvation. A trembling frozen hand reached toward the surface—and touched clear ice.

The surface of the open lake had frozen over during the storm.

Matt's buoyancy carried him upward. His head struck a roof of ice. He pawed around and over him, then pounded a fist against the ice. It was thick, at least six inches. Too solid to punch through from below.

He stared upward toward the light, to the salvation denied him by a mere six inches.

Like father . . . like son . . .

Despair set into him. His gaze drifted down, following the light into the icy depths below.

Deep down, movement drew his eye. Shapes glided into view. First one, then another . . . and another. Large, graceful despite their bulk, perfectly suited to this hellish landscape. The white bodies spiraled upward toward their trapped prey, climbing toward the light.

Grendels.

Matt's back pressed against the ice roof overhead as he stared downward.

At least he wouldn't die like Tyler.

5:23 P.M.

Amanda raked her sails forward, struggling to skate her boat past the rain of blasted ice. A blue boulder, the size of a cow, landed a yard in front of the prow, bounced, then rolled ahead of the boat.

She leaned into the keel with her hip, fighting to angle off to the side. They flanked past the rolling boulder as it lost momentum and slowed.

Twisting around, Amanda watched more ice rain silently down from the skies. Behind them, a deep divot had been blasted out of the cap. The two hover-cycles circled to either side, continuing the chase.

Amanda worked the boat's foot pedals, sweeping them back and forth at erratic intervals. It slowed the boat's forward progress, but they couldn't count on pure speed to escape the minirockets or the cycles. The best course was a crooked, jagged path, to make them as hard a target as possible.

Amanda concentrated on the landscape ahead of them. Jenny and Craig had rolled to their bellies and watched behind her. They kept their faces turned so she could read their lips when needed.

Jenny mouthed to her, "Damn fancy sailing."

She allowed a grim smile to form, but they weren't safe yet.

Craig wiggled around and extracted his hidden radio ear-piece. He pushed it in place, then pulled up the collar of his parka. His lips were covered as he spoke.

Amanda could not read what he said, but she could imagine he was frantically calling in help from the Delta Force unit. Craig was free of the station. The "football" he carried was safely away from the Russians' clutches for the moment. Craig dared not risk a fumble and interception so late in the game. Not when he was so close to the goal.

Jenny waved to her, pointing back. *Trouble*.

Amanda swiveled in her seat. The hovercraft to the right was angling closer, swinging in, blazing across the flat snowscape.

She turned back around and straightened the boat, speeding faster now, taking advantage of a fiercer gusting of wind. She tried to put more distance between the boat and the cycle.

Jenny's lips moved. "They're lining up to fire again."

Amanda peeked back over a shoulder. The rider on their tail was bent over his bike, as was his passenger. They had to be pushing the limits of their cycles.

She would have to do the same.

Amanda glanced to her boat's laser speedometer. She was clocking up toward sixty. The fastest she had ever sailed this craft.

She tried to ignore the danger and focused on the boat under her: fingers on ropes, toes on foot pedals, palm on the keel bar. She felt the winds tugging at the sails, at the boat. She attuned her entire form to match the racer. She extended her senses outward, listening with the boat in a way only someone deaf could. Through her connection, she *heard* the whistle of the runners, the scream of winds. Her handicap became her skill.

She eked out more speed, watching the speedometer climb past *sixty . . . sixty-five . . .*

"They're firing!" Jenny shouted soundlessly at her.

. . . seventy . . . seventy-five . . .

A flash of fire struck to the right; ice shattered skyward. Amanda shifted the boat, turning the sails to catch the blast's force.

. . . eighty . . .

They struck a lip of ice. The boat jumped high in the air, like a Windsurfer catching the perfect wave. Fire exploded under them, taking out the ridge.

But the boat flew clear and away. Amanda lifted in her seat, but still trimmed her sail to carry them level. They hit the ice again, skating at impossible speeds.

. . . ninety . . . ninety-five . . .

Ice again rained down around them, but they were beyond the worst of the blast area. The boat flew across the ice, one with the storm, one with its pilot.

Craig pointed an arm. "Christ, they're turning back. You did it!"

Amanda didn't even bother to glance around. She knew she had succeeded. The racer skated, barely touching the ice now. She let the craft glide, blown by the storm. Only as their speed began to edge downward on its own did she touch the brake.

From the flaccid response of the handle, she immediately recognized the danger. The last jump had shattered the ice brake.

She continued to pump the handle. No response. She tried to reef the sail a bit, but the winds had too tight a grip. The ropes were taut bands of iron, jammed in their racks. The boat was not built for these speeds.

The others saw her struggle, eyes widening.

The winds gusted up. The needle on the speedometer crept up again.

. . . ninety-five . . . one hundred . . .

That was as high as the speedometer could read.

They rocketed over the frozen plain. They were at the mercy of the storm winds, flying headlong out into the ice, at speeds at which a single mistake could kill.

There was only one course left to them.

Something Amanda loathed to do.

She yelled to the others. "We need an ax!"

5:26 P.M.

Near to blacking out, Matt faced the rising pod of grendels. They circled up from below, slow, patient. They were in no hurry. Like Matt, they knew he could not escape. He was trapped between the ice above and the teeth below.

He remembered Amanda's trick of luring the monsters away with her helmet and heating mask. If he could only find a way to bait them away . . . something hot . . . something bright . . .

Then a thought struck him. Something *forgotten*.

He pawed into the pocket of his parka, praying it hadn't fallen loose, an object he had nabbed from the severed hand of a Russian soldier while fleeing the ice station. It was still there.

He pulled out the black pineapple. It was one of the Russians' incendiary grenades, the same as had killed Pearlson.

As Matt's vision tunneled from lack of oxygen, he flipped up the trigger guard and pressed the button that glowed beneath it. He stared at the closest grendel, a white shadow spiraling upward, and dropped the grenade toward it, trusting the explosive's weight to carry it down into the depths.

It dropped quickly, rolling down toward the waiting pod.

Unsure of the timer on the grenade, Matt curled into a tight ball. He covered his ears and exhaled all the stale air out of his chest, leaving his mouth open afterward. Seawater swamped into his throat. He kept one eye toward the rising sea monster.

The grendel nosed the grenade as it rolled past, nudging it. Matt closed his eyes. *Please . . .*

Then the world below blew with blinding fire. Matt saw it

through his closed eyelids at the same time as the concussion wave struck him like a Mack truck, driving him upward, collapsing his chest, squeezing his skull in a vise grip. He felt a wash of fiery heat, searing his frozen limbs.

Then his body was blown upward. As the ice roof shattered with the explosion, he flew into open air, limbs flailing. He took one shuddering breath, caught a glimpse of the open ice plains, then fell back toward the sea, now covered in block and brash. Fire danced over the surface in oily patches.

Matt hit the water, sank, then sputtered up, dazed, his head throbbing. He paddled leadenly in the wash.

Ahead, a large form hummocked out of the depths, sluicing ice and flames from its back. It was pale white. Black eyes stared at him.

Matt scrambled away.

Then the bulk rolled . . . and sank down into the sea.

Dead.

Shaking from both cold and terror, Matt stared up at the column of steam rising into the air. So much for his clandestine escape. As he searched for a way to climb out, figures appeared at the edge of the pit.

Russians.

Rifles pointed at him.

Matt clung to a chunk of ice. He was out of tricks.

16

Fathers and Sons

ᐊᐹᐸᐃᑦ ᐃᕐᓂᑦᓗ

APRIL 9, 5:30 P.M.
ON THE ICE . . .

Staying low, Jenny freed the ice ax trapped under her body. As she lifted up, she peeked beyond the boat's rail at the landscape whipping by. They were flying under the full force of the storm. Winds screamed. The hiss of the runners sounded like an angry nest of snakes under the keel. The vibrations through the hull set her skin to itching.

The ax in one hand, Jenny clung to the handrail with the other. She felt like she'd be kited off the shallow deck at any moment. "What do you want me to do?" she yelled into the wind.

Amanda pointed an arm to the boom. "We need to cut the sail loose! Rope's jammed! It's the only way to slow down!"

Jenny stared up at the ballooned sail, then back to Amanda so she could read her lips. "Tell me what to do," she mouthed.

Amanda pointed, leaning forward so she could be understood. "I need the sail to break, but not tear away. We still need to power the boat. To do that, you must chop through some of the ties, get the sail to flutter. Once it's loosened, I'll be able to work the ropes. At least, I hope." She indicated which ties she wanted Jenny to ax.

The first were easy. They were where the sail was secured to the boom. Jenny simply had to lie on her back and hack at them. As each rope was cut, the ties snapped away, popping from the tension. The sail shuddered, but held tight.

The next were trickier. Jenny had to crawl up to her knees, then lean into the wind. With one hand clutched to the mast, she swung up with the ax and sliced ropes that secured the sail to the mast. She worked her way up the pole, holding her breath. One lash point exploded, whipping out, striking her cheek.

She fell back, losing her grip on the mast. She headed overboard.

But Craig caught her by the waistband, pulling her back to the mast.

Jenny regained her grip. Blood trickled hotly down her chin.

Rather than succumbing to fear, Jenny got angry. She pulled herself closer and hacked determinedly.

"Careful!" Amanda yelled to her.

The sail flapped as its conformation suddenly altered. The boom quaked.

Amanda fought a rigged line. Suddenly the capstan spun loose, ropes lashed out. "Down!" she yelled.

Jenny turned to obey, but it was too late. The boom sprang around in a deadly arc. She could not get out of its way in time. Instead of dropping, she leaped up.

The boom missed her, but the loose sail slammed into her. She snatched an edge, grabbing what she could. Fingers found a few lash points near the mast to cling to as the boom carried her beyond the boat's hull.

Ice raced under her toes as she hung from the rigging.

Then the sail caught the wind again and punched out at

her, swelling full. She was torn from her perch, flying through the air. A scream blew from her lips.

Then she hit—not the ice, but the boat.

Amanda had expertly maneuvered the shell under Jenny, catching her as she fell.

"Are you okay?" Craig asked.

Jenny couldn't speak, unsure of the answer anyway. She panted where she lay, knowing how close she had come to dying.

"I've got control of the sail!" Amanda called to her. "I'm slowing us down."

Thank God.

Jenny remained where she fell, but she sensed the boat decelerating. The winds didn't seem as fierce, and the hiss of the runners gentled.

She sighed with relief.

Then a new noise intruded: a deep, sonorous *whump-whump*.

Jenny rolled around and peered beyond the prow. From out of the low storm clouds, a white helicopter appeared. She spotted the American flag emblazoned on it.

"The Delta Force team," Craig said from across the way.

Only now did Jenny allow tears to rise to her eyes.

They had made it.

Craig spoke into his throat mike. "Osprey, here. We're safe. Heading to home base now. Someone put on a big pot of coffee for us."

6:04 P.M.
ICE STATION GRENDEL

Matt sat in a cell, groggy. He wore a set of dry Russian underway clothes: pants, a green hooded sweatshirt, and boots a size too large. He vaguely remembered putting them on. Still he shivered and tremored from the recent dunking in the Arctic Ocean. His wet clothes were piled in the corner of the guardroom outside the cell. Every piece and pocket had been thoroughly searched.

One guard stood by the exit door. The pair of men who had stripped him, roughly searched him, and tossed the dry clothes to him had already left, vanishing with his identification papers. But before leaving, they had emptied his wallet and pocketed the soggy bills themselves. So much for their old Communist ideals.

He stared over to the neighboring cells. Though he had been dazed when brought down here, he knew where he was. He had glimpsed the line of cells when fleeing from the Russians earlier. He was back on Level Four, in the containment cells that must have once housed the poor folk frozen in the tanks.

Each cell was a cage of bars. The only solid wall was the one at the back of the cell. No privacy. No toilets. Just a rusted bucket in the corner. The only other furniture in the room was a steel cot. No mattress.

He sat on the bed now, holding his head in his hands. The concussion of the grenade still throbbed behind his ears. His jaw ached from the strike of a rifle butt to his face. His nose still leaked blood. But he wasn't sure if it was from the blast or the pistol whipping.

"Are you all right?" his neighbor asked from the adjacent cell.

He tried to remember the boy's name. One of the biologists. He couldn't think straight yet. ". . . mm fine," he mumbled.

Sharing the boy's cell were the other two biologists: Dr. Ogden and the girl. He vaguely wondered where the other student was. Hadn't there been a third? He groaned. *What did it matter?*

"Pike," a firmer voice said behind him. He twisted around.

In the other cell, Washburn stood by the front bars. Her lower lip was split, her left eye swollen shut.

"What happened to Commander Bratt?" she asked.

He simply shook his head. His brain rattled inside. Nausea washed over him. He swallowed back bile.

"Shit . . ." Washburn murmured.

They were the only survivors.

Ogden stepped to the bars that separated their two cells. "Mr. Pike . . . Matt . . . there's something you should know. Your wife . . ."

Frowning, Matt's head sprang up. "What . . . what about her?"

"She was with us," Ogden said. "I saw her, that CIA guy, and Dr. Reynolds fleeing in a boat."

Matt heard the bitterness in the other's voice, but he could not comprehend what the biologist was saying. There were too many things that made no sense. He recalled seeing the ice racer chased by two hover-cycles. "Jenny . . ."

Ogden told him his story.

Matt did not want to believe the man, but he remembered Bane's sudden appearance . . . and end. His fingers crept over his face both to hide his grief and hold it back. *Jenny . . . she had been so close. What had happened to her?*

Ogden continued, his voice dropping to a whisper, "I speak some Russian. I overheard what the guards were saying when they were searching us. They're looking for some books. Books that the CIA guy took with him."

"I heard the same," Washburn said, edging closer, keeping her words low.

Matt frowned. "What CIA guy?"

One of the students answered. Matt finally remembered his name. Zane. The boy mumbled, "He said his name was Craig Teague."

Stunned, Matt felt a surge of heat flow through him. He blustered for a moment, trying to find his tongue. "Craig . . . Teague is CIA?"

Ogden nodded. "Sent here to secure the Russian data on suspended animation and escape."

Matt thought back on all his dealings with the supposed reporter. All along, he had sensed some deeper strength in the man, some hidden well of resourcefulness that would shine through occasionally. But he had never even suspected . . .

Matt clenched a fist. He had saved the jackass's life and this is how he repaid him. "Goddamn bastard . . ."

"What do we do now?" Washburn asked.

Matt had a hard time concentrating, balanced between fury and fear for Jenny.

"Why are they keeping us here?" Washburn continued.

Before anyone could answer, the guardroom door swung open. It was the pair of guards who had left with their identification papers. They pointed and spoke to the lone armed guard. The group approached Matt's cell. "You come with us," one said in halting English.

The guard keyed open the lock and pulled the door wide. The other two bore pistols in their hands. Matt judged what it would take to make a grab for one of the weapons. He stood. His legs wobbled under him. He almost fell. So much for a full frontal attack.

He was waved out at the point of a pistol.

I guess this answers Washburn's question. They were going to be interrogated. And after that? Matt eyed the pistol. The prisoners' usefulness would surely be at an end. They had seen too much. There was no way they would be allowed to live.

Flanked by the two guards, Matt was led deeper into the heart of Level Four. Rather than going out to the encircling hall with their dreaded tanks, Matt was led to an inner hall. The passage ended at a solitary room.

He was waved inside.

Matt stepped through the door into a small office, exquisitely appointed in mahogany furniture: wide desk, open shelves, cabinets. There was even a thick bearskin rug on the floor. Polar bear. Its head still attached.

The first sight that drew his eye was of a small boy,

dressed in a baggy shirt. It fit him like a full-length robe. He knelt on the rug and was petting the polar bear's head, whispering in its ear.

The boy glanced up to him.

Matt gasped and tripped on the edge of the rug, going down on one knee. He could not mistake that face.

One of the guards barked at him in Russian, grabbing him by the scruff of the neck.

Matt was too stunned to respond.

A new voice spoke, cold and commanding. Matt raised his eyes, focusing on the room's other occupant. He stood up from the leather chair he had been sitting on and waved the guard away.

The man was tall, six-foot-five, broad of shoulder, wearing a black uniform. But his most striking features were his pale white hair and storm-gray eyes. Those eyes pierced through him now.

"Please take a seat," the man said in perfect English.

Matt found himself rising, obeying reflexively. But once up, he refused to sit. He knew who stood behind the desk. The leader of the Russian forces.

The door to the office clicked shut behind him, but one guard remained in the room. Matt also spotted the pistol holstered at the leader's hip.

Hard gray eyes stared back at him. "My name is Admiral Viktor Petkov. And you are?"

Matt spotted his wallet resting atop the desk. There was no reason to lie. It would get him nowhere. "Matthew Pike."

"Fish and Game?" This was spoken with thick doubt.

Matt kept his voice firm. "That's what my papers say, don't they?"

One eye twitched. Clearly the Russian admiral was not someone who was faced with insolence very often. His voice steeled. "Mr. Pike, we can do this civilly or—"

"What do you want?" He was too tired to play the cordial adversary. He was no James Bond.

The admiral's pale face colored, his lips thinning.

Before anything more could be said, the child rose from his seat on the rug and wandered over to the older man. The admiral's eyes tracked the Inuit lad. The boy touched his hand.

"That's the child from the ice tanks," Matt said, unable to keep the true amazement from his voice.

The admiral's hand curled around the tiny fingers, protective. "The miracle of my father's research here."

"Your father?"

Petkov nodded. "He was a great man, one of Russia's leading Arctic scientists. As the head of this research station here, he was delving into the possibility of suspended animation and cryogenic freezing."

"He experimented on human subjects," Matt accused.

Petkov glanced down to the boy. "It is easy to judge now. But it was a different time. What is considered *myerzost,* or an 'abomination,' today was science back then." His words grew softer, half ashamed, half proud. "Back in my father's time, between the two World Wars, the dynamics of the world were tenser. Every country was trying to discover the next innovation, the next bit of technology to revolutionize their economies. With war pending, world tensions high, the ability to preserve life on the battlefield could make a difference between victory and defeat. Soldiers could be frozen until their wounds could be attended to, organs could be preserved, entire armies could be put into cold storage. The possibilities for medical uses and military innovations were endless."

"So your government forced some of your own native peoples into servitude here. To be experimental guinea pigs."

Petkov's eyes narrowed. "You *truly* don't know what was going on here, do you?"

"I don't know a goddamn thing," Matt admitted.

"So you don't know where my father's stolen journals are? Who has taken them?"

Matt thought about lying, but he was not feeling particularly protective of Craig Teague. "They're gone."

"In the iceboat that escaped."

Escaped? Dare he hope? Jenny was supposedly on that boat. He struggled to find his voice. "They got away?"

Petkov stared tightly at him, as if trying to weigh the risk of telling the truth, too. Perhaps he heard the pleading in Matt's voice or maybe he simply considered Matt no threat. Either way, he answered the question. "They outran my men and reached Omega."

Matt stepped back and sank into the seat he had refused a moment ago. Relief washed through him. "Thank God. Jen . . . my ex-wife was on that boat."

"Then she's in more danger than you."

Matt's brow pinched, tensing again. "What do you mean?"

"This isn't over. Not for any of us." Petkov's gaze flicked to the boy. "This ice station. It's not a Russian research base."

Matt felt a heavy weight settle in his gut.

Petkov's eyes returned to Matt. "It's American."

6:16 P.M.
OMEGA DRIFT STATION

Jenny climbed from the skate boat, her feet settling to the ice. She stared over at the ruin of the nearby polynya. It was blasted, stained with black soot and rusty trails of oil. Fires still burned within the wreckage of two helicopters crumpled on the ice. The air reeked of smoke and fuel.

The thunderous *whump* of the lone remaining helicopter echoed over the frozen terrain as it circled to land near the iceboat. Amanda busied herself with securing the boat, tying down the sails and finding a spare set of wooden chocks to brace the runners. She glanced over her shoulder as the

Sikorsky Seahawk glided out of the blowing winds and settled to the ice.

Craig crossed toward the helicopter, leaning against the
rotor wash. He held his throat mike under his chin as he
spoke to the Delta Force leader inside the craft.

From out of the cluster of Jamesway huts, a group of soldiers in white snow gear ambled out, weapons in hand, but
not raised. They were taking no chances with the Russians
so near.

One of the men approached the two women by the boat.
"Ma'am, if you'll follow me, I'll get you inside with the others. The Russians planted a slew of incendiary devices
throughout the base. We don't know if any of them are
booby-trapped."

Jenny nodded, glad to follow, but fearful to discover the
fate of her father. Was he okay?

They wound back through the nest of buildings. The
snowfall had stopped, but the winds continued to gust
fiercely through the Jamesway huts. Jenny almost lost her
footing, too worried with her goal so close. As they walked,
she knew where they were being taken. To the same barracks
from which she and Kowalski had escaped.

This thought generated more tears. She had thought herself done crying on the boat ride here, relieved, but at the
same time full of grief. Kowalski was missing. Tom was
most likely dead. Bane, too. And Matt . . .

Now all were gone.

She needed someone to still be alive.

Her pace hurried as the guard opened the door to the hut.
Jenny crossed through, followed by Amanda. The soldier
walked them down the hall to the double doors leading to
the barracks.

Jenny noted the two armed soldiers posted by the doorway.

"For your protection," their escort said as he led them
past. "We're trying to keep everyone in one place until we

know the base is safe. And with the Russians entrenched only thirty miles away, nowhere else is safe."

Jenny was not about to object to a little protective custody. After what she had just gone through, the more, the merrier.

The warmth of the barracks struck her like a wet blanket to the face. The heat was stifling from both the heaters and the number of bodies. Jenny quickly glanced through the crowds.

She spotted Commander Sewell immediately. He sat in front. Half his face was bandaged. His arm was in a sling. She stepped in front of him, her eyes wide.

He stared at her with the one good eye that peeked from the bandages. "You just couldn't stay away, could you?"

"What happened?" Her gaze traveled over his beaten form.

"You ordered me to protect your father." He shrugged. "I take orders seriously."

The crowd parted and a familiar figure pushed through. Tired-eyed, but unharmed.

She hurried into his arms. "Papa!"

He hugged her tight. "Jen . . . honey."

She could not say anything more. Something broke inside her. She began to sob. Not simply tears, but racks of pain and gulping breath. It was uncontrollable, rising from a well deep inside her. It hurt so much. She had survived. So many others had not. "M-Matt," she managed to sob out.

Arms tightened.

She continued to cry while her father drew her back to a bed and pulled her down beside him. He didn't try to console her with words. Words would come later. Right now she simply needed someone to hold and someone to hold her.

Her father gently rocked her.

After a period of time, she became aware of her surroundings again, emptied and numb. She slowly lifted her face. At some point, Craig had joined them. He was seated with Amanda, Commander Sewell, and a man in a storm suit.

This last fellow carried a helmet under one arm. His hair was black, short, slicked back. He appeared to be in his midthirties, but a *hard* midthirties. His skin was ruddy with a wicked scar that trailed under his ear to his neckline. He fingered the scar as he leaned beside Craig, studying something on a table that had been dragged over. "I don't see that any of this matters," the soldier said. "We should strike now before the Russians can entrench any further."

Jenny extracted herself, concerned about what they were discussing. She patted her father's hand.

"Jen . . . ?"

"I'm better." *At least for the moment,* she added silently. She stood and walked over toward the group. Her father followed.

Craig glanced up at her. "Are you okay?" he asked.

"As well as can be expected."

He turned back to his discussion with the others. "These are the journals I was assigned to acquire. But they're coded. I can't make any headway deciphering them."

Amanda glanced over to Jenny. "He can't be sure he has the right ones."

"What does it matter?" the storm-suited newcomer asked. "My team can take the station in under two hours. Then you can send in as many encryption experts as you'd like."

Jenny eyed him. He must be the head of the Delta Force team.

Craig answered, "The Russian admiral is no fool. He'll blow the station before letting us commandeer it. Before we go in shooting blindly, we need more intelligence."

Jenny agreed. *Intelligence* was definitely in short supply here. She stared down at the open book resting atop two others. The stolen journals. She glanced to line after line of symbolic markings, her eyes settling on the title line:

ᚘᐅᑎᐸᑎᕐᐱᐅ ᒥᐊᔭᖁᐱ ᒪᕐ ᖁᒃᐁᖁᒃᔭᖁᐱ
ᐅᑎᒪᐅᔭᖃᐊᐅᒋᒃ (ᑭᖁᖁᕐᖁᒃ

She leaned over and picked up the book. Craig frowned at her. She ran a finger over the lines. "This last word is *Grendel*."

Craig swung around in his seat. "You can read the code?"

Jenny shook her head. "No. It makes no sense to me." She turned and showed it to her father.

He shook his head. "I can't read it."

Craig stared between them. "I don't understand."

"Neither do I," Jenny said, flipping through the book. "This is all written in Inuktitut—or rather the Inuit script, but it's not the Inuit *language*. This last word, *Grendel,* I can read because it's a proper name, spelled phonetically in Inuit symbols."

Craig stood up next to her. "Phonetically?"

She nodded.

"Can you read the opening line? How it would sound spoken aloud?"

Jenny shrugged. "I'll try." She pointed to the title line and read it, slowly and haltingly. " 'Ee—stor—eeya—led—yan—noy—stan—zee Grendel.' "

Craig jerked straighter, listening with a bent ear. "That's Russian! You're speaking Russian." He repeated her words more clearly. "*Istoriya ledyanoi stantsii Grendel.*" It translates 'History of the Ice Station Grendel.' "

Jenny stared up at him, her eyes widening.

Craig hit his forehead with the heel of his hand. "Of course, the doctor who ran the station would know Inuit. They were his test subjects. He would need to communicate with them. So he used their symbolic code to record his own Russian notes." He turned to Jenny. "I need you to translate the books for me."

"All of them?" she asked, daunted.

"Just some key sections. I must know if we have the right books."

Amanda had been following their discussion intently. "To ensure the research data is secure."

Craig nodded, barely hearing her, glancing down at the book in Jenny's hands.

Edgy from all that had happened, Jenny risked a glance toward Amanda, unsure she understood all that was going on here. Over Craig's shoulder, she mouthed words at Amanda. Not speaking, merely moving her lips: *Do you trust him?*

Amanda remained still, then gave the tiniest shake of her head.

No.

6:35 P.M.
ICE STATION GRENDEL

Viktor Petkov enjoyed the look of surprise on the prisoner's face. He was so sick of Americans blithely ignoring their own histories, their own atrocities, while vilifying the same actions among other governments. The hypocrisy sickened him.

"Bullshit. There's no way this is an American base," the man insisted. "I've crawled all through here. Everything's written in Russian."

"That's because, Mr. Pike, the discovery here in the Arctic was our own. The Russian government refused to allow you Americans to steal what we found. To claim all the glory." He waved a hand. "But we did allow the United States to fund and oversee the research."

"This was a joint project?"

A nod.

"We put up the dough, and you spent it."

"Your government supplied more than just money." Viktor pulled the small boy onto his knee. The boy leaned into him, sleepy, seeking the solace of the familiar. Viktor stared over to the American. "You supplied the research subjects."

A horrified expression widened the man's eyes as understanding dawned. His gaze took in the boy in his lap. "Impossible. We would never take part in such actions. It goes against everything the United States stands for."

Viktor educated him. "In 1936, a crack unit of the United States Army was dropped near Lake Anjikuni. They emptied a remote village. Every man, woman, and child." He stroked the boy's hair. "They even collected dead bodies, preserved in frozen graves, as comparative research material for the project. Who would miss a few isolated Eskimos?"

"I don't believe it. We wouldn't participate in human experiments."

"And you truly believe this?"

Pike glared, defiant.

"Your government has a long history of using those citizens it considers *less desirable* as research subjects. I'm sure you're familiar with the Tuskegee Syphilis Study. Two hundred black men with syphilis are used as unwitting research subjects. They are not told of their disease and treatment is withheld from them so that your American researchers could study how painfully and horribly these men would die."

The prisoner had the decency to glance down. "That was back in the thirties. A long time ago."

"It didn't stop in the thirties," Viktor corrected him. "Nineteen-forty, Chicago. Four hundred prisoners are intentionally sickened with malaria so experimental drugs could be evaluated. It was this very experiment that the Nazis used later to justify their own atrocities during the Holocaust."

"You can't compare that to what the Nazis did. We condemned the Nazis' actions and prosecuted all of them."

"Then how do you justify Project Paperclip?"

The man frowned.

"Your intelligence branches recruited Nazi scientists, offering them asylum and new identities, in exchange for their employment into top-secret projects. And it wasn't just the German scientists. In 1995, your own government admitted doing the same to Japanese war criminals, those who had firsthand involvement with human experimentation on your own soldiers."

By now, the color had drained from Pike's face. He stared at the Inuit boy, beginning to comprehend the truth here. It was painful to have one's innocence ripped away so brutally. "That was long ago," he mumbled, struggling to justify what was too hard to accept. "World War Two."

"Exactly." Viktor lifted his hands. "When do you think this base was built?"

Pike simply shook his head.

"And don't delude yourself that such secret experimentation upon your own people was ancient history, something to be dismissed. In the fifties and sixties, it is well documented that your CIA and Department of Defense sprayed biological and chemical agents over major U.S. cities. Including spreading mosquitoes infected with yellow fever over cities in Georgia and Florida, then sending in Army scientists as public health officials to test the unwitting victims. The list goes on and on: LSD experiments, radiation exposure tests, nerve-gas development, biological research. It is going on right now in your own backyards . . . to your own people. Does it still surprise you it was done here?"

The man had no answer. He stared, trembling slightly—whether from his recent near drowning in the Arctic Ocean or from the truth of what really had gone on here, it didn't matter.

Viktor's voice deepened. "And you judge my father. Someone forced at gunpoint into service here, torn away from his family . . ." Viktor had to choke back his anger and bile. It had taken him years to forgive his father—not for the atrocities committed at the station, but for abandoning his family. Understanding had come only much later. He could

expect no less from the man seated before him. In fact, he
didn't know why he was even trying. Was he still trying to
justify what happened here to himself? Had he truly forgiven his father?

He stared into the face of the boy on his lap. His voice
grew tired, fingers waved. "Take him away," he called to the
guard. "I have no further use for this man."

The motion startled the little boy. A tiny hand raised to a
cheek. "Papa," he said in Russian. The child had imprinted
to him like a gosling after first hatching.

But Viktor knew it was more than that. He knew what the
child must think. Viktor still had a few worn pictures of his
father. He knew now how much he looked like his father did.
Same white hair. Same ice-gray eyes. He even wore his hair
like the last picture of his father. For the boy, fresh from his
frozen slumber, no time had passed. He awoke to find the
son had become the father. No difference to the boy.

Viktor touched the child's face. *These eyes looked upon
my father. These hands touched him.* Viktor felt a deep bond
with the child. His father must have cared for the boy to en-
gender such clear affection. How could he do any less? He
ran a finger along one cheek. After losing all his family, he
had finally found a connection to his past.

Practicing a smile, the boy spoke to him, softly. It was not
Russian. He didn't understand.

The American did. "He's speaking Inuit." Pike had
stopped by the door, held at gunpoint, staring back.

Viktor crinkled his forehead. "What . . . what did he say?"

The man stepped back into the room. He leaned toward
the boy, bowing down a bit. *"Kinauvit?"*

The child brightened, sitting straighter and turning to
Pike. "Makivik . . . *Maki!"*

The man glanced to Viktor. "I asked him his name. It is
Makivik, but he goes simply by Maki."

Viktor pushed a wisp of hair from his face. "Maki." He
tried the name and liked it. It fit the boy.

The child reached up and pulled a lank of his own hair. *"Nanuq."* This was followed by a giggle.

"Polar bear," the prisoner translated. "From the color of your hair."

"Like my father," Viktor said.

Pike stared between them. "He mistakes you for your father?"

Viktor nodded. "I don't believe he knows how much time has passed."

Maki, now with an audience, chattered blearily, rubbing an eye.

Pike frowned.

"What did he say?" Viktor asked.

"He said that he thought you were supposed to still be sleeping."

"Sleeping?"

The men stared at each other, realization dawning on both of them.

Could it be?

Viktor's gaze flicked off in the direction of the outer hall, toward the circle of frozen tanks. *"Nyet.* It is not possible." His voice trembled—something it never did. "A-ask him. *Where?"*

Pike stared silently at him, clearly knowing what he wanted, then concentrated on the child. "Maki," he said, gaining the boy's attention. *"Nau taima?"*

The exchange continued, ending with the boy crawling off Viktor's lap.

"Qujannamiik," Pike whispered to the boy, then in English. "Thank you."

Viktor stood. "Does he know where my father might be?"

As answer, Maki waved. *"Malinnga!"*

Pike translated. "Follow me . . ."

7:18 P.M.
OMEGA DRIFT STATION

Amanda sat at the table as the decoding of the journals continued. Jenny read from the text, translating the Inuktitut symbols, speaking slowly so Craig could decipher the spoken Russian.

The first book was skimmed. It was the history behind the founding of the station, dating back to the infamous tragedy of the *Jeannette* back in 1879.

The U.S. Arctic steamer *Jeannette,* captained by Lieutenant George W. DeLong, had been sent to explore for a new route between the United States and Russia, but the boat became trapped in the polar ice cap, frozen in place. The steamer remained icebound for two winters until it was crushed by the floes in 1881. The survivors escaped in three life rafts, dragging the boats over the ice until they reached open water. But only two boats ever reached landfall in Siberia.

The fate of the third was lost to history—but apparently not to the Russians. "Saturday, the first of October, in the year of Our Lord, 1881." Jenny and Craig translated a bit of a diary entry included in the journal. "We are blessed. Our prayers have been answered. After a night of storms, huddled under a tarp, bilging our boat hourly, the day broke calm and bright. Across the seas, an island appeared. Not land. God is not that kind to sailors. It was a berg, pocked with caves, enough to get out of the storms and seas for a spell. We took what refuge we could and discovered the carcasses of some strange sea beasts, preserved in the ice. Starving as we were, any meat was good meat, and this was especially tasty. Sweet on the tongue. God be praised."

Jenny glanced around the room. Everyone in the barracks room knew what "beasts" had been discovered on that lone iceberg. *Grendels.* Even the meat being notably sweet was consistent with Dr. Ogden's comparison of the grendel's physiology to that of the Arctic wood frog. Like the frogs, it was a glucose, or sugar, that acted as the cryoprotectant. But Amanda kept quiet about this as Jenny and Craig continued.

"October second . . . we are only three now. I don't know what sins we cast upon these seas, but they have returned a hundredfold. In the night, the dead awoke and attacked our sleeping party. Creatures that had been our meals became the diners that night. Only we three were able to make it to the lifeboat and away. And still we were hunted. Only a fortuitous harpoon stab saved us. We dragged the carcass behind our boat until we were confident it was deceased, then took its head as our trophy. Proof of God's wrath to show the world."

This last decision proved not a wise choice. After three more days at sea, the survivors made landfall at a coastal village of Siberia, bearing their prize and story. But such villagers were a superstitious lot. They feared that bringing the head of the monster into their village would draw more beasts to them. The three sailors were slain, and the head of the monster was blessed by the village priest and buried under the church to sanctify it.

It wasn't until three decades later that the story reached a historian and naturalist. He traced the tale to its source, exhumed the skull of the monster, and returned to St. Petersburg with it. It was added to the world's most extensive library of Arctic research: the Arctic and Antarctic Research Institute. From there, a search began to discover the whereabouts of this infamous ice island. But even using the maps of the slain sailors, it would take another two decades to rediscover the berg—now frozen and incorporated into the ice pack. But it was worth the search.

The sailors' story proved true. The grendels were found again.

At that part of the story, Craig, growing impatient, had Jenny stop reading the history text and jump ahead to the last two journals, the research notes of Vladimir Petkov, the father of the admiral who had attacked Omega and the ice station.

"That's what we really need to know about," Craig said.

As the new translations began, the Delta Force team leader—who gave his name only as Delta One—entered the barracks room, pushing through the double doors, flanked by two of his men.

He strode over and reported to Craig. Amanda read his lips. "The bird's ready to fly on your word. All we need is the go-ahead to proceed to Ice Station Grendel."

Craig held him off with a raised hand. "Not yet. Not until I know for sure that we have all we need."

As time was critical, they did a quick scan through the next sections, looking to make sure they had the final notes on the research here. But what quickly became apparent was that Dr. Vladimir Petkov was no fool. Even in the coded text, the researcher had been wary of revealing all.

His scientists had isolated a substance from the deep glands of the grendel's skin, a hormone that controlled the ability to send the beasts into suspended animation. It seemed these glands responded to ice forming on the skin and released a rush of hormones that triggered the cryo-preservation.

But all attempts to inoculate test subjects with this hormone had met with disastrous failure. There were no successful resurrections after freezing.

Craig recited, troubling over some of the words: " 'Then I made an intuitive leap. A . . . a cofactor that activated the hormone. This led to my first successful resuscitation. It is the breakthrough I had been hoping for.' "

The victim had been a sixteen-year-old Inuit girl, but she did not live long, dying in convulsions minutes later. But it was progress for Dr. Petkov.

Jenny paled with the telling of this last section. Amanda understood why. These were the woman's own people, used so cruelly and callously.

According to the dates of the journal, Dr. Petkov spent another three years refining his technique, going through test subjects. Craig had Jenny skim these sections, much of it ancillary research into sedatives and soporifics. Sleep formulas that had no bearing on the main line of research.

But near the very end, Craig found what he had been looking for. Vladimir finally hit upon the right combination, as he stated, "an impossible concoction that would be maddening to reconfigure, more chance than science." But he had succeeded. He synthesized one batch of this final serum.

Then the journal abruptly ended. What had become of those samples and the fateful end of the station remained a mystery.

Jenny closed the last book. "That's all there is."

"There must be more," Craig said, taking the book.

Amanda answered, speaking from experience with scientists. "It looks like Dr. Petkov became more and more paranoid as his successes grew. He split his discovery into notes and samples."

Craig frowned.

Delta One stood straighter. "Sir, what are your orders?"

"We'll have to go back," Craig mumbled. "We only have half the puzzle here. I have the notes, but the Russians control the samples. We must get to them before they're destroyed by Admiral Petkov."

"On your word, we're ready to head out," Delta One said gruffly.

"Let's get it done," Craig said. "We can't give the Russians time to find the sample."

Delta One barked orders to his two flanking men, heading away.

"I'll join the team in a moment," Craig called to him. "Ready the bird." He continued to study the books, then turned to Jenny, wearing a pained expression. "I can't leave the journals here. They must be protected. But I also need them reviewed in more detail. In case we're missing any obvious clues."

"What are you asking?" Jenny said.

"I need someone to come with us who can read the Inuktitut." His gaze flicked between her and her father. "We must know if there are any directions or hints in the books."

"You want one of us to go with you?" Jenny stepped in front. "Don't you think we've put our necks out far enough in this matter? Sacrificed enough?"

"And your knowledge could still save lives. Dr. Ogden, his students, and anyone else holed up over there. I won't force you to come, but I do need you."

Jenny glanced to her father, then back to Craig. Her eyes were full of suspicion, but she was clearly a woman of strong reserves. "I'll go under one condition."

Craig looked relieved.

Jenny patted her empty holster. "I want my goddamn pistol back."

Craig nodded. "Don't worry. This time around, we're all going armed."

This seemed to relieve her.

Amanda stood to the side as final preparations were made. Through a window, she watched Craig hunch next to Delta One out in the snow. The storm was kicking up again, but she could almost make out their lips. She turned to Lieutenant Commander Sewell. He was overseeing his own men. They would defend the base until the Delta team returned. The entire team was leaving on this last mission.

"Commander Sewell," she said. "Could I borrow your field binoculars?"

He frowned but passed her his pair from a pocket of his parka.

Amanda focused on Craig and Delta One as they conversed under one of the lamp poles.

"Is everything ready here?" Craig asked.

A curt nod. Amanda read the tension at the corner of

Delta One's eyes. She also read his lips. "All is ready. The Russians will be blamed."

A figure stepped to her side, startling her. She turned. It was John Aratuk.

"What are you watching?" he asked.

Amanda prepared to answer, ready to voice her fear and suspicions. But as terror iced through her, a new sensation arose—a familiar one.

No . . . it wasn't possible.

The tiniest hairs vibrated on her arms. She felt the telltale tingle behind her deafened ears. But it sounded like alarm bells to her now.

Could the grendels have traveled all the way here?

"What's wrong?" John asked, sensing her panic.

She turned to him, rubbing the tingling hairs on her arms. *"Sonar . . ."*

7:31 P.M.
ICE STATION GRENDEL

Matt held the boy's hand and followed him down the hall, back through the prison wing, and around to the outer circular hall.

"Malinnga!" the boy repeated. *Follow me!*

Behind Matt, the Russian admiral followed. Viktor Petkov was accompanied by the two armed guards. There was no chance of a quick escape. Matt feared for little Maki's safety. He would not abandon the boy.

While they passed through the prison section, his fellow captives cast questioning glances toward him. Dr. Ogden's gaze traveled to the boy. Matt saw the shock of surprise on his face.

Matt clutched the tiny fingers, so warm in his palm. It seemed impossible that this was the same child who'd been frozen in ice only hours ago. He flashed back on his own son, Tyler, walking with him hand in hand. Both boys had died in ice, but now one had returned.

As the two entered the curving wall of tanks, the boy stared at the hazy figures inside. Did he know what they held? Were his own parents inside one of these tanks?

Maki pushed a thumb in his mouth, eyes round and wide. He hurried past, scared.

Petkov spoke behind them. "Does he know where he's going?"

Matt relayed the question in Inuktitut.

"Ii," Maki answered around his thumb, nodding his head.

The hall curved to its end. A wall appeared ahead, blocking the way. They had circled the entire level. There was no way forward. No door.

The boy continued toward the passage's end. To the right, the tanks finally ended. Maki led Matt toward the blank section of wall. It appeared seamless and solid, but the boy's tiny fingers found a small hidden panel. It swung in, revealing a foot-wide brass control wheel.

Maki played with the panel, swinging it back and forth. He spoke in Inuktitut. Matt translated for Petkov. "He says past here is your secret room."

The admiral gently moved the boy's arm out of the way and stared at the brass wheel. He stepped back and waved Matt forward. "Open it."

Matt bent to the hole and grabbed the wheel. It wouldn't budge, frozen solid. "I need a crowbar," he gasped as he struggled.

The boy reached under the wheel and flipped a hidden catch. The wheel immediately spun in his hand, well oiled and preserved.

As the wide handle revolved to a stop, seals popped with a slight hiss. A full section of the wall cracked open. A secret door.

Matt was guided back at gunpoint. Another of the guards stepped forward and pulled the door open.

The cold flowed out as if from an open freezer. Lights flickered on, revealing that it was indeed an icebox inside. Similar to the service huts, it was another room cut directly out of the island. But it was no maintenance closet, but a lab sculpted from the blue ice.

Abutting the three walls were worktables carved from the ice. Shelves of slab ice rose above them, covered with an assortment of stainless-steel equipment: crude centrifuges, measuring pipettes, graduated cyclinders. But the shelves of the back wall, lit by a row of bare lightbulbs, had cored receptacles drilled into them. Inserted into each of the holes were glass syringes, their plungers sticking up. The ice was glassy enough to see through to the amber-colored liquid filling each of the syringe's chambers. There had to be over fifty of the loaded doses.

Matt stared around as he stepped into the ice lab. Work must have been done in a totally frozen state.

The boy entered, still sucking his thumb. His eyes grew wider. He stared into the room, then back out toward the Russian admiral.

Matt understood his confused expression.

"Papa," the boy said in Inuktitut, then repeated it in Russian.

Upon the floor slumped a figure, seated, legs out, head lolled. Even through the frost on the features, there could be no doubt who it was. The family's snow-white hair was unmistakable.

A gasp from Petkov confirmed the identity. He shoved forward, dropping to his knees before the body and reaching out.

The elder Petkov's face was tinged blue, the clothes frosted with rime and ice. One sleeve had been rolled up. A cracked syringe lay on the floor. Blood trailed from a puncture on the inside of the arm to the needle.

Matt crossed to the wall of syringes. He pulled one free. The liquid was unfrozen, impervious to the subzero cold. He

glanced down to the figure. "He dosed himself," he muttered.

Petkov glanced between the boy and his father. Then to
Matt. From his expression, his thoughts were easy to read.
Like the boy, could my father still be alive?

Matt spotted a journal, like all the others, on the table
under the shelves. He flipped open the brittle cover to find
line after line of Inuktitut script scrawled across the pages,
until the notes ceased. Taught by Jenny and her father to
read the language, Matt could make it out, but it made no
sense. He mumbled aloud, trying to determine the meaning.

Petkov glanced up to him. "You speak Russian."

Matt frowned and indicated the book. "I'm just reading
what's written here."

Still on his knees beside his father's remains, Petkov gestured for the journal. He flipped through what was clearly
the last of the journals. Petkov passed it to him. "Read it . . ."
His voice cracked. "Please."

Maki wandered to the admiral's side and leaned into him,
tired and needing reassurance. Petkov put an arm around the
boy.

Matt was in no position to argue with two pistols pointed
at him. Plus he was curious. He read as Petkov translated
aloud. The admiral paused every now and then to question
and to ask Matt to reread a section.

Slowly the truth came out.

The journal was the final testament of Vladimir Petkov. It
seemed that in the decade he'd spent here, Viktor's father
had slowly grown a conscience. Mostly because of the boy
Maki. The child was born here, orphaned when his parents
died during the tests. Missing his own son back in Mother
Russia, Vladimir had developed an attachment and affection
for the boy, which was always a mistake in research. Never
name your test animals. Through this lapse of judgment,
however, Vladimir inadvertently rediscovered his humanity,
losing his professional detachment.

This occurred about the same time he answered the puzzle of activating the grendel hormone. The hormone had to be collected from living specimens, thawed and unfrozen. If collected from dead specimens or frozen ones, it would be rendered inert. Furthermore, once a sample had been drawn by syringe directly from a living grendel, it had to be treated carefully, maintained at a constant temperature.

The temperature of the ice caverns.

Matt glanced around the special lab, understanding its necessity now.

The answer to the puzzle was fire and ice again: the *fire* of a living grendel and the *ice* of the island. Nowhere else could such a discovery be made.

It was this realization that had finally broken Vladimir Petkov. Sickened by his own complicity in what went on here, in the lives lost, he had refused to allow his discovery to reach the outside world, especially after hearing about the Holocaust in Germany.

"We have Russian Jews in our own family," Petkov quietly added.

Matt understood. When it was your people being persecuted, it opened your eyes to the inhumanity of your actions. But understanding wasn't enough. Vladimir needed a final act of contrition. The world could never benefit from what had been done here. So he and a handful of others made the ultimate sacrifice. They sabotaged their own base: damaging the radios and scuttling the station's transport sub. Cut off and adrift on currents, they would allow themselves to disappear into the silent Arctic. Several base members attempted an overland escape, but clearly they never made it.

To protect the innocent prisoners here, Vladimir sent them into a frozen sleep.

Matt glanced out to the hall, weighing whether such an act was mercy or further abuse. Still, from the syringe in the scientist's arm, it was clear that Vladimir took the same medicine. But had it worked?

Petkov mumbled, aghast. "My father destroyed this station. It wasn't treachery."

"He had no choice, not if he was to live with himself," Matt answered. "He had to bury what had been gained so foully."

Petkov stared down at his father. "What have I done?" he mumbled, and fingered a thick wristwatch on his right arm. Tiny lights blinked on its face. Some form of radio device. "I've brought everyone here. Fought to thwart my own father's sacrifice. To bring his discovery back to light."

A commotion at the door drew their attention around. A Russian soldier pushed inside, then stood stiffly before the admiral. He spoke rapidly in Russian, clearly agitated.

The admiral answered, climbing to his feet. The soldier fled away.

Petkov turned to Matt. "We've just confirmed hearing the bell beat of an approaching helicopter over the UQC hydrophone. It just left the vicinity of the Omega base."

The Delta Force team, Matt guessed silently. The cavalry was finally en route. But did that mean Jenny was safe? He could only hope.

Petkov motioned to the guards to move Matt out. "My father gave his life to hide his discovery here. I won't let it be stolen now. I will finish what my father started." He shoved his coat sleeve over his large wrist radio. "This is not over yet."

7:48 P.M.
EN ROUTE OVER ICE . . .

Jenny rode in the back of the Sikorsky Seahawk. She stared outside the window. Not that there was much to see. The rotor wash from the helicopter's blades whirled snow about the rising craft. They lifted from the ice in a whiteout cloud.

But as they cleared from the surface, the snow fell away. Winds buffeted the Seahawk, but the pilot was skilled, compensating, holding the craft steady.

Craig spoke to Jenny from the front. She couldn't see him, but his voice reached her through the radio built inside her sound-dampening earphones. "We should be at the station in twenty minutes. If you could continue to read from the last journal, I've set your microphone to record. I'll also listen as we ride. Any clue could mean the difference between success and failure."

Jenny touched the journal in her lap and glanced across the crew bay. Delta One was strapped in the jump seat, ready to respond with the rest of his twelve-man team at a moment's notice. The stern man stared dully out at the snowfields.

Jenny followed his thousand-mile gaze. The red buildings of Omega were now a hazy smear on the ice. The sun was near the horizon, still up as the days grew longer, heading toward the round-the-clock sunlight of midsummer.

Would this long day ever end?

She returned to the journal in her lap, ready to continue the translation, but a flash of fire drew her eyes back to the window.

The horizon flared up in a rose of flame and swirling snow.

Then the concussion hit her. Even through the earphones, she heard the low boom. It thudded against her chest, a mule kick.

God . . . no . . . no . . .

Jenny leaned against the straps, pressing toward the window, her eyes open with raw shock. It was too horrible to believe. Her hearing stretched, all sounds hollowing out as something inside her wailed.

The helicopter banked, swinging around.

For a moment the view was gone. Jenny prayed it was not what she feared. Then the fiery tornado reappeared out in the ice fields, a swirling column of flame, twisting on thermals. Where Omega had once stood, flames leaped as high as the retreating helicopter.

Slowly, the blazing cascade fell back earthward, consumed by the winds and snow.

Jenny's hearing returned. Cries of surprise and dismay spread through the cabin. Men shifted for better views, wearing masks of anger and pain.

Across the frozen wasteland, lit by the smoldering flames, a huge hole smoked like some Arctic volcano. The surrounding ice was covered in burning pools.

There was no sign of Omega. It was obliterated, blasted off the face of the world.

Jenny could not breathe. *Her father . . . all the others . . .*

Craig yelled over the radio on a general channel. "Goddamn it! I thought you said all the Russian booby traps had been disabled!"

A sergeant answered, "They were, sir! Unless . . . unless I missed one . . ."

Jenny still could not breathe. Tears welled but remained trapped in her eyelashes. She read the honest surprise in everyone's face—all except one person.

The Delta Force team leader still stared out at the flaming landscape. His expression had not changed, still stoic, unaffected . . . not surprised.

He glanced to her.

With dawning horror, Jenny understood the true situation here.

She listened to Craig yell at the sergeant. She heard the lie in his voice. It had all been a setup. The team leaders here were operating under the same guise as the Russians: grab the prize and leave no one to tell the tale. A clean-sweep operation.

No witnesses.

Jenny maintained the fixed look of shock on her face, hiding her comprehension. She stared over at Delta One. He faced her now, trying to read her. She would live only as long as she was useful. Her immediate knowledge of the Inuktitut script was all that stood between her and a bullet in the head.

Craig whispered condolences in her ears, but she remained deaf to him. Instead, she stared down at the book.

From the corner of her eye, flames danced. Tears rolled down her cheek—born of both grief and anger. *Papa* . . .

One hand crept to her belt holster. Another promise not kept.

It was still empty.

Trial by Fire

ᐅᑉᐳᐃᓂᑉ ᐃᒃᐊᑕ ᕐᑉ

Matt sat in his cell, having been returned at gunpoint. Oddly the boy had been left with him. The child, Maki, lay curled on the bed, in a cocoon of blankets. Perhaps the admiral had wanted the boy and his translator close by. Matt had not objected to his role as baby-sitter. At the foot of the bed, he kept vigil on the lad, watching the boy sleep, his tiny fingers curled by his lips as if in prayer.

Maki's features were clearly Inuit: the olive complexion, the ebony hair, the brown almond eyes. As Matt watched over him, he was struck by memories of Tyler, the same dark hair and eyes, like his mother. His heart ached, beyond terror and fear, only a deep sense of loss.

"It's hard to believe . . ." Dr. Ogden murmured from the neighboring cell, looking on. Matt had related the findings in Vladimir Petkov's journal.

Matt merely nodded, unable to take his eyes from the boy.

"What I wouldn't give to study the boy . . . maybe a sample of his blood."

Matt sighed and closed his eyes. *Scientists*. They never lifted their noses from their research to see who was affected.

"A *hormone* from the grendels," Ogden continued. "That makes sense at least. To produce the cryosuspension, it would require an immediate enzymatic cascade of the gene sequence. And skin glands would be perfect vehicles to initiate the event. The skin ices up, it triggers a hormonal release, the genes are activated through the body's cells, glucose pours into cells to preserve them, then the body freezes. And with the grendels being mammals, their hormonal chemicals would be compatible with other mammalian species. Like insulin from cows and pigs that's been used to treat human diabetes. The work here was ahead of its time. Brilliant, in fact."

Matt had had enough. He swung around. "*Brilliant?* Are you fucking mad? Try *monstrous*! Do you have any idea what was done to these people? How many were killed? Goddamn it!" He pointed to Maki as he stirred. "Does that look like a damn lab rat?"

Ogden backed from the bars. "I didn't mean to suggest—"

Matt noted the shadows under the doctor's eyes. Ogden's hands trembled as they dropped from the bars. Matt knew the man was as tired and frightened as any of them. He didn't need someone yelling at him. Lowering his voice, he continued: "Someone has to take responsibility. A line has to be drawn. Science cannot ignore morality in its desire to leap forward. We all lose when that happens."

"Speaking of losing," Washburn said behind him, "what's up with the Delta Force team? Can they take this place?"

Matt saw the two biology students stir at her question. It was their only hope: *rescue*. But he also remembered the fierce determination of Admiral Petkov. The Russian commander was not about to surrender, not even against superior forces. Matt had also noted a glint in his eyes, a cold dispassion that frightened the American more than the guns or the grendels.

Only the boy seemed to warm that edge from the man. Matt glanced at Maki. As with Vladimir Petkov, the child might hold the key to the admiral's salvation. But such a transformation required time . . . time they didn't have. Petkov was a Russian bear cornered in its den. There was nothing more dangerous—or unpredictable.

Matt turned back to Washburn. "I counted at least twelve soldiers. And the Russians have the advantage of being entrenched in here. It would take a full frontal assault to breach this place, then a bloody, brutal, level-by-level clearing."

Magdalene spoke from her cot. "But they'll still come, won't they?"

Matt stared at the small number of survivors. Five of them, six if the child Maki was counted. If the Delta Force team was returning here, it was for more than just a rescue mission. Craig must have heard about the samples. The ultimate success of his mission would require obtaining them.

Washburn knew this, too. "They aren't coming for us," she said, answering Magdalene's question. She met Matt's eye. "We're not the priority."

The door to the prison wing opened. Admiral Petkov strode inside, accompanied by the same two guards. The trio approached Matt's cell.

Here we go again, Matt thought, standing to face them.

Petkov spoke with his usual bluntness. "Your Delta Force team blew up the drift station."

Matt took a breath to assimilate what had just been said.

Washburn swore off to the side. "Bullshit."

"We recorded the explosion minutes after their helicopter took off."

Washburn scowled, but Matt knew Petkov was not lying. It was not his way. Omega had been destroyed. *But why?*

Petkov answered his silent question with two words. "Plausible deniability."

Matt weighed this answer. He sensed the truth to it. Delta Force teams were covert, operating with minimal supervision, surgical-strike teams. They entered a combat zone, completed their mission, and left no witnesses behind.

No witnesses . . .

Inhaling sharply, Matt realized what this news meant. He stumbled, hitting the back of his legs on the bed, jarring it. The child woke with a start.

Petkov pointed for a guard to open the cell. "It seems your government seeks the same objective as my own. To seize the research for themselves, and leave no one to claim otherwise. At any and all cost."

The cell was opened. Pistols were again pointed at him.

"What do you want with me?" Matt asked.

"I want you to stop them both. My father sacrificed all to bury his research. I will not let either government win."

Matt narrowed one eye. If what the admiral had related was true—if this truly *was* a black ops mission—then perhaps he had just found an ally. They shared a common enemy. He faced the admiral. Anger churned in him. If the Delta team had murdered everyone at Omega . . . it seemed unfathomable, but also horribly possible . . . he would do what he could to avenge them all.

He pictured dark eyes, staring at him with love.

Jenny . . .

Fury built in him. He saw a matching determination in Petkov's eyes. But how far could he trust this cold fellow?

"What do you propose?" Matt finally choked out.

Petkov answered icily, "That you bear the white flag. I would talk with this Delta Force team leader, the one who stole my father's journals. Then we will see where we stand."

Matt frowned. "I don't think Craig will be in the talking mood when he gets here. I imagine he and his team will do all their talking with M-sixteens."

"You will have to convince him otherwise."

"What makes you think he'll listen?"

"You'll be taking someone with you whose presence he can't dispute."

"Who's that?"

Petkov's eyes settled upon the small boy on the bed.

7:59 P.M.
EN ROUTE OVER ICE . . .

Through tears, Jenny read the text on her lap. She had no idea what she was saying. She simply translated the Inukti-tut symbols in phonetic Russian. It was all she could do to keep from screaming. She knew Craig was listening, record-ing, seeking some clue.

Across from her, Delta One continued his vigil by the window. The flames of the incinerated drift station had long faded into the twilight. Before leaving, the helicopter had circled the blast zone. But there had been no survivors.

Words cut off her recitation, coming over the general radio. "Ice station dead ahead!" the pilot reported.

"Ready for missile attack," Craig said. "On my word."

Missile attack? Jenny sat straighter.

"Coordinates locked."

"Fire."

Before she could react, a hissing explosion sounded from outside the door. A flash of flame accompanied it.

She leaned forward as the Seahawk banked into the wind.

Out the window, a spiraling trail marked the passage of a rocket. It struck the peaks to the left of the station entry. Ice and fire blasted upward and rolled out into the open ice fields. A flutter of orange, a tent, flapped up in the gale.

Jenny knew the target. It was the site from which the Rus-sians had fired rockets at them. It seemed Craig was clear-ing the field to land the helicopter—and perhaps getting payback.

Under the roil of steam and smoke, the Seahawk rotored down toward the ice.

"Ready Team One!" Delta One yelled, startling Jenny.

The doors on the opposite side swung open. Winds howled into the cabin. The cold bit at her exposed flesh. Then soldiers began bailing out, rappelling down, one after the other. They zipped out of view, vanishing below in seconds.

"Team Two!"

The door on Jenny's side swung open, and the crosswinds tore at her. Nearly losing her grip on the journal in her hand, she clutched it to her chest.

Men pushed past her, grabbing lines and leaping free as fast as the ropes themselves were unfurled. The cabin emptied out of all but three men, including Delta One.

"Man the side guns!" the leader barked.

Already in place, two soldiers swung up huge cannons by the doors.

"Strafe on my command!" Delta One ordered. "Full perimeter fire!"

Jenny risked leaning forward to stare below. The smoke from the rocket attack had begun to disperse. Below, she spotted the off-loaded men. White-camouflaged figures scurried and dropped to bellies.

"Fire!" Delta One ordered.

The guns roared, chattering, spitting fire. Spent cartridges dropped like brass rain. Below, the ice was torn apart in a wide swath around the men, protecting them.

A lone soldier, Russian, fled from a hidden bunker in the ice. He was cut in half by the gunfire, staining the ice red like a squashed bug on a windshield. There seemed to be no other survivors out on the ice.

"Take us lower," Craig ordered the pilot, still on the general line.

The Seahawk descended, retreating slightly to put the ground forces between them and the mouth of the station.

Delta One held one of his earphones firmly to his head. "Reports coming in!" he relayed. "Surface is ours! Station's entrance under heavy guard!"

"Is it safe to land?" Craig asked.

"I'd rather keep the bird in the air until the station is taken," Delta One answered. "But fuel's a concern. We've a long haul back to Alaska. *Hold on!*" He leaned into his earphone, listening. He pressed his throat mike, conversing with someone below. Finally he pulled up his radio microphone. "Sir, ground teams report movement by the station entry. Someone's coming out. Unarmed. He's waving a truce flag."

"What? Already? Who is it?"

The helicopter turned as it hovered. Jenny spotted the figure a hundred yards off. He stood out against the snow, though traces of smoke still smudged across the view. He was wearing a green jacket, bright against the snow. Even across the distance, she recognized the faded coat. She had washed, mended, patched, ironed the damn thing for ten years.

She could not keep the joy and amazement from her voice. "It's Matt!" A sob of relief followed.

The general channel was still open. Craig heard her. "Jen, are you sure?"

Delta One spoke up from across the cabin. "Sir, there's a boy with him."

Now brought to her attention, she saw the child clinging to Matt's leg. He kept one arm around the boy; the other held a pole with a scrap of white parka waving from it.

"Land!" Craig ordered.

The Seahawk began its descent.

Delta One urged caution. "Perhaps we should remain airborne until the matter is cleared up."

"He's been sent out as an envoy. We may be able to use this to our advantage."

Fear wormed through Jenny's relief. Since the beginning,

she and Matt had been pawns in this game between super-powers. It seemed their duty was not over yet.

The skids settled onto the ice. Snow swirled and eddied around the craft. The rotors slowed.

Delta One passed on an order to the pilot. "I want this engine kept hot."

"Yes, Commander."

Craig squeezed back from the cockpit into the main cabin. "We'll leave the journals here." He pointed at Delta One. "They're going to be your responsibility to guard."

"What are you going to do?" he asked.

"I'm going to meet that man out there. He's pulled my butt out of the fire often enough. Let's see if he can do it again." He turned to Jenny. "I'd prefer you to stay put."

"Like hell I will." She unbuckled her seat harness. They'd have to shoot her to keep her here.

Craig watched her a moment, plainly judging her sincerity, then shrugged. He probably preferred all his targets together anyway.

The pair climbed out of the Seahawk and onto the ice. They ducked under the rotors and were met by a trio of Delta Force team members, who were moving forward under an armed escort.

Jenny barely noticed these others. Her eyes were on the figure standing thirty yards from the station opening. Matt! She had to restrain herself from running toward him. She feared such a sudden action would get them both shot.

So she kept to the group, flanked and led by the soldiers. They crossed the ice, passing beyond the circle of defense and out into neutral territory.

Matt was down on one knee, sheltering the boy, his attention on the child. The little guy hugged Matt. He was swaddled from head to toe in someone's parka, wearing it like a full-length greatcoat. The sleeves hung to the ground. In Matt's arms, he wiggled around to stare wide-eyed at the approaching party.

Jenny saw the boy's face clearly for the first time: the black hair, the large brown eyes, the tiny features. She tripped, her legs going suddenly weak. "Tyler!"

8:07 P.M.
OUT ON THE ICE . . .

Matt had his hands full with the boy. As soon as they had stepped out of the tunnel and into the wind, Maki had clung to him like an eel. The explosions and roar of the gunship's 50mm weapons had already spooked the kid. And now out in the open, he acted agoraphobic, panicking at the wind and snow. Matt could guess why. He had probably spent all his young years isolated below, possibly even limited to Level Four. Here in the open, with the entire world spread out around him, he came unhinged.

He needed something to cling to, an anchor—and that was Matt.

Matt hardly noted the approach of the others. He had spotted Craig among the soldiers, then had to keep Maki from bolting back toward the station.

"Tyler!"

The familiar cry tore him around.

From out of the group of soldiers, Jenny shoved free. Her eyes were wild, but she quickly collected herself as she stepped out. She recognized her mistake as soon as she uttered it. Pure reflex, Matt understood.

"His . . . his name's Maki," Matt gasped out as he stood. The child clung to his knee, but Matt didn't object this time. His legs weak from the relief of seeing Jenny alive, he needed the boy's support now.

She rushed at him.

Matt didn't know what to expect, cringing slightly at her approach.

Then she was in his arms, pulling tight to him, her own

arms around his neck. It came so naturally that it surprised Matt. She fit to him, as if she always belonged there. It was as if no time had passed between them at all. Drawing Jenny even tighter to him to make sure it wasn't all a dream, he smelled her hair, the nape of her neck. She was real . . . she was in his arms.

She sobbed in his ear. "Back at the base . . . Papa . . ."

Matt stiffened. John wasn't with her, or on the helicopter. Her father had been left back at Omega. From Jenny's reaction, Petkov's earlier report had not been a lie. The place *had* been blown up.

"Jenny, I'm so sorry." Even to him, the words sounded lame. All he could do was offer her his strength, his shoulder, his arms.

She shook in his grip. Words reached up to him, whispered, meant for his ears only. "It was Craig. Don't trust him."

Matt's fingers clutched her parka. He stared past Jenny to the figure in the familiar blue parka. He kept his face stoic, pretending he hadn't heard the words whispered in warning.

It was all true. Everything.

He slowly peeled himself from Jenny, but he kept one arm around her.

Craig stepped forward. "Matt, it's good to see you alive. But what's going on? What are you doing out here?"

Matt fought back the urge to punch the man square in the face. But such an action would only get him killed. To survive from here on out, it would take an artful game of half-truths and lies.

So first, a *lie*. "God, it's good to see you all here."

Craig's tentative grin firmed up.

"The Russian admiral remains in control down there, but he sent me up here. He figures if you all were going to shoot blindly and ask questions later, then it might as well be one of us Americans that gets killed."

"Why did he send anyone?"

"To parley a truce. To quote the admiral, both sides have half the key to the miracle here. You have the technical notes. He controls the samples. Either is useless without the other."

Craig stepped closer. "Is he telling the truth?"

Matt stepped aside and pushed little Maki between his and Jenny's legs. The boy kept tight to Matt's thighs. "Here's the proof I was sent up with."

Craig frowned and bent down to stare closer at the boy. "I don't understand."

Matt shouldn't have been surprised. Craig had been trained to be single-minded, to tunnel-vision toward the goal and ignore all the rest. Especially the bodies left by the way-side.

"It's the boy from the tank," he explained. "The ice tank that Dr. Ogden activated."

Craig's gaze flicked up to him. "My God, that's the boy? He resuscitated? It actually works?"

Matt kept himself composed. He couldn't let the man know that he understood the deadly intent of the Delta Force team. "It worked, but the only surviving samples of the elixir are secured in a hidden vault down below. I've seen the place myself. But Admiral Petkov has wired the base to explode. He'll destroy it all."

Craig's gaze darkened. "What does he want?"

"A truce. A parley between the two of you. On Level One. He'll pull his men down below. You can come in with five of your men, armed as you like. But if any harm comes to the admiral, his men have orders to shoot the prisoners and ex-plode the vault. I don't see that you have much choice. It's either lose everything or make a pact with this devil."

Matt waited, unsure if he had overplayed his hand.

Craig snorted and turned away. He raised the collar of his jacket and spoke into it, then pulled his hood's drawstring and held it to his ear. A hidden radio, Matt realized.

Jenny sidled closer to him. "He's consulting with the

Delta Force commander. The stolen journals are in the helicopter with the man. But what about this parley? Is there anyone we can trust?"

"The only person I trust is standing next to me."

She squeezed his hand. "If we get out of this—"

"When," he corrected her. "When we get out of this."

"Matt . . ."

He leaned in and gently pressed his lips to hers. It wasn't so much a kiss as a promise of more to come. A promise he intended to keep. He tasted the salt of her tears on her mouth. They would survive this.

Craig turned to him as more men gathered around him. They readied weapons. "You're right. It looks like we have no choice but to meet with the bastard."

Matt counted Craig's team. *Five.* "You have one too many," he said, nodding to the soldiers.

Craig crinkled his brow. "What do you mean? You said five."

Matt gestured toward Jenny. "She's coming in with us. You'll need to get her a sidearm."

"But—"

"Either she comes or I don't go back. And if I don't return as ordered, Petkov will blow the vault."

Shaking his head, Craig waved off one of the men. "Fine, but she's safer out here."

Matt didn't respond. For better or worse, they were sticking together. Jenny gave his hand a final squeeze and held out an open palm for a pistol.

One of the soldiers passed her his sidearm. Matt had to guide Jenny's hand to her holster. As angry as she was, she might just shoot Craig where he stood.

Once ready, they set off toward the station. Matt pulled the boy up in his arms. Maki stared over at Jenny, his small eyes haunted. They trudged through the blasted opening and down the tunnel again. The warmth of the station breathed out at them.

Matt wondered if Petkov was prepared. The Russian admiral had been vague about his plans. *Get Craig inside* was his mission objective. Petkov would do the rest. But what could the admiral hope to do? The Russian contingent was outnumbered and outgunned.

Matt led the way onto Level One. The lights were back on. Someone must have found spare fuses and powered up the level. The place was too bright. The blood on the floor stood out garishly. Bodies lined one wall. The tables had been pushed away.

In the center of the room, Petkov stood by the spiral stair. The elevator had been raised from below. The Russian admiral stood with one foot on the elevated platform.

"Welcome," he said coldly.

Petkov stepped onto the platform. He shared the space with a strange device. It was a titanium globe on a tripod. A small series of blue lights raced across the sphere's equator. Though it was unmarked, it had *bomb* written all over it.

Matt had a sudden sinking feeling that his newfound ally in this war between superpowers had not been as forthcoming as he would have wished. What game was being played now?

Behind Matt, footsteps suddenly pounded. He swung around. Another five Delta Force soldiers raced into the room, fanning out. It seemed neither side was going to honor the truce.

Matt shouldn't have been surprised, but he was.

Petkov remained stoic, unreadable. He continued to stand on the elevator stand. "You risk your mission," he finally said. "On my word or death, the samples will be destroyed."

Craig strode up beside Matt. He picked Maki out of his arms, earning a startled yelp from the boy. "This is all I need," he said, holding the boy aloft. "An *issledovatelskiy subyekt*. A research subject. Jenny here was kind enough to read more of your father's journal while en route here. It seems the hormone remains active in a revived specimen for a full week. Between his notes and the boy, we will distill the hormone on our own. What you hold is worthless. But I'll still make an offer. Your life in exchange for the samples you hold. The offer will last for exactly one minute."

"Thank you for your gracious offer," Petkov said, "but I won't need the minute."

The explosion rocked the level, bucking the floor and tossing them all skyward. Smoke rolled out from behind them. Matt landed in a pile beside Jonny. He twisted around.

The exit to the surface was gone. A tumble of broken ice blocked the way, caved in, spilling out onto this level. He rolled to his feet, ears ringing. Craig and what was left of the Delta Force team picked themselves off the floor. Two men were dead, crushed by falling ice near the shaft.

Lights flickered. Smoke set everyone to coughing.

Matt searched the central staircase. Petkov was gone, having fled down the staircase. Matt glanced between Craig and the vanished Russian. He was trapped between two madmen, buried with them.

He stared across to the titanium sphere resting on the elevator platform. The blue flashing lights raced around and around the device.

This was not going to end well.

8:15 P.M.
UNDER THE ICE . . .

Aboard the *Polar Sentinel,* Amanda crouched beside Captain Greg Perry. Together they studied the monitor of the sub's DeepEye sonar. Others gathered behind them, some watching the screen, others staring out the Lexan eye of the sub.

Greg rested a hand on her knee. He was clearly not letting her out of his reach . . . and she was fine with this arrangement.

Half an hour ago, back at Omega, she had been in full panic. She had struggled to raise the alarm among the others—about the deceit planned by the Delta Force leaders and of the nerve-jangling sonar frequency, indicating the presence of grendels. But it hadn't been grendels. It had been the *Polar Sentinel* activating its DeepEye sonar.

Before she could even get Commander Sewell's attention, the double doors to the barracks had popped open and Greg had rushed into the room with a small squad. He had ordered everyone to remain quiet.

Too shocked by the miracle, Amanda had flown into his arms. Ignoring decorum, he had pulled her to him, kissed her, and whispered that he loved her.

Together, they had waited until the Delta Force helicopter lifted off. Then they were all running. With Greg in the lead, they raced through the shadows to the oceanography shack. Inside, Amanda found a strange sight. Thrust up within the lab's main research room stood the conning tower of the *Polar Sentinel*. The sub had surfaced its tower through the square hole cut in the ice. The small port was normally used by the oceanographers to raise and lower their two-man bathysphere. But now it serviced the sub's tower, the proverbial square peg in a round hole.

With time ticking down, the party had fled into the submarine.

As soon as all were aboard, Greg had ordered the submarine to crash-dive. The *Polar Sentinel* fell away like a brick. They were at forty fathoms when the Russian V-class incendiaries blew off the top of their world.

Amanda had been in Cyclops at the time. She had witnessed the blinding flash, the impossible sight of flames shooting down through the water. The submarine had been rocked, shoved deep, but with the insulation of almost three hundred feet of water, they had survived, no more than rattled.

Greg had then related her father's frantic VLF message,

his warning about the ultimate mission of the Delta strike team. "I was already here, planning a rescue attempt under the Russians' noses. I never imagined that I'd have to rescue you from our own forces." This last was spoken bitterly.

He had also shared the news about her father's medical condition. A heart attack. But he was recovering well in the naval hospital on Oahu. "Even before he'd let them treat him, he insisted the warning be sent first."

The timing had saved them.

Now once again, the *Polar Sentinel* spied from below. This time the submarine hovered beside the inverted mountain of ice that hid Ice Station Grendel. Through the Deep-Eye's penetrating sonar, they had watched the assault upon the buried station. It was eerie watching the silent play unfold on the screen, the ghostly images of men and gunfire.

Then the explosion erupted, appearing as a wash of yellow on the monitor.

It slowly cleared.

Greg squeezed her knee, indicating he wanted to speak to her. She turned and looked at him. "I don't know what we can do to help," he said. "It looks like the entrance collapsed. They're trapped in there."

Over Greg's shoulder, a figure stirred, moving forward. "Jenny." It was the woman's father. He pointed to the screen and tapped one of the phantoms, the form billowy from the sonar. "That's my daughter."

Amanda glanced back to him. "Are you sure?"

He leaned forward and ran his finger down the figure's lower half. "She broke her leg when she was twenty-two. They had to pin it back together."

Amanda focused the DeepEye slightly. The old man could be right. The penetrating sonar was similar to X rays. And there appeared to be a distinct metallic density in the lower extremities. It could be her.

She turned to John and read the raw fear in his face. He *knew* it was his daughter. Amanda struggled to think of some other way to rescue Jenny and any other folk trapped between the two forces.

Greg pointed to the monitor. Throughout the upper levels of the station, spats of yellow appeared on the monitor. She didn't have to read his lips to know what it was. *Gunfire*.

A large flare of amber flashed midlevel in the station.

She turned to him.

"Grenade," he mouthed.

She turned back as flashes and flares continued to descend into the depths of the station.

It was all-out war.

8:22 P.M.
ICE STATION GRENDEL

Another grenade exploded, rocking the floor under Jenny. In her arms, she held the Inuit boy. He screamed and sobbed, covering his ears, squeezing his eyes tightly closed. She rocked him as she crouched.

Matt hovered over them both, a rifle in his hand.

Screams and shouts wafted up the central shaft, along with billows of smoke and soot. Fires were raging somewhere below. Most of the base was steel, brass, and copper. But a significant part of its infrastructure was straw and flammable composites.

It was burning.

Even if the Delta Force team could commandeer the station, what then? They would either die in flames or be buried in the ice as the station collapsed.

And then there was always the third possibility.

Hovering amid the column of smoke, the large titanium sphere rested on the elevator platform. One of the soldiers, a demolition expert, knelt in front of an open hatch at the bottom of the sphere. He had been studying it for the past ten

minutes, tools spread at his knees, untouched. It was not a
good sign.

Craig barked at her shoulder as the gunfire ebbed below.
He was yelling into his radio while he surveyed the level.
Two other Delta Force soldiers held positions by the shaft.
The remainder of the squad continued its guerrilla war down
below.

Lowering his throat mike, Craig stepped to them. He eyed
the collapsed exit. "There's no way for the few men left
above to dig us out. It would take days. Any attempt to blast
a way through with a missile would just get us all killed."

"So what are they going to do?"

Craig closed his eyes, then opened them. He stared over
to the bomb. "I ordered them to stand down, to retreat thirty
miles off. I can't risk losing the journals."

"Thirty miles?" Matt asked. "Isn't that overkill?"

Craig nodded to the device being examined over the shaft.
"It's nuclear. That's as much as Sergeant Conrad can tell us
right now. Unless we can deactivate it . . ." He shrugged.

Jenny had to give the guy credit. He was one cold fish.
Even in their current straits, his mission was his first priority.

Matt continued to watch over them, eyes sweeping all
around. "The shooting . . . I think it's slowing . . ."

Jenny realized he was right. She cradled the boy. The gunfire had died to sporadic bursts.

Over by the central shaft, the two guards stirred. One
yelled back to them. "Friendlies coming up!"

A pair of Delta Force team members clambered up the
steps. They led a Russian soldier, hands on top of his head,
at gunpoint. A young man, no older than eighteen, he
blinked at the blood that ran down his face. Soot covered his
clothes.

One of his captors snapped at him in Russian. He dropped
to his knees. The other came to report to Craig. "They're
surrendering. We've another two prisoners on Level Three."

"And the others?"

"Dead." The soldier glanced back to the stairwell. The gunfire had ended. "We cleared all the tiers, except for Level Four. Men are sweeping it now."

"What about Admiral Petkov?" Matt asked.

The man nudged the prisoner. Weak with terror and loss of blood, he fell on his side, afraid even to lower his hands to catch himself. "He says that the admiral fled into Level Four. But so far, we've not found him. The prisoner might be lying. He may need a little encouragement."

Before the matter could be addressed, Sergeant Conrad approached from his examination of the nuclear bomb.

Craig turned his full attention toward the man. "Well?"

The soldier shook his head. "It's like nothing I've ever seen. As far as I can tell, it's a low-yield nuclear device. Minimal radiation risk. But it's certainly no standard bomb. I'm guessing more of a disrupter of some type. Like the EM-pulse weapons under development. The explosive capability is small for a nuclear weapon, but its energy could generate a massive pulse. But I don't think it's an *electromagnetic* pulse. Something else. I don't know what."

Matt interrupted his report. "You said the explosion would be *small*. That's the part I want to know about. How small?"

He was answered with a shrug. "Small for a *nuclear* device. But it'll crack this island like a hard-boiled egg. If it blows, we're all dead, no matter what pulse it sends out."

"Can you deactivate it?"

The sergeant shook his head. "The trigger is based on subsonics. It's tied to an external detonator. Unless we can get the abort code to turn this thing off, this baby's going to blow in"—he checked his watch—"in fifty-five minutes."

Craig rubbed his left temple. "Then we need to find the admiral. He's our only chance." His gaze settled on the frightened youth at his feet. He nodded to the soldier who had kicked the man. "Find out what he knows."

The prisoner must have understood. He babbled in Russian, terrified, his hands still on his head.

Matt stepped between the prisoner and the soldier. "Don't bother. I can find Petkov. I know where he must be holed up."

Craig turned to him. "Where?"

"Down on Level Four. I'll have to show you."

Craig narrowed his eyes, glancing between the youth and the shaft. "All right. I doubt this fellow knows anything anyway." He pulled out his pistol and shot the man in the head.

The retort was loud in the silent station. Skull, brains, and blood splattered across the floor.

"Jesus Christ!" Matt yelled, stumbling back as the blast echo died. "Why did you do that?"

Craig's eyes narrowed. "Don't play me for a fool, Matt. You know why." He headed toward the shaft, waving for a pair of soldiers to flank him. "It's either us or them. Pick sides and let's go."

Matt remained frozen but stared toward Jenny, who had twisted from the body, shielding the boy.

The gunshot had sent the boy into another bout of wailing. Jenny held him tightly.

Matt stepped over and leaned down, hugging them both. "Go," she whispered, defying her own heart's desire. She wanted him to stay with them. "But watch your back."

A small nod. He understood her. The biggest danger right now was the bomb. Once that was nullified, they'd find some way to survive both the Russians and the Delta Force strike team.

Matt stood, shouldering his rifle.

Jenny closed her eyes, not wanting to see him leave. But as he stepped away, she opened her eyes. She watched his every movement: the set of his shoulders, the length of his stride. She drank him in, not knowing if she'd ever see him again, regretting the waste of bitter years.

Then they were gone. Two guards watched the shaft. Otherwise she was alone with the gently sobbing boy. She comforted him, as she had not been able to comfort Tyler. She ran fingers through his hair, whispered wordless sounds to soothe.

Across the way, the two guards by the stairs talked softly together. There was no more gunfire, no more explosions. Smoke still hazed the level. Through the oily fog, the lone beacon still shone, beating like a titanium heart, counting down.

As she cradled the boy, a voice whispered behind her, ghostly and vague. She was not even sure she heard it. Then her name was spoken.

"Jenny . . . can you hear me?"

She cautiously glanced behind her. She did not recognize the voice. It came from an overturned set of electronics.

"Jenny, it's Captain Perry of the Polar Sentinel."

8:32 P.M.
USS *POLAR SENTINEL*

Perry stood in the communication shack by the bridge. He spoke into the UQC underwater telephone. "If you can hear me, move toward the sound of my voice."

As he waited, he switched to the shipboard intercom. He hailed the Cyclops chamber. "John, can Amanda see Jenny on the monitor? Is your daughter responding?"

A short pause, then an answer came through. "Yes!" He heard a father's hope in the man's voice.

For the past five minutes, they had waited, spying with the DeepEye until Jenny was alone. Earlier, Perry had eavesdropped on communication between the station and the *Drakon* through the underwater phone. He had hoped the rubber landline that draped into the ocean had not been severed by the blast.

"Jenny, we can see you with our sonar. Is there any way

you can transmit? There should be a receiver. Just like an old-fashioned phone. If you find it, simply talk into it."

Perry waited, praying. He didn't know what help they could offer, but he needed to know the situation in the station to formulate a plan.

The line remained quiet.

C'mon . . . we need some break. A bit of luck.

The silence stretched.

8:33 P.M.
ICE STATION GRENDEL

Jenny clutched the telephone receiver in her hand. Tears of frustration welled in her eyes. The cord was cut. There was no way to communicate out. She wanted to bang the handset on the ground in frustration. Instead she simply set it down.

So far the two guards remained busy with their own discussion. She kept one arm around little Maki, not wanting to attract attention.

The captain's voice returned. *"There must be a problem at your end. But we're monitoring all means of communication coming from the station. We have all our ears up. You simply need to find a radio of any sort. Even a walkie-talkie. Our ears are very good out here. Get to it. But don't let any of the Delta team see you."*

Jenny closed her eyes.

"Just know we're watching you. We'll do what we can to help."

She listened to his confidence, but it shed from her like water off a seal's fur. Even if she could reach a radio, what good would it do? How could they help?

She stared at the blue lights circling around and around the titanium sphere. A sense of despair and hopelessness settled over her. She was too tired to fight any longer. She had been up almost two days straight. The constant terror and tension had burned all substance from her. She felt hollow and empty.

Then a new voice whispered from the tiny speaker. *"Jenny, we're here. We won't leave until we get you all out of there."* She barely heard the words, it was the voice that held her attention: the familiar slight slurring, the drawled consonance.

"Amanda . . ." She was naming a ghost.

"I have someone who wants to speak to you."

There was a pause during which Jenny sought to make sense of it all.

"Honey . . . Jen . . ."

Tears flowed, filling the hollow space in her heart. "Papa!"

Her outburst drew the guards' attention. She leaned over the boy, speaking to him, covering her mistake.

Behind her, her father spoke to her . . . alive! *"Do as Captain Perry says,"* he urged her. *"We won't leave you."*

Jenny hunched over the boy, rocking, hiding her sobs. Her father still lived. The miracle of it pushed back her despair. She would not give up.

She lifted her head and stared over to the dead Russian teenager. From the upper pocket of his fatigues, a black walkie-talkie protruded.

Jenny stood up, pulling the boy in her arms. As she paced with Maki, softly humming, she edged closer to the body. Once near enough, she waited until the guards' backs were turned. Then she darted down, snatched the walkie-talkie, and sprang back up.

She hid the radio where no one would think to look.

But what now?

Across the room, the titanium sphere continued its deadly countdown. There could be no rescue until that threat was addressed.

It was all up to the man she loved.

Matt led the way down the long curving hall of frozen tanks.

Craig followed with his two men. Other members of Delta Force manned key positions throughout this level. With all the remaining Russians executed, the base was once again an American station . . . all except for one Russian admiral.

Matt reached the end of the hall, where the line of tanks stopped. He crossed to the secret panel. Pausing, he weighed the evils here: Craig versus the Russian admiral. But he also pictured Jenny and the little boy. He took strength from her heart, her will to protect the innocent. Before any other matters could be decided, the bomb had to be deactivated.

His fingers tightened on the rifle in his hand.

"There's nothing here," Craig said suspiciously.

"Nothing?" Matt reached and swung open the hidden panel, revealing the wheeled latch to the ice lab's door. He glanced over to Craig with one eyebrow raised. "Then you go in first, because I doubt we're going to get a very warm welcome."

Craig waved Matt aside and had one of the Delta Force guards work the wheel. Matt allowed him to struggle a moment, remembering his own frustration. But time was critical. He leaned forward and hit the secret switch that unlocked the wheel. It spun free. The door cracked open.

No one moved to open it farther.

Craig stepped closer. "Admiral Petkov!" he called. "You asked for us to meet, to parley a solution. I'm still willing to talk if you are."

There was no answer.

"Maybe he killed himself," one of the guards mumbled.

This theory was quickly disproven as Petkov called out, "Come in."

Craig frowned, unsettled by the admiral's yielding. He glanced to Matt.

"I'm not going in there first. This is *your* goddamn game."

Craig motioned everyone to either side, then pulled the door open himself, shielding his body behind the door. There was no gunfire.

One of the soldiers, a sergeant, extended a small spy mirror around the corner. He studied the room for a few moments. "All clear," he said, not hiding his surprise. "He's just sitting in there. Unarmed."

Making the soldier prove his words, Craig waved him in first. Raising his rifle, the sergeant slid from his vantage point and ducked low through the doorway. Dropping to a knee, he swept his weapon around, ready for any threat. None arose.

"Clear!" he yelled.

Craig cautiously stepped around the door, his pistol pointing forward. He crossed into the room. Matt followed, while the other guard remained posted in the hall.

Little had changed inside the ice lab. Nothing had been moved or destroyed. Matt had at least expected Petkov to have smashed the samples, but the glass syringes were still secured across the back shelves.

Instead, the admiral sat on the ice floor beside his father. The two could have been brothers, rather than father and son.

"Vladimir Petkov," Craig said.

There was no need to confirm the obvious.

Craig's eyes took in the wall of syringed samples. He kept his gun pointed at the admiral. "It doesn't have to end this way. Give us the abort code to the bomb upstairs and you can still live."

"Like you allowed my men to live, like you allowed your own people at Omega to live." Petkov scowled. He lifted an arm and shook back his sleeve, revealing the hidden wrist monitor. "The bomb upstairs is a sonic charge, set to go off in another forty-two minutes."

Craig no longer even tried to lie. "I can turn those forty-two minutes into a lifetime of pain."

Petkov laughed bitterly at the threat. "You can teach me nothing about pain, *huyok*."

Craig bristled at the clear insult.

"What do you mean a *sonic* charge?" Matt interrupted. "I thought it was a nuclear bomb?"

Petkov's gaze flicked to him, then back to Craig. The Russian admiral knew the true enemy here. "The device has a nuclear *trigger*. After a sixty-second sonic pulse, the main reactor will go critical and blow. It'll take out the entire island."

Craig shoved his pistol closer, threatening. The hammer cocked back.

Unfazed, Petkov simply tapped his exposed wrist monitor. "The trigger is also tied to my own heartbeat. A fail-safe. Kill me and the time before detonation will drop to one minute."

"Then maybe something else will persuade you." He shifted his pistol and pointed it at Petkov's father's head. "Matt told me your story. Your father took the elixir along with the Eskimos. If he did that, then a part of him wanted to live."

Petkov remained unreadable, stone. But there was no response this time.

"Like the boy, he may still be alive even now. Would you take that chance at rebirth from him? I understand the shame and grief that drove your father to his decision, but there can be no redemption in death, only in life. Would you deny your father that?" Craig stepped forward and crushed the glass syringe Vladimir had used decades ago. "He *injected* himself. He *wanted* to live."

Petkov glanced to his father. One hand twitched up, then down, plainly wavering.

Matt pressed, "And what about little Maki? Your father put him to the final test himself, the boy he took as his foster son. He wanted the boy to live. So if not for yourself or your father, consider the boy."

Petkov sighed. His eyes closed. The silence became a physical weight on them all. Finally, tired words flowed from the admiral. "The abort code is a series of letters. They must be entered forward, then reentered backward."

"Tell me," Craig urged. "Please."

Petkov opened his eyes. "If I do, I want one promise from you."

"What is that?"

"Do with me what you will, but protect the boy."

Craig narrowed one eye. "Of course."

"No research labs. You mentioned using him again as an *issledovatelskiy subyekt*, a research subject." He indicated the wall of syringes. "You have more than enough here. Just let the boy live a normal life."

Craig nodded. "I swear."

Petkov sighed again. "I suggest you write the code down."

Craig pulled a small handheld device from his pocket. "A digital recorder."

Petkov shrugged. "The code is L-E-D-I-V-A-Y-B-E-T-A-Y-U-B-O-R-G-V."

Craig played it back to make sure he got it right.

The admiral nodded. "That's it."

"Very good." Craig lifted his pistol and pulled the trigger.

The noise in the small space sounded like a grenade. Several of the syringes shattered.

Again, Matt was startled from the sudden violence. He stumbled back. The guard at the door, obeying some hidden signal, snatched the rifle from his fingers. The other soldier's weapon pointed at his face.

Petkov remained on the floor. His father's body had fallen over his legs, headless now. The frozen skull had shattered half away from the point-blank shot.

Matt gaped at Craig.

The man shrugged. "This time I did it because I was pissed off."

8:49 P.M.

Victor held his father's body. Parts of his skull littered his lap, the floor, the shelves. A shard had sliced his own cheek, deeply, but he barely felt the sting. He clutched the cold flesh.

A moment ago, there had been hope that some part of his father yet lived, suspended in time. But now all such hopes had been shattered away as thoroughly as the frozen skull.

Dead.

Again.

How could the pain be so fresh after so many years?

Though his heart thudded painfully in his chest, no tears came. He had shed his tears for his father when he was a boy. He had no more.

Craig spoke by the door to one of his guards. "Take them both to the cells to join the others. Bring the woman and boy down, too."

The boy . . .

Viktor stirred, finding purpose. "You swore," he called out hoarsely.

Craig paused at the door. "I will keep my promise as long as you haven't lied."

8:50 P.M.

Matt watched the admiral struggle to his feet and noted there was still a strength to him. Petkov's hands were bound so that he couldn't access the wrist monitor, and in short order, he and Petkov were escorted at gunpoint from the room.

It was over. Craig had won.

With the bomb deactivated, the bastard had plenty of time to recall the remainder of the Delta team and dig himself free. And with the notes and samples, he had all he needed from the ice station.

All that was left was to clean up the mess.

Returned to their cell, Matt and Petkov drew stunned gazes from the other prisoners, Ogden and the two biology students in one cell, Washburn alone in the other.

It didn't take long for Jenny and Maki to be herded down as well. They were thrust into the cell with Washburn.

Matt met Jenny at the bars. "Are you okay?"

She nodded. Her face was ashen, but her eyes were twin sparks of hellfire. Washburn took Maki from Jenny and sat with the boy on the bed. He seemed fascinated by the lieutenant's dark skin.

"What happened?" Jenny asked.

"Craig got the samples, the books, and the abort code."

Petkov stirred behind Matt, speaking for the first time. "The *huyok* got nothing," he spat out thickly.

Matt turned to the man. His face was pure ice. "What do you mean?"

"There is no abort code for the Polaris Array."

It took half a second for Matt to assimilate the information. The admiral had tricked Craig, outfoxed him at his own game. And while Matt might have appreciated it in other circumstances, the outcome was bleak for all of them.

"In twenty-nine minutes," Petkov said, "the world ends."

North Star

ᑲᓇᖅᓯᖅ ᐅᕝᔪᓂᐊᖅ

Perched on the elevator platform, Craig typed in the code on the electronic keyboard wired to the titanium sphere. He hurried. They had wasted a precious ten minutes hooking up the connection.

Still, despite the urgency, Craig carefully listened to the digital recording. He typed in each letter as dictated. Then, as directed by the admiral, he retyped the same sequence in *reverse* this time. His fingers moved quickly and surely.

V-G-R-O-B-U-Y-A-T-E-B-Y-A-V-I-D-E-L

Once done, he hit the "enter" button.

Nothing happened.

He hit it again with the same result.

"Is this hooked properly?" he asked Sergeant Conrad, the demolition expert.

"Yes, sir. I'm registering that the device has accepted the code, but it's not responding."

"Maybe I typed it in wrong," he mumbled. If there was any mistake, it was probably when he typed the sequence in backward. He looked at those letters more closely. Then he saw his mistake.

"Goddamn it!" he swore, clenching a fist.

The reversed letters separated into Russian words: *V grobu ya tebya videl*. The translation was a common Russian curse. *I will see you in your grave*.

"Nothing appears wrong," Conrad said, bent half under the device, misinterpreting his outburst.

"Everything's wrong!" Craig snapped back, leaping off the platform. "We've got the wrong code."

He pounded back down the steps. He knew one way to make the bastard talk.

The boy.

8:53 P.M.

Matt listened as Admiral Petkov finished his description of Polaris. The sonic bomb on Level One was only *one* of the devices. There were another five amplifiers out on the ice, ready to spread the destruction in all directions. The pure ambition struck him dumb—to destroy the entire polar ice cap, to bring ruin down upon the globe, and potentially trigger the next great ice age.

He finally found his tongue. "Are you nuts?" It wasn't the most diplomatic response, but he was way beyond diplomacy at this point.

Petkov merely glanced toward him. "After all you've seen, is this truly a world you want to protect?"

"Hell, yes. I'm in it." He reached between the bars and took Jenny's hand. "Everything I love is in it. It's fucked up. No question there, but hell, you don't throw the damn baby out with the bathwater."

"No matter," Petkov said. "Polaris cannot be stopped. The detonation will commence in twenty minutes. Even if we could escape here, the secondary amplifiers are planted fifty kilometers away, all around the island. You'd have to disable and remove at least *two* of the five to break the array's full effect. That could never be done. It is over."

Matt had tired of the admiral's defeatism, but it was beginning to spread to him, too. What could they do?

Jenny slipped her hand from his. "Hold on." She eyed the pair of Delta Force guards. They stood by the prison-wing door, one watching out, one in. They were sharing a smoke, passing it between them, ignoring them.

With no one watching, Jenny crossed the cell and reached out to Maki. The boy was half asleep in Washburn's arms, exhausted and shell-shocked. Jenny parted the child's parka, and with her back to the guards, she removed a black walkie-talkie.

She tucked the radio in her own jacket and crossed back.

"Who do you think you're going to call with that?" Matt asked.

"The *Polar Sentinel* . . . I hope."

Washburn heard her. "Captain Perry's here?" she hissed, stirring from the bed.

Jenny waved her back down. "He's been monitoring everything here, seeking a way to rescue us." She shook her head. "If what this guy says is true, rescuing us is impossible—but maybe they can do something about this Polaris Array."

Matt nodded. It was a long shot, but they had no other option. "Try to raise them."

Washburn helped shield Jenny. The lieutenant carried Maki, singing a lullaby to cover her attempt to communicate.

Matt stepped toward the Russian. "If we are to have any hope for this to work, we need the exact coordinates of the secondary amplifiers."

Petkov shook his head, not so much in refusal as hopelessness.

Matt resisted the urge to throttle the man. He spoke rapidly, sensing the press of time, the falling ax. "Admiral, please. We are all going to die. Everything your father sought to hide will be destroyed. You've won there. His research will be forever lost. But the revenge you seek upon the world . . . because of an atrocity you thought was committed upon your father by your government or mine . . . it's over. We both know what truly happened. The tragedy here was your father's own doing. He cooperated in the research, and only at the end found his humanity."

Petkov's expression was tired, his head sagging a bit.

Matt continued, pointing over to the boy. "Maki saved your father. And your father attempted to save him, preserving the boy in ice. Even at the end, your father died with hope for the future. And right there lies that hope." Matt stabbed a finger toward Maki. "The children of the world. You have no right to take that from them."

Petkov stared over at the boy. Maki lay in Washburn's arms, head cradled against her neck. She sang softly. "He is a beautiful boy," Petkov conceded. His gaze flicked to Matt, then a nod. "I'll give you the coordinates, but the sub will never make it there in time."

"He's right," Jenny said this as she stepped back to the bars, covering the radio with her jacket. "I've raised the *Sentinel*. Perry doesn't think he could even run to one of the amplifiers, let alone two. But he's heading away at full steam. He needs the exact positions."

Matt rolled his eyes. He'd give his right arm for one optimist in the damn group. He waved for the radio. "Pass it here."

Jenny slipped the walkie-talkie through the bars. Matt pressed the transmitter and held the radio toward Petkov's lips. The admiral's hands were still bound behind his back. "Tell them."

Before the man could speak, a loud thud sounded by the door. All eyes turned back to the entrance. One of the guards was on the floor. A dagger hilt protruded from his left eye socket. The other fell back, someone on top of him. An attempt to shout an alarm was cut from the soldier's throat by a wicked long knife. Blood shot across the floor.

As the soldier gurgled, grabbing at his own bloody throat, his attacker shoved up. He was a true gorilla of a man.

Jenny rushed to the front of the cell. "Kowalski!"

The man wiped the blood from his meaty hands on his jacket. "We have to stop meeting like this."

"How . . . I thought . . . the rocket attack?"

He worked rapidly, searching the guard. "I was blown into a snowbank. I burrowed down deep when I saw the situation out there. Then I found another ventilation shaft. Way the fuck out there."

"How?"

Kowalski jabbed a thumb toward the door. "With a little help from my friends."

Another man entered the room, a bandage around his head and a rifle in his hands. He covered the door.

"Tom!" Jenny called out. She clearly knew the pair.

But the fellow was not alone. At the man's knee, a shaggy form loped into the room, tongue lolling, eyes bright.

"My God!" Matt said, dropping to the floor. "Bane." His voice caught in his throat. The dog leaped on the cell door, pushing his nose through the bars, trying to squeeze through, whining, squirming.

"We found him in the ice peaks." Kowalski spoke rapidly as he keyed open the cell doors "Or rather, *he* found us. The Russians left Tom as dead meat in the snow, but he was only knocked out. I dragged him off."

"You survived," Jenny said, still sounding incredulous.

Kowalski straightened with a handful of keys. "No thanks to you guys . . . running off and leaving us for dead. Next time check a goddamn pulse, for God's sake."

As Matt's cell was unlocked, he pushed open the door and worked fast. Time was against them. He removed the dagger from the corpse and sliced the admiral's hands free, then searched the guards for further weapons, taking everything he could find. He passed weapons around as the other cells were opened. "We'd better haul ass."

"This way," Tom said, rushing the line of prisoners out and around to the curving exterior hallway. The group hurried to the same service duct through which Matt and the others had fled hours ago.

As they were ducking away, a commotion sounded from across the level. Yelling. Matt straightened, listening as he waved the biology group into the tunnels. It was Craig. He must have realized the abort code was a ruse. Matt didn't want to be here when Craig found out they had escaped.

Matt dove through the vent, following Bane and Jenny.

Kowalski led them into the service shafts. "We've been rats in the walls ever since the attack started. Tom knows this station like the back of his hand. We were waiting for a chance to break you free."

"Where's this ventilation shaft?" Washburn asked as the group piled into one of the service huts. She still held Maki in her arms. The boy was silent, eyes wide.

"About half a mile," Tom said. "But we're safer down here."

Matt turned to the admiral. "What's the blast range of the Polaris bomb?"

Kowalski swung toward them, eyes wide. "Bomb? What bomb?"

Petkov ignored the man. "The danger is not so much the *blast* as the *shock wave*. It'll shatter the entire island and the ice for miles around. There's no escape."

"What *fucking* bomb?" Kowalski yelled.

Jenny told him.

He shook his head as if trying to deny the truth. "Fucking fantastic, that's the last time I rescue you guys."

"How much time do we have left?" Tom asked.

Matt checked his watch. "Fifteen minutes. Not nearly enough time to get clear."

"Then what are we going to do?"

Matt removed one of the confiscated weapons. One of the black pineapples. "I may have an idea."

"Buddy, that grenade's not strong enough to blast a hole to the surface," Kowalski said.

"We're not going up."

"Then where?"

Matt answered, then led them off in a mad dash as time was running out.

Kowalski pounded after him. "No *fucking* way."

9:10 P.M.

Craig stared at the empty row of cells, the pair of dead guards. Everything was unraveling. He spun on the pair of soldiers at his side. "Find them!"

Another soldier rushed through the door. "Sir, it looks like they fled into the service shafts."

Craig clenched a fist. "Of course they did," he mumbled. But what were they trying to do? Where could they go? His mind spun. "Send two men in there. The Russian admiral must not—"

A muffled blast cut him off. The floor under his feet rattled. The guards stiffened.

Craig stared down between his toes. "Shit!"

9:11 P.M.

A floor below, Matt tested the docking bay's hatch. The others were lined up along the wall on Level Five. A moment ago, he had opened the hatch and tossed in a pair of the incendiary grenades, one collected from each of the two dead guards.

Matt touched the metal door with his bare fingers. It had

gone from ice cold to burning hot. The blast of the V-class incendiaries continued to impress him. But were they strong enough to do the job here?

There was only one way to find out.

As the blast echoed away, Matt swung open the door. It led to the docking lake for the Russian transport sub, an old I series. A moment ago, the room had been half filled with ice, completely encasing the docked conning tower. Matt remembered Vladimir's final confession. Petkov's father had scuttled the sub, blowing all ballast, driving the sub up and jamming it in place. Over the years, the room had flooded and frozen.

Matt stared into the room. The pair of grenades had transformed the frozen tomb into a fiery hell. Water bubbled on the surface. Pools of flame dotted the new lake formed around the sub. The smell of phosphor and steam rolled out.

As Matt studied the chamber, his eyes and face burned. It was still too hot to enter.

"Next time," Kowalski groused, shielding his face, "let's try just *one* grenade.

Despite the residual heat, at least the mound of ice covering the conning tower had melted away. The sub's hatch was uncovered.

Now if only they could get to it.

Matt checked his watch. *Thirteen minutes*. With his face sweating, he turned to the others. They didn't have time to spare. "Everyone inside!"

Washburn splashed into the room first, followed by the biology group. The water was knee-deep. Tom went with them. "Get that hatch open!" Matt called to the Navy pair.

Kowalski and Matt covered the door, keeping their weapons fixed toward the stairs. Despite the thick insulation of the docking bay, everyone had to have heard the grenade explosion.

Matt motioned Jenny. "Get everybody into the sub!"

Jenny nodded, starting across with Bane at her side and Maki in her arms. Beside her, Petkov still spoke into the walkie-talkie, passing the coordinates to the *Polar Sentinel*.

Jenny called back to him: "Matt!" He heard the distress in her voice and turned. "The water's getting deeper! It's filling up!"

She was right. The level had risen to her thighs. Suddenly a geyser of water shot up from the half-frozen lake, exploding up with a soft *whoosh*.

"Damn it," Matt swore, understanding what was happening. The Russian incendiaries had been *too* good. They had melted spots down to the open ocean, weakened others. The outside water pressure, held back by thick ice, was breaking through. Another geyser erupted. Water flooded into the room.

Jenny and the admiral stood halfway across the burning lake. The level had already climbed waist-high.

"Hurry," she called back to him.

Gunfire erupted at Matt's side. Kowalski had his rifle raised to his cheek, the barrel smoking. "They're coming after us!" he hissed.

No surprise there.

Matt retreated a step with Kowalski.

Behind them, Washburn and Tom had gotten the sub's hatch open. The biology group was already clambering down inside. The sub was dead, defunct. Their only hope of survival was to hole up in the old vessel, trusting its thick hide to insulate them as the ice shattered from the device's shock wave. The chance of survival was slim, but Matt still had a stubborn streak.

Until he was dead, he'd keep fighting.

A metallic pinging drew his full attention back to the outer corridor. A grenade bounced down the stairwell.

"Crap!" Kowalski yelled. He reached out, grabbed the hatch handle, and yanked the door shut. "Jump!"

Matt leaped to one side, Kowalski to the other.

The grenade blew the door off its hinges. The bay's hatch flew up, hit the sea cave's ice ceiling, and rebounded into the water with a crash.

Matt scrambled away from the open door.

Kowalski waved an arm, firing with the other. "Everybody! Inside!"

Matt trudged across the rapidly flooding chamber, half dog-paddling, half kicking. Kowalski retreated with him.

Jenny and the admiral had almost reached the sub. Bane was already being hauled up and in by Tom and Washburn.

Then a geyser blew, throwing Jenny and Petkov apart.

Jenny landed in the water, cradling the boy. She came up sputtering. Maki wailed.

The admiral slogged toward her.

Then a large white hummock surfaced between them. At first Matt thought it was a chunk of ice. Then it thrashed and vanished under the dark water. Everyone knew what it was, freezing in place in terror.

A grendel.

The predator must have slipped through the opening water channels, coming to search the new territory.

Jenny clutched Maki higher in her arms.

Matt stared around. There was no way of knowing where the beast was. They feared moving, attracting it. But it was also death to stay where they were.

Matt glanced to his watch. *Twelve minutes*.

He stared back out. Across the deepening lake, the water remained dark and still. The grendel could be anywhere, lurking in wait.

Fearing to attract it, they dared not move.

9:12 P.M.
USS *POLAR SENTINEL*

Perry studied the computer navigation and mapping. "Are you certain those are the coordinates of the closest amplifier?" he asked the ensign.

"Yes, sir."

Damn. He recalculated in his head what the computers

confirmed. He checked his watch, a Rolex Submariner, wishing for once that it weren't so accurate. *Twelve minutes* . . .

They'd never make it. Even at their top-rated speed of fifty-two knots, they'd barely reach *one* of the Polaris amplifiers, not the necessary two. At their current speed, the entire sub vibrated as the nuclear engines generated steam at ten percent above design pressure. There was no need to run silent now. It was a brutal race to the finish.

"We need more power," he said.

"Engineering says—"

"I know what the engineers said," he snapped, tense. He would risk the entire boat if they pushed her any harder. There were limits that carbon plate and titanium could withstand. And he didn't have the time to surface and get instructions from Admiral Reynolds. The decision was his.

"Chief, tell engineering we need to press the engines another ten percent."

"Aye, sir." His orders were relayed.

After a few more moments, the shuddering in the boat set clipboards and pens to rattling. It felt as if they were riding over train tracks.

Everyone sat tensely at their stations.

Perry climbed the periscope stand and paced its length. Earlier he had consulted with Amanda. As an expert in ice dynamics, she had confirmed at least the *theory* behind the Polaris Array. Such a global threat was possible.

The sub's speed was called out as it climbed. "Sixty knots, sir."

He glanced to the ensign at the map table. The young officer shook his head. "Still ten miles out from the first set of coordinates."

He had to push the boat harder.

"Get me engineering," he ordered.

Matt stood in water up to his armpits. Pools of flaming oil lit the room but failed to reveal the grendel hidden in the dark waters around them. Occasional ripples marked its passage as it stalked among them.

They were trapped as time pressed down on them.

Ten minutes.

They were doomed if they fled, doomed if they stayed.

A voice suddenly called from beyond the smoky, blasted doorway. "Don't move!"

"Great," Kowalski growled. "Just great."

"We have you covered!" Craig yelled. "Any aggression and we'll start shooting."

Emphasizing this threat, razor-sharp lines of laser sights crisscrossed the hazy room and settled on their chests. "Don't move," Craig repeated.

No one dared disobey him—but it wasn't the guns that held them all frozen in place.

The waters continued to remain dark and quiet.

"Like I'm going to move," Kowalski grumbled.

Beyond the doorway, figures shifted within the smoke.

Craig called out to them. "I want the admiral over here now!"

Ten feet from Matt, the waters welled with movement.

Matt met Jenny's eyes, urging her not to move. It was death to do so.

He checked his watch. *Nine minutes . . .*

The choices were not great: guns, grendels, or nuclear bombs.

Take your pick.

Matt glanced to Jenny one more time. There was only one chance for the others. *I'm sorry,* he wanted to say—then turned and stepped toward the doorway.

9:16 P.M.

Viktor knew what the American was attempting. *A sacrifice.* He intended to draw the grendel to him, allowing the others to break free and make for the sub. His eyes lingered on the boy in the woman's arms.

His father had adopted the boy as his son, and at the end, sacrificed so much to keep him safe. Anger flared in him, some of it selfish, a bit of jealousy at the affection given the boy and denied him. But mostly, he felt a connection to his father through the small child. One forms a family where one can. His father had lost so much up here, but at the end, not his humanity.

Viktor turned away. He had brought this ruin upon them all.

Like his father before him, Viktor knew what he had to do.

He yelled over to the blasted doorway. "I'm coming out!" he bellowed, stopping the American in mid-stride.

"What are you—" the other began.

"Here," Viktor said, and tossed the walkie-talkie toward Pike.

He caught it easily.

"Take care of the boy," Viktor called, and began splashing toward the exit, pushing through the water. "I'm coming out!" he yelled again, placing his now empty hands atop his head. "Don't shoot."

"Admiral," Pike warned.

His gaze flicked to the man. "One minute," he said under his breath, tapping a finger atop his wrist monitor. "You have one minute."

9:17 P.M.

One minute? Matt frowned and glanced to his own wrist. According to his watch, they still had a full *eight* minutes before the bomb went—

Then it dawned on him.

He spotted the wake that appeared in the water. It began in a lazy S, then focused and tracked in on the wading admiral.

Matt's gaze fell back to Petkov's wrist monitor. Once his heart stopped beating, the bomb's timer would drop immediately to one minute.

The wake in the water sped toward Petkov's splashing form.

He was taking the bullet for Matt—but it would shorten the time before the bomb exploded.

Matt swung to face Jenny. Her eyes were confused, terrified.

"Be ready to run," he warned Jenny and Kowalski.

Craig appeared at the doorway, flanked by two guards. They were on higher ground. The flooding water had barely reached their knees. Rifles followed the admiral. All attention was on Petkov.

He was only four yards from Craig when the grendel struck. It surged out of the water, jaws wide, striking him from behind.

The admiral's head snapped back from the impact at the same time as his body was rammed forward. Propelled by the grendel, he flew high, lifted out of the water. Then the monster rolled, its prey caught in its jaws. Petkov was slammed back into the water.

Craig and his men fell back in horror.

"Run!" Matt yelled.

Jenny was closest, but she was also in the deepest water, up to her neck. She swam with Maki in her arms, kicking with her legs. Once she was within reach of the conning tower, Tom lunged out, snatched the boy from her and pulled him to safety.

Her arms free, Jenny grabbed the outside rungs of the ladder and clambered upward.

Matt retreated with Kowalski.

By the door, the waters thrashed as the grendel whipped its prey, bashing it through the water. A stain of blood pooled around the creature's white bulk. An arm flailed weakly.

Craig and his guards sheltered back from the savage attack, forgetting about the others for the moment.

Kowalski reached the sub first. Matt waved him up.

The seaman mounted the ladder, scrambling. He glanced back, then stumbled a step. One arm shot out. "Behind you!"

Matt twisted in the water. Another white shape surfaced. Then another. The blood was drawing more of the pod.

Matt weighed caution versus speed. He opted instead for panic. He kicked and paddled, fighting his way toward the sub.

Kowalski reached the top of the tower. He began to fire into the lake, offering some defense.

Matt finally reached the sub and grabbed the lower rung of the ladder. Pulling himself up, he struggled to get his legs under him.

His toes slipped, numb from the cold and slippery from the water.

Kowalski leaned down, grabbed him, half hauling him up the ladder.

Beneath Matt, something struck the tower, clanging into it. Jarred, Matt lost his footing and fell free of the wet ladder. But Kowalski still had a fist wrapped in the hood of Matt's sweatshirt, holding him from a plunge into the waters below.

Matt sought to plant his feet on the rungs. Between his toes, a large white shape surged out of the water.

A grendel, jaws wide, lunged up at him.

With a groan of effort, Kowalski heaved Matt higher. Jaws snapped, catching Matt's boot heel. The weight of the falling beast yanked the boot clean off. The beast disappeared with its prize.

Matt snatched the ladder and climbed the rest of the way up. "Damn bastard!"

Kowalski was already rolling into the hatch. "What?"

Matt glanced back to the waters below. He had recognized the grendel who had just attacked him. He had noted the pocked and macerated bullet holes. It was the same creature that had hunted Amanda and him in the Crawl Space, the one that had stolen his pants.

"Now the greedy bastard's got my goddamn boot, too!"

Kowalski shook his head and dropped down the hatch.

Following him, Matt twisted to climb down the ladder when bullets ricocheted off the plate near his head. He ducked lower, crab-crawling down into the hatch.

He looked back to the docking-bay doorway, spotting Craig. A rifle was leveled at Matt. Between them swam a small pod of grendels.

There was no trace of the admiral's body.

How much time until—

The answer came a moment later. The grendels suddenly went crazy. The waters churned as the monsters thrashed, rolling, leaping, snapping at the air.

Matt understood what had upset the beasts, driving them to a frenzy. He felt it, too. From his head to his toes. A vibration through the station, like a tuning fork struck by a sledgehammer.

A sonic pulse.

Matt knew what it meant.

Polaris had activated.

Just as the admiral had described, the device would generate a sonic pulse. And according to Petkov, the pulse would last sixty seconds, then the nuclear trigger would blow, destroying the island and concussing out in a deadly shock wave.

Across the churning lake, Craig had backed a step away, his rifle still in his hands, his head cocked, listening.

Matt pushed up higher. "One minute!" he called over to Craig, tapping his empty wrist, repeating Petkov's earlier warning.

Craig's gun dropped as the realization struck him.

The admiral was dead . . . the sonic pulse . . .

Time had just run out for all of them.

Satisfied by Craig's look of horror, Matt dropped through the hatch, clanging it shut behind him. He dogged it tight and climbed down to the others.

Kowalski sealed the inner hatch, locking it tight. Tom and Washburn held flashlights. No one spoke. Bane sensed the tension, whining at the back of his throat.

There was no stopping Polaris now.

9:17 P.M.
USS *POLAR SENTINEL*

"We have less than a minute?" Perry asked, incredulous.

Scratchy static came over the phone as he listened. *"Yes,"* the man confirmed. *". . . can't say . . . only seconds left!"*

Perry glanced over to Amanda. She had read his lips, saw his expression. She mirrored his reaction. The race was over before it began. They were defeated.

". . . nuclear trigger . . ." the man continued. *"Get clear . . ."*

Before Perry could answer, Amanda's fingers dug into his arm. Her voice slurred at her sudden anxiety. "Get us deep! Now!"

"What?" he asked.

But she was already running. "As deep as the boat will go!" she yelled back at him.

Perry responded, trusting the woman's urgency. "Emergency dive!" he yelled to the crew. "Flood negative! Now!"

Klaxons rang throughout the sub.

9:17 P.M.
ICE STATION GRENDEL

Craig pounded down the hall of Level Four. He knew his
destination, but did he have time? There was no telling. He
patted his parka's pocket, hearing a satisfying clink.

He ran past one of the Delta Force team members. The
sergeant major called to him as he fled past. "Sir . . . ?"

He didn't slow, running headlong around the curving hall.
His goal came in sight. He needed a secure place to hide,
somewhere to ride out the blast wave, someplace waterproof. He knew only one sure place.

The door to the solitary tank was still open, empty of its
recent occupant, the Inuit boy. Craig dove inside. He twisted
around and yanked the glass door closed. Still powered on
the generators, it automatically locked down and was sealed,
closing him in.

But was it secure enough? He touched the glass. It vibrated from the sonic pulse of Polaris.

Craig sank to the bottom of the cylinder, bracing himself.
How much time was left?

9:17 P.M.
RUSSIAN I-SERIES SUB

Matt lay with Jenny. In each other's arms, the pair was nestled between two mattresses, crammed and sandwiched in
one of the bunks. The others were similarly padded, limited
two to a bunk. Washburn watched over Maki. Even Bane
had been penned in a padded cell of mattresses.

After boarding the sub, there had been no time for niceties
or plans. They had all fled to the sub's berths and found
ways to secure themselves from the coming explosion.

And now the waiting.

Matt buried himself into Jenny. The admiral must have

survived longer than he'd guessed. Or perhaps the lag time on the device was a bit longer than one minute.

He clutched Jenny, and she him. Hands sought each other, moving from memory, reflexively. His mouth found hers. Soft lips parted under him. They murmured to each other, no words, merely a way to share their breath, reaching out to each other in all ways, a promise unspoken but heartfelt.

He wanted more time with her.

But time had run out.

9:17 ᴘ ᴍ,
OUT ON THE ICE . . .

Under the twilight sky, Command Sergeant Major Edwin Wilson, currently designated Delta One, stood on the ice. The Sikorsky Seahawk rested five paces behind him. Its rotors slowly spun, engines kept hot, ready for immediate action. As ordered, he had retreated thirty miles from the submerged ice island. With the discovery of the bomb at the station, it was up to him to protect the stolen journals. He was only to return if an all clear was dispatched by the mission's operational controller.

Until then, he waited. No further updates had been transmitted.

Under his feet, the ice had begun to vibrate. At first he thought it was his imagination, but now he was not so certain. The trembling persisted.

What was happening?

He faced northeast, staring through high-powered binoculars, equipped with night vision. The terrain was so flat and featureless that he was able to make out the tall line of pressure ridges near the horizon.

Nothing. No answers there.

He checked his watch. According to the timetable of the original report, there were only a few more minutes to spare.

Frowning, he lifted the binoculars again.

Just as he raised them to his face, the world ignited to the north. The flash of green through the scopes whited out the view, blinding him. Stumbling back, he let the scopes drop around his neck.

He blinked away the glare and stared to the north. Something was wrong with the horizon. It was no longer a smooth arc. It now bowed up, rising like a wave.

He snatched the binoculars and stared again. A deep green glow marked the center of the cresting wave, like a signal buoy riding a wave.

Then it was gone.

A roar like the end of the world rumbled over the ice.

He continued to stare. The bomb had clearly gone off, but what was happening? He couldn't understand what he was seeing through the scopes.

Then it hit him. He suddenly understood why the glow at the center of the explosion had vanished. It was blocked from his view—by a wall of ice rolling toward him, as wide as the horizon.

As he stared, the cresting wave spread out from ground zero, like a boulder dropped into a still lake.

A tidal wave of ice.

His heart leaped to his throat as he ran for the idling helicopter. "Go!" he screamed as the world continued to rumble ominously. Instead of the explosion fading and echoing away, it was growing louder.

He fled to the Seahawk's door.

One of his men pushed the door open. "What's happening?"

Wilson dove in. "Get this bird in the air! Now!"

The pilot heard him. The rotors immediately began to kick up, spinning faster, rotating toward lift off.

Wilson dove to the copilot's seat.

The blast wave of ice raced toward them.

He stared upward, praying. Overhead, the rotors spun to a

blur. The Seahawk lifted from its skids, bobbling a bit as the rotors dug at the frigid air, trying to find purchase.

"C'mon!" Wilson urged.

He stared as the horizon closed in on them.

Then the bird took to the air, shooting straight up.

Wilson judged the distance of the surging ice-tsunami. *Was its speed slowing? Fading?*

It seemed to be.

It was!

They were going to make it.

Then a half mile away, something blew under the ice. The entire cap slammed up at them, striking the skids of the helicopter. It tilted savagely.

Wilson screamed.

The amplified wave struck the helicopter, swatting it out of the sky.

9:18 P.M.
USS *POLAR SENTINEL*

Amanda stared at the screen of the DeepEye. A moment ago, the monitor's resolution had fogged from a deep sonar pulse, wiping out detail. Then worse—the screen went suddenly *blue*.

Only one effect registered that hue on a sonar device.

A nuclear explosion.

John Aratuk stood beside her. The elderly Inuit maintained his vigil in the Cyclops room. He stared up through the dome of Lexan glass. The seas lay dark around them. They were nearly at crush depth. Here the world was eternally sunless.

John pointed.

A star bloomed in the darkness. Off to the south, high above.

Ground zero.

The old man turned to Amanda. He didn't speak. He didn't have to. His grief was plain in every line of his face. He had aged decades in a single moment.

Amanda spoke. "I'm so sorry."

He closed his eyes and turned away, inconsolable.

Amanda turned back to the DeepEye. The man's daughter, all the others, they had sacrificed everything in an attempt to save the world.

But had they wasted their lives?

The Polaris trigger had blown. That was plain on the DeepEye monitor. But what of Amanda's attempt to block the two amplifiers?

She stared at the blued-out screen. Her idea had been a simple one, employed rapidly. She had ordered the *Polar Sentinel* to dive deep. She needed distance from the surface.

As the submarine had plummeted into the Arctic depths, she had rapidly punched in the coordinates and aligned the DeepEye toward the locations of the two nearest amplifiers in the array. Once it was deep enough, she had pointed the DeepEye and widened the breadth of the sonar cone to encompass both devices, needing the distance and depth to accomplish this. Then she had turned the full strength of the DeepEye upon the pair of amplifiers and prayed.

For Polaris to work, the array had to propagate a perfect harmonic wave, just the right frequency to generate an ice-shattering effect. But if the DeepEye was transmitting across the wave front, it could alter the harmonics just enough to disrupt and perhaps jangle the wave front from igniting the two amplifiers within the DeepEye's cone.

Amanda stared over at the monitor, waiting for it to clear. Had her plan worked?

Burrowed between two mattresses, Jenny clung to Matt. The world cartwheeled around them both, not smoothly, but jarringly, like a paint shaker. Even with the cushioning, she felt battered and bruised. Her head rang from the concussion of the explosion.

But she was still alive.

They both were.

Matt hugged her tight, his legs and arms wrapped around her. "We're heading down," he yelled in her ears.

She also felt the increasing pressure.

After a long minute, the world slowed its spin, settling out into a crooked angle.

"I think we've stabilized." Matt slid an arm from her and peeled away one edge of the mattress to peek out.

Jenny joined him.

In a berth across from them, Kowalski had already poked his head out. He waved a field flashlight up and down the crew quarters. The floor was tilted down and canted to the side, still rolling slightly. "Is everyone okay?" he called out.

Like butterflies leaving cocoons, the rest of the party emerged. Muffled barking confirmed Banc's status.

Magdalene cried from farther back. "Zane . . . he fell out . . . !"

Zane answered faintly from the other direction, "No, I'm okay. Broke my wrist."

Everyone slowly crawled free, checking their own limbs. Washburn carried Maki. She sang softly to the child, soothing him.

Tom worked his way up the narrow passage between the stacked bunks. His eyes were on the walls and ceilings. Jenny knew why. She heard the creak of seams, the pop of strained joints. "We're deep," he muttered. "The explosion must have thrust us straight down."

"But at least we *survived* the explosion," Ogden said.

"It was the ice around the sub," Tom said dully. "It shielded us. The hollow sea cave was a structural weak point of the station. It simply shattered away, carrying us with it."

"Are we going to sink to the bottom?" Magdalene asked.

"We've positive buoyancy," Tom answered. "We should eventually surface like a cork. But . . ."

"But what?" Zane asked, cradling his arm.

All of the Navy crew stared at the walls as they continued to groan and scrape. Kowalski answered, "Pray we don't reach crush depth first."

9:20 P.M.
UNDER THE ICE . . .

With a start, Craig woke in darkness, upside down. He tasted blood on his tongue, his head ached, and his shoulder flared with a white-hot fire. *Broken clavicle*. But none of this stimulation woke him.

It was the spray of cold water in his face.

In the darkness, it took him a moment to orient himself. As he righted himself, his hands reached out to glass walls. He felt the source of the jetting spray. A crack in the tank's glass door. The water was ice-cold.

His eyes strained for any sign of where he was. But the world remained as dark as oil. Water rose under him, filling the tank. He could hear the bubble of escaping air. The tank was no longer intact. He had survived the shockwave of the bomb, but he was deep underwater.

And still falling.

The spray grew fiercer as the depth grew deeper.

Ice water soaked through him, thigh-high now. His teeth chattered, half from cold, half from shock, but mostly from growing panic.

He secretly feared being buried alive. He had heard tales of agents being eliminated in such a manner.

This was worse.

The cold rose through him faster than the water. Which would kill him first, he wondered, hypothermia or drowning?

After a full minute, the answer came.

The loud bubbling stopped, and the spray of water slowed to a trickle, then stopped. He had reached some equilibrium point. The pocket of air was holding the water back . . . at least for now.

But he was far from safe. The small pocket would quickly stale, and even before that, the cold would kill him.

Or maybe not.

Fingers scrambled into the pocket of his parka. The clink of glass sounded. His fingertips touched broken glass, cutting. Still, he searched and found what he sought. He pulled out one of the glass syringes, unbroken. He had taken two samples from the ice lab, insurance at the time.

Now it was survival.

He thumbed off the needle cap.

There was no way he could find a vein in the dark.

With both hands, he stabbed the long point into the flesh of his belly. The pain was exquisite. He shoved the plunger, pushing the elixir into his peritoneal cavity. From there, it should slowly absorb into his bloodstream.

Once emptied, he pulled the syringe free and dropped it into the icy pool at his waist. His teeth chattered uncontrollably, his limbs soon followed.

A fear rose through his panic.

Would the cryogenic elixir absorb fast enough?

Only time would tell.

9:21 P.M.
RUSSIAN I-SERIES SUB

Holding his breath, Matt stood with the others. The old sub groaned and popped. Kowalski swung his flashlight up and down the passage. Distantly a soft hiss of water whispered in the boat. A leak. The darkness pressed down upon them.

Jenny held his hand, fingers tight, palms damp.

Then Matt felt the shift under his legs, a slight rolling of his stomach. He turned to Kowalski and Tom, trusting the Navy men's senses more than his own.

Tom confirmed his hope. "We're rising."

Jenny's fingers squeezed his. They were heading back up. Murmurs of relief echoed among the others.

But Kowalski's face remained tight. Tom did not look any more relieved.

"What's wrong?" Matt asked.

"There's no way to alter our buoyancy," Tom answered.

Kowalski nodded. "It's an uncontrolled ascent. We're going to keep climbing faster and faster."

Matt understood, remembering Tom's earlier analogy. The sub was like a cork shoved deep into the water. It was now back on its way up, gaining speed, propelled by its own buoyancy. Matt's gaze drifted up, picturing what would happen.

Once they reached the surface, the speed of their ascent would be deadly. They'd strike the underside of the polar ice cap like a train wreck.

"Back into the mattresses?" Matt asked.

"That won't do much good," Kowalski said. "It'll be pancake city once we hit the surface."

Still they had no other recourse. The party fled back to the padding and security of the mattresses. Matt pushed in next to Jenny. He sensed their rate of ascent accelerating. He felt it in his ears, a popping sensation. The incline of the sub grew steeper as it rose.

Jenny sought him with her hands. He curled into her, not knowing if this would be his last chance to do so. His hands reached to her cheeks. They were damp.

"Jen . . ."

She shook in his arms.

"I love you," he whispered. "I always have. I never stopped."

Her body quaked with silent sobs, but still she reached him with her lips, seeking his mouth. She kissed him deeply, hugely. She didn't have to speak. She answered with her entire body and soul.

They clung to each other, shutting out the world, the terror. Here, in this moment, there was only forgiveness and love and simple need. One for another. How could they have forgotten something so simple?

The moment stretched to a crystalline eternity.

Then the sub hit the surface.

9:23 P.M.

ABOVE THE ICE . . .

The moon was full, a bright coin breaking through the storm clouds. Its light cast the Arctic stillness into silver, shining off the ice. The only blemish was a half-mile-wide dark hole, still smoldering and smoking. The rest of the world remained a perfect plain of sterling silver.

But it was not to last. Perfection never did.

A mile from the hole, something smashed through from below, a black whale breaching from the water. It thrust itself high into the air, leaving the seas fully behind. It hung in the air until gravity claimed it again.

The length of iron and steel crashed, belly first, to the sea, vanishing under the ice for a moment, then rolling back up, sloshing and rocking in the slush.

9:24 P.M.
RUSSIAN I-SERIES SUB

Matt lay in a tangle with Jenny. In the darkness, pressed between mattresses, it was hard to say whose limbs were whose.

A moment ago, they had struck the surface. They must have. Locked in each other's arms, they had been thrown upward, held weightless for a long breath as if they were flying. Then they were inexplicably falling again.

The crash jarred them back to their berth, landing them in a pile.

Cries of surprise reached them from the others.

The sub rolled and canted.

Matt extracted himself from Jenny and helped them both from their nest. His feet were unsteady—or was it the rocking sub? Matt kept one hand clutched to the frame of his berth. "What just happened?" he asked.

Kowalski scratched his head with his flashlight. "We should be dead. Crushed." He sounded oddly disappointed, his firm faith in the physics of buoyancy and ice betrayed.

"Well, I'm not complaining," Matt said, gaining his balance as the sub settled. "Let's see where we are."

Keeping a firm grip on Jenny's hand, he led the party back to the center of the boat. The inner hatch was unlocked. It dropped open, drenching Kowalski with water.

"Crap," he swore. "Why am I the one always getting soaked?"

Matt climbed the ladder to the top of the boat's sail, cracking the upper hatch of the conning tower. He threw it open with a clang. Cold air swept over him. He had never felt anything more wonderful.

He climbed out to the flying bridge to make room for the others below. As he stood, he gaped at the sight beyond the submarine.

The storm had broken. Moonlight turned the world silver.

But it wasn't *solid* silver.

The submarine lolled in a sea of slush. Ripples spread out from the rocking boat. A hundred yards away, the gentle waves lapped against a shore of solid ice. It marked the boundary between two worlds—one of regular ice and one of decomposed slush.

Matt stared out. A huge black hole separated these two worlds.

Jenny joined him, slipping her hand back into his. "What happened?"

"The Polaris Array did what it was supposed to do," he said, waving a hand over the vast sea of slush and broken ice. "But it was only half a success. It looks like the other half of the array didn't blow."

"Was it the *Polar Sentinel*?"

Matt shrugged. "Who else could it be?"

Kowalski echoed Jenny's words. "The *Polar Sentinel*."

Matt glanced to him. He was pointing out into the slushy sea. A black bulk shoved upward, shedding ice as it rose. The submarine's large eye, aglow from the lights inside, stared back at them, as if surprised to see them alive.

Matt pulled Jenny under his arm, recognizing how well she fit against him, two becoming one once again.

He had to admit, he was surprised, too.

EPILOGUE

It was too damn early.

Matt burrowed under the worn quilt comforter, refusing to forsake the warmth beneath the thick down. Though it was already spring, mornings in the Alaskan high country were as cold as any Midwestern winter. He sought the warmest spot in the bed, next to his wife's naked body.

He spread his length next to Jenny, spooning against her, skin to skin, nuzzling her neck, legs entwining.

"We already had your honeymoon last night," she murmured into her pillow.

He grumbled but was unable to squash his smile. He had not stopped grinning like a love-addled teenager since he had spoken his vows beside the river yesterday afternoon. It had been a small ceremony. A few friends and family.

Amanda and Greg had flown in, newly married themselves. Captain Perry had been decorated for his heroics up north. Though half the polar ice cap had been destroyed by the Polaris Array, the other half had been preserved through his efforts and Amanda's timely use of the Deep-Eye sonar.

As for the cap's actual damage, it was significant but not irreparable. Each year, over the course of a summer, the cap normally melted in half anyway, yet recovered in winter, proving the earth's remarkable resilience. The same proved true again. Over the past winter, the cap had re-formed, spreading intact over the northern seas once again.

However, the healing of the two governments—Russia and the United States—was neither as easy, nor as quick. Throughout the halls of power in Washington and Moscow, repercussions and punishments still rattled. Daily hearings, judicial inquiries, and military court-martials continued. But even this turmoil would eventually subside, freeze over.

Matt only hoped that something better came of it all.

As to what happened in the north, there was no sign. The schematics for the Polaris Array were never found, destroyed by Admiral Petkov before he ever left port. And the grendels were gone, too, wiped out in the nuclear blast.

In the end, the war had no lasting result.

Well, *almost* no result . . .

Laughter again echoed out from the main room of the family cabin. It was the pure delight that only a child could call forth. It was this merriment that had awakened Matt from his short sleep.

Jenny stirred this time. "It sounds like Maki's up."

The clank of pots and pans sounded from the neighboring room, too. Matt pulled the cover back, ready to shout for another couple hours of sleep. Then the aromas reached him. He inhaled deeply, sighing.

"Coffee . . . that's not playing fair."

Jenny rolled against him, sitting. "I guess we should be getting up."

Matt shifted to one elbow. He stared at his new wife, sunlight streaming through the window, bathing her. He was the luckiest man in the whole damn world.

Childish giggles again drifted to them.

Jenny smiled at the sound. There was not even a hint of old sorrow. Like her, he knew how good it was to hear laughter again in the cabin, if even for only a short time.

Together, they slipped into pajamas and robes, then crossed to the bedroom door. Matt opened the way for her, then followed her out.

Maki was in the middle of the room, playing with Bane. The large wolf mix lay sprawled on his back, his belly exposed to be petted. The boy would scratch it, but when he reached the sweet spot, Bane's back leg would twitch and scratch reflexively. This triggered another peal of laughter.

Matt smiled at the simple pleasure. A boy and a dog.

"You're up!" a voice spoke from the kitchen. It was Belinda Haydon.

"Where's your husband?" he asked.

"Bennie and Jen's dad headed out with their poles an hour ago."

Maki climbed to his feet. He crossed to the kitchen. "Mama," he said in Inuit. "Can I have a Pop-Tart?" This last was in English. He was learning the language quickly.

"After you have your cereal, honey," Belinda answered firmly.

Maki stuck out his lower lip and headed back to Bane.

Matt followed him with his eyes. After the ordeal a year ago, he and Jenny had considered adopting the boy, but they had too much to heal between themselves first. It was not a time for them to raise such a traumatized child.

Instead, the perfect family had been found for the boy: Bennie and Belinda. Jenny had told Matt about the couple's miscarriage and infertility. The pair had enough love for ten children. If any two people could help the boy recover and grow, this was the couple.

Matt found himself staring at Jenny. And they could always have more children themselves. It was something they had already tentatively discussed, whispered in the night, sharing their hopes under the covers.

There was still time for all of them.

"Uncle Matt," Maki called over to him, "Bane wants a Pop-Tart, too."

Matt laughed.

Jenny smiled at him, at both of them.

He met her bright eyes.

He truly was the luckiest man in the world.

6:55 A.M

UNDER THE ICE . . .

The tank rested on the ocean floor, full of water, crushed and cracked. The lone occupant was a frozen lump of bone and hardened tissue. There was no light. No sound.

None could hear the screaming inside the man's head.

The cryoprotectant had worked, preserving and protecting him. But there was a side effect he had not anticipated. A horrible, monstrous side effect. The figure now understood the years the Russian scientists had spent researching sedatives and soporifics. *Sleep drugs.* The research was not ancillary, but critical to the suspended animation.

For the state created by the elixir was *not* sleep.

Consciousness remained—frozen, too, but intact.

Sleep was denied him.

He screamed and screamed, but even he heard nothing.

Deaf, dumb, blind.

Yet his body remained, preserved for all time. Deep in the black depths of the Arctic Ocean, one thought persisted as madness ate at what was left of him.

How long? How long is eternity?

AUTHOR'S NOTE

Over the past years, I have been asked many times about where the line lies between truth and fiction in my stories. So here at the end of *Ice Hunt*, I thought it might be interesting to share some of those details.

Let's start at the beginning. The novel opens with a fictitious newspaper article detailing the disappearance of an Inuit village on Lake Anjikuni. The details of the tribe's sudden and mysterious disappearance are based on fact. The fate of the poor people is, of course, of my own imagining. The same could be said for the story and fate of the unfortunate sailors aboard the *Jeannette* back in 1881. The tragedy was real; the fate of the crew of the lone missing lifeboat is pure fiction.

As to the threat posed by the Polaris Array, this scenario is based on scientific theory, but the practical application of the star-shaped harmonic device was my own invention. The stated effect of such an annihilation of the northern polar cap—the creation of a new ice age—is also based on projections by leading Arctic researchers.

Now, as to the derivation of the "grendels," the species is a blend of fact and fiction, too. The species *Ambulocetus natans,* known as the walking whale, has been documented in the fossil record. Additionally, the biological oddity of the

Arctic wood frog is factual. These strange frogs do indeed freeze solid for months at a time, then revive upon thawing. Ken Storey of Carleton University has been researching the mechanism for this miraculous adaptation. The role of simple sugar in this "suspended animation" process is also factual, as is the singular and surprising fact about its genetic mechanism: that all vertebrate species carry these genes. I then mixed these facts and species to create the grendels.

Lastly, a comment on the one detail I thought would be the hardest for folks to believe: Could the United States, along with Russia, be involved with something as heinous as secret human experimentation? In the novel, Admiral Petkov states his case based on historical facts, but even he barely scratches the surface of the truth. So, as a cautionary note, let me end this book by documenting a partial list of historical abuses collated and copyrighted by the Health News Network (www.healthnewsnet.com):

1932 The Tuskegee Syphilis Study begins. Two hundred black men diagnosed with syphilis are never told of their illness, are denied treatment, and instead are used as human guinea pigs. They all subsequently die from syphilis.

1935 The Pellagra Incident. After millions of individuals die from pellagra over a span of two decades, the U.S. Public Health Service finally acts to stem the disease. The director of the agency admits it had known for at least twenty years that pellagra is caused by a niacin deficiency but failed to act since most of the deaths occurred within poverty-stricken black populations.

1940 Four hundred prisoners in Chicago are infected with malaria in order to study the effects of new and experimental drugs to combat the disease. Nazi doctors later on trial at Nuremberg cite this American study to defend themselves.

1945 Project Paperclip is initiated. The U.S. State Department, Army intelligence, and the CIA recruit Nazi scientists and offer them immunity and secret identities in exchange for work on top-secret government projects.

1947 The CIA begins its study of LSD as a potential weapon. Human subjects (both civilian and military) are used with and without their knowledge.

1950 In an experiment to determine how susceptible an American city would be to biological attack, the U.S. Navy sprays a cloud of bacteria from ships over San Francisco. Many residents become ill with pneumonia-like symptoms.

1956 The U.S. military releases mosquitoes infected with yellow fever over Savannah, Georgia, and Avon Park, Florida. Following each test, Army agents posing as public health officials test victims for effects.

1965 Prisoners at the Holmesburg State Prison in Philadelphia are subjected to dioxin, the highly toxic chemical component of Agent Orange used in Vietnam. The men are later studied for development of cancer.

1966 U.S. Army dispenses *Bacillus subtilis* variant *niger* throughout the New York City subway system. More than a million civilians are exposed when Army scientists drop lightbulbs filled with the bacteria onto ventilation grates.

1990 More than 1,500 six-month-old black and Hispanic babies in Los Angeles are given an "experimental" measles vaccine that had never been licensed for use in the United States. CDC later admits that parents were never informed that the vaccine being injected into their children was experimental.

1994 Senator John D. Rockefeller issues a report revealing that for at least fifty years the Department of Defense has used hundreds of thousands of military personnel in human experiments and for intentional exposure to dangerous substances.

1995 The U.S. government admits that it had offered Japa-

nese war criminals and scientists who had performed
human medical experiments salaries and immunity from
prosecution in exchange for data on biological warfare
research.

1995 Dr. Garth Nicolson uncovers evidence that the biological agents used during the Gulf War had been manufac-
tured in Houston, Texas, and Boca Raton, Florida, and
tested on prisoners in the Texas Department of Correc-
tions.

1996 The Department of Defense admits that Desert Storm
soldiers were exposed to chemical agents.

1997 Eighty-eight members of Congress sign a letter demanding an investigation into bioweapons use and Gulf
War syndrome.

An ancient angelic script.
Holds the secret to patterns in our DNA?
A great explorer in the jungles of Southeast Asia.
Discovered a fate so horrifying he never spoke of it.
An intrinsic basis for evil.
Buried in our own genetic code,
can mankind survive . . .

THE JUDAS STRAIN
Available Now
Wherever Books Are Sold

Nothing stays buried forever—and it will be up to Sigma
Force to face what will be unearthed: a plague beyond any
cure, a scourge that turns all of Nature against mankind.

From the high seas of the Indian Ocean to the dark jungles
of Southeast Asia, from the canals of Venice to the crypts of
ancient kings, Sigma Force must piece together a mystery
that, unless solved, will end all life on our planet. But even
this challenge may prove too large for Sigma Force alone.
With a worldwide pandemic growing, Director Painter
Crowe and Commander Gray Pierce turn to their deadliest
adversaries for help, teaming up with a diabolical foe who
thwarted them in the past.

But can the enemy be trusted even now? Or will they
prove to be another Judas?

James Rollins—for the thrill of it!

> **"I have not told half of what I saw."**
> —the last words of Marco Polo,
> spoken upon his deathbed
> when asked to recant his stories of the Far East

May 12, 1293
Island of Sumatra
Southeast Asia

The screams had finally ceased.

Twelve bonfires blazed out in the midnight harbor.

"Il dio, li perdona . . ." his father whispered at his side, but Marco knew the Lord would not forgive them this sin.

A handful of men waited beside the two beached long-boats, the only witnesses to the funeral pyres out upon the midnight lagoon. As the moon had risen, all twelve ships, mighty wooden galleys, had been set to torch with all hands still aboard, both the dead and those cursed few who still lived. Flakes of ash rained down upon the beach and those few who bore witness. The night reeked of burned flesh.

"Twelve ships," his uncle Masseo mumbled, clutching the

silver crucifix in one fist. "The same number as the Lord's Apostles."

At least the screams of the tortured had ended. Only the crackle and low roar of the flames reached the sandy shore now. Marco wanted to turn from the sight. Others were not as stout of heart, kneeling on the sand, backs to the water, faces as pale as bone.

All were stripped naked. Each had searched his neighbor for any sign of the mark. Even the great Khan's princess, who stood behind a screen of sailcloth for modesty. Her maids, naked themselves, had searched their mistress, a maiden of seventeen. The Polos had been assigned by the Great Khan to safely deliver her to her betrothed, the Khan of Persia, the grandson of Kublai Khan's brother.

That had been in another lifetime.

Had it been only four months since the first of the galley crew had become sick, showing welts on groin and beneath the arm? The illness had spread like burning oil, unmanning the galleys of able men and stranding them here on this island.

With the cruel fire, the disease was at last vanquished, leaving only this small handful of survivors.

Seven nights ago, the remaining sick had been taken in chains to the moored boats, left with water and food. The others remained on shore, wary of any sign among them of fresh affliction. All the while, those banished to the ships called out across the waters, pleading, crying, praying, cursing, and screaming. But the worst was the occasional laughter, bright with madness.

Better to have slit their throats with a kind and swift blade, but all feared touching the blood of the sick. So they had been sent to the boats, imprisoned with the dead already there.

Then as the sun sank this night, a strange glow appeared

in the water, pooled around the keels of two of the boats, spreading like spilled milk upon the still black waters. They had seen the glow before, in the canals beneath the stone towers of the cursed city.

The disease sought to escape its wooden prison.

It had left them no choice.

The boats—all the boats, except one—had been torched.

Marco's uncle, Masseo, moved among the remaining men. He waved for them to again cloak their nakedness, but simple cloth and woven wool could not mask their deeper shame.

"What we did . . ." Marco said.

"We must not speak of it," his father said and held forth a robe toward Marco. "Breathe a word of contagion and all lands will shun us. But now we've burned away the last of the pestilence with a cleansing fire. We have only to return home."

As Marco slipped the robe over his head, his father noted what the son had drawn earlier in the sand with a stick. With a tightening of his lips, his father quickly ground it away under a heel and stared up at his son. "None must ever know what we found . . . it is cursed."

Marco nodded and did not comment on what he had drawn. He only whispered, *"Città dei Morti."*

His father's countenance, already pale, blanched further. But Marco knew it wasn't just plague that frightened his father.

A hand gripped his shoulder, squeezing to the bone. "Swear to me, my son. For your own sake."

He recognized the terror reflected in his fire-lit eyes . . . and the pleading. Marco could not refuse.

"I will keep silent," he finally promised. "To my deathbed and beyond. I so swear, Father."

Marco's uncle finally joined them, overhearing the younger

man's oath. "We should never have trespassed there, Niccolò," he scolded his brother, but his accusing words were intended for Marco.

Silence settled between the three, heavy with shared secrets.

His uncle was right.

Marco pictured the river delta from four months back. The black stream had emptied into the sea, fringed by heavy leaf and vine. They had only sought to renew their stores of fresh water. They should never have ventured farther, but Marco had spotted a stone tower deep within the forest, thrusting high, brilliant in the dawn's light. It drew him like a beacon, ever curious, brave with two score of the Khan's men from the galleys.

Still, the silence as they rowed toward the tower should have warned him. No bird calls, no scream of monkeys. The city of the dead had simply waited for them.

It was a dreadful mistake to trespass.

And it cost them in more than blood.

The three stared out as the galleys smoldered down to the waterlines.

"The sun will rise soon," his father said. "Let us be gone. It is time we went home."

"And if we reach those blessed shores, what do we tell Tedaldo?" Masseo asked, using the original name of the man, once a friend and advocate of the Polo family, now styled as Pope Gregory X.

"We don't know he still lives," his father answered. "We've been gone so long."

"But if he does, Niccolò?" his uncle pressed.

"We will tell him all we know about the Mongols and their customs and their strengths. As we were directed under his edict so long ago. But of the plague here . . . there remains nothing to speak of. It is over."

Masseo sighed, but there was little relief in his exhalation. *Plague had not claimed all of them.*

His father repeated more firmly, as if saying would make it so, "It is over."

Marco glanced up at the two older men, his father and his uncle, framed in fiery ash and smoke against the night sky. It would never be over, not as long as they remembered.

Marco glanced to his toes. Though the mark was scuffled off the sand, it burned brightly still behind his eyes. He had stolen a map painted on beaten bark. Painted in blood. Temples and spires spread in the jungle.

All empty.

Except for the dead.

The ground had been littered with birds, fallen to the stone plazas as if struck out of the skies in flight. Nothing was spared. Men and women and children. Oxen and beasts of the field. Even great snakes had hung limp from tree limbs.

The only living inhabitants were the ants.

Teeming across stones and bodies, slowly picking apart the dead.

Upon discovering what Marco had stolen from one of the temples, his father had burned the map and spread the ashes into the sea. He did this even before the first man aboard their own ships had become sick.

"Let it be forgotten," his father had warned then.

Marco would honor his word, his oath. This was one tale he would never speak. Still, he touched one of the marks in the sand. He who had chronicled so much . . . was it right to vanquish such knowledge?

If there was another way to preserve it . . .

As if reading Marco's thoughts, his uncle Masseo spoke aloud all their fears. "And if the horror should rise again, Niccolò, should someday reach our shores?"

"Then it will mean the end of man's tyranny of this

world," his father answered bitterly. He tapped the crucifix resting on Masseo's bare chest. "The friar knew better than all. His sacrifice . . ."

The cross had once belonged to Friar Agreer. Back in the cursed city, the Dominican had given his life to save theirs. A dark pact had been struck. They had left him there, abandoned him, at his own bidding.

The nephew of Pope Gregory X.

Marco whispered as the last of the flames died into the dark waters. "What God will save us next time?"

"Who wants another bottle of Foster's while I'm down here?" Gregg Tunis called from belowdecks.

Dr. Susan Tunis smiled at her husband's voice as she pushed off the dive ladder and onto the open stern deck. She skinned out of her BC vest and hauled the scuba gear to the rack behind the research yacht's pilot house. Her tanks clanked as she racked them alongside the others.

Her husband climbed up with three perspiring bottles of lager, pinching them all between the fingers of one hand. He grinned broadly upon seeing her. "Thought I heard you bumping about up here."

He climbed topside, stretching his tall frame. Employed as a boat mechanic in Darwin Harbor, he and Susan had met during one of the dry-dock repairs on another of the University of Sydney's boats. That had been eight years ago. Just three days ago they had celebrated their fifth anniversary aboard the yacht, moored a hundred nautical miles off

Kirimiti Atoll, better known as Christmas Island.

He passed her a bottle. "Any luck with the soundings?"

She took a long pull on the beer. "Not so far. Still can't find a source for the beachings."

Ten days ago, eighty dolphins, *Tursiops aduncus*, an Indian Ocean species, had beached themselves along the coast of Java. Her research study centered on the long-term effects of sonar interference on Cetacean species, the source of many suicidal beachings in the past. She usually had a team of research assistants with her, a mix of postgrads and undergrads, but the trip up here had been for a vacation with her old mentor. It was pure happenstance that such a massive beaching occurred in the region—hence the protracted stay here.

"Could it be something other than manmade sonar?" Professor Applegate pondered, drawing sigils with his fingertip in the condensation on his beer bottle. "Micro-quakes are constantly rattling the region. Perhaps a deep-sea subduction quake struck the right tonal note to drive them into a suicidal panic."

"There was that bonzer quake a few months back," her husband said. He settled into a lounge beside the professor and patted the seat for her to sit with him. "Maybe some aftershocks?"

Susan couldn't argue against their assessments. Between the series of deadly quakes over the past two years and the major tsunami in the area, the seabed was greatly disturbed. It was enough to spook anyone. But she wasn't convinced. Something else was happening. The reef below was oddly deserted. What little life was down there seemed to have retreated into rocky niches, shells, and sandy holes. It was almost as if the sea life here was holding its breath.

She frowned and joined her husband.

A sharp bark startled her, causing her to jump. She had

not known she was that tense. Apparently the strange, wary behavior of the reef life below had infected her.

"Oy! Oscar!" the professor called.

Only now did Susan notice the lack of their fourth crewmate on the yacht. The dog barked again. The pudgy Queensland Heeler belonged to the professor.

"I'll see to him," Applegate said. "Leave you two love-birds all cozied up. Besides, I could use a trip to the head before I find my bed."

The professor gained his feet with a groan and headed toward the bow, intending to circle to the far side—but he stopped, staring off toward the east, away from where the sun had just set.

Oscar barked again.

Applegate did not scold him this time. Instead, he called over to Susan and Gregg, his voice low and serious. "You both should come see this."

Susan scooted up and onto her feet. Gregg followed. They joined the professor.

"Bloody hell . . ." her husband mumbled.

"I think you may be looking at what drove those dolphins out of the seas," Applegate said.

To the east, a wide swath of the ocean glowed with a ghostly luminescence, rising and falling with the waves. The silvery sheen rolled and eddied. The old dog stood at the starboard rail and barked, trailing into a low growl at the sight.

"What the hell is that?" Gregg asked.

Susan answered as she crossed closer. "I've heard of such manifestations. They're called *milky seas*. Ships have reported glows like this in the Indian Ocean, going all the way back to Jules Verne. In 1995, a satellite even picked up one of the blooms, covering hundreds of square miles. This is a small one."

"Small, my ass," Gregg grunted. "But what exactly is it? Some type of red tide?"

She shook her head. "Not exactly. Red tides are algal blooms. These glows are caused by bioluminescent bacteria, probably feeding off algae or some other substrate. There's no danger. But I'd like to—"

A sudden knock sounded beneath the boat. Oscar's barking became more heated. The dog danced back and forth along the rails, trying to poke his head through the posts.

All three of them joined the dog and looked below.

The glowing edge of the milky sea lapped at the yacht's keel. From the depths below, a large shape rolled into view, belly up, but still squirming, teeth gnashing. It was a giant tiger shark, female, over six meters. The glowing waters frothed over its form, bubbling and turning the milky water into red wine.

Susan realized it wasn't *water* that was bubbling over the shark's belly, but its own *flesh*, boiling off in wide patches. The horrible sight sank away. But across the milky seas, other shapes rolled to the surface, thrashing or already dead: porpoises, sea turtles, fish by the hundreds.

Applegate took a step away from the rail. "It seems *these* bacteria have found more than just algae to feed on."

Gregg turned to stare at her. "Susan . . ."

She could not look away from the deadly vista. Despite the horror, she could not deny a twinge of scientific curiosity.

"Susan . . ."

She finally turned to him, slightly irritated.

"You were diving," he explained. "All day."

"So? We were all in the water at least some time. Even Oscar."

Her husband would not meet her gaze. He remained focused on where she was scratching her forearm. The worry in his tight face drew her attention to her arm. Her skin was

pebbled in a severe rash, made worse by her scratching.
As she stared, bruising red welts bloomed on her skin.
She gaped in disbelief. "Dear God . . ."
But she also knew the horrible truth.
"It's . . . it's *in* me."